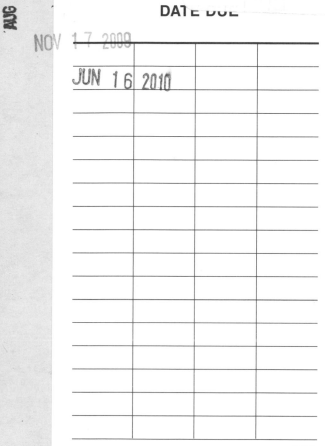

THE
WEAVERS
OF SARAMYR

CHRIS WOODING

Copyright © Chris Wooding 2003
All rights reserved

The right of Chris Wooding to be identified as the
author of this work has been asserted by him in accordance
with the Copyright, Designs and Patents Act 1988.

First published in Great Britain in 2003 by

Gollancz
An imprint of the Orion Publishing Group
Orion House, 5 Upper St Martin's Lane, London WC2H 9EA

This paperback edition first published in Great Britain
in 2004 by Gollancz

A CIP catalogue record for this book is
available from the British Library

ISBN 0 575 07542 2

Typeset at The Spartan Press Ltd,
Lymington, Hants

Printed in Great Britain by
Clays Ltd, St Ives plc

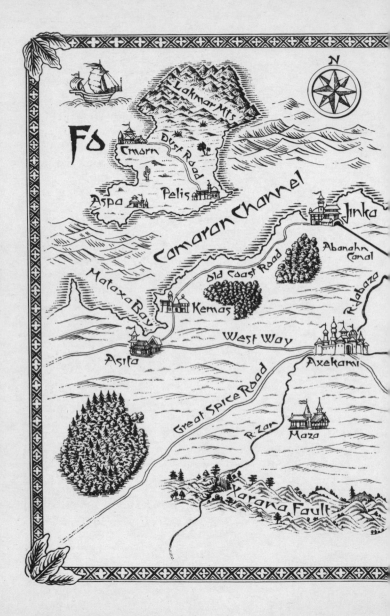

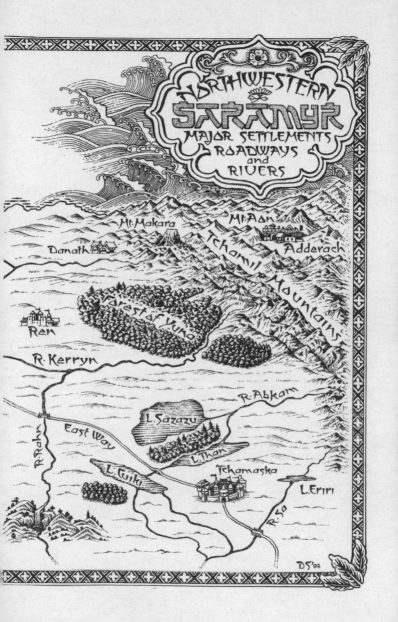

ONE

Kaiku was twenty harvests of age the first time she died.

There was no memory of how she had come to this place. Recollection evaded her, made slippery by ecstasy, the sensation of tranquillity that soaked every fibre of her body. And the sights, oh, such sights as would have made her weep if she could. The world to her was a golden shimmer, millions upon millions of tiny threads crowding her gaze, shifting, waving. They tugged and teased her gently, wafting her unhurriedly onward towards some unseen destination. Once they parted to delineate a shape that slid through them, a distant glimpse of something vast and wondrous, like the whales she used to watch off the coast at Mishani's summer house. She tried to catch it with her eye, but it was gone in a moment, and the tapestry had sewn shut behind it.

These are the Fields of Omecha, she thought. Yet how could that be so? She had not passed through the Gate yet, not met the guardian Yoru, the laughing, pot-bellied dwarf with his red skin and piggy tusks and ears, carrying the endless jug of wine given to him by Isisya to ease his long vigil. No, not the Fields, then; merely the approach to the Gate, the soft path to the entrance of the realm of the blessed dead.

She felt no remorse or sorrow. She was full of such harmony that she had space in her heart for nothing else. She thought she might burst from the wonder of the golden, glittering world she drifted through. This was what the monks strived for when they crossed their legs and sat for years upon a pillar in contemplation; this was what the old addicts in their smokehouses sought when they sucked on their pipes of burnt amaxa root. This was completeness.

1

But suddenly there was a wrench, a terrible burning in her breast. She felt a shudder through the shimmering fibres that caressed her, felt them draw back . . . and then, appallingly, she was being pulled away, down, back to where she had come from. She thought she saw the outline of the Gate in the distance, and Yoru laughing and raising his jug in farewell to her. She wanted to scream, but she had no voice. The beauty was deserting her, fleeing her heart, draining like water through a holed bucket. She fought to resist, but the force pulled harder now, the burning stronger, and she was sucked away . . .

Her eyes flew open, unfocused. Lips were on hers, soft lips pressing hard, and her lungs seared as agonising breath was forced into them. A face, too close to determine; black hair lying against her cheek.

She twitched, a single brief spasm, and the lips left hers. The owner drew back, and Kaiku's vision finally found its focus. They were on her sleeping-mat, in her room, and straddling her hips was her handmaiden Asara. She brushed the long, sleek fall of her hair back over her shoulder and regarded her mistress with eyes of liquid darkness.

'You live, then,' she said, strangely.

Kaiku looked about, her movements frightened and bewildered. The air felt wrong somehow. Flashes of purple flickered in the night outside, and the thrashing of rain underpinned the terrible screeching roars from the sky. It was no ordinary thunder. The moonstorm her father had been predicting for days had finally arrived.

Her surroundings slotted themselves into place, assembling an order from her fractured consciousness. The once-familiar sights seemed suddenly alien now, disjointed by a slowly settling unreality. The intricately carved whorls and loops of the shutters looked wrong, subtly off-kilter, and when they rattled in the wind the clacking was like some desert snake. The deep night-shadows that gathered among the polished

2

ceiling beams seemed to glower. Even the small shrine to Ocha that rested in one corner of the minimally furnished bedroom had changed; the elegantly laid guya blossoms seemed to nod in sinister conspiracy with the storm, and the beautifully inlaid pictographs that spelt the name of the Emperor of the gods seemed to swarm and shift subtly.

Behind Asara, she could see a sandalled foot poking from the hem of a simple white robe. The owner lay inert on the hard wooden floor.

Karia.

She sat up, pushing Asara off her. Karia, her other hand-maiden, was sprawled as if in sleep; but Kaiku knew by some dread instinct that it was a sleep she would never wake from.

'What is this?' she breathed, reaching out to touch her erstwhile companion.

'There's no time,' Asara said, in a tone of impatience that Kaiku had never heard before. 'We must go.'

'Tell me what has happened!' Kaiku snapped, unaccustomed to being talked to in such a way by an inferior.

Asara grabbed her hard by the shoulders, hurting her. For a moment, Kaiku was seized by the wild notion that she might be struck by her handmaiden. 'Listen,' she hissed.

Kaiku obeyed, mostly out of shock at the way she was being treated by the usually meek and servile Asara. There *was* another sound over the awful screeching of the moon-storm and the pummelling tattoo of the rain. A slow, insectile tapping, coming from above; the sound of something moving across the roof. She looked up, then back down at Asara, and her eyes were full of terror.

'*Shin-shin,*' her handmaiden whispered.

'Where's Mother?' Kaiku cried, suddenly springing up and lunging for the curtained doorway. Asara grabbed her wrist and pulled her roughly back. Her expression was grim, and it told Kaiku that all the things she feared were true. She could not help her family now. She felt her strength desert her, and she fell to her knees and almost fainted.

When she raised her head, tears streaked her face. Asara was holding a rifle in one hand, and in her other she held a mask, an ugly thing of red and black lacquer, the leering face of a mischievous spirit. She stuffed it unceremoniously inside her robe and then looked down at her mistress. Kaiku's feathered brown hair was in disarray, forming a messy frame around her face, and she wore only a thin white sleeping-robe and the jewelled bracelet at her wrist she never took off. For a moment, Asara pitied her. She had no conception of what was happening, what stakes she was playing for. Less than five minutes ago she had been dead, her heart stopped, her blood cooling. Perhaps she wished now she had stayed that way; but Asara had other plans for her.

A scream sounded from somewhere in the house; thin, cracked. The grandmother. She seized Kaiku and pulled her towards the doorway. A sawing scrape from outside cut through the house, the voice of the moonstorm. A moment later came the sound of a shin-shin, rattling across the roof slates. Something darted past the shutters, crawling down the outside wall of the building. Kaiku saw it and shuddered.

Asara took her hand and looked into her eyes. They were wild and panicked.

'Listen to me, Kaiku,' she said, her voice firm but calm. 'We must run. Do you understand? I will take you to safety.'

Trembling, she nodded. Asara was satisfied.

'Stay with me,' she said, and she slid aside the thin curtain in the doorway and stepped out on to the balcony beyond.

The country retreat of Ruito tu Makaima – Kaiku's father and a scholar of some renown – was built in a clearing in the midst of lush woodland, a hollow square enclosing a central garden. It was built with an eye for aesthetics, in the fashion of the Saramyr folk, ensuring ostentation was kept to a minimum while the spare beauty of its form was picked out and assembled in harmony with its surroundings. The austere simplicity of its pale walls was contrasted by ornate wooden shutters and curved stone lintels shaped into graceful horns at either end. It sat in eerie serenity even amid the howling storm. A ruthlessly tamed lawn surrounded it, with a simple bridge vaulting a stream and a path leading from the front door that was so immaculate it might have been laid only yesterday. Within the boundaries of the clearing, the more untidy edges of nature had been excised for the sake of perfection; it was only where the clearing ended that the forest regained dominance again, crowding around the territory jealously.

The upper floor had a long balcony running around its inside wall, looking out over rockeries and miniature waterfalls, tiny bridges and sculpted trees. All the rooms, Kaiku's included, faced on to this balcony; and it was on to that balcony they emerged, Asara with her rifle held ready.

The night was hot, for it was early summer, and the rain that lashed the house ran off carven gutters to pour down in torrents to the garden below. Thin pillars stretched from the waist-high wooden barrier to the sloping roof. The air was full of drumming and rattling, the voice of a thousand drips and splatters; and yet to Kaiku it seemed eerily silent, and she could hear the pounding of her heart loud in her ears.

Asara looked one way, then another, distrusting the empty balcony. Her hands gripped hard on the rifle. It was a long, slender piece of metal, its barrel decorated with sigils and a sight cleverly fashioned in the form of a breaking wave. Far too expensive and elegant for a handmaiden like Asara to own; she had stolen it from elsewhere in the house.

Kaiku jumped as Asara moved suddenly, levelling the barrel down at the garden. Something dark moved across the rockeries, inhumanly fast, racing on four spindly legs; it was too quick for Asara, and she withdrew without firing.

They edged along the balcony towards the stairs. Kaiku was almost paralysed with fright, but she forced herself to move. Too much had happened, too quickly. She felt overwhelmed and helpless; but Asara, at least, seemed to be in control. She followed her servant. There was nothing else she could do.

They reached the top of the stairs without incident. Below it was dark. No lanterns had been lit tonight, and there was no sign of movement. The sky howled again; Kaiku looked up instinctively. The clouds were being torn ragged up there, tossed about by the changing winds, swirling and curling, occasionally reaching out to each other as a bolt of purple lightning bridged a gap or lanced down to earth.

She was about to say something to Asara when she saw the shin-shin.

It was creeping out of the darkness at one end of the balcony, a demon of shadow that made Kaiku quail in terror. She could barely see it, only its outline, for it seemed part of the blackness that concealed it; but what she could see was enough. Its torso was like that of a human, but its forelegs and forearms were terribly elongated and tapered to a thin spike, so that it seemed like a man walking on four stilts. It was tall, much taller than she was, and it had to crush itself down to fit under the roof of the balcony. She could see no other detail except the eyes; they glittered in the darkness like lamps, twin points of burning brightness in the gloom.

Asara swore an impolite oath and pulled Kaiku after her, down the stairs. Kaiku needed no second prompting; all else had fled her mind at that moment, and the only remaining urge was to get away from the demon that stalked towards them. They heard the clatter as it gave chase, and then they were thundering down the stairs into the shadowy room below.

The entrance hall was wide and spacious, with elaborately carved wooden archways to the other ground-floor rooms. This house was built for the stifling heat of summer, so there were no interior doors, and attractively dyed screens stood about which could be moved to better allow the warm evening breezes through. The unnatural lightning of the moonstorm flickered through the ornamental shutters, stunning the room in brightness.

Kaiku almost fell down the final few steps, but Asara

pushed her aside and aimed her rifle up the stairs at the
archway leading on to the balcony. A moment later, the
spindly silhouette of the shin-shin darted into view, eyes
blazing in the dark oval of its face. Asara fired, and the report
of the rifle cracked deafeningly through the house. The
doorway was suddenly empty; the demon had been deterred,
at least for a short time. Asara reprimed the bolt on her
weapon and hurried Kaiku towards the door to the outside.

'Asara! More of them!' Kaiku cried, and there they were,
two of the creatures, hiding in the shadowy archways of the
entrance hall. Asara clutched her mistress's wrist and they
froze. Kaiku's hand was on the door, but she dared not tear it
open and run, for the creatures would cut her down before
she had gone ten metres. The raw, choking fear that had
attended her ever since her eyes had opened tonight began
to claw its way up her throat. She was blank with panic,
disorientated, caught in a waking nightmare.

Slowly the shin-shin came into the hall, ducking their
torsos beneath the archways as they angled their long, tapered
limbs with insectile grace. They were the more terrible
because Kaiku's gaze refused to fix on them properly, allowing only hints of their form; only the glitter of their eyes was
solid and visible. She was conscious of Asara reaching for
something: a lantern, dormant and unlit on a window-ledge.
The demons crept closer, keeping to the deepest darknesses.

'Be ready,' Asara whispered; and a moment later, she threw
the lantern into the centre of the room. The shin-shin whirled
at the sound, and in that instant Asara brought up her rifle
and fired it into the slick of lantern oil on the floor.

The room was suddenly bright, a roaring sheet of flame,
and the demons shrieked in their unearthly tongue and
scattered clumsily away from the brilliance. But Kaiku was
already through the door and out into the storm, racing
barefoot across the grass towards the trees that surrounded
the house. Asara came close behind, leaving the fire to lick at
the wooden walls and paper screens. They rushed through the

rain, cringing at the great screeches coming from the sky. Not daring to look back, not knowing if Asara was following or not, Kaiku plunged into the forest.

The three moons were out tonight, clustered close above the slowly writhing clouds. Vast Aurus, the largest and eldest of the sisters; Iridima, smaller but brighter, her skin gullied with blue cracks; and the tiny green moon Neryn, the shyest of them all, who rarely showed her face. Legends told that when the three sisters were together, they fought and tore the sky, and that the screeching was Neryn's cries as her siblings teased her for her green skin. Kaiku's father taught a different tale, that the moonstorms were simply a result of the combined gravity of the moons playing havoc with the atmosphere. Whatever the reason, it was accepted wisdom that when the three moons were close moonstorms would follow. And on those nights, the Children of the Moons walked the earth.

Kaiku panted and whimpered as she ran through the trees. Thin branches whipped at her from all sides, covering her arms and face with wet lashes. Her sleeping-robe was soaked through, her chin-length hair plastered to her cheeks, her feet muddied and slimed. She fled blindly, as if she could outrun reality. Her mind still refused to grip the enormity of what had occurred in the previous few minutes. She felt like a child, helpless, alone and terrified.

Finally, the inevitable happened. Her bare foot found a rock that was more slippery than it looked, and she fell headlong, landing heavily against a root that was steadily emerging from washed-away layers of mud. Fresh tears came at the pain, and she lay in the dirt, filthy and sodden, and sobbed.

But there was no rest for her. She felt herself gripped from behind, and there was Asara, dragging her upright. She shrieked incoherently, but Asara was merciless.

'I know a safe place,' she said. 'Come with me. They are not far behind.'

Then they were running again, plunging headlong through

the trees, stumbling and slipping as they went. The air seemed to pluck at them, trying to lift them up, charged with a strange energy by the storm. It played tricks on their senses, making everything seem a little more or less than real. Grandmother Chomi used to warn her granddaughter that if she jumped too high in a moonstorm she might never come back down, but drift into the sky. Kaiku pushed the thought away, remembering instead the scream she had heard earlier. Her grandmother was gone. All of them were gone. She knew without knowing, by the void in her heart.

They came out of the trees at the edge of a rocky stream, swollen and angry with the rains. Asara looked quickly left and right, her long hair soaked to deepest black and sluggish with moisture. She made her decision in moments, heading downstream, tugging Kaiku after her. The latter was almost at the limit of exhaustion, and it told in her staggering steps and lolling head.

The stream emptied into a wide clearing, a shallow bowl of water from which humped several grassy islands and banks, scattered with the bald faces of half-buried rocks and taut clusters of bushes. The largest island by far was the pedestal for a vast, ancient tree, overwhelmingly dominating the scene by its sheer size. Its trunk was twice as thick as a man was tall, knotted and twisted with age, and its branches spread in a great fan, leaves of gold and brown and green weeping a delicate curtain of droplets across the water below. Even in the rain, the clearing seemed sacred, a place of untouched beauty. The air here was different, possessed of a crystalline fragility and stillness, as of a held breath. Even Kaiku felt the change, the sensation of a presence in this place, some cold and slow and gentle awareness that marked their arrival with a languid interest.

The sound of a breaking twig alerted Asara, and she spun to see one of the shin-shin high up in the trees to their right, moving with impossible dexterity between the boughs while its lantern eyes stayed fixed on them. She pulled Kaiku into the water, which came up to their knees and soaked through their robes. Urgently, they splashed across to the largest island, and there they clambered out. Kaiku collapsed on the grass. Asara left her there and raced to the tree. She put her palms and forehead against it and murmured softly, her lips rapid as she spoke.

'Great ipi, venerated spirit of the forest, we beg you to grant us your protection. Do not let these demons of shadow defile your glade with their corruption.'

A shiver seemed to run through the tree, shaking loose a cascade of droplets from the leaves.

Asara stepped back from the trunk and returned to Kaiku's side. She squatted down, wiping the lank strands of hair from her face, and scanned the edge of the glade. She could sense them out there, prowling. Three of them, and maybe more, stalking around the perimeter, hiding in the trees, their shining eyes never leaving their prey.

Asara watched, her hand near her rifle. She was no priest, but she knew the spirits of the forest well enough. The ipi would protect them, if only because it would not let the demons near it. Ipis were the guardians of the forest, and nowhere was their influence stronger than in their own glades. The creatures circled, their stiltlike legs carrying them to and fro. She could sense their frustration. Their prey was within sight, yet the shin-shin dared not enter the domain of an ipi.

After a time, Asara was satisfied that they were safe. She hooked her hands under Kaiku's shoulders and dragged her into the protection of the tree's vast roots, where the rain was less. Kaiku never woke. Asara regarded her for a moment, soaked as she was and freezing, and felt a kind of sympathy for her. She crouched down next to her mistress and stroked her cheek gently with the back of her knuckles.

'Life can be cruel, Kaiku,' she said. 'I fear you are only just beginning to learn that.'

With the moonstorm raging high overhead, she sat in the shelter of the great tree and waited for the dawn to come.

TWO

Kaiku awoke to a loud snap from the fire, and her eyes flickered open. Asara was there, stirring a small, blackened pot that hung from an iron tripod over the flames. A pair of coilfish were spitted on a branch and crisping next to it. The sun was high in the sky and the air was muggy and hot. A fresh, earthy smell was all about as damp loam dried from last night's downpour.

'Daygreet, Kaiku,' Asara said, without looking at her. 'I went back to the house this morning and salvaged what I could.' She tossed a bundle of clothes over. 'There was not a great deal left, but the rain put out the blaze before it could devour everything. We have food, clothes and a good amount of money.'

Kaiku raised herself, looking around. They were no longer in the waterlogged clearing. Now they sat in a dip in the land where the soil was sandy and clogged with pebbles, and little grew except a few shrubs. Trees guarded the lip of the depression, casting sharply contrasting shadows against the dazzling light, and the daytime sounds of the forest peeped and chittered all about. Had Asara carried her?

The first thing she noticed was that her bracelet was missing.

'Asara! Grandmother's bracelet! It must have fallen . . . it . . .'

'I took it. I left it as an offering to the ipi, in thanks for protecting us.'

'She gave me that bracelet on my eighth harvest!' Kaiku cried. 'I have never taken it off!'

'The point of an offering is that you sacrifice something

11

precious to you,' Asara said levelly. 'The ipi saved our lives. I had nothing I could give, but you did.'

Kaiku stared at her in disbelief, but Asara appeared not to notice. She made a vague gesture to indicate their surroundings. 'I thought it best not to start a fire in the ipi's glade, so I moved you here.'

Kaiku hung her head. She was too drained to protest any further. Asara watched her in silence for a time.

'I must know,' Kaiku said quietly. 'My family . . .'

Asara put down the spoon she had been using to stir the pot and knelt before Kaiku, taking her hands. 'They are dead.'

Kaiku's throat tightened, but she nodded to indicate she understood. 'What happened?'

'Would you not rather eat first, and compose yourself?'

Kaiku raised her head and looked at Asara. 'I must know,' she repeated.

Asara released her hands. 'Most of you were poisoned,' she said. 'You died as you slept. I suspect it was one of the kitchen servants, but I cannot be sure. Whoever it was, they were inefficient. Your grandmother did not eat at the evening meal last night, so she was still alive when the shin-shin came. I believe that somebody sent the demons to kill the servants and remove the evidence. With no witnesses, the crime would go unsolved.' She settled further on her haunches.

'Who?' Kaiku asked. 'And why?'

'To those questions I have no answers,' she said. 'Yet.'

Asara got up and returned to the pot, occasionally turning the fish. It was some time before Kaiku spoke again.

'Did I die, Asara? From the poison?'

'Yes,' replied the handmaiden. 'I brought you back.'

'How?'

'I stole the breath from another, and put it into you.'

Kaiku thought of Karia, her other handmaiden, who she had seen lying dead on the floor of her room.

'How is that possible?' she whispered, afraid of the answer.

'There are many things you do not understand, Kaiku,' Asara replied. 'I am one of them.'

Kaiku was beginning to realise that. Asara had always been the perfect handmaiden: quiet, obedient and reliable, skilled at combing out hair and laying out clothes. Kaiku had liked her better than the more wilful Karia, and often talked with her, shared secrets or played games. But there had always been the boundary there, a division that prevented them from becoming truly close. The unspoken understanding that the two of them were of a different caste. Kaiku was high-born and Asara was not, and so one had a duty to serve and obey the other. It was the way in Saramyr, the way it had always been.

And yet now Kaiku saw that the last two years had been a deception. This was not the person she thought she knew. This Asara had a steely calm, a core of cold metal. This Asara had saved her life by stealing another's, had burned down her house, had taken her most valuable token of her grandmother's love and given it away with impunity. This Asara had rescued her from demons.

Who was she, truly?

'The stream is nearby, Kaiku,' Asara said, pointing with her spoon. 'You should wash and change. You will catch a chill in that.' It had not escaped notice that since last night she had ceased to call Kaiku 'mistress', as was proper.

Kaiku obeyed. She felt she should be ashamed of the state of herself, half undressed with her thin white sleeping-robe mussed and filthy. Yet it seemed insignificant in the wake of what had gone before. Weary despite her sleep, she went to the stream, and there she threw away the soiled robe and washed herself clean, naked in the hot sunlight. The feel of the water and warmth on her bare skin brought her no pleasure. Her body felt like only a vessel for her grief.

She dressed in the clothes Asara had brought her, finding that they were sturdy attire for travelling in. Leather boots, shapeless beige trousers, an open-throated shirt of the same colour that would belong better on a man. She had no complaints. She had always been a tomboy, and she fitted as easily into the trappings of a peasant as those of a noble lady. Her elder brother had been her closest companion, and she had competed with him at everything. They had fought to outride, outshoot and outwrestle each other constantly. Kaiku was no stranger to the gun or the forest.

When she returned to the campfire, the air was alive with sparkling flakes, drifting gently from the sky like snow. They glittered as the sun caught them, sharp flashes of light all about. It was called starfall: a phenomenon seen only in the aftermath of a moonstorm. Tiny, flat crystals of fused ice were created in the maelstrom of the three sisters' conflict, thin enough to float on their way down. Beauty after chaos. Much prose had been written of starfall, and it was a recurring theme in some of the finest love poetry. Today, it held no power to move her.

Asara handed her a bowl of coilfish, vegetables and saltrice. 'You should eat,' she said. Kaiku did so, using her fingers in the way she had as a child, barely tasting it. Asara arranged herself behind, and gently untangled Kaiku's hair with a wooden comb. It was an act of surprising kindness, in the face of everything; a gesture of familiarity from a girl who now seemed a stranger.

'Thank you,' Kaiku said, when Asara was done. The words meant more than simple gratitude. There was no need to thank a servant for a duty that was expected to be rendered. What seemed a mere pleasantry was a tacit acceptance that Asara was no longer subservient to her. The fact that Asara did not correct her proved it.

Kaiku was unsurprised. Asara had altered her mode of address towards Kaiku, and was now talking to her as if she was social equal, albeit one who was not close enough to be called a friend. It spoke volumes about the new state of their relationship.

The Saramyrrhic language was impenetrably complex to an outsider, a mass of tonal inflections, honorifics, accents and qualifiers that conveyed dense layers of meaning far beyond the simple words in a sentence. There were dozens of different modes of address for different situations, each one conveyed by minute alterations in pronunciation and structure. There were different modes used to speak to children, one each for boys, girls, and a separate one for infants of either sex; there were multiple modes for social superiors, depending on how much more important the addressee was than the speaker, and a special one used only for addressing the Emperor or Empress. There were modes for lovers, again in varying degrees with the most intimate being virtually sacrilegious to speak aloud in the presence of anyone but the object of passion. There were modes for mother, father, husband, wife, shopkeepers and tradesmen, priests, animals, modes for praying and for scolding, vulgar modes and scatological ones. There were even several neutral modes, used when the speaker was uncertain as to the relative importance of the person they were addressing.

Additionally, the language was split into High Saramyrrhic – employed by nobles and those who could afford to be educated in it – and Low Saramyrrhic, used by the peasantry and servants. Though the two were interchangeable as a spoken language – with Low Saramyrrhic being merely a slightly coarser version of its higher form – as written languages they were completely different. High Saramyrrhic was the province of the nobles, and the peasantry were excluded from it. It was the language of learning, in which all philosophy, history and literature were written; but its pictographs meant nothing to the common folk. The higher strata of society was violently divided from the lower by a carefully maintained boundary of ignorance; and that boundary was the written form of High Saramyrrhic.

'The shin-shin fear the light,' Asara said in a conversational tone, as she scuffed dirt over the fire to put it out. 'They will not come in the daytime. By the time they return we will be gone.'

'Where are we going?'

'Somewhere safer than this,' Asara replied. She caught the look on Kaiku's face, saw her frustration at the answer, and offered one a little less vague. 'A secret place. Where there are friends, where we can understand what happened here.'

'You know more that you say you do, Asara,' the other accused. 'Why won't you tell me?'

'You are disorientated,' came the reply. 'You have been to the Gates of Omecha not one sunrise past, you have lost your family and endured more than anyone should bear. Trust me; you will learn more later.'

Kaiku crossed the hollow and faced her former servant. 'I will learn it now.'

Asara regarded her in return. She was a pretty one, despite the temporary ravages of grief on her face. Eyes of brown that seemed to laugh when she was happy; a small nose, slightly sloped; teeth white and even. Her tawny hair she wore in a feathered style, teased forward over her cheeks and face in the fashionable cut that young ladies wore in the capital. Asara had known her long enough to realise her stubborn streak, her mulish persistence when she decided she wanted something. She saw it now, and at that moment she felt a slight admiration for the woman she had deceived all this time. She had half expected the grief of the previous night to break her, but she was finding herself proven wrong. Kaiku had spirit, then. Good. She would need it.

Asara picked up a cured-leather pack and held it out. 'Walk with me.' Kaiku took it and slid it on to her back. Asara took the other, and the rifle, from where it had been drying by the fire. The previous night's rain had soaked the powder chamber, and it was not ready to use yet.

They headed into the forest. The branches twinkled with starfall as it gently drifted around them, gathering on the ground in a soft dusting before melting away. Kaiku felt a fresh upswell of tears in her breast, but she fought to keep them down. She needed to understand, to make some small sense of what had happened. Her family were gone, and yet it did not seem real yet. She had to hold together for now. Resolutely, she forced her pain into a tight, bitter corner of her mind and kept it there. It was the only way she could continue to function. The alternative was to go mad with sorrow.

'We've watched you for a long time,' Asara said eventually. 'Your house and family, too. Partly it was because we knew your father was one who was sympathetic to our cause, one who might be persuaded to join us eventually. He had connections through his patronage in the Imperial Court. But mostly it was because of you, Kaiku. Your condition.'

'Condition? I have no *condition*,' Kaiku said.

'I admit I had my doubts when I was sent here,' replied her former handmaiden. 'But even I have noticed the signs.'

Kaiku tried to think, but her head was muddled and Asara's explanation seemed to be throwing up more questions than answers. Instead, she asked directly: 'What happened last night?'

'Your father,' Asara said. 'You must have remembered how he was when he returned from his last trip away.'

'He said he was ill . . .' Kaiku began, then stopped. She sounded foolish. The illness he had feigned had been an excuse. She *did* remember the way he had seemed. Pale and wan, he was also quiet and lethargic; but there was a haunted look about him, a certain absence in his manner. Grandmother had been that way when Grandfather died, seven years ago. A kind of stunned disbelief, such as she had heard soldiers got when they had been too long exposed to the roar of cannons.

'Yes,' she agreed. 'Something happened, something he would not speak of. Do you know what it was?'

'Do you?'

Kaiku shook her head. They trudged a few more steps in silence. The forest had enshrouded them now, and they walked a zigzagging way through the sparsely clustered trees, stepping over roots and boulders that cluttered the wildly uneven ground. A dirt ridge had risen to waist-height on their right, fringed with gently swaying shadowglove serviced by fat red bees. The sun beat down from overhead, baking the wet soil in a lazy heat that made the world content and sluggish. On any other day Kaiku would have been lost in tranquillity, for she had always had a childlike awe of nature; but the beauty of their surroundings had no power to touch her now.

'I watched him these last few weeks,' Asara said. 'I learned nothing more. Perhaps he wronged someone, a powerful enemy. I can only guess. But I am in no doubt that it was he who brought ruin on you last night.'

'Why? He was just a scholar! He read *books*. Why would someone want to kill him . . . all of us?'

'For this,' Asara said, and with that she drew from her heavy robe the mask Kaiku had seen her take from the house. She brandished it in front of Kaiku. Its red and black lacquer face leered idiotically at her. 'He brought it with him when he returned last.'

'That? It's only a mask.'

Asara brushed her hair back from her face and looked gravely at the other. 'Kaiku, masks are the most dangerous weapons in the world. More than rifles, more than cannon, more than the spirits that haunt the wild places. They are—'

Asara trailed off suddenly as Kaiku's step faltered and she stumbled dizzily.

'Are you unwell?' she asked.

Kaiku blinked, frowning. Something had turned in her gut, a burning worm of pain that shifted and writhed. A moment later it happened again, stronger this time, not in her gut but lower, coming from her womb like the kick of a baby.

'Asara,' she gasped, dropping to one knee, her hand splayed on the ground in front of her. 'There's . . . something . . .'

And now it blossomed, a raw bloom of agony in her

18

stomach and groin, wrenching a cry from her throat. But this one did not recede; instead it built upon itself, becoming hotter, a terrifying pressure rising inside her. She clutched at herself, but it did not abate. She squeezed her eyes shut, tears of shock and incomprehension dripping from the corners.

'Asara . . . help . . .'

She looked up in supplication, but the world as she knew it was no longer there. Her eyes saw not tree and stone and leaf but a thousand million streams of light, a great three-dimensional diorama of glowing threads, stirring and flexing to ebb and flow around the objects that moved through it. She could see the bright knot of Asara's heart within the stitchwork frame of her body; she could see the ripple in the threads of the air as a nearby bird tore through it; she could see the lines of the sunlight spraying the forest as it slanted through the canopy, and the sparkle of starfall all about.

I'm dying again, she thought, *just like the last time.*

But this was not like the last time, for there was no bliss, no serenity or inner peace. Only something within, something huge, building and building in size until she knew her skin must split and she would be torn apart. Her irises darkened and turned red as blood; the air stirred around her, ruffling her clothes and lifting her hair. She saw Asara's expression turn to fear, the threads of her face twisting. Saw her turn and run, fleeing headlong into the trees.

Kaiku screamed, and with that venting, the burning force found its release.

The nearest trees exploded into flaming matchwood; those a little further away ignited, becoming smoking torches in an instant. Grass crisped, stone scorched, the air warped with heat. The power tore from her body, seeming to rip through her lungs and heart and sear them from the inside; but she never stopped screaming until she blacked out.

She did not know how long unconsciousness held her before releasing her back into reality, but when it did calm had returned. The air was thick with smoke, and there came the harsh crackle and heat of burning trees.

She levered herself up, her muscles knotting and twitching, her insides scoured. Panting, she found her feet and her balance. She was alive; the pain told her so. Slowly she looked around the charred circle of destruction that surrounded her, and the sullenly smouldering trees beyond. Already the dampness from yesterday's rains was overcoming the hungry tongues of flame, and the fire was subsiding gradually.

She fought to reconcile the scene with the one she had been walking through when the pain struck her, and could not. Blackened rock faces hunkered out of soil gone hard and crisp. Scorched leaves curled into skeletal fists. Trees had been split in half, roughly decapitated or smashed aside. The very suddenness of the obliteration was almost impossible to understand; she could scarcely believe she was still in the same place as she had been when she had fainted.

The mask, unharmed, lay on the ground nearby, its empty gaze mocking. She stumbled over to it and picked it up. There was a terrible weariness in her body, a hazy blanket over her senses that smothered her towards sleep or unconsciousness or death – she was not sure which, and welcomed all equally.

Her eyes fell upon the crumpled white shape lying nearby. Numb, she staggered over to it, absently stuffing the mask into her belt as she went.

It was Asara. She lay strewn in a hollow where she had been thrown by the blast. One side of her had caught the brunt, evidently. Her robe was seared, her hair burned and smoking. Her hand and cheek were scarred terribly. She lay limp and still.

Kaiku began to tremble. She backed away, tears blurring her eyes, her fingers dragging at her face as if she might pull the flesh off and find the old Kaiku underneath, the one that had existed only yesterday, before chaos and madness took her in a stranglehold. Before she had lost her family. Before she had killed her handmaiden.

A choking sob escaped her, a sound not sane. She shook her head as she retreated, trying to deny what she saw; but the weight of truth crushed down on her, the evidence of her eyes accused. Panic swam in and seized her, and with a cry, she ran into the forest and was swallowed.

Asara lay where she was left, amid the smoke and the ruin, the gently drifting starfall settling on her to twinkle briefly and then die.

THREE

The roof gardens of the Imperial Keep might have seemed endless to a child at first, a vast, multi-levelled labyrinth of stony paths and shady arbours, of secret places and magical hidey-holes. The Heir-Empress Lucia tu Erinima, next in line to the throne of Saramyr, knew better. She had visited all of its many walls, and found that the place was as much a prison as a paradise, and it grew smaller every day.

She idled slowly down a rough-paved trail, her fingers dragging over a vine-laden trellis to her left. Somewhere nearby she could hear the rustle of a cat as it chased the dark squirrels that wound around the thin, elegant boles of the trees. The garden was an assembly of the most delicate foliage and flowers from all over the known world, arranged around a multitude of sheltered ornamental benches, statues and artful sculpture. Sprays of exotic foreign blooms stirred in the minute breeze; birds hop-swooped back and forth, their gullets vibrating as they chattered staccato songs to each other. Distantly, the four spires of the Keep's towers lanced upward, rendered pale by haze; and closer by the dome of the great temple that surmounted the centre of the Keep's roof was visible over the carefully placed rows of kamaka and chapapa trees. Today it was hot and balmy with the promise of a summer soon to come. The sun rode high in the sky, the single eye of Nuki, the bright god, whose gaze lit the world. She basked in his radiance as she watched the squirrels jumping through the treetops and spiralling along the boughs.

The Saramyr people ever tended towards tanned skin and a smooth beauty, and Lucia's paleness was striking by contrast.

More so was her hair, for true blonde was rare among the Saramyr, and her round face was framed by a flaxen cascade that fell down her back. She wore a dress of light green and simple jewellery; her tutors demanded that she learned to present herself elegantly, even when there was nobody to see her. She listened, as she always did, with a dreamy vacancy of expression, and they retreated in exasperation. She obeyed them, though. The look in her eyes was often mistaken for inattention, but it was not so.

She envied her tutors sometimes. They had a marvellous ability to focus their concentration on one thing to the exclusion of all others. It was inconvenient that they could not understand her situation in the way that she understood theirs; but Zaelis, at least, knew why she rarely seemed to be more than partially interested in any one thing. She had a lot more to think about than those with only five senses.

By the time she had learned to speak – at six months old – she already knew this to be a bad thing. She sensed it in the instinctive way of infants, in the sadness her mother's eyes held when she looked down at her baby. Even before Lucia had begun outwardly to manifest her talent, her mother the Empress knew. She was hidden from the world and put inside this gilded cage deep in the dark, sprawling heart of the Imperial Keep. She had been a prisoner ever since.

The cat emerged from a cluster of trees nearby on to the path, with an insouciantly casual walk. It looked her over with an insulting lack of respect and then turned its attention to the squirrels that raced about above it, watching those who were heading dangerously near to ground level. A moment later, it sprang off after them. She felt the alarm of the squirrels as it blundered in, their fast animal thoughts blaring. It had been months since the cat had been in the gardens, having found its way from who knew where, yet the squirrels were as surprised by its presence now as they had been the first time. Squirrels never learned.

Her animals were her friends, for she had no others. Well,

she supposed Zaelis was her friend, and her mother in a strange way. But them aside, she was alone. The solitude was all she knew. She was quite content with her own company; and yet when she dreamed, she dreamed of freedom.

Her mother Anais, Blood Empress of Saramyr and ruler of the land, visited her at least once a day, when she was not constrained by official business. As the author of her confinement, Lucia sometimes considered hating her; but she hated nobody. She was too forgiving for that, too ready to empathise. There was not a person she had met yet who was so black-hearted that she could find no redeeming quality to them.

When she told Zaelis this, he reminded her that she hadn't met many.

It was her mother who taught her to keep her talents secret, her mother who had seen to it that her tutors were kept silent about the true nature of the child they taught. It was her mother also who had confirmed what she already knew: that people would hate her, fear her, if they knew what she was. That was why she was hidden.

The Empress had begged her daughter's forgiveness a hundred times for keeping her locked away from the world. She wanted nothing more than to let Lucia run free, but it was simply too dangerous. Anais's sorrow was, she said, as great as Lucia's own. Lucia loved her mother because she believed her.

But there were dark clouds massing beyond the horizon; this she knew. Her dreams of late had been plagued by an unseen menace.

Often, as she slept, she walked the corridors of the Imperial Keep, beyond the confines of her rooms. Sometimes she visited her mother, but her mother never saw her. Lucia would watch the Empress sew, or bathe, or gaze out of the windows of the Keep. Sometimes Lucia would listen to her consult with advisors about the affairs of the realm. Other times she would walk through the rooms of the servants as

they gossiped and cooked and coupled. Occasionally someone would see her, and panic ensued; but most just looked
straight through her.

Once she asked her mother about some things she had seen
in her dreams, and her mother's face grew a little sad, and she
kissed her daughter on the forehead and said nothing. From
this, Lucia knew not to mention them again; but she also
knew that these were no ordinary dreams, and that what she
was witnessing was real.

Through her dreams she learned about the world outside,
without ever leaving her room. And yet still she was con-
founded by the perimeter of the Keep, unable to roam
beyond it. The city of Axekami, that surrounded the Imperial
Keep, was simply too far outside her experience. She could
not dream it. She had only widened the walls of her pen.

It had been a little over a year since she had first begun
dream-walking; and not long after that the dream lady had
appeared. But a fortnight ago, she had suddenly discovered
that there was a new stranger who visited her in the dark.
Now she woke sweating and shaking, her body taut with fear
at the nameless presence that stalked her through the corridors of nightmare, prowling inexorably behind.

She did not know what it was, but she knew what it meant.
Something bad had found her; perhaps the very thing her
mother had tried to hide her from. Change was coming. She
did not know whether to feel joyous or afraid.

On the far side of the roof garden, something stirred. The
gardeners had been working here of late, digging up the
dying winter blooms to replace them with summer flowers.
A wheelbarrow sat idle by the path, forks and spades laid
askew within it. Beneath the thick screen of trees, newly
turned earth lay moist and black and fertile in the sun,
waiting for the seeds it could impart its life to.

The turf shuddered. First a small movement, and then a
great disturbance as the man buried beneath it rose up,

sloughing off dirt. A tall, thin man, nearing his fortieth harvest, with short, greying hair and stubbled cheeks. Silently, he pulled himself free and spat out the short, thick bamboo tube that had been his breathing apparatus. He dusted himself off as best he could and straightened.

Purloch tu Irisi had always been lucky, but this was ridiculous. Already he had evaded enough dangers to put off even the most determined intruder. He had slipped past sentries, rappelled down sheer walls, crept past observation posts. He had made a blind jump across a fifty-foot drop to a lightless wall, trusting only his instincts to find and grip the edge. Frankly, he believed he should have been caught or dead by now. He had always prided himself on being the most adept cat-burglar in the city, capable of getting into anywhere; but even he had been a whisker's breadth from discovery three times since last night, and twice had edged by death with barely an inch to spare. The Heir-Empress was guarded more closely than the most precious jewel.

His confidence had been badly shaken by the events of the night before. He could hardly credit the luck that had brought him this far, but he doubted it would take him much further. He was living on borrowed time. All he wanted to do was to have this business over and done with and get out in one piece.

The person who had come to him with the offer was an obvious middleman, a hireling sent to protect the identity of the real brain behind the plan. Purloch had met enough to know. And the offer was so intriguing, especially to a man who prided himself on his work as Purloch did. To get to the Heir-Empress's chambers . . . such a thing was close to impossible!

But the middleman was remarkably well informed, with detailed plans of the castle to hand and information about sentry movements and blind spots; and the price he offered was enough for Purloch to retire on and live wealthy for the rest of his days. Think of it! To end his illustrious career on such a dizzying high! He would be left a legend among the underworld, and his days of risk-taking would be done.

It was a potent lure, but the mission was too dangerous to be taken on faith. So he shadowed the middleman back to his home, and observed as he met another man later that day, and that man met another the next night, and through him Purloch finally traced the offer to its source. It had taken all his skill just to keep up with them, even though they had been unaware he was following. They were undoubtedly good. He was assuredly better.

The source, then: Barak Sonmaga, head of Blood Amacha. They were powerful among the high families, and old antagonists to Blood Erinima, to which the Empress and her daughter belonged. Purloch could divine nothing of Blood Amacha's plans, but he could surmise that he was being made part of something huge, a pawn in the game between two of the empire's greatest families.

It was a terrible risk, now that he knew the stakes. But he could not turn it down, though he had to admit he was puzzled by the nature of his task. He had taken every precaution he could – including what retribution he could muster against his employer if he should be double-crossed in some way – but in the end, the money and glory were too great to ignore.

Now he was wishing he had listened to sense, and turned down the offer.

He had spent days posing as a servant, observing the forms and rhythms of the castle before he moved. Getting into the Keep had been the easy part; there were forgotten ways, paths that history had lost but which he had unearthed again. But it was the slow process of planning a way to penetrate the defences at its core that was the true art. Even with the detailed information his employer had given him, it was abominably hard to conceive of how he might get to the Heir-Empress. Only a select few had ever seen her at all – the most trusted guards, the most honoured tutors – and the circle of people surrounding her was so small that infiltration by disguise or deception was not even remotely viable.

But Purloch was patient, and clever. He talked with the right people, asked the right questions, without ever drawing suspicion to himself. And soon his opportunity came.

He had made a special point of befriending some of the gardeners, a guileless, honest group whose loyalty to their liege was beyond question, inspired by the almost religious awe that the peasantry felt towards their masters and mistresses. They were forbidden on pain of death to talk about the Heir-Empress, even though they had never seen her, for the gardening was done only in those hours of the day when Lucia was not outside; but they were still informative enough, in their way. It was clear they were honoured to be gardeners to the future ruler of Saramyr, and they talked about the minutiae of their jobs endlessly. The day before yesterday, Purloch had learned they were soon to be digging new beds to plant a fresh batch of summer flowers that would not wilt in the heat. It had given him the idea he needed. And so the plan had formed.

He had infiltrated the garden at night, for it would certainly have been impossible during the day. There were too many guards, too many rifles, even for him; it would be simply suicide. But with the cover of darkness, and the moons all but hidden beneath the horizon, he had made it. Barely.

Once inside, he had searched for his place to hide. A light poison in the drinks of the gardeners had seen to it that they were forced to spend the next day in bed – he wouldn't like to find his guts pierced by a fork as he lay under the turf. He buried himself expertly before the dawn came, and then waited in his earthen cocoon for daybreak.

His contact had informed him that guards searched the garden in the morning, before the Heir-Empress was allowed up. They were just as aware as Purloch was that the concealing shadows of night might afford an intruder a slim chance of getting past the sentries, and even that slim chance was too much. The information was good. Purloch heard the clatter of pikes as they passed him by. But they had searched the garden a thousand times before and never found a thing, so their search was only cursory. They never suspected. The newly turned soil of the flower bed showed no sign of the disturbance Purloch had created while digging himself into it.

Now the guards were gone, and the child was here alone. Time to do what had to be done. Slipping silently along, he undid the clasp of the dagger at his belt.

He found the girl in a small paved oval hemmed in by trees. A cat was chasing its tail, while the Heir-Empress watched it with a strangely detached look on her face. The cat was absorbed in its own capering, so much so that it did not hear his approach. Lucia did, however, though he had made not a sound. She slowly looked into the foliage, right at him, and said: 'Who are you?'

The man slid out from behind a tumisi tree, and the cat bolted. Lucia regarded the newcomer with an unfathomable gaze.

'My name is of no consequence,' Purloch replied. He was clearly nervous, glancing about, eager to be gone.

Lucia watched him placidly.

'My lady, I must take something from you,' he said, drawing his dagger from its sheath.

The air around them exploded in a frenzy of movement, a thrashing of black wings that beat at the senses and caused Purloch to cry out and fall to his knees, his arm across his face to shield it from the tumult.

As quickly as it had begun, it was over. Purloch lowered his arm, and his breath caught in his throat.

The child was cloaked in ravens. They buried her, perching on her shoulders and arms: a mantle of dark feathers. They surrounded her, too, a thick carpet of the creatures. Dozens more perched in the branches nearby. Now and then one of them stirred, preening under a wing or shuffling position; but all of them watched him with their dreadful black, beady eyes.

Purloch was dumbstruck with terror.

'What did you want to take?' Lucia asked softly. Her expression and tone reflected none of the malevolence the ravens projected.

Purloch swallowed. He was aware of nothing more than the ravens. The birds were *protecting* her. And he knew, with a fearful certainty, that they would tear him to bloody rags at a thought from the child.

He tried to speak, but nothing came out. He swallowed and tried again. 'A . . . a lock of your hair, my lady. Nothing more.' He looked down at the dagger still in his hand, and realised that his haste to get his prize and escape had made him foolish. He should not have drawn the blade.

Lucia walked slowly towards him, the ravens shuffling aside to let her pass. Purloch stared at her in naked fear, this monster of a child. What *was* she?

And yet what he saw in her pale blue gaze was anything but monstrous. She knew he was not a killer. She did not think him evil; she felt sympathy for him, not hate. And beneath it all was a kind of sadness, an acceptance of something inevitable that he did not understand.

Gently, she took the dagger from his hand, and with it cut away a curl of her blonde, tumbling hair. She pressed it into his palm.

'Go back to your masters,' she said quietly, the ravens stirring at her shoulder. 'Begin what must be begun.'

Purloch drew a shuddering breath and bowed his head, still kneeling. 'Thank you,' he whispered, humbled. And then he was gone, disappearing into the trees, with Lucia watching after and wondering what would come of what she had done.

FOUR

It was four days after the murder of her family that Kaiku was found. The one who discovered her was a young acolyte of the earth goddess Enyu, returning to the temple from a frustrating day of failed meditation. His name was Tane tu Jeribos.

He had almost missed her as he passed by, buried as she was under a drift of leaves at the base of a thick-boled kiji tree. His mind was on other things. That, he supposed, was the whole problem. The priests had taught him the theory behind attuning himself to nature, letting himself become blank and empty so he could hear the slow heart of the forest; yes, he understood the theory well. It was just that putting it into practice was proving next to impossible.

You cannot feel the presence of Enyu and her daughters until you are calm inside. It was the infuriating mantra that Master Olec droned at him every time he became agitated. But how calm could he be? He had relaxed to the best of his ability, evacuated his mind of all the clutter, but it was never enough. Doubly frustrating, for he excelled at his other studies, and his other masters were pleased with his progress. This lesson seemed to elude him, and he could not understand why.

He was turning over sullen thoughts in his mind when he saw the shape buried beneath the leaves. The sight made him jump; his first reaction was to reach for the rifle slung across his back. Then he saw what it was: a young woman, lying still. Cautiously he approached. Though he saw no threat from her, he had lived his whole life in the forests of Saramyr, and he knew enough to assume everything was dangerous until proven otherwise. Spirits took many forms, and not all of them were friendly. In fact, it seemed they were getting more and more hostile as the seasons glided by, and the animals grew wilder by the day.

He reached out and poked the girl in the shoulder, ready to jump back if she moved suddenly. When she did not respond, he shoved her again. This time she stirred, making a soft moan.

'Do you hear me?' he asked, but the girl did not reply. He shook her again, and her eyes flickered open: fevered, roving. She looked at him, but did not seem to see. Instead she sighed something incoherent, and murmured her way back to sleep again.

Tane looked around for some clue about her, but he could see nothing in the balmy evening light except the thick forest. She seemed starved, exhausted and sick. He brushed back her tangled brown hair and laid a hand on her forehead. Her skin burned. Her eyes moved restlessly beneath their lids.

As he was examining her, his hand brushed across the leaves that were covering her, and he paused to pick one up. It was fresh-fallen. In fact, all of them were. The tree had shed them on the girl as she lay, not more than half a day past. He smiled to himself. No tree-spirit would harbour an evil thing in such a way. He straightened and bowed.

'Thank you, spirit of the tree, for sheltering this girl,' he said. 'Please convey my gratitude to your mistress Aspinis, daughter of Enyu.'

The tree made no response; but then, they never did. These were young trees, not like the ancient ipi. Barely aware, all but senseless. Like newborn children.

Tane gathered up the girl in his arms. She was a little heavier than he had expected, but by her lithe figure it was apparent that it was muscle and not fat. Though Tane was no great size himself, forest life had toughened him and tautened his own muscles, and he had no trouble carrying her. It was a short walk to the temple, and she did not wake.

*

The temple was buried deep in the forest, situated on the banks of the River Kerryn. The river flowed from the mountains to the north-east, winding through the heart of the Forest of Yuna before curving westward and heading to the capital. The building itself was a low, elegant affair, with little ostentation to overshadow the scenery all around. Temples to Enyu and her daughters were intentionally kept simple out of humility, except in the cities where gaudiness was a virtual prerequisite for a place of worship. It was decorated in simple shades of cream and white, supported by beams of black ash, artfully describing lines and perimeters across the structure. It was two storeys high, the second one built further back than the first to take advantage of the slant of the hill. Gentle invocations were inscribed in the henge-shaped frame of the main doors, picked out in unvarnished wood, a mantra to the goddess of nature that was as simple and peaceful as the temple itself. A prayer-bell hung above a small shrine just to one side of the doors, a cairn of stones with bowls of smouldering incense inside, long-stemmed lilies and fruit laid out on a ledge before an icon of Enyu: a carved wooden bear statuette, with one mighty paw circling a cub.

A curving bridge arced from one side of the Kerryn to the other, carven pillars etched with all manner of bird, beast and fish sunk deep into the river bed. The river was a deep, melancholy blue, its natural transparency made doleful by the salts and minerals it carried down from the Tchamil Mountains. It threw back the sun in fins of purple-edged brightness, dappling the smooth underside of the bridge with an endless play of shifting water-light. The effect, intentionally, was that of calm and beauty and idyll.

Tane consulted with his masters, and an aged priest examined her. He concluded that she was starving and fevered, much as Tane had said, but there were no more serious afflictions. She would recover with care.

'She is your responsibility,' Master Olec told him. 'See if you can keep your mind on something for a change.'

Tane knew Olec's withered old tongue too well to be offended. He put her in a guest room on the upper storey. The room was spare and white, with a sleeping-mat in a corner beneath the wide, square windows, whose shutters were locked open against the heat of oncoming summer. Like most windows in Saramyr, there was no need for glass – much of the year it was too hot, and shutters worked just as well against adverse weather.

As evening wore on to a dark red sunset, Tane brewed a tea of boneset, yarrow and echinacea for her fever. He made her sip and swallow it as hot as he dared, half a cup every two hours. She muttered and flinched, and she did not wake, but she did drink it down. He brought a bucket of cool water and mopped her brow, cleaned her face and cheeks. He examined her tongue, gently holding her mouth open. He checked the flutter of her pulse at her throat and wrist. When he had done all he could, he settled himself on a wicker mat and watched her sleep.

The priests had undressed her – it was necessary to determine if she had suffered from poison thorns, insect bites, anything that might influence her recovery – and given her a sleeping-robe of light green. Now she lay with a thin sheet twined through her legs and resting on her ribs, pushed out of place by her stirrings. It was too hot to lie under anyway, especially with her fever, but Tane had been obliged to provide it out of respect for her modesty. He had cared for the sick before, young and old, male and female, and the priests knew it and trusted him. But this one interested him more than most. Where had she come from, and how had she got into the state she was in? Her very helplessness provoked in him the need to help her. She was incapacitated and utterly alone. The spirits knew what kind of ordeals she had gone through wandering in the forest; she was lucky even to be alive.

'Who are you, then?' he asked softly, fascinated.

His eyes ranged over the lines of her cheekbones, a little too pronounced now but they would soften with the return of her health. He watched her lips press together as she spoke half-formed dream-words. The light from outside began to fade, and still he stayed, and wondered about her.

The fever broke two days later, yet there was no immediate recovery. She had beaten the illness, but she had not overcome whatever it was that plagued her waking hours and haunted her dreams. For a week she was nearly catatonic with misery, unable to lift herself from the bed, crying almost constantly. Very little of what she said made sense, and the priests began to doubt her sanity. Tane believed otherwise. He had sat by her while she sobbed and raved, and the few fragments of what he could understand led him to the conclusion that she had suffered some terrible tragedy, endured loss such as no human should have to undergo.

He was excused from some of his less pressing duties while he cared for his patient, though there was little he could do for her now that she was physically well again. He made her eat, though she had no appetite. He prepared a mild sedative – a tincture of blue cohosh and motherwort – and gave it to her to gentle down some of her worse fits of grief. He made an infusion of hops, skullcap and valerian to put her to sleep at night. And he sat with her.

Then one morning, as he came into her room with a breakfast of duck eggs and wheatcakes, he found her at the window, looking out over the Kerryn to the trees beyond. Insects hummed in the morning air. He paused in the doorway.

'Daygreet,' he said automatically. She turned with a start. 'Are you feeling better?'

'You are the one who has been looking after me,' she said. 'Tane?'

He smiled slightly and bowed. 'Would you like to eat?'

Kaiku nodded and sat down cross-legged on her mat, arranging her sleeping-robe about her. She had little recollection of the past two weeks. She could remember impressions, unpleasant moments of fright or hunger or sadness, but not the circumstances that attended them. She remembered this face, though: this bald, shaven head, those even, tanned features, the pale green eyes and the light beige robes he always wore. She had never imagined a young priest – to her, they had always been old and snappy, hiding their wisdom inside a shell of cantankerousness. This one had some of the air of gravity she usually associated with the holy orders, but she remembered moments of light-heartedness too, when he had made jokes and laughed at them himself when she did not. By his speech, she guessed he had come from a moderately affluent family, somewhere above the peasantry though probably still local. While he was educated, he was certainly not high-born. The complexities of the Saramyrrhic language meant it was possible to guess at a person's origins simply by the way they used it. Tane's speech was looser and less ruthlessly elocuted than hers.

'How long has it been?' she asked, as she slowly ate.

'Ten days since we found you. You were wandering for some time before that,' Tane replied.

'Ten days? Spirits, it seems like it was forever. I thought it would never pass. I thought . . .' She looked up at him. 'I thought I could never stop crying.'

'The heart heals, given time,' Tane said. 'Tears dry.'

'My family are gone,' she said suddenly. She had needed to say it aloud, to test herself, to see if she could. The words provoked no new pain in her. She had mastered her grief, sickened of it; though it had taken a long time, her natural wilfulness would not let her be kept down. Her sorrow had spent itself, and while she doubted it would ever leave her entirely, it would not swallow her again. 'They were murdered,' she added.

'Ah,' said Tane. He could not think of anything else to say.

'The mask,' she said. 'I had a mask with me . . . I think.'

'It was in your pack,' said Tane. 'It is safe.'

36

She handed her plate back to him, having eaten only a little. 'Thank you,' she said. 'For taking care of me. I would like to rest.'

'It was my honour,' he replied, getting up. 'Would you like a tea to help you sleep?'

'I do not think I will need it, now,' she said.

He retreated to the door, but before he reached it he stopped.

'I don't know your name . . .'

'Kaiku tu Makaima,' came the reply.

'Kaiku, there was someone you mentioned several times in your delirium,' he said, turning his shoulder to look at her. 'Someone you said was with you in the woods. Asara. Perhaps she is still—'

'A demon killed her,' Kaiku replied, her eyes on the floor. 'She is gone.'

'I see,' Tane replied. 'I'll come back soon.' And with that he left.

A demon killed her, Kaiku thought. *And I am that demon.*

She did rest for a time, for she was weakened by her ordeal. She felt more drained than she had ever thought it was possible to feel, more exhausted than she could ever remember. The feeling spurred a memory that she had not come across for months, a random jag of pain that emerged to worry at the fresh wound of her loss. She steeled herself against it. She would not forget. Some things were worth remembering.

It had been at Mishani's summer house by the coast, where she and her brother Machim often stayed. They had always been competitive, and growing up with a brother had left her with some hopelessly unfeminine tendencies – one of which was a stubbornness that verged on mule-headed. One morning, she and Machim had become embroiled in their usual game of boasting who was better at what. The stakes were raised and raised until between them they had devised an

endurance course involving archery, swimming, cliff-climb-
ing, running and shooting that was far beyond the capacity of
most athletes, let alone two youths who had rarely tasted
hardship. Out of sheer unwillingness to concede, they both
agreed to attempt it.

The archery they handled easily – they had to shoot ten
arrows, and a bullseye meant that they could run down to the
beach and swim across the bay to the cliffs. Machim
succeeded before she did. The swimming was hard work, for
she was trying to catch up with her brother and narrow his
head start. She gained ground on the cliffs, but by now the
ache in their bodies was evident, and their muscles were
trembling. Machim was flagging badly, and he barely made it
over the top before collapsing in a panting heap. Kaiku could
have given up then and claimed the victory; but it was not
enough for her. She began to run back along the cliff top to
Mishani's house, where they had set up a makeshift rifle
range. Her body burned, her vision blurred, she wanted to be
sick, but she would not let herself stop. She reached the
house, but the effort of picking up the rifle was too much for
her, and she fainted.

She was put to bed then, and until now she had never felt
anything like the exhaustion she had experienced on that day.
The challenge had taken everything out of her, and it seemed
like there was barely enough left to go on surviving. Mishani
chided her for her stubbornness. Her brother sneaked in and
congratulated her on her victory when nobody else was
around.

But however bad that had been, this was worse. Her very
soul felt exhausted, used up in the effort to expel the grief of
her family's death. She found that thinking of her brother
now brought no tears, only a dull ache. Well, she could
endure that, if she must.

It was not only the loss of her family that troubled her,
however. It was the power . . . the terrible force that had
claimed Asara's life in the forest. Something had come from

within her, something agonising and evil, a thing of raw destruction and flame. *Was* she a demon? Or had she one inside her? Could she even let herself be around other people, after what she had done to—

'No,' she said aloud, to add authority to her denial. It was useless to think that way. She had fled from the horror once already; now she had to face it. Whatever was the cause of Asara's death, it would not be exorcised by hiding herself away from the world. Besides, it had shown no sign of re-occurring in the time since that first cataclysmic event. She felt a hard coil of determination growing inside her. Suddenly she resented the presence of this side of herself that she had never known before. She would understand it, learn about it, and destroy it if necessary. She would not carry around this unnamed evil for the rest of her life. She refused to.

Asara. She had been the key. She had spoke of a cause. They had been watching her father, hoping to persuade him to join them. And they had been watching her, for two whole years.

Mostly it was because of you, Kaiku. Your condition.

Condition? Could she have meant the cruel flame that took her life? How long had it slumbered inside her, then, since Asara had come to her two years before this *condition* ever manifested itself? She thought back to the circumstances that might have attended her arrival. One of her previous hand-maidens had disappeared without word or warning, that was true. Was there anything suspicious in that? Not at the time – after all, she was only a servant – but in retrospect it made her uneasy. No, she had to think before that. She had heard the tales of the spirits of the forest turning bad. She knew the stories of the achicita, the demon vapours that came in the swelter of summer and stole in through the nostrils of sleeping men and women, making them sick on the inside. She knew about the baum-ki, who bit ankles like snakes and left their poison dormant in the body, to be passed on through saliva or other, more personal fluids, hopping from person to person and becoming lethal only when it came across a baby in a womb, killing mother and child in one terrible haemorrhage.

It was the only sense she could make. There was something within, something unknown, something that had lashed out and killed. Had the shin-shin been after her, to claim whatever was inside her? What was she carrying? What was the *condition* Asara had spoken of?

But Asara was gone, and all she had left behind were questions. What manner of thing was she, who could suck the breath from one person and give it to another? Another demon, sent to look after her own? Who were her masters, the ones who had sent her? And what had her father been involved in, that such a tragedy should be visited on their house?

She slept, and her dreams were full of a face of black and red, a cackling spirit that haunted her in the darkness with the voice of her father.

The priests allowed her to use their sacred glade to make an offering to Omecha, the silent harvester, god of death and the afterlife. It lay along a narrow, winding trail that wove up the hill to the rear of the temple. Tane led the way, taking her hand when she stumbled. Having spent so long in convalescence, her muscles were shockingly weak, and the incline was almost too much for her to take. But Tane was there, keeping a respectful silence, and with his help she made it.

The glade was a spot of preternatural beauty, scattered with low, smooth white stones that peeped from the undergrowth, upon which complex pictograms were carved and painted red. There appeared to be no man-made boundary or border to separate it from the surrounding forest – in fact, were it not for the stones and the shrine, Kaiku would have not recognised it as a sacred place at all. There was a thin stream running through the glade, with the far bank rising higher than the near side, and a great old kamaka tree surmounting it, its thick roots knotted through the soil and its pendulous leaf-tendrils hanging mournfully over the water in flowery ropes. On the near side of the stream was the shrine, little bigger than the one that sat in front of the temple. It had been carved from the bole of a young tree, and the interior was hung with wind-chimes and tiny prayer scrolls; fresh flowers had been laid inside it, and incense sticks smouldered in little clay pots to either side.

She gave Tane a nod and a wan smile, and he bowed, murmured a swift prayer to Enyu to excuse himself from the glade, and retreated down the trail.

Alone, Kaiku took a breath and assembled her thoughts. There was no emotion involved in this; she had spent that entirely by now. This was ritual. Her sorrow had eaten her from the inside and then turned and devoured itself into emptiness. All that was left was what was inevitable, what honour and tradition demanded she do. She acceded without complaint. Everything had fallen apart around her, but this at least was inviolable, and there was some comfort in that.

She knelt among the incense in the grey votive robe the priests had given her, for she had no formal wear and it was necessary to be respectful here. She prayed to her ancestors to guide her family through the Gate, past laughing Yoru into the golden Fields. She named each of them aloud to Omecha, so that his wife Noctu might write them in her great book, and record their deeds in life. And finally she prayed to Ocha, Emperor of the gods and also god of war, revenge, exploration and endeavour. She begged for strength to aid her purpose, asking for his blessing in finding the one that struck down her family. If he would aid her, she swore to avenge them, no matter the cost.

And with that oath, her course was set.

When she left the glade, she felt exorcised somehow. She had left a part of herself behind there, the part that was confused and frightened and heavy with grief. She had a new path now. It was what her family's honour demanded.

She would not let them die forgotten; she would right the injustice. There was no other course open to her.

After she had walked back to the temple with Tane, she reclaimed the mask from the priests and looked at it often, turning it about in her hands. Asara said her father had been killed for this mask. What was it, and what did it mean? Sometimes she toyed with the idea of putting it on, but she knew better. Even if Asara had not warned her, she had heard enough tales of the Weavers to learn caution.

Masks are the most dangerous weapons in the world.

The next morning, Tane brought her clothes with her breakfast.

'You've been lying about too long,' he said. 'Come outside. You should see this.'

Kaiku nodded muzzily. She had no particularly strong inclination to do anything, but it seemed easier to go along with his suggestion than to refuse it. When he had gone, she stood up and stretched her limbs, then clambered into her travel clothes that the priests had washed and mended. Someone – presumably Tane – had added a purple silk sash to the bundle, a splash of colour amid the beige and brown. She tied it loosely round her waist, letting it hang down her thigh. It made her attire a little more feminine, at least. She laced up the open-throated shirt and gave herself a perfunctory examination. A smile touched her lips, more wry than humorous. The sash made her look like some flamboyant bandit.

She joined Tane outside in the bright glare of the sun. It was a good time to be out, before the ascending heat became uncomfortable. She appreciated the warmth of Nuki's gaze on some dim and distant level, but it did not seem to penetrate as it had done in the days when her family were still alive. Rinji birds were drifting down the Kerryn, their long, white necks twisting down to snap at fish and beetles that strayed too close. Tane was watching them distractedly.

'They're early this year,' he observed. 'It's going to be a long, hot summer.'

Kaiku shaded her eyes and followed the languid procession with her gaze. Several of the priests had paused in their work and were studying the birds with contemplative expressions. As children, she and Machim used to head out to the river-bank every morning in early summer, to wait for the rinji to come down from their nesting sites in the mountains, down to the plains where the better feeding was. With their long, gangly legs tucked beneath them and their massive wings folded, they glided with effortless grace, riding the currents of the Kerryn towards the lowlands.

When the first rinji had drifted out of sight – there were only a dozen or so, the vanguard of the impending exodus – Tane led Kaiku down to the bank; but at her request, they crossed over the bridge and sat on the south side instead, looking over the shimmering deep-blue expanse towards the unassuming temple.

'This is the way we always watched them,' she said by way of explanation. 'Machim and I.' Watching the birds going from left to right instead of the opposite had jarred with her memories and made her unaccountably uncomfortable.

Tane nodded. Whether it was simple preference, or if she was consciously trying to recapture the fond moments she shared with her dead sibling, he was prepared to indulge her.

'It seems there are fewer and fewer each year,' Tane said. 'Word comes down from the mountains that their nesting grounds aren't so safe any more.'

Kaiku raised an eyebrow. 'Why not?'

'Fewer of the eggs hatch, that's one thing,' he replied, rubbing his bald scalp, rasping his palm against the stubble. 'But they say there are things in the mountains now that can climb up to where they lay. And those things are multiplying. It wasn't like that ten years ago.'

Kaiku found herself wondering suddenly why Tane had

troubled to bring her out here at all, why they were sitting together and talking about birds.

'I have watched them every year since I can remember,' she said. 'And I used to stay up in the autumn and look out for them flying back.'

It was an aimless comment, a lazy observation thrown out into the conversation, but Tane took it as a cue to continue his train of thought.

'The beautiful things are dying,' he said gravely, looking upstream to where the Kerryn bent into the trees and was lost to sight. 'More and more, faster and faster. The priests can sense it; *I* can sense it. It's in the forest, in the soil. The trees know.'

Kaiku was not quite sure how to respond to that, so she kept her silence.

'Why can't we *do* anything about it?' he said, but the question was rhetorical, an expression of impotent frustration.

They watched the birds come down the river all that day, and it did seem that there were fewer than Kaiku remembered.

She stayed another week at the temple while she regained her strength. The waiting was chafing her, but the priests insisted, and she believed they were right. She was too weak to leave, and she needed time to formulate a plan, to decide where to travel to and how to get there.

There was never really any doubt as to her destination, however. There was only one person who might be able to help her learn the circumstances that surrounded her father's death, and only one person who she felt she could trust utterly. Mishani, her friend since childhood and daughter of Barak Avun tu Koli. She was part of the Imperial Court at Axekami, and she was privy to the machinations that went on there. Kaiku had not seen her much since they both passed their eighteenth harvest, for Mishani had been enmeshed in the politics of Blood Koli; yet despite everything, she found herself growing excited at the thought of seeing her friend again.

She walked with Tane often during that week, traipsing through the forest or along the river. Tane was interested in her past, in who she was and how she had come to be under that tree where he had found her. She talked freely about her family; it made her feel good to recall their triumphs, their habits, their petty foibles. But she never spoke of what happened at her house that night, and she made no mention of Asara's fate again. He was light-hearted company, and she liked him, though he tended to swing into unfathomably dark moods from time to time, and then she found him unpleasant and left him alone.

'You're leaving soon,' Tane said as they walked side by side in the trees behind the temple. It was the hour between morning oblations and study, and the young acolyte had asked her to join him. Birds chirruped all around and the forest rustled with hidden animals.

Kaiku fiddled with a strand of her hair. It was a childhood habit that her mother used to chide her for. She had thought she had grown out of it, but it seemed to have returned of late. 'Soon,' she agreed.

'I wish you would tell me what you are hurrying for. Are you fleeing your family's murderers, or trying to find them?'

She glanced at him, faintly startled. He had never been quite so blunt with her. 'To find them,' she said.

'Revenge is an unhealthy motive, Kaiku.'

'I have no other motives left, my friend,' she said. But he was a friend in name only. She would not let him close to her, would not divulge anything of true worth to him. There was no sense inviting more grief. She knew she was leaving him; it was necessary, for she still did not know the nature of the demon inside her, and she feared she might harm him as she had Asara. By the same token, she was terribly afraid of endangering Mishani by her presence; but she knew if

45

Mishani were asked, she would willingly take that chance, and so would Kaiku for her. There was some comfort in that, at least. Their bonds of loyalty went beyond question. And there was scarcely any other choice, anyway; it was the only course she could see.

'I'd like it if you stayed,' he said solemnly. She stopped and gave him a curious look. 'For a while longer,' he amended, colouring a little.

She smiled, and it made her radiant. For a moment, she felt something like temptation. He was physically attractive to her, there was no doubt of that. His shaven head, his taut and muscular body honed by outdoor chores and an ascetic diet, his deep-buried intensity; these were qualities she had never encountered in the high-borns she had met in the cities. But though they had spent much time together in the past week, she felt she had not learned anything about him. Why had he become a priest? Why was he driven to heal and help others, as he professed? He was as closed to her as she was to him. The two of them had fenced around each other, never letting their guards down. This was the nearest he had got to real honesty. She exploited the opening.

'What is it I mean to you, Tane?' she asked. 'You found me, you saved my life and sat with me through it all. You have my endless gratitude for that. But why?'

'I'm a priest. It's my . . . my calling,' he said, frowning.

'Not good enough,' she said, folding her arms beneath her breasts.

He gave her a dark look, wounded that she would pressure him this way. 'I lost a sister,' he said. 'She would not be much younger than you are. I could not help her, but I could help you.' He looked angrily at the ground and scuffed it with his sandals. 'I lost my family too. We have that much in common.'

She wanted to ask how, but she had no right. She would not share her secrets with him, nor he with her. And therein lay the barrier between them, and it was unassailable.

'One of the priests is going downriver to the village of Ban tomorrow,' she said, unfolding her arms. 'I can get a skiff from there to the capital.'

'And you think your friend Mishani will be able to help you?' Tane asked, somewhat bitterly.

'She is the only hope I have,' Kaiku replied.

'Then I wish you good journey,' said Tane, though his tone suggested otherwise. 'And may Panazu, god of the rain and rivers, guard your way. I must return to my studies.'

With that, he stalked away and back to the temple. Kaiku watched him until he was obscured by the trees. In another time, in another place . . . maybe there could have been something between them. Well, there were greater concerns for now. She thought of the mask that lay in her room, hidden behind a beam on the ceiling. She thought of how she would get to Axekami, and what she might find there.

She thought of the future, and she feared it.

FIVE

It had to come to this, Anais thought. *I was only putting off the inevitable. But by the spirits, how did they find out?*

The Blood Empress of Saramyr stood in her chambers, her slender profile limned in the bright midday sunlight, the hot breath of the streets reaching even here, so far above. Below her lay the great city of Axekami, heart of the Saramyr empire. It sprawled down the hill and away from her, a riot of colours and buildings: long red temples shunting up against gaudy markets; smooth white bathhouses huddling close to green-domed museums; theatres and tanneries, forges and workhouses. Distantly, the sparkling blue loop of the River Kerryn cut through the profusion on its way to meet its sister, the Jalaza, and combine to form the Zan. Axekami was built on the confluence of the three rivers, and their sweeping flow served to carve the city neatly up into districts, joined by proud bridges.

She let her eyes range over the capital, over *her* city, the centrepiece of a civilisation that stretched thousands of miles across an entire continent and encompassed millions of people. The life here never ceased, an endless, beautiful swelter of thronging industry, thought and art. Orators held forth in Speaker's Square while crowds gathered to jeer or clap; manxthwa and horses jostled in their pens while traders harangued passers-by and jabbered at each other; philosophers sat in meditation while across the street new lovers coupled in fervour. Scholars debated in the parks, blood spewed on to tiles as a bull banathi's throat was slashed by a butcher's blade, entertainers leered as they pulled impossible contortions, deals were made and broken and reforged.

Axekami was the hub of an empire spread so wide that it was only possible to maintain it via the medium of instantaneous communication through Weavers, the administrative, political and social fulcrum on which the entire vastness of Saramyr balanced. Anais loved it, loved its constant ability to regenerate, the turbulence of innovation and activity; but she knew well enough to fear it a little too, and she felt a ghost of that fear brush her now.

The Imperial Keep stood high and magnificent on the crest of a hill, looking out over all. It was a vast edifice of gold and bronze, shaped like a truncated pyramid, with its top flattened and surmounted by a wondrous temple to Ocha, Emperor of the gods. It swarmed with pillars and arches, broken up by enormous statues that grew out of the walls, or which snaked along the grandiose façade to wind around shining columns. At the four points of the compass stood a tall, slender tower, reaching high above the main body of the Keep, each one dedicated to one of the Guardians of the Four Winds. Narrow bridges ran between the towers and the Keep, spanning the chasms between. The whole was surrounded by a great wall, decorated with carvings and scrollwork all along its length, and broken only by a mighty gate, with its soaring arc of gold inscribed with blessings.

Anais turned away from the vista. The room was wide and airy, its walls and floor made from a smooth, semi-reflective stone known as *lach*. Three tall arches gave her the view of her city; several smaller ones provided access to other rooms. A trickling fountain was the centrepiece, fashioned in the shape of two manta rays, their wings touching as they danced.

Messages had been arriving all day, both by hand and across the Weave, calling for a council. Her allies felt betrayed, her enemies incensed, and nothing she could do would assuage them. The only heir to the throne of Saramyr was an Aberrant. She should have been killed at birth.

Weave-lord Vyrrch was in the room with her; the very last

person she wanted to see right now. The Weavers were the ones who did the killing, and she could feel glowering disapprobation in every syllable he spoke. He was, however, wise enough not to berate her for hiding her child away from them, even though she knew that was what he was thinking. Did that foul ghoul seriously expect her to give up her only child to their tender mercies?

'You must be very cautious, Mistress,' he gurgled. 'Very cautious indeed. You have few options if you wish to avert a disaster.'

The Weave-lord was wearing his Mask, and for that, at least, she was thankful. His horribly deformed features were hidden behind a bronze visage, and though the Mask itself was distressing to look upon, it was far preferable to what lay beneath. It depicted a demented face, its features distorted in what could be pain, insanity or leering pleasure; the very sight of it made her skin crawl. She knew that it was old, very old; and where the True Masks were concerned, age meant power. She dreaded to think how many minds had been lost to that Mask, and how much of Vyrrch's remained . . .

'What do you advise then, Weave-lord?' she replied, concealing her distaste with a skill born through many years of practice. Silently, she dared him to suggest having her daughter executed.

'You must appear conciliatory, at least. You have deceived them, and they will expect you to acknowledge that. Do not underestimate the hatred that we of Saramyr bear for Aberrants.'

'Don't be ridiculous, Vyrrch,' she snapped. Though slender and willowy, with petite features and an innocent appearance, she could be iron when she wanted to be. 'She's not an Aberrant. She's just a child with a talent. *My* child.'

'I know well the semantics of the word, Mistress,' he wheezed, shifting his hunched body. He was clothed in ragged robes, a patchwork of fibres, beads, bits of matting and animal hide cannibalised together in an insane fashion.

All the Weavers wore similar attire. Anais had never had the desire to delve deep enough into their world to ask why.

The Weavers had been responsible for the practice of killing Aberrant children for more than a hundred years. They were gifted at tracking down the signs, searching with their unearthly senses across the Weave to root out corruption in the purity of the human form. Though they were reclusive as a rule, preferring to remain in the comfort of noble houses or in their monasteries in the mountains, they made exception where Aberrants were concerned. Weavers travelled from town to village to city, appearing at festivals or gatherings, teaching the common folk to recognise the Aberrant in their midst, urging them to give up the creatures that hid among them. The visit of a Weaver to a town was an almost religious event, and the people gathered in fear and awe, both repulsed and drawn by the strange men in their Masks. While there, they listened to the Weaver's teachings, and passed on that wisdom to their children. Though the content of the teachings never varied, the Weavers were tireless, and their word had become so ingrained in the psyche of the people of Saramyr that it was as familiar as the rhymes of childhood or the sound of a mother's voice.

Vyrrch waited for Anais's gaze to cool before continuing. 'What I think of the matter is not relevant. You must be prepared for the wrath of the families. The child you have borne is an Aberrant to them. They will make little distinction between Lucia and the twisted, blind, limbless children that we of the Weavers must deal with every day. Both are . . . *deviant*. Until today, they believed the line of Erinima had an heir. Sickly, perhaps – I believe that was your excuse for hiding her away from us? – but an heir nonetheless. Now they find it does not, and many possibilities will—'

'It *does*, Vyrrch,' Anais smouldered. 'My child *will* take the throne.'

'As an Aberrant?' Vyrrch chuckled. 'I doubt that.'

Anais turned to the fountain to cover the tightening of her jaw. She knew Vyrrch spoke the truth. The people would never suffer an Aberrant as ruler. And yet, what other choice was there?

Apart from her phenomenal speed at picking up speech, Lucia had displayed few outward signs of her abilities until she reached two harvests of age; but Anais knew. If she was honest with herself, she had known instinctively, early in the pregnancy, that the child in her womb was abnormal. At first she did not dare believe; but later, when she faced the reality of the situation, she did not care. She would not consider telling her doctor; he would have counselled poisoning the child in the womb. No, she would not have given Lucia up for anything.

Perhaps that would be her downfall. Perhaps, if she *had* given up Lucia, she would have borne many healthy babies afterward. But she made her choice, and through complications she was rendered barren in giving birth. She could have no more children. Lucia was the only one there would ever be. The sole heir to the realm of Saramyr.

And so she had hidden her child away from the world, knowing that the world would despise her. They would ignore her gentle nature and dreamy eyes, and see only a creature *not human*, something to be rooted out and destroyed before its seed could pollute the purity of the Saramyr folk. She had thought that the child might learn to hide her abnormalities, to control and suppress them; but that hope was dashed now. Heart's blood, how did they learn of it? She had been so careful to keep Lucia from the eyes of those that might harm her.

This land was sick, she thought bitterly. Sick and cursed. Every year, more children were born Aberrant, more were snatched by the Weavers. Animals, too, and plants. Farmers griped that the very soil was evil, as whole crops grew twisted. The sickness was spreading, had been spreading for decades and nobody even knew what it was, much less where it came from.

The door was thrown open with a force that made her judder, and her husband thundered in, a black tower of rage.

'What is this?' he cried, seizing her by the arm and dragging her roughly to him. '*What is this?*'

She tore free from his grip, and he let her. He knew where the power lay in this relationship. She was the Blood Empress, ruler by bloodline. He was Emperor only by marriage; a marriage that could be annulled if Anais wished it.

'Welcome back, Durun,' she replied sarcastically, glowering at him. 'How was your hunt?'

'What has happened while I've been gone?' he cried. 'The things I hear . . . our child . . . what have you done?'

'Lucia is *special*, Durun. As you might know, if you had seen her more than once a year. Do not claim that she is *our* child: you have taken no hand in her parenting.'

'So it's true? She's an Aberrant?' Durun roared.

'No!' Anais snapped, at the same time that Vyrrch said 'Yes.'

Durun gazed in astonishment at his wife, and she, unflinching, gazed back. A taut silence fell.

She knew how he would react. The Emperor was nothing if not predictable. Most days she despised him, with his tight black attire and his long, lustrous black hair that fell straight to either side of his face. She hated his proud bearing and his hawk nose, his knife-thin face and his dark eyes. The marriage had been purely political, arranged by her parents before their passing; but while it had gained her Blood Batik as staunch and useful allies, she had paid for it by suffering this indolent braggart as a husband. Though he did have his moments, this was not one of them.

'You gave birth to an Aberrant?' he whispered.

'You fathered one,' she countered.

A momentary spasm of pain crossed his face.

'Do you know what this means? Do you know what you've done?'

'Do you know what the alternative was?' she replied. 'To kill my only child, and let Blood Erinima die out? Never!'

'Better that you had,' he hissed.

There was a chime outside the door then, forestalling her retort.

'Another messenger awaits you,' Vyrrch said in his throaty gurgle.

Flashing a final hot look at her husband, Anais pulled open the door and strode past the servant before he had time to tell her what she already knew. Durun stormed away to his chambers. For that, Anais was thankful. She still had no idea how she would handle the anger of the high families, but she knew she would do it better without Durun at her side.

The chambers of Weave-lord Vyrrch were a monument to degradation. They were dingy and dark, hot and wet as a swamp in the heat of early summer. The high shutters – sealed closed when they should have been open to admit the breeze – were draped in layers of coloured materials and tapestries. The vast, plush bed had collapsed and settled at an angle, its sheets soiled and stained. In the centre of the room was an octagonal bathing pool. Its waters were murky, scattered with floating bits of debris and faeces. At the bottom, staring sightlessly upward, was a naked boy.

Everywhere there was evidence of the Weave-lord's terrible appetites when in his post-Weaving rages. All manner of food was strewn about in varying states of decay. Fine silks were ripped and torn. Blood stained the tiled floor here and there. A scourge lay beneath the broken bed. A corpse lay *in* the bed, several weeks old, its sex and age mercifully unidentifiable now. A vast hookah smoked unattended amid a marsh of spilled wine and wet clothes.

And in the centre, his white, withered body cloaked in rags, the Weave-lord sat cross-legged, wearing his Mask.

The True Mask of the Weave-lord Vyrrch was an old, old thing. Its lineage went all the way back to Frusric, one of the greatest Edgefathers that had ever lived. Frusric had formed it from bronze, beaten thin so it would be light enough to wear. It was a masterpiece: the face of some long-forgotten god, his expression at once demented and horribly, malevolently sane, his brows heavy over eyes like dark pits. The face appeared to be crying out in despair, or shrieking in hate, or calling in anger, depending on what angle the light struck it.

Frusric had given the new Mask to Tamala tu Jekkyn, who had worn it till his untimely death; it was then handed on to Urric tu Hyrst, a master Weaver himself. From Urric, it could be traced through seven subsequent owners over one hundred years, until it had come into the possession of Vyrrch, given to him by his master, who recognised in the boy a talent greater than any he had seen.

The True Masks took all their owners had, draining them, rotting them from the inside out; and they kept a portion of what they took, and passed it on to the next wearer. It *changed* them, imbuing shreds of its previous owner's mind and memories and personality; with each owner, it took more and passed more on, until the clash of influences, dreams and experiences became too much for the mind to bear. The older the Mask, the greater the power it gained, and the swifter it drove the wearer to insanity. Lesser apprentices would have died of shock at just putting this Mask on; Vyrrch was laid low three seasons, but he mastered it. And the power it had granted him was nothing short of magnificent.

What it had taken from him, though, was less glorious. He was nearly forty harvests of age, but he creaked and wheezed like a man of thrice that. His face had been made hideous. A thousand more minor corruptions and cancers boiled in his broken body, and the pain was constant. And though he did not realise it, the Mask had subtly been eroding his sanity like all the others, until he teetered daily on the brink of madness.

But he felt none of the pains in his body now, for he was Weaving, and the ecstasy of it took him away on a sea of bliss.

Like all Weavers, he had been taught to visualise the

sensation in his own way. The raw stuff of the Weave was overwhelming, and many novices had found its beauty more than they could bear, and lost their will to leave. They wandered forever somewhere between its threads, lost in their own private paradise, bright ghosts mindlessly slaved to the Weave.

For Vyrrch, the Weave was an abyss, a vast, endless blackness in which he was an infinitesimal mote of light. And yet it was far from empty. Great curling tunnels snaked through the dark, grey and dim and faintly iridescent, like immense worms that thrashed and swayed, their heads and tails lost in eternity. The worms were the threads of the Weave, and he floated in the darkness in between, where there was nothingness, only the utter and complete joy of disembodiment. A creature of sensation alone, he felt the sympathetic vibration of the threads, a slow wind that swept through him, charging his nerves. On the edge of vision, huge whale-like shapes slid through the darkness. He had never understood what they were: a product of his own imagining, or something else altogether? Nor had he ever found out, for they eluded him effortlessly, remaining always out of his reach. Eventually he had given up trying, and for their part they ignored him as being beneath their notice.

Swiftly he glided between the immense threads, a gnat against their heaving flanks. By reading their vibrations he found the thread he sought and, steeling himself, he plunged into it, tearing through its skin into the roaring tumult inside, where chaos swallowed him.

Now he was a spark, a tiny thing that raced along the synapses of the thread with dizzying speed, selecting junctions here and jumping track there, flitting along faster than the mind could comprehend. From this thread to that he flickered, racing down one lane after another, a million changes executed in less than a second, until finally he reached the terminator of a single thread, and burst free.

His vision cleared as his senses reassembled themselves,

and he was in a small, dimly lit chamber. It was unremarkable in any way, except for the crumbling yellow-red stone of its walls, and the pictograms daubed haphazardly across it, spelling out nonsense phrases and primal mutterings, dark perversions and promises. The ravings of a madman. A pair of lanterns flickered fitfully in their brackets, making the shadow-edges of the bricks shift and dance. A peeling wooden door was closed before him. Though he was far from any mark by which to recognise his surroundings, the walls exuded a familiar resonance to his heightened perception. This was Adderach, the monastery of the Weavers.

The room was empty, but he sensed the approach of three of his brethren. While he waited, he thought over the news he had to report.

He could not imagine how she had stayed hidden for so long. That the Heir-Empress could be an Aberrant . . . how could he have not seen it before? It was only when he began to hear reports from frightened servants of a spectral girl walking the corridors of the Keep at night that he began to suspect something was amiss. And so he had begun to investigate, searching the Keep for evidence of resonances, tremors in the Weave that would indicate that someone was manipulating·it, in the way a spider feels the thrashings of the fly through her web.

He found nothing. And yet something was there. Whatever was causing these manifestations was either too subtle to be detectable even by him, or was of a different order altogether.

Eventually his searching bore fruit, and he found the trail of the wandering spectre as she prowled the corridors of the Keep, a tiny tremor in the air at her passing that was so fine it was almost imperceptible. Yet though he sensed himself drawing close time after time, he never caught up with her; he was always evaded. Frustration gnawed at him, and his efforts became more frantic; yet this only seemed to make her escapes seem all the easier. Until one day one of his spies overheard Anais consulting a physician about her daughter's odd dreams, and the connection was made.

Like many, he had never laid eyes on the Heir-Empress, but he had spied on her from time to time. The Heir-Empress was far too important for him to abide by her mother's wish for her to be kept sheltered and secret. He knew at once that she was not so sickly as Anais made out, but he also knew there were many good reasons why a child as important as this one should be kept safe from harm. He had simply attributed it to Anais's paranoia about her only daughter – the only child she could ever have – and forgotten about it. It had not seemed urgent at the time, and as the seasons came and went he forgot about it, the thoughts slipping through the gauze of his increasingly addled mind and fading away.

It was his assurance of his own abilities that had led him to discount the little Heir-Empress from his initial investigations concerning the spectre; surely, he would have sensed something if she had been unusual in any way. He had not looked closer at first, because he should have detected it when he first spied on her.

The night he heard about the Heir-Empress's dreams, he had used his Mask to search for her, to divine what she truly was. It was something he should have done a long time ago. Yet when he tried, she was impossible to find. He knew who and where she was, but she was still invisible to him. His consciousness seemed to slip over her; she was unassailable. The rage at his failure was immense, and cost the lives of three children. All this time, there had been an Aberrant under his very nose; but it had taken him eight years to see it.

He knew now that he was dealing with something unlike anything he had encountered before. He considered what she was and what it might mean, and he feared her.

And yet still he needed proof, and it must be a proof that could not be connected to him in any way. So he had sent a message to Sonmaga tu Amacha's Weaver, who had advised the Barak, who had employed a series of middlemen to obtain a lock of the Heir-Empress's hair. Anyone who followed the trail would find it led to Sonmaga tu Amacha's door; the only one who knew of Vyrrch's involvement was Sonmaga's Weaver, Bracch.

The conclusive proof of Aberration could only be carried out by a Weaver if he were physically within sight of the person, or if he had a piece of the person's body to study. With the lock of hair Bracch was able to convince Sonmaga of the truth.

The girl was a threat that had to be eliminated. Though the situation was yet far from desperate, she had the potential to become a great danger to the Weavers. With good fortune, the Baraks and high families would deal with her for him, but if not . . . well, maybe then more direct methods would have to be employed.

The door to the chamber opened then, and the shambling, ragged figures of the three Weavers came inside. To them, he appeared as a floating apparition, barely visible in the dim, flickering light.

'Daygreet, Weave-lord Vyrrch,' croaked one, whose mask was a tangle of bark and leaves shaped into a rough semblance of a bearded face. 'I trust you have news?'

'Grave news, my brothers,' Vyrrch replied softly. 'Grave news . . .'

SIX

The townhouse of Blood Koli was situated on the western flank of the Imperial Quarter of Axekami. The original building had been improved over the years, adding a wing here, a library there, until the low, wide mass sprawled across the expanse of the compound that protected it. Its roof was of black slate, curved and peaked into ridges; the walls were the colour of ivory, simple and plain, their uniformity broken up by a few choice angles or an ornamental cross-hatching of narrow wooden beams. Behind the townhouse was a cluster of similarly austere buildings: quarters for guards, stables, and storage rooms. The remainder of the compound was taken up by a garden, trimmed and neat and severe in its beauty. Curving pebble paths arced around a pond full of colourful fish, past a sculpted fountain and a shaded bench. The whole was surrounded by a high wall with a single gate, that separated the compound from the wide streets of the Imperial Quarter. The morning sun beat down on the city, and the air was humid and muggy. Not too distantly, the golden ziggurat of the Imperial Keep loomed at the crest of a hill, highest of all the buildings in the city.

Within the townhouse, Mishani tu Koli sat cross-legged at her writing desk and laboured through the last season's fishing tallies. Blood Koli owned a large fishing fleet that operated out of Mataxa Bay, and much of their revenue and political power was generated there. It was common knowledge that crabs and lobsters stamped with the mark of Blood Koli were the most tender and delicious (and hence the most expensive) in Saramyr. It was a benefit of the unique mineral content of the bay's waters, so Mishani's father said. For two years now she had been rigorously educated in every aspect of the family's holdings and businesses. As heir to the lands of Blood Koli and the title of Barakess upon her father's death, she was expected to be able to handle the responsibility of heading them. And so she tallied, her brush flicking this way and that as she made a mark here, crossed a line there, with a single-minded focus that was alarming in its intensity.

Mishani was a lady of no great height, slender and fine-boned to the point of fragility. Her thin, pale face, while not beautiful, was striking in its serenity. No involuntary movement ever crossed her face; her poise was total. No flicker of her pencil-line eyebrows would betray her surprise unless she willed it so; no twitch of her narrow lips would show a smirk unless she wished to express it. Her small body was near-engulfed by the silken mass of black hair that fell to her ankles when she stood. It was tamed by strips of dark blue leather, separating it into two great plaits to either side of her head, and one long, free-falling cascade at her back.

A chime sounded outside the curtained doorway to her room. She finished the tally line she was working on and then rang a small silver bell in response, to indicate permission to enter. A handmaiden slipped gracefully in, bowing slightly with the fingertips of one hand to her lips and the other arm folded across her waist, the female form of greeting to a social superior. 'You have a visitor, Mistress Mishani. It is Mistress Kaiku tu Makaima.'

Mishani looked blandly at her handmaiden for a moment; then a slow smile spread across her lips, becoming a grin of joy. The handmaiden smiled in response, pleased that her mistress was pleased. 'Shall I show her in, Mistress?'

'Do so,' she replied. 'And bring fruit and iced water for us.'

The handmaiden left, and Mishani tidied up her writing equipment and arranged herself. In the two years since her eighteenth harvest, she had been kept busy and with little time for the society of friends; but Kaiku had been her companion through childhood and adolescence, and the long separation had pained her. They had written to each other often, in the florid, poetic style of High Saramyrrhic, explaining their dreams and hopes and fears. It did not seem enough. How like Kaiku, then, to turn up unannounced like this. She never was one to follow protocol; she always seemed to think herself somehow above it, that it did not apply to her.

'Mistress Kaiku tu Makaima,' the handmaiden declared from without, and Kaiku entered then. Mishani flung her arms around her friend and they embraced. Finally, she stepped back, holding Kaiku's hands, their arms a bridge between them.

'You've lost weight,' she said. 'And you seem pale. Have you been ill?'

Kaiku laughed. They had known each other too long to be anything less than brutally honest. 'Something like that,' she said. 'But you look more the noble lady than ever. City life must agree with you.'

'I miss the bay,' Mishani admitted, kneeling on one of the elegant mats that were laid out on the floor. 'I will admit, it is galling that I have to spend my days counting fish and pricing boats, and being reminded of it every day. But I am developing something of a taste for tallying.'

'Really?' Kaiku asked in disbelief, settling herself opposite her friend. 'Ah, Mishani. Dull, repetitive work always was your strong suit.'

'I shall take that as a compliment, since it was you who was always too flighty and fanciful to attend to her lessons as a child.'

Kaiku smiled. Just the sight of her friend made the terrors that she had endured seem more distant, fainter somehow. She was a living reminder of the days before the tragedy had struck. She had changed a little: shed the last of her girlhood, her small features become womanly. And she spoke with a more formal mode than Kaiku remembered, presumably picked up at court. But for all that, she was still that same Mishani, and it was like a balm to Kaiku's sore heart.

The handmaiden gave a peremptory chime and entered;

she needed no answering bell when she had already been invited by her mistress. She laid a low wooden table to one side of Kaiku and Mishani, placed a bowl of sliced fruit there, and poured iced water into two glasses. Finally, she adjusted the screens to maximise the tiny breaths of the wind that stirred the hot morning, and unobtrusively slipped away. Kaiku watched her go, reminded of another handmaiden from a time before death had ever brushed her.

'Now, Kaiku, to what do I owe this visit?' Mishani said. 'It is not a short way from the Forest of Yuna to Axekami. Are you staying long? I will have a room prepared. And you will need some proper clothes; what are you *wearing*?'

Kaiku's smile seemed fragile, and the sadness within showed through. Mishani's eyes turned to sorrow and sympathy in response. 'What has happened?' she asked.

'My family are dead,' Kaiku replied simply.

Mishani automatically suppressed her surprise, showing no reaction at all. Then, remembering who it was that she was talking to, she relaxed her guard and allowed the horror to show, her hand covering her mouth in shock. 'No,' she breathed. 'How?'

'I will tell you,' Kaiku said. 'But there is more. I may not be as you remember me, Mishani. Something is within me, something . . . *foreign*. I do not know what it is, but it is dangerous. I ask for your help, Mishani. I *need* your help.'

'Of course,' Mishani replied, taking her friend's hands again. 'Anything.'

'Do not be hasty,' Kaiku said. 'Listen to my story first. You are in danger just by being near me.'

Mishani sat back, gazing at her friend. Such gravity was not Kaiku's way. She had always been the wilful one, stubborn, the one who would take whatever path suited her. Now her tone was as one convicted. 'Tell me, then,' she said. 'And spare nothing.'

So Kaiku told her everything, a tale that began with her own death and ended in her arrival at Axekami, having bought passage on a skiff downriver from Ban with money she found in her pack. She talked of Asara, how her trusted handmaiden had revealed herself to be something other than what she seemed; and she told of how Asara died. She spoke of her rescue by the priests of Enyu, and the mask Asara had taken from her house, that her father had brought back from his last trip away. And she told of her oath to Ocha: that she would avenge the murder of her family.

When she was finished, Mishani was quite still. Kaiku watched her, as if she could divine what was going on beneath her immobile exterior. This new poise was unfamiliar to Kaiku; it was something Mishani had acquired accompanying her father in the courts of the Empress these past two years. There, every movement and every nuance could give away a secret or cost a life.

'You have the mask?' she asked at length.

Kaiku produced it from her pack and handed it to her friend. Mishani looked it over, turning it beneath her gaze. The mischievous red and black face leered back at her. Beautiful and ugly at the same time, it still looked no more remarkable than many other masks she had seen, worn by actors in the theatre. It seemed entirely normal.

'You have not tried to wear it?'

'No,' Kaiku said. 'What if it were a True Mask? I would go insane, or die, or worse.'

'Very wise,' Mishani mused.

'Tell me you believe my story, Mishani. I have to know you do not doubt me.'

Mishani nodded, her great cascade of black hair trembling with the movement. 'I believe you,' she said. 'Of course I believe you. And I will do all I can to help you, dear friend.' Kaiku was smiling in relief, tears gathering in her eyes. Mishani handed the mask back. 'As to that, I have a friend who has studied the ways of the Edgefathers. He may be able to tell us about it.'

'When can we see him?' Kaiku asked, excited.

Mishani gave her an unreadable look. 'It will not be quite as simple as that.'

The chambers of Lucia tu Erinima were buried deep in the heart of the Imperial Keep, heavily guarded and all but impregnable. The rooms were many, but there were always Guards there, or tutors pacing back and forth, or nannies or cooks hustling about. Lucia's world was constantly busy, and yet she was alone. She was trapped tighter than ever now, and the faces that surrounded her looked on her with worry, thinking how the poor child's life must be miserable, for she was hated by the world.

But Lucia was not sad. She had met many new people over the last few weeks, a veritable whirl compared to her life before the thief had taken a lock of her hair. Her mother visited often, and brought with her important people, Baraks and ur-Baraks and officials and merchants. Lucia was always on her best behaviour. Sometimes they looked on her with barely concealed disgust, sometimes with apprehension, and sometimes with kindness. Some of those who came prepared to despise her departed in bewilderment, wondering how such an intelligent and pretty child could harbour the evil the Weavers warned of. Some left their prejudices behind when they walked out of the door; others clutched them jealously to their breast.

'Your mother is being very brave,' said Zaelis, her favourite of all the tutors. 'She is showing her allies and her enemies what a good and clever girl you are. Sometimes a person's fear of the unknown is far, far worse than the reality.'

Lucia accepted this, in her dreamy-eyed, preoccupied kind of way. She knew there was more, deeper down; but those answers would come in time.

It was while she was with Zaelis one balmy afternoon that the Blood Empress Anais brought the Emperor.

She was sitting on a mat by the long, triangular windows in her study room, with the sunlight cut into great dazzling teeth and cast on to the sandy tiles of the floor before her. Zaelis was teaching her the catechisms of the birth of the stars, recounting the questions and answers in his throaty, molten bass tones. She knew the story well enough: how Abinaxis, the One Star, burst and scattered the universe, and from that chaos came the first generation of the gods. Sitting neatly and with her usual appearance of inattentiveness, Lucia was listening and remembering, while in the back of her head she heard the whispers of the spirits of the west wind, hissing nonsense to each other as they flowed across the city.

Zaelis paused as a gust ruffled through the room, and Lucia looked quickly upwards, as if someone had spoken by her shoulder.

'What are they saying, Lucia?' he asked.

Lucia looked back at Zaelis. He alone treated her abilities as if they were something precious, and not something to be hidden. All the tutors, nannies and staff were sworn to secrecy on pain of death with regards to her talents; they looked away if they caught her playing with ravens, and shushed her if she spoke of what the old tree in the garden was saying that day. But Zaelis encouraged her, believed her. In fact, his fervour worried her a little at times.

'I don't know,' she said. 'I can't understand them.'

'One day maybe you will,' said Zaelis.

'Probably,' Lucia replied offhandedly.

She sensed Durun's arrival a moment before she heard him. He frightened her with his intensity of passion. He was a knot of fire, always burning in anger or pride or hate or lust. In the absence of anything that heated his blood, he lapsed into boredom. He had no finer emotions, no intellectual interests or stirrings of mild introspection. His flame roared blindingly or not at all.

The Emperor strode into the room and halted before them, his black cloak settling reluctantly around his broad shoulders. Anais was with him. Zaelis stood and made proper obeisance; Lucia did so as well.

'So this is she,' Durun said, ignoring Zaelis completely.

'It is the same *she* as you saw previously, on every occasion you bothered yourself to visit her,' Anais replied. It was clear by their manner that they had just argued. Anais's face was flushed.

'Then I had no idea that I was harbouring a viper,' Durun answered coldly. He looked Lucia over. She returned his gaze with a placid calm. 'If it weren't for the distance in those eyes,' he mused, 'I would think her a normal child.'

'She *is* a normal child,' Anais snapped. 'You are as bad as Vyrrch. He breathes down my neck, eager for the chance to—' She stopped herself, glanced at Lucia. 'Must you do this in front of her?'

'You've told her, I suppose? About how the city is rising against her?'

Zaelis opened his mouth and shut it again. He knew better than to interfere on behalf of the child. If the Emperor would not listen to his wife, he certainly would not listen to a scholar.

'You'll bring this land to ruin with your ambition, Anais,' Durun accused. 'Your arrogance in making this abomination the heir to the throne will tear Saramyr apart. Every life lost will be on your head!'

'So be it,' she hissed. 'Wars have been fought for less important causes. Look at her, Durun! She is a beautiful child . . . *your* child! She is all you could hope for in a daughter, in an heir! Don't be blinded by a hatred wrapped up in *tradition* and *lore*. You listen too much to the Weavers, and think too little for yourself.'

'So did you,' he replied. 'Before you spawned *that*.' He flung out a finger at Lucia, who had been watching the exchange impassively. 'Now you use arguments that you would have scorned in days gone by. She's an Aberrant, and she's no child of mine!'

With that, he turned with a melodramatic sweep of his cloak and stalked away. Anais's face was tight with rage, but one look at her daughter and it softened. She knelt down next to Lucia, so that their faces were level, and hugged her.

'Don't listen, my child,' she murmured. 'Your father doesn't understand. He's angry, but he'll learn. They all will.'

Lucia didn't reply; but then, she seldom did.

SEVEN

Six sun-washed days had passed in the temple of Enyu on the banks of the Kerryn, and Tane felt further from inner peace with every dawn.

He had wandered far today, after his morning duties were performed. As an acolyte, the priests gave him leisure to do so. The way to Enyu was not made up of rituals and chores, but of community with nature. Everyone had their own way to calm their spirit. Tane was still looking for his.

The world was tipping over the heady brink between spring and summer, and the days were hot and busy with midges. Tane laboured through the pathways of the forest with his shirt tied around his waist and his torso bare, but for the strap of the rifle that was slung across his back. His lean, tanned body trickled with sweat in the humid confines of the trees. The sun was westering; soon he would have to head back, or risk being caught in the forest after dark. Ill things came with the night, more so now than ever.

All around was discontent. The forest seemed melancholy, even in the sunlight. The priests muttered about the corruption in the land, how the very soil was turning sour. The goddess Enyu was becoming weak, ailing under the influence of some unknown, sourceless evil. Tane felt his frustration grow at the thought. What good were they as priests of nature, if they could only sit by and lament the sickness in the earth as it overtook them? What use were their invocations and sacrifices and blessings if they could not stand up to defend the goddess they professed to love? They talked and talked, and nobody was doing anything. A war was being fought beyond the veil of human sight, and Tane's side was plainly losing.

But such questions were not the only things that preyed on his mind and ruined his attempts at attaining tranquillity. Though he worked hard to distract himself, he found he was unable to forget the young woman he had found buried in leaves at the base of a kindly tree. Pictures, sounds and scents, frozen in memory, refused to fade as others did. He remembered the expression of surprise, the whip of her hair, as she whirled to find him standing unexpectedly behind her; the sound of her laugh from another room, her joy at something unseen; the smell of her tears as he watched over her during her grief. He knew the shape of her face, peaceful in sleep, better than his own. He cursed himself for mooning over her like a child; and yet still he thought on her, and the memories renewed themselves with each visit.

He found his feet taking him to a spring, where cold water cascaded down a jagged rock wall into a basin before draining back into the stone. He had been here a few times before, on the hotter days of summer; now it seemed a wonderful idea to cool himself off before returning home. A short clamber up a muddy trail brought him to the basin, hidden among the crowding trees. He stripped and plunged into the icy pool, relishing the delicious shock of the impact. Sluicing the salty sweat off his body with his palm, he dived and surfaced several times before the temperature of the pool began to become uncomfortable, and he swam to the edge to climb out.

There was a woman in the trees, leaning on a rifle and watching him.

He stopped still, his eyes flickering to his own rifle, laid across the bundle of clothes near the edge of the pool. He might be able to grab it before she could raise her own weapon, but he would have no chance of priming and firing before she shot him. If indeed that was her intention. She appeared, in fact, to be faintly amused.

She was exceedingly beautiful, even dressed in dour brown travelling clothes. Her hair was long, with streaks of red amid the natural onyx black, and was left to fall naturally about her face. She wore no makeup, no hair ornaments; the dyed strands of her hair were the only concession to artificiality. Her beauty was entirely her own, not lent to her by craft.

'You swim well,' she commented dryly.

Tane hesitated for a moment, and then climbed out to retrieve his clothes. Nudity did not bother him, and he refused to be talked down to while he trod water in the pool. She watched him – equally unfazed – as he pulled on his trousers over the wet, muscular curves of his legs and buttocks. He stopped short of picking up his rifle. She did not seem hostile, at least.

'I am looking for someone,' the stranger said after a time. 'A woman named Kaiku tu Makaima.' He was not quick enough to keep the reaction off his face. 'I see you know that name,' she added.

Tane ran his hands over his head, brushing water from his shaven scalp. 'I know that she suffered a great misfortune at someone's hands,' he said. 'Are you that someone?'

'Assuredly not,' she replied. 'My name is Jin. I am an Imperial Messenger.' She slung her rifle over her back and walked over to him, pulling back her sleeve to expose her forearm. Stretching from her wrist to her inner elbow was a long, intricate tattoo – the sigil of the Messengers' Guild. Tane nodded.

'Tane tu Jeribos. Acolyte of Enyu.'

'Ah. Then the temple is not far.'

'Not far,' he agreed.

'Perhaps you could show me? It will be dark soon, and the forest is not safe.'

Tane looked her over with a hint of suspicion, but he never really considered refusing her. Her accent and mode spoke of an education, and possibly high birth, and besides, it was every man and woman's duty to offer shelter and assistance to an Imperial Messenger, and the fact that her message was for Kaiku intrigued him greatly. 'Come with me, then,' he said.

'Will you tell me of this . . . misfortune on the way?' Jin asked.

'Will you tell me the message you have for her?'

Jin laughed. 'You know I cannot,' she replied. 'I am sworn by my life to deliver it only to her.'

Tane grinned suddenly, indicating that he had been joking. His frustrated mood had evaporated suddenly and left him in high spirits. His humours were ever mercurial; it was something about himself that he had learned to accept long ago. He supposed there was a reason for it, somewhere in his past; but his past was a place he had little love of revisiting. His childhood was darkened by the terror of the shadow that stood in his doorway at night, breathing heavily, with hands that held only pain.

They talked on the way back to the temple, as night drew in. Jin asked him about Kaiku, and he told her what he knew of her visit. He made no mention yet of her destination, however. He had no wish to reveal everything to a stranger, Imperial Messenger or not. He felt protective towards Kaiku, for it was he who had saved her life, he who nursed her to health again, and he treasured that link. He would make sure of Jin before he sent her on the trail to Axekami.

As they walked, Tane realised to his chagrin that he had misjudged the time it would take to travel back from the spring. Perhaps he had unconsciously been slowing his pace to match Jin's, and he had been so preoccupied in conversation that he had not noticed. Whatever the reason, the last light bled from the sky with still a mile to go. The looming bulk of Aurus glowed white through the trees, low on the horizon. Iridima, the brightest moon, was not yet risen, and Neryn would most likely stay hidden tonight.

'Is it far yet?' Jin asked. She had politely restrained from asking him if he was lost for some time now.

'Very close,' he said. His embarrassment at the miscalculation had not diminished his good humour one bit. The single moon was enough to see by. 'Don't concern yourself about losing the light. I grew up in the forest; I have excellent night vision.'

'So do I,' Jin replied. Tane looked back at her, about to offer further words of encouragement, but he was shocked to see her eyes shining in a slant of moonlight, two saucers of bright reflected white, like those of a cat. Then they passed into shadow, and it was gone. Tane's voice went dry in his throat, and he turned away, muttering a quiet protective blessing. He reaffirmed his resolve to tell her nothing of Kaiku's friend Mishani until he was certain she meant no harm.

They were almost at the temple when Tane suddenly slowed. Jin was at his shoulder in a moment.

'Is something wrong?' she whispered.

Tane cast a fleeting glance at her. He was still a little unnerved by what he had seen in her eyes. But this was nothing to do with her, he surmised. The forest felt *bad* here. The instinct was too strong to ignore.

'The trees are afraid,' he muttered.

'They tell you so?'

'In a way.' He did not have the time or inclination to elaborate.

'I trust you, then,' Jin said, brushing her hair back over her shoulder. 'Are we close to your home?'

'Just through these trees,' muttered Tane. 'That's what worries me.'

They went carefully onward, quietly now. Tane noted with approval how Jin moved without sound through the forest. His mood was souring rapidly into a dark foreboding. He unslung his rifle, and his hands clasped tightly around it as they stepped through the blue shadows towards the clearing where the temple lay.

At the edge of the trees, they crouched and looked out over the sloping expanse of grassy hillside that lay between the river on their left and the temple. Lights burned softly in some of the temple windows. The wind stirred the trees gently. The great disc of Aurus dominated the horizon before them, lifting her bulk slowly clear of the treeline. Not an insect chittered, and no animal called. Tane felt his scalp crawl.

'Is it always so quiet?' Jin whispered.

Tane ignored her question, scanning the scene. The priests were usually indoors by nightfall. He watched the temple for some time more, hoping for a light to be lit or extinguished, a face to appear at one of the windows, anything that would indicate signs of life within. But there was nothing.

'Perhaps I'm being foolish,' he said, about to stand up and come out of hiding.

Jin grabbed his arm with a surprisingly strong grip. 'No,' she said. 'You are not.'

He looked back at her, and saw something in her expression that gave her away. 'You know what it is,' he said. 'You know what's wrong here.'

'I suspect,' she replied. 'Wait.'

Tane settled himself back into his hiding place and returned his attention to the temple. He knew each of its cream-coloured planes, each beam of black ash that supported each wall, each simple square window. He knew the way the upper storey was set back from the lower one, to fit snugly with the slope of the hill. This temple had been his home for a long time now, and yet it never felt as if he belonged here, no matter how much he tried. No place had ever truly been home for him, however much he tried to adapt himself.

'There,' Jin said, but Tane had already seen it. Coming over the roof from the blind side of the temple, like some huge four-legged spider: *shin-shin*. It moved stealthily, picking its way along, its dark torso hanging between the cradle of its stiltlike legs, shining eyes like lanterns. As Tane watched with increasing dread, he saw another one come scuttling from the trees, crossing the clearing in moments to press itself against one of the outer walls, all but invisible. And a third now, following the first one over the roof, its gaze sweeping the treeline where they crouched.

'Enyu's grace . . .' he breathed.

'We must go,' said Jin urgently, laying a hand on his shoulder. 'We cannot help them.'

But Tane seemed not to hear, for he saw at that moment one of the priests appear at an upper window, listening with a frown to the silence from the forest, unaware of the dark, spindly shapes that crouched on the roof just above him.

'You cannot fight!' Jin hissed, 'You have no weapon to use against them!'

'I won't let my priests die in their beds!' he spat. Shaking her off, he stood up and fired his rifle into the air. The report was deafening in the silence. The glowing eyes of the shin-shin fixed on him in unison.

'Demons in the temple!' he cried. 'Demons in the temple!' And with that he primed and fired again. This time the priest disappeared from the window, and he heard the man's shouts as he ran into the heart of the building.

'Idiot!' Jin snarled. 'You will kill us both. Run!' She pulled him away, and he stumbled to his feet and followed her, for the sensation of the shin-shin's eyes boring into him had drained his courage.

One of the demons hurled itself from the roof of the temple and came racing towards them. Another broke from the treeline and angled itself in their direction. Two more shadows darted across the clearing, slipping into the open windows of the temple with insidious ease, and from within the first of the screams began.

Tane and Jin ran through the trees, dodging flailing branches and vaulting roots that lunged into their path. Things whipped at them in the night, too fast to see. Behind they could hear the screeches of the shin-shin sawing through the hot darkness as they called to each other. Tane's head was awhirl, half his mind on what was happening back at the temple, half on escape. To run was flying in the face of his instincts – he wanted to help the priests, that was his way, that was his *atonement* for the crimes of his past. But he knew enough of the shin-shin to recognise the truth in Jin's words. He had no effective measure against them. Like most demons, they despised the touch of iron; but even the iron in a rifle ball would not stop them for long. To attack them would be suicide.

'The river!' Jin cried suddenly, her red and black hair lashing about her face. 'Make for the river. The shin-shin cannot swim.'

'The river's too strong!' Tane replied automatically. Then the answer came to him: 'But there is a boat!'

'Take us there!' Jin said.

Tane sprang past her, leading them on a scrabbling diagonal slant down the hillside. The decline sharpened as they ran, and suddenly he heard a cry and felt something slam into him from behind. Jin had tripped, unable to control her momentum, and the two of them rolled and bounced down the slope. Tane smacked into the bole of a tree with enough force to nearly break a bone, but somehow Jin was entangled with him, and as she slithered past he was dragged down with her. They came to rest at the bottom of a wide, natural ditch; a stream in times gone by. Jin hardly paused to recover herself; she was up on her feet in an instant, dragging Tane with her. She scooped up her rifle as it clattered down to rest nearby. The screeches of the shin-shin were terrifyingly close, almost upon them.

'In here!' Tane hissed, pulling against her. There was a large hollow where the roots of a tree had encroached on the banks of the ditch, forming an overhang. Tane unstrapped his rifle – which had miraculously stayed snagged on his shoulder during the fall – and scrambled underneath, wedging his body in tight. There was just enough space for Jin to do so as well, pressing herself close to him. Mere moments later, they heard a soft thud as a shin-shin dropped out of the trees and landed foursquare in the ditch.

Both of them held their breath. Tane could feel Jin's pulse against his chest, smell the scent of her hair. Ordinarily, it might have aroused him – priests of Enyu had no stricture of celibacy, as some orders did – but the situation they were in robbed him of any ardour. From where they hid at ground level, they could see only the tapered points of the shin-shin's stilt-legs, shifting as it cast about for its prey. It had lost sight of them as they tumbled, and now it sought them anew. A slight fall of dirt was the only herald of the second demon's arrival in the ditch; that one had followed their trail down the slope, and was equally puzzled by their disappearance.

Tane began a silent mantra in his head. It was one he had not used since he was a child, a made-up nonsense rhyme that he pretended could make him invisible if he concentrated hard enough. Then he had been hiding from something entirely different. After a few moments, he adapted it to include a short prayer to Enyu. *Shelter us, Earth Goddess, hide us from their sight.*

The pointed ends of the shin-shins' legs moved this way and that in the moonlight, expressing their uncertainty. They knew their prey should be here; yet they could not see it. Tane felt the cold dread of their presence seeping into his skin. The narrow slot of vision between Jin's body and the overhang of thick roots and soil might be filled at any moment with the glowing eyes of the shin-shin; and if discovered, they were defenceless. He fancied he could sense their gaze sweeping over him, penetrating the earth to spot them huddled there.

Time seemed to draw out. Tane could feel his muscles tautening in response to the tension. One of the shin-shin moved suddenly, making Jin start; but whatever it had seen, it was not them. It returned to its companion, and they resumed their strange waiting. Tane gritted his teeth and concentrated on his mantra to calm himself. It did little good.

Then, a new sound: this one heavy and clumsy. The shin-shin stanced in response. Tane knew that sound, but he could not place it in his memory. The footsteps of some animal, but which?

The yawning roar of the bear decided the issue for him.

The shin-shin were uncertain again, their reaction betrayed by the shifting of their feet. The bear roared once more, thumping on to its forepaws, and began to advance slowly. The demons screeched, making a rattling noise and darting this way and that, trying to scare it away; but it was implacable, launching itself upright and then stamping down again with a snarl. There was the loping gallop as the bear ran towards them, not in the least cowed by their display. The shin-shin scattered as it thundered along the ditch, squealing and hissing their displeasure; but they gave the ground, and in moments they were gone, back into the trees in search of their lost prey.

Tane released the pent-up breath he had been storing, but they were not out of danger yet. They could hear the bear coming down the wide ditch, its loud snuffling as it searched for them.

'My rifle . . .' Jin whispered. 'If it finds us . . .'

'No,' he hissed. 'Wait.'

Then suddenly the bear poked down into the hollow, its brown, bristly snout filling up their sight as it sniffed at them. Jin clutched for the trigger of her rifle to scare it away; but Tane grabbed her wrist.

'The shin-shin will hear,' he whispered. 'We don't fear the bears in Enyu's forest.' He was less confident in his heart than his words suggested. Where once the forest beasts had been friends to the priests of Enyu, the corruption in the land had made them increasingly unpredictable of late.

The bear's wet nose twitched as it smelt them over. Jin was rigid with apprehension. Then, with a final snort, the snout receded. The bear lay heavily down in front of their hiding place, and there it stayed.

Jin shifted. 'Why did it not attack us?' she muttered.

Tane was wearing a strange grin. 'The bears are Enyu's

creatures, just as Panazu's are the catfish, Aspinis's the monkeys, Misamcha's the ray or the fox or the hawk. Give thanks, Jin. I think we've been saved.'

Jin appeared to consider that for a time. 'We should stay here,' she said at length. 'The shin-shin will be waiting for us if we emerge before dawn.'

'I think she has the same idea,' Tane said, motioning with his eyes towards the great furred bulk that blocked them in.

The bear lay in front of their hollow throughout the night, and in spite of their discomfort the two of them slept. Jin's dreams were of fire and a horrible scorching heat; Tane's, as always, were of the sound of footsteps approaching his bedroom doorway, and the mounting terror that came with them.

EIGHT

Weave-lord Vyrrch shuffled along the corridors of the Imperial Keep, his hunched and withered body buried in his patchwork robes, his ruined face hidden behind the bronze visage of an insane and ancient god. Once he had walked tall through these corridors, his stride long and his spine straight. But that was before the Mask had twisted him, warped him from the inside. Like all the True Masks, its material was suffused with the essence of witchstone, and the witchstones gave nothing without taking something away. His body was thronged with cancers, both benign and malignant. His bones were brittle, his knees crooked, his skin blemished all over. But such was the price of power, and power he had in abundance. He was the Weave-lord, the Empress's own Weaver, and he wanted for nothing.

The Weavers were a necessity of life in the higher echelons of Saramyr society. Through them, nobles could communicate with each other instantly over long distances, without having to resort to messengers. They could spy on their enemies, or watch over their allies and loved ones. The more effective Weavers could kill invisibly and undetectably, a convenient way to remove troublesome folk; the crime could only be traced by another Weaver, and even then there were no guarantees.

But the most important role of a Weaver was as a deterrent; for the only defence against a Weaver was another Weaver. They were there to stop their fellows spying on their employers, or even attempting to kill them. If one noble had a Weaver in their employ, then his enemies must have one to keep themselves safe. And so on with their enemies, and theirs. The first Weavers had begun to appear around two and a half centuries ago, and in the intervening time they had become a fixture of noble life. Not one of the high families lacked a Weaver; to be without one was a huge handicap. And while they were widely reviled and despised even by their employers, they were here to stay.

The price paid to acquire a Weaver was steep indeed, and the employer never stopped paying till the Weaver died. Money was an issue, of course; but that money was not paid to the Weavers themselves, but to the Edgefathers in the temples, for they made the Masks that the Weavers wore, and such was the purchase price of the Mask. For the Weaver, there was only this: that whatever comfort he sought would be attended to, every need fulfilled, every whim satisfied. And that he would be cared for, when he could not care for himself.

Weaving was a dangerous business. The Weavers brushed close to madness each time they used their powers, and it took years of training to deal with the energies inherent in their Masks. The Masks were essentially narcotic in effect. The sublime delights of the Weave took the mind and body to a dizzying high; but when the Weaver returned to himself, there was a corresponding backlash. Sometimes it manifested itself as a terrible, suicidal depression; sometimes as hysteria; sometimes as insane rage or unquenchable lust. Each Weaver's needs were different, and each had different desires that had to be satisfied lest the Weaver turn on himself. No employer wanted that. A dead Weaver was merely a very expensive corpse.

The Weavers were mercenaries, selling their services to the highest bidder. To their credit, once bought they were loyal; there had never been a case of one Weaver defecting to another family for a higher price. But all owed a higher loyalty, and that was to Adderach, the great mountain monastery that was the heart of their organisation. The Weavers would do anything and everything for their employers, even kill other Weavers – it was hard to maintain a conscience in the face of the atrocities they committed in their post-Weaving periods – but they would not compromise Adderach or its plans. For Adderach was the greatest of the monasteries, and the monasteries kept the witchstones, and without the witchstones the Weavers were nothing.

Vyrrch reached the door to his chambers, which were high up at the south end of the Keep. He encountered few people here. Though there were servants within calling distance whose job it was to satisfy whatever desire took him, they had learned that it was safer to stay out of his way unless needed. Vyrrch's preferences were unusual, but then it was common for a Weaver's requests to become more random and bizarre as the insanity took hold.

He had become increasingly paranoid about theft of his belongings one summer, convinced that whispering figures were conspiring to strip his chambers of their finery. He gnawed on his thoughts until he had reached the point of mania, and several servants were executed for stealing things which had never existed in the first place. After that, he declared that no servant would be allowed to enter his chambers; they were accessible by only one door, which was kept locked, and he was the sole owner of a key. Beyond that door was a network of rooms in which no servant had trodden for several years now.

He drew out the heavy brass key from where it hung around his scrawny white neck, and unlocked the massive door at the end of the corridor. With a heave, he pushed it open. A moment later, something darted out and shot past his feet. He whirled in time to see a cat, its fur in burned patches, racing away down the corridor. A momentary frown passed beneath the still surface of his Mask. He did not even remember asking for a cat. He wondered what he had done to it.

He stepped into the dim chambers, closed and locked the door behind him. The stench coming from within was imperceptible to him; it was the smell of his own corrupted flesh, mixed with a dozen other odours, equally foul. The light from outside was muted by layers of hung silks, now besmirched by dust and hookah smoke, making the rooms gloomy even at midday. He shuffled into the main chamber, where the octagonal bathing pool was. Vyrrch had rid it of its centrepiece of a drowned, naked boy by ordering a tank full of scissorfish and dumping them in the pool. They made short work of the boy, and later of each other, but now the water was dark red and chunks of flesh floated in it. The decayed lump that shared his broken bed was still there, he noted with distaste. It was beginning to offend him. He would do something about it soon. For now, though, he had a more important task of his own.

The Empress was facing the council on the morrow. It was a dangerous time for her, and potentially ruinous to Blood Erinima. The nobles and high families had assessed the Lucia situation by now; they had formed into alliances, struck deals. They were ready with threats which they were fully prepared to deliver, ready to declare their intentions regarding Lucia's claim to the throne: support, or opposition.

Vyrrch had spent the last few days relaying communiqués between Blood Erinima's allies, of which there were more than he expected. The news that Lucia's Aberration was not overtly dangerous, nor outwardly visible, had gentled the storm somewhat, and many of Blood Erinima's staunchest friends had opted to stand by them. Even Blood Batik, the line to which Anais's husband belonged, had given their support, despite Durun's obvious abhorrence to the child. They believed the tradition of inheritance by blood should be adhered to. Other, smaller families, seeking the opportunity of raising themselves, had also shown their colours in Lucia's defence. They hoped that allying themselves to the Empress in her time of need would win them reward and recognition.

Vyrrch was a little dismayed, but not put off. The opposition – who believed in the good of the country over tradition – were easily as strong, and there were still many families drifting undecided. The debate could swing either way.

It was Vyrrch's intention to lend his own weight to the swing, and not in his employer's favour. For the accession of

Lucia was dangerous to the Weavers and to Adderach, and so he worked quietly to betray the Empress and her daughter.

He settled himself in his usual spot near the pool, cross-legged and hunched over, curled up small. Once he had become still, he waited while the ache in his joints slowly faded, allowing his phlegmy breathing to deepen. He relaxed as much as was possible, for his body constantly pained him. Gradually, he meditated, allowing even the pain to numb and retreat, feeling the eager heat of the witchstone dust embedded in his Mask. It seemed to warm his face, though its temperature did not rise; and its surface began to shimmer with an ochre-green cast.

The sensation of entering the Weave was like swimming upward through dark water to bright skies above. The pressure of the held breath expanding in the lungs, the feeling of being near bursting, the anticipation of the moment of relief; and then, breaking water with a great expulsion of air, and he was floating once again in the euphoric abyss between the gargantuan threads of the Weave.

The bliss that swamped him was unearthly, making all sensation pale by comparison. For a time, he shuddered in the throes of a feeling far past any joy that physical pleasure could provide. Then, with a great effort of will, he reined himself in, keeping the ecstasy down to a level he could tolerate and function in. The Weaver's craft was born of terrible discipline; for the Weave was death to the untrained.

He took himself to a territory often visited by him at his mistress's behest. It was the domain of Tabaxa, a young and talented Weaver who worked in the service of the Barak Zahn tu Ikati. This time, though, he was coming not to convey a message or to parley. This time he was entering unnoticed.

Blood Ikati were a sometime ally of Blood Erinima. The two families had too many conflicting interests ever to become loyal friends, but they were rarely at odds; more often, they remained respectfully neutral with each other. Blood Ikati, while not being especially rich or owning much land, had an impressive array of vassal families who had sworn allegiance to them. In their heyday, they had been the ruling family, and many treaties forged then still held today through careful management. Blood Ikati by themselves were not the most powerful family in the land by a long shot, but when one counted in the forces they brought to the table they became a factor to be reckoned with.

Barak Zahn had struck a deal with the Empress – in secret – meaning that he would declare his support for her during tomorrow's council. Anais knew better than to send a message through Vyrrch if she did not have to, and she had wisely decided not to rely on his loyalty in this affair. It pleased Vyrrch to see her distaste at being forced to use him to communicate over distance, for she was well aware of the Weaver's standpoint on the matter of Lucia. Instead she had invited the Barak to meet with her in person in the Keep. But this was Vyrrch's domain, and there was little that went on within these walls that he did not know about; so he listened in from afar anyway, unbeknownst to the plotters.

Anais was relying heavily on Blood Ikati's support to help her win over the council; or at least to stop them becoming openly hostile. Vyrrch had other ideas. He planned to change the Barak's mind.

It was a dangerous undertaking, but these were dangerous times. If he was discovered, it would mean scandal for the Empress – which was no bad thing – but it would also give Anais the excuse she needed to get rid of him. There were rules to prevent employers throwing Weavers out once they became an annoyance, as they inevitably did; but committing sabotage without her order was breaking those rules.

The Weavers' position depended on their trustworthiness. The nobles resented them for their necessity, and despised the fact that they had to take care of the Weaver's ugly and primal needs; yet without them the vast empire would be hopelessly crippled. It was a curious balance, a symbiotic relationship of mutual distaste; and yet, for all the strength of the Weavers, they were still only involved in Saramyr society as mere tools of the nobles who employed them, and like tools they could be discarded. No one could feel safe with creatures which could read their innermost secrets, and yet it would be worse to have those secrets read by a rival.

The Weavers balanced on a knife edge, and if one as prominent as Vyrrch was shown to be undermining his employer the repercussions would set Adderach's plans back decades. If they were suspected of being less than absolutely loyal, the retribution would be terrible, and their security relied on the nobles not acting in concert to remove them. Anais would love to have a new Weaver, and Vyrrch was too infirm to survive without a patron now.

Tread carefully, he thought to himself, but the words seemed as mist in the bliss of the Weave.

Tabaxa was no easy opponent, and so the strategy relied entirely upon stealth. The Barak or his watchdog must not realise that Vyrrch had been there, subtly tinkering with his thoughts, turning them against the Empress.

Tabaxa had woven his domain as a network of webs, their gossamer threads reaching into infinity. It was the most common visualisation of the Weave, taught by the masters to their pupils, but Vyrrch could not help a small stir of awe at the sight.

The vastness of the web defied perspective. It hung in perfect blackness, layer over layer stretching away at angles that baffled logic, anchored by threads chained somewhere so distant that perspective had thinned them to oblivion. It was far more complex than the simple geometry of a spider's construction; here, unconstrained by laws of physics, webs bent at impossible angles that the eye refused to fix on, joining in abstractions that could not have existed in the world outside the Weave. Between the thick strands, gauzy curtains of filmy gossamer seemed to sway in a cold wind, the tomblike breath of the abyss. A faint chiming sounded as the massive construction murmured and shifted.

Vyrrch was forced to adapt, shifting his perception to match that of his opponent. He knew it was not really there, only a method of allowing his frail human brain to see the complexities of the Weave without being driven mad. He hovered in nothingness, a disembodied mind, probing gently with his senses, seeking gaps in the defence. Net upon net of webwork spread before him, each one representing a different alarm that would bring Tabaxa. Vyrrch was impressed. It was subtly and carefully laid; but not so carefully that a Weave-lord could not penetrate it.

He shifted his vision to another frequency of resonance, and saw to his delight that much of the webbing was gone. Clearly Tabaxa had not been careful enough to armour his domain across the entire spectrum. There were very few Weavers who could alter their own resonance to a different level – in a sense, enter a new dimension within the Weave. Vyrrch could. Gratified, he gentled his way forward, invisible antennae of thought reaching out all around him, brushing near the threads but never touching them. He could feel the thrum of Tabaxa's presence, a fat black spider many hundreds of times his size, brooding somewhere near.

A tremor caught the edge of his senses, and in his mind he saw something descending from above, a ghostly veil, flat and transparent, drifting through the gaps between the webbing. Almost immediately, he sensed others nearby. None seemed to be heading for him, so he remained still until they passed by, like ethereal wisps of smoke.

He's clever, Vyrrch thought. *I've never seen that before.*

The things were sentinels, roaming alarms that existed on a plane high up in the resonance of the Weave. They were invisible at normal resonance. If Vyrrch had tried to penetrate the web as he had originally found it, he would have been unable to see them until they bumped into him and alerted their creator.

The Weave-lord was enjoying this. Slowly, patiently, he penetrated deeper into the gossamer shell of Tabaxa's domain. The illusory wind sighed through the framework of alarms, shifting them from side to side. In reality, Tabaxa had set the alarm network to vary slightly across the Weave, the better to catch unsuspecting intruders, but the effect manifested itself to Vyrrch's senses as a stirring of the web. Vyrrch had to dodge aside as a huge thread of silver lunged past him. He kept himself small, a tight focus of consciousness, and crept through, deeper, inward.

That was when the alarm was tripped.

Vyrrch panicked as the web around him erupted in a deafening din, a stunning cacophony of resonances. For an instant, he flailed; then he regained himself, and cast about for the cause. Nothing! There was nothing! He had been careful! He could feel the sudden, urgent movement of Tabaxa as he hefted his bulk up and came racing down the web, searching for the intruder. Vyrrch tried to move, to get out before he was identified, but he was trapped, his consciousness snared. Frantically, he shifted back down to normal resonance, and there, to his horror, he found himself engulfed in some grotesque, slippery thing, half mist and half solid, a vile amoeba that was clutching his mind tightly.

Vyrrch cursed. Tabaxa had not only employed alarms that were visible exclusively in the higher spectrum – the filmy ghosts he had seen before – but he had used ones that could only be seen in the normal spectrum too. Vyrrch had been caught out; he should have been switching between the two resonances.

Enraged suddenly, he annihilated the amoeba with a thought, disassembling its threads in fury. But Tabaxa was almost upon him now, a dark, massive shape, eight legs ratcheting as he raced along the threads of his weave to see what was amiss. It was too late to avoid a conflict, too late to escape and remain anonymous. Tabaxa would know he, Vyrrch, had been here.

Heart's blood! he thought furiously. *There's nothing else for it now.*

He tore out through the webbing of alarms, tattering it

behind him, and crashed into the spider-body of his opponent. His world dissolved into an impossible multitude of threads, a rushing, darting tapestry of tiny knots and tangles, and he was *in* the threads, controlling them. Tabaxa was here too; Vyrrch sensed his angry defiance. He was puzzled as to why Vyrrch had come into his domain, but eager to demolish the older Weaver. There would be no quarter given, and none asked.

The conflict was conducted faster than consciousness could follow. Each sought a channel into the other, so they dodged and feinted down threads, finding one suddenly knotted against them, untangling this one or that, reaching dead-ends and loops that had been laid as traps or decoys. Each wanted to confuse the other long enough to break through the defences, while simultaneously shoring up their own. By manipulating the threads of the Weave, they jabbed and parried, darting back and forth, creating labyrinths for their opponent to get lost in or frantically unwinding a complex knot to create a channel into their enemy.

But in the end experience won out, and Tabaxa slipped up. Vyrrch had left him a tempting channel as a lure, and he impetuously took it; but it came up against a dead-end, and Vyrrch was waiting. With a speed and skill unmatched among the Weavers, he fashioned an insoluble knot behind Tabaxa, trapping him. Tabaxa tried to skip threads, to get out of the trap, but he only came up against another trap, and another, and by that time it was too late. Vyrrch was already away, burrowing through his defences, and Tabaxa could not get out in time. Vyrrch had identified a knot in Tabaxa's wall that was fraying, and he tore it open and raced through, into Tabaxa's mind like a meathook into a carcass, lodging in there and *rending* . . .

He could feel the force of his enemy's haemorrhage as he withdrew, feel the flailing embers of Tabaxa's consciousness as they were pulled back to his dying body. Tabaxa was even now spasming on the floor of his chamber, his brain ripped from the inside by the force of Vyrrch's will. The Weave-lord himself was retreating, the agony receding behind him rapidly as he raced out of the Weave, following the threads back to his own body, cursing and raging.

Vyrrch's eyes snapped open in the dim, filthy room where he sat. He shrieked in frustration, consumed by an anger that could not be borne. He had been careless! He, Vyrrch, the Weave-lord, had been caught by a trap he should have avoided with ease, *would* have avoided a year ago. What was wrong with him? Why could his mind not assemble his thoughts, lessons, instincts as it used to? He was perhaps the most formidable Weaver in the land, and yet he had blundered into Tabaxa's trickery, and been forced to kill him to protect his own identity. And all without getting close to Barak Zahn. A failure; an unmitigated failure.

Vyrrch rose suddenly, another shriek coming from beneath his Mask. He picked up the unidentifiable corpse on his bed and tossed it into the bloodied pool. He swatted aside a crystal ornament that stood in the corner of the room, one he did not recall seeing before. It dashed into shards on the tiles, a fortune destroyed in an instant. Like a whirlwind he swept through his chambers, breaking and throwing anything he could pick up, screaming like a child in a tantrum before flinging himself to the floor and scratching at it until his fingernails snapped.

The pain of his broken nails brought him to a momentary calm, a lull in the storm. He lay panting for a moment, before getting to his feet and stumbling to where a mouthpiece was set into the wall, connected by an echoing pipe to the quarters of his personal servants.

'Get me a child!' he rasped. 'A child, I don't care what sort. Get me a child, and . . . and bring me my bag of tools. And food! I want meat! Meat!'

He did not wait for a response. He threw himself to the floor again and lay there, his emaciated ribs heaving, waiting, drooling in anticipation. He did not know what would happen when the child got here. He never knew what would happen. But he thought he was going to enjoy it.

NINE

The compound of Blood Tamak was on the other side of the
Imperial Quarter from Blood Koli's, but Mishani chose to
walk anyway. For one thing, it was a beautiful day, with cool
breezes from the north offering relief from the usual stifling
heat of the city. For another, she preferred that her business
this afternoon remained a secret.

The streets of the Imperial Quarter were wider than the
usual thoroughfares of the city, and less trafficked. Tall,
ancient trees lined the roadside, and the rectangular flagstones were swept for leaves every morning. Fountains or
ornamental gutters plashed and trickled, collecting in basins
where passers-by could drink to quench their thirst. Carts
rattled by with deliveries piled high upon them. Mishani
passed many gates, each one belonging to an important
family, each one with their ancestral emblem wrought upon
them somewhere. The Imperial Quarter was made up mainly
of the townhouses of the various families – not only the high
families who sat on the councils, but a multitude of minor
nobles as well.

She glanced up at the Imperial Keep, its angled planes
sheening in the sunlight. One such council was going on now,
and it was one that she should well be attending. The Heir-
Empress was an Aberrant, and the Empress in her hubris still
seemed intent on putting her on the throne. Mishani would
never have believed it possible – not only that Lucia had been
allowed to reach eight harvests of age in the first place, but
also that the Empress was foolish enough to think the high
families would allow an Aberrant to rule Saramyr. Her father
would be angry that she had not been there to lend her

support to his condemnation of the Empress; but she had something else to attend to, and it had to be done while all eyes were on the Keep.

The divisions brought about by the revelations in the Imperial Family had come swift and savage. Longtime allies had separated in disgust, driven apart by their inability to condone the other's viewpoint. Arguments had erupted and turned to feuds. Most of it was down to men and their posturing, Mishani thought with a wrinkle of contempt. Her father was an example. He and Barak Chel of Blood Tamak had been political allies and good friends a month ago. Mishani had often accompanied him on visits to the town-house of Blood Tamak. Then Chel's support of the Empress in the matter of the succession sparked a debate in which both said regretful things to each other, and now they were bitter enemies and would not speak.

That, unfortunately, was contrary to Mishani's interests, for within the house of Blood Tamak lived a wise old scholar by the name of Copanis, whose particular field of expertise was antique masks. And whatever the state of play between their two families, she intended to see him. The risk to herself was not inconsiderable. Her reputation would suffer greatly if she was caught in defiance of her father's wishes, not to mention the embarrassment that would be caused by her presence in her enemy's house. But there were greater matters at play here. Kaiku's only clue to her father's murder was the mask, tucked now beneath Mishani's blue robes; and if anyone could tell them about it, it was Copanis.

She just had to get to him.

She worried about her friend as she walked a winding route through the Imperial Quarter: across sunlit, mosaic-strewn plazas with restaurants in the shady cloisters, down narrow and immaculate alleyways where thin, short-furred cats prowled and slunk, through a small park in which couples strolled and artists sat cross-legged on the grass, their brushes hovering above their canvases. She had a great affinity for the

Imperial Quarter, and on most days she found it tantalising, a place of beauty and intrigue, where the peripheral machinations of the court were played out in the gardens and under the arches. She was aware that it was heavily sanitised and rigidly policed in comparison to the sweaty bustle of the rest of the city, but she was content to avoid the crush and press when she could, and she preferred the calm and beauty of these streets to those of the Market District or the Poor Quarter.

But today her mind was not on the sights and sounds surrounding her. Her concern for Kaiku consumed her thoughts entirely. If what Kaiku had told her was true – and she had no doubt that Kaiku, at least, believed it – then her situation was grave. She was convinced she was possessed by something, which was bad enough; the alternative – that she was mad, and had merely created the story of the shin-shin and the burning of Asara as a hysterical reaction to the death of her family – was scarcely better. And yet she seemed lucid, which tended to discount either of those possibilities; unless the madness or possession was of a more insidious kind, that did not show itself as raving lunacy but in a subtle mania instead.

A chill ran through her, a cool bloom that counteracted the bright afternoon sun on her skin. Heart's blood, what if she *was* possessed? Mishani knew the stories of the dark spirits that haunted the forests and mountains, the deep and high and secret places of the world; but they had always seemed distant, powerless to affect her. She had heard about the gathering hostility of the beasts; it had been a small but persistent concern in court circles for a long time now. Enyu's priests and their sympathisers never stopped talking about it. Was it so much of a stretch, then, to believe the possibility that her friend had become . . . *infested* by the emboldened spirits?

She shook her head. What did she know about spirits? She was frightening herself with conjecture and guesswork. There would be answers, there *had* to be answers, and she and Kaiku would hunt them out; but first, she had another task to perform.

Blood Tamak's compound was set on a hillside, the main body of the townhouse supported by a man-made cliff of stone to make it sit level. It was a squat, flat-roofed building, its beige walls sparsely panelled in dark, polished wood, without any of the ornamentations, votive statues or icons that were usually present somewhere around the exterior of Saramyr households. Beneath it were the gardens, an unprepossessing lawn with curving flagstone paths and sprays of blooms, spartan even by the minimalist norms of Saramyr.

Mishani knew the layout well, for she had been shown around it often during her father's visits. At the side of the compound, a narrow set of sandstone steps ran from the street in front to the one behind, which was set higher in the hill. There was a servants' gate there, used for unobtrusive errand-running. It was here that Mishani took herself and waited.

She had timed her arrival excellently. Less than five minutes later, a short, sallow servant girl appeared, half opening the gate. Recognition widened her eyes as she saw who was outside.

'Mistress Mishani,' she gaped, blanching. She looked up and down the steps. 'You should not be here.'

'I know, Xami,' she replied. 'Heading to the market for flour?' Xami nodded. 'I thought so. Ever punctual. Your master would approve.'

'My master . . . your father . . . we must not be seen talking!' Xami stammered.

Mishani was the picture of elegant calm. Her tone was unhurried but firm. 'Xami, I have a favour to ask.'

'Mistress . . .' she began reluctantly, still standing in the gateway with the gate obscuring her partway, like a shield between them.

Mishani reached in and took the servant girl's hands in

hers, and within was the crinkle of money. *Paper* money, which meant Imperial shirets. 'Remember the services I performed for you, in days when the heads of our houses were friends.'

Xami put the money inside her robe without looking at it. Her wide, watery eyes wavered in indecision. Mishani had passed love letters between her and a servant boy in the Koli house many times. It had seemed an interesting diversion then – and, additionally, Xami's clumsy attempts at poetry in the vulgar script of Low Saramyrrhic always made her smirk – but now it seemed it might serve a useful political purpose as well.

'Let me in, Xami,' Mishani said. 'You did not see me; you will not be blamed if I am caught. I promise you.'

Xami deliberated a few moments longer. Then, more because she feared somebody seeing them together than because she wanted to, she opened the gate fully. Mishani went in, and Xami slipped out and shut the gate behind her.

Mishani found herself in a narrow, vine-laden passageway that led around to the back of the main house, where the servants' quarters were. Most of the servants – indeed, much of the household – would be at the Keep now, for in matters of state the nobles liked to arrive in full pomp and splendour whenever they could. Copanis would not. He was a scholar, not a servant; the Barak Chel was his patron.

The thought brought uncomfortable resonances of Kaiku's father, Ruito tu Makaima. If he had had a patron, maybe there would have been somewhere to start, somebody that suspicion might devolve upon who might have a reason to kill him and his family; but it was a dead-end. Ruito had been in the rare position of being independently wealthy enough to survive without patronage, having had several works of philosophy in circulation among the literati of the empire that had generated enough income for him to buy himself free a long time ago.

Mishani made her way around to the back. She refused to

sneak; she walked instead as if she owned the place, her long, dark hair swaying around her ankles as she went. Those servants that were still about would be engaged in menial duties now, but thankfully none seemed to have taken them outside, and she was able to slip into the house through the rear entrance undetected.

The interior of the house was very spare and minimal, with polished wooden floorboards and only the occasional wall hanging or mat to draw the eye. Chel liked his house as he liked his pleasures – respectable and sparse. Upstairs lay the family rooms and the ancestral chambers, where the house's treasures were kept. She would have no chance of getting up there; they were always guarded. But Copanis's study was on the ground floor, near the back of the house. Trusting to luck and Shintu, god of fortune, she made her way down a wide corridor, hoping that no one would come to challenge her.

Shintu smiled upon her, it seemed; for she reached the study without seeing another soul. Unusually, it had a door instead of a curtain or screen, but then the old scholar valued his privacy. She tapped on it. An instant later it was opened irritably, as if he had been lurking on the other side for just such an opportunity to surprise those who dared to interrupt him.

His face turned from annoyance to puzzlement as he saw who it was. Before he could protest, she laid a finger on her lips and slid inside, shutting the door behind her.

Copanis's study was uncomfortably hot, even with the shutters open to admit the breeze from outside. A low table was scattered with scrolls and manuscripts, but everywhere were concessions to ornamentation that were not present in the rest of the house. A sculpted hand; a skull with glass jewels for teeth; an effigy of Naris, god of scholars and son of Isisya, goddess of peace, beauty and wisdom. All was a clutter, but it conveyed the intensity of its author.

'My, my,' he said. 'Mistress Mishani, daughter of my master's newly embittered enemy. I take it you have something very important you need, to come see me like this. And miss the council with the Empress, too.'

Mishani looked over the old man with an inner smile that did not show on her face. He always was quick, this leathery, scrawny walnut of a scholar. His clothes seemed to sag off his lean frame, as his flesh did; but his eyes were still feverishly bright, and he was capable of running rings round intellectuals half his age.

Mishani decided to dispense with the preamble. She drew out the mask. 'This belongs to a dear friend of mine,' she said. 'Our need is most pressing to discover all we can about it. I can tell you no more than that.'

Copanis scrutinised her for a short while. He was making a show of deliberation, but it was not hard to see how his eyes were drawn to the mask. He was too cantankerous to fear to balk the authority of his master, and he was never one to hoard his knowledge when he could share it. With a mischievous quirk of one eyebrow, he took the mask and turned it around in his hands.

'You take a great risk, coming here,' he murmured.

'I seek to right a grave wrong, and aid a friend in desperate straits,' she replied. 'The risk is little, weighed against that.'

'Indeed?' he said. 'Well, I won't inquire, Mistress Mishani. But I dare to say I can help you in my small way.'

He placed the mask in a small wooden cradle, so that it faced the sunlight from the windows. After that, he found himself a small ceramic pot of what looked like dust. This he sprinkled over the face of the mask. Mishani watched with fascination – disguised, as ever, behind a wall of impassivity – as the dust seemed to glitter in the sun.

'Draw the shutters,' he said. 'Not this one; the others.'

Mishani obeyed, darkening the room until only a single shutter remained, shining light on to the mask's dusty face. After a time, Copanis shut that one himself, plunging the room into darkness. He turned the mask so they could both see it. The dust glowed dimly, phosphorescent in the darkness – but its life was momentary, and it faded.

Copanis harumphed. He told Mishani to open the shutters again. She did so, enduring his peremptory tone because she needed his help. After that, he sat cross-legged at his desk and brushed the dust off the mask, then turned it over in his hands and studied it. He held it near to his face without letting it touch. He closed his eyes and spent a short time chanting softly, as if in meditation. Mishani waited patiently, kneeling opposite him with her hair pooled around her.

Eventually he opened his eyes. 'This is indeed a True Mask,' he said. 'It has been infused with witchstone dust, and there is power here. However, it is very young. Less than a year old; I would estimate no more than two previous wearers, neither of them possessing any remarkable mental strength. It is valuable, of course; but as far as the True Masks go, it is weak, like a newborn.'

'You can tell all that? I am impressed,' Mishani said.

He shrugged. 'I can only tell you in the vaguest of terms. A True Mask picks up strength from its wearers . . . or, rather, it saps it from them. There are ways to tell a True Mask from an ordinary one, and guess at its age; but little else can be done. There is a simple way to learn more, of course, but I cannot counsel it.'

'And that is . . . ?'

'To put it on, Mistress,' said Copanis with a sour smile.

'Surely anyone who did that would die, unless they were a Weaver and trained in the arts.'

'Ah, not so. A common misconception,' Copanis replied, stretching. His vertebrae cracked like fireworks. 'The older the Mask, the greater the peril; but one as young and weak as this . . . why, you or I might put it on and suffer no ill effects. Nightmares, maybe. Disorientation. That said, I repeat I cannot counsel it. There is still an element of risk. Should the mind prove to be susceptible, insanity and death would surely follow. The chance is small, but it exists.'

Mishani considered this. 'Can you tell me where it comes from?'

'Ah, that is easy. The hallmarks are obvious. See this wave pattern in the wood on the inside? And the indentation here, to accommodate the wearer's philtrum? This comes from one of the Edgefathers at Fo; although from which part of the isle, I cannot say. I would guess at the north, simply because of the marked lack of mainland influences on the carving. The one who carved this either had little contact with the ports in the south of Fo and the people there, or he spurned the craft of the mainland Edgefathers.' He passed it back to her, the red and black face seeming to grin mockingly. 'That is all I can tell you.'

'It was more than enough,' she replied, bowing. 'You have my gratitude. Now I must go; I've put you in peril already.'

He stood up, knee joints popping, and cackled. 'Hardly peril, Mistress. Here, I'll help you get out,' he said. 'Let me spy out the lie of the land for you, then you can make it to the servants' gate. You know where it is?'

'I know,' replied Mishani, standing also, her hair cascading around her.

'I thought you might,' he replied.

Kaiku was unused to spending the summer months in the city; her father had always sent his family to their cooler property in the Forest of Yuna while he worked. Though it was only just climbing the slope towards the truly miserable heat of midsummer, Kaiku had become drowsy and felt the need for a siesta, and she had slept while she waited for Mishani to return.

In her dreams, the shin-shin came.

This time they were even more dark and nebulous than she remembered. They stalked unseen in the corridors of her mind, fearful presences that emanated dread, which she could not see but sense. She fled through a labyrinth that resembled her father's house in the forest, but seemed infinitely bigger and endless. She found doors, hatches, corners that brought her shuddering to a stop, for she knew with dream-certainty that death was lurking there, *felt* them waiting just beyond with a terrifying, hungry patience. And each time she came up against one of these invisible barriers of fear, she turned and ran the other way, her skin clammy with the proximity of the end. But no matter how far she went, they were every-where, and inescapable.

Flailing helplessly, trapped forever, she knew there was no escape for her, and still she tried. At some point, she became aware of another presence, one even more malevolent than the shin-shin. This one lived inside her, in her belly and womb and groin, and it grew whenever she thought about it, feeding on her attention. She desperately tried to distract herself, but it was impossible not to feel the thing inside her skin, and she sensed its mad glee as it suckled on her terror. Desperate, driven by some illogical prescience that she had to get out of the house before this new entity consumed her, she raced onward, trying new routes with increasing panic, find-ing all blocked against her by the lurking, unseen shin-shin. Her chest ached, and her heart pounded harder and harder, but she could not stop even though her body burned with fatigue, and suddenly it was all too much and—

Her eyes flew open to agony, and the room ignited.

She threw herself off her sleeping-mat with a shriek, warned by some instinct that caused her to react before her conscious mind could arrange itself. She was fortunate: so quick was she that the ripples of flame that sprang from the weave of the mat only licked her, and it was too brief to do more than singe her sleeping-robe. She scrambled to her feet, gazing wildly around the room. The curtain that hung in the doorway was ablaze; the window shutters smoked and charred, blue flames invisible in the bright sunlight. The timbers of the room had blackened but not caught light; an arrangement of guya blossoms in a vase had crisped to cinders. A wall-hanging, that had once depicted the final victory of the first Emperor, Jaan tu Vinaxis, over the primitive Ugati people that had occupied this land in the past, ran with fire. Thin, deadly smoke was rising all around her.

She dashed immediately for the doorway, an automatic response, and then retreated as she saw it was impassable while the curtain still burned. The windows were no option either. More terrifying than her animal fear of fire was the knowledge that she was trapped by it. She tried to cry for help, but the intake of breath made her chest blaze in pain. Her every muscle was in agony, and the blood seemed to boil and scorch as it pumped through her veins. The demon inside her had returned in her sleep and tormented her with fires inside and out.

Steeling herself against the torture, she found her voice and shouted, hoping to alert the servants to her plight. But no sooner had she done so than the flaming curtain began to thrash, and she saw Mishani beyond it, slashing at it with a long, bladed pike that had been part of an ornamental set in the corridor outside. She hacked at the disintegrating cloth and it came to pieces, falling to the floor where a servant girl threw a bucket of suds across it and reduced it to a black mush. Shielding her face with one blue-robed arm, Mishani called to her friend; Kaiku ran to her in desperate relief. Mishani pulled her clear of the room, out into the corridor. Voices were raised all about the household as servants ran for water.

Kaiku would have embraced her friend then, if it were not for the gasp of horror that the servant girl gave. Kaiku looked to her, confused, and the girl quailed and made a sign against evil. Mishani's face was stony. She grabbed the servant girl's wrist, pulling her roughly to face her mistress.

'On your life, you will speak of this to no one,' she said, her voice heavy with threat. 'On your *life*, Yokada.'

The servant girl nodded, frightened.

'Go,' Mishani commanded. 'Find more water.' As Yokada gratefully fled, she turned to Kaiku. 'Close your eyes, Kaiku. Let me lead you. Feign that you are smoke-blinded.'

'I—'

'As I am your friend, trust me,' Mishani said. Kaiku, shaken and scared still, did what she was told. Mishani was several inches shorter than Kaiku, but she seemed many years older then, and her tone brooked no argument. She took her friend by the hand and led her away, hurrying so that Kaiku feared to trip. She opened her eyes to see where her feet were, and Mishani caught her and hissed at her to keep them shut. Servants rushed past them in a clatter of feet, and she heard the swill of water in buckets. After a time, Mishani drew back a curtain and led her into a room.

'Now you can open them,' Mishani said, sounding weary.

It was Mishani's study. The low, simple table was still occupied by neat rows of tally charts, an inkpot and a brush. Several shelves held other scrolls, not one of them out of place. Sketch paintings of serene glades and rivers hung on the walls, next to a large elliptical mirror, for Mishani often entertained guests in here and she understood the importance of appearance.

'Mishani, I . . . it happened again . . .' Kaiku stammered. 'What if you had been with me? Spirits, what if—'

'Go to the mirror,' Mishani said. Kaiku quieted, looked at her friend, then at the mirror. Suddenly, she feared what she might see. She shuddered as a spasm of pain racked her body.

'I need to rest, Mishani . . . I'm so tired,' she sighed.

'The mirror,' Mishani repeated. Kaiku turned, bowing her head as she stood before it. She did not dare see whatever it was that Mishani wanted her to.

'*Look at yourself!*' Mishani hissed, and there was an edge to her voice that Kaiku had never heard before, one that made her afraid of her friend. She looked up.

'Oh,' she murmured, her fingers coming up to rest on her cheek.

Her eyes, gazing back at her, were no longer brown. The irises were a deep and arterial red, the eyes of a demon.

'Then it's true,' she said, slowly, brokenly. 'I am possessed.'

Mishani was standing at her shoulder in the mirror, her head tilted down so that her hair fell across her face, her gaze averted.

'No, Kaiku,' she said. 'You are not possessed. You are Aberrant.'

TEN

The council chamber of the Imperial Keep was not vast, but what it lacked in size it made up for in opulence. The walls and tiers of the semi-circular room were drenched in grandeur, from the enormous gold and crystal chandelier overhead to the ornate scrollwork on the eaves and balconies. The majority of the room was lacquered in crimson and edged in dark gold; the ceiling was sculpted into a relief of an ancient battle, while the floor was of reflective black stone. The flat wall at the back – where the speaker stood to talk to those on the semi-circular tiers above – bore a gigantic mural of two scaled creatures warring in the air, their bodies aflame as they locked in mortal combat above a terrified city below.

The assembly was silent as Anais tu Erinima, Blood Empress of Saramyr, walked to stand in front of the mural, her dress a dark red like that of the room. She wore her flaxen hair in her customary long plait, with a silver tiara across her brow. Next to her walked an old man in robes of grey, his hood masking his face so that only his hooked nose and long, salt and pepper beard could be seen. High, arched windows lit the scene, brighter on the west side where the sun was heading toward afternoon.

Anais hated this room. The colours made her feel angry and aggressive; it was a poor choice for a place of debate. But this had been the council chamber for generations past, through war and peace, famine and plenty, woe and joy; tradition had kept it virtually unaltered for centuries.

Maybe I will be the one to change it, Anais thought to herself, masking her nervousness with bravado. *Maybe I will change many things, before my days are done.*

She took her place on the central dais, a petite and deceptively naïve-looking figure in the face of the assembly. The Speaker in his grey robes stood next to her. Facing her, on three tiers that rose up and away, were representatives of the thirty high families of Saramyr. They sat behind expertly carven stalls, looking down on their ruler. She scanned the room, searching out her supporters, seeking her enemies . . . and finally finding Barak Zahn tu Ikati, whom until a few minutes ago had been the former. Now she had no idea where she stood in his regard.

She had in her pocket a letter from the Barak, informing her of the sudden and extremely suspicious death of his Weaver, Tabaxa. It said nothing more than that. The letter had been delivered to her by a servant just before she entered the chamber. If the move had been calculated to unnerve her, it had succeeded admirably. Now she studied him in the stalls, a tall man with a short white beard and pox-pitted cheeks, trying to divine what he meant by it; but his face was blank, and gave no indication of his thoughts.

By the spirits, does he think I did it? she asked herself, and then wondered what she would do if the Barak withdrew his support, when her position was precarious enough already.

'The Blood Empress of Saramyr, Anais tu Erinima,' the Speaker announced, and then it was her time to speak. She took a breath, showing nothing of the fear she felt.

'Honourable families of Saramyr,' she began, her usually soft and gentle voice suddenly strong and clear. 'I bring this council to session. Thank you for coming; I know some of you have travelled far to be here today.' She paused, allowing the echoes of her pleasantries to fade before she launched into the fray.

'I am certain you are aware of the matter before us. The issue of my daughter is of great importance to all of you, and to Saramyr as a whole. I know of the division over this situation, both among the high families and those not of noble birth. If compromise can be reached to heal this division, then

I am willing to compromise. There are many aspects to this matter that will bear negotiation. But know this as a fact: my daughter is of Blood Erinima, and the daughter of the Blood Empress. Some may call her Aberrant, some may not: it is a matter of opinion. But the point is moot in the laws of succession. She is the sole heir to my throne, and she will be Blood Empress after me.'

The council, predictably, broke out in uproar. Anais faced them without flinching or lowering her gaze. Many of them had been hoping that she had seen sense and decided to abdicate, if only to spare her daughter's life. But Anais had never been more sure of anything. Her child would be as good a ruler as any, better than most. Whatever the dangers to herself, she would bring her child to throne.

Unless, of course, she was deposed by the council.

The thirty high familes were nominally vassals to the ruling family, but it rarely worked exactly that way. Blood Erinima ruled Saramyr, meaning that they – in theory – spoke for all the families. The Baraks each owned vast tracts of land, effectively dividing up Saramyr into manageable chunks. The Baraks further subdivided their land to ur-Baraks, who dealt with smaller portions, and the ur-Baraks left the management of villages within their territory to the Marks. With as many powerful families as there were in Saramyr, the question of loyalty was never clear-cut.

The council of the high families represented only the Baraks, and some of the more influential ur-Baraks who were related by blood. Though there was a strong tendency to support the ruling family, fuelled by tradition and concepts of honour, it was by no means a guarantee. The council had turned against their lieges before, and for much less. A vote of no confidence from the council was damning, and left only two real options: abdication, or civil war. Saramyr's history was spotted with bloody coups. Though the ruling family always had the greatest army by far – for their post entitled them to the protection of the Imperial Guards, who owed allegiance only to the throne and not Blood – an alliance of several strong Baraks could still challenge them and win.

The Speaker raised his arm, and in his hand was a small wooden tube on a thin red rope. He spun it quickly, and a high keening wail cut through the room. When it died, silence had returned. Anais's eyes flickered over the assembly. She could see other members of Blood Erinima in the stalls, approving of her declaration. Her old enemies in Blood Amacha looked furious; though she noted that Barak Sonmaga's expression was almost smug. He relished the fight.

'To those who oppose me, I say this!' she cried. 'You are blinded by your prejudices. Too long have you listened to the Weavers, too long have you been told what to think on this matter. Many of you have never even seen an Aberrant. Many of you are ill educated in what makes an Aberrant at all. Those of you who have met my daughter know her to be gentle and kind. She bears no deformities. She may possess perceptions greater than ours, senses that we do not under-stand: but don't the Weavers have the same? She has harmed no one and nothing; she is as well-adjusted as a child can be. And if exceptional intelligence is an undesirable trait for a ruler of Saramyr, then let us be ruled by half-wits instead, and see how long our proud country lasts!'

There was silence again for a short moment. She was coming dangerously close to defying the Weavers outright, and who knew the ruin that would bring? Anais was only glad that no Weavers were present; they played no part in the country's politics. Still, she was sure that they were listening somewhere . . .

Barak Sonmaga tu Amacha stood. She might have known he would be the first. The Speaker announced his name.

'Empress, nobody doubts the love you have for Lucia,' Sonmaga said. He was a broad-chested, black-bearded man with heavy eyebrows. 'Which of us could say that we would not do the same, were it our own son or daughter? Who among us could bear to deliver our own child to the Weavers, even if they were . . . unnatural?'

Anais did not react to his choice of words. They were intended to provoke.

'But this is a matter greater than your feelings, Empress,' he continued, his voice lowering in tone. 'Greater even than ours, here in this council. The *people* are the issue here. The people of Saramyr. And I tell you they *will not bear* an Aberrant to sit on the throne. She might have the potential to be a great ruler – I'm sure no mother would think any less of her child – but how long will she rule, how effectively, when she is reviled by the people beneath her?'

Anais kept her face calm. 'Barak Sonmaga, the people have a long time to get used to her. By the time she sits the throne, they will have learned to accept. They, like many of the honourable Baraks and Barakesses in this chamber, will find their opinions changed upon seeing my daughter, and witnessing her nature.'

Sonmaga opened his mouth to speak again, but Anais suddenly remembered another point she had meant to make, and got in first. 'And never forget, Barak Sonmaga, the lessons of the past. Our people have suffered tyranny under the madness of Emperor Cadis tu Othoro. They have been brought to famine and ruin by the ineptitude of Emperor Emen tu Gor; and then suffered terrible and entirely preventable plagues under his successor, because he refused to clean up the cities. None of these brought the people to revolution. I offer a child with extraordinary intelligence, impeccable sanity and a kind nature, and the only count against her is that she is unusual. I hardly think the people will take up arms at that. I say you exaggerate, Barak Sonmaga tu Amacha. It is no secret that you have your own preferences as to who should sit on the throne.'

Sonmaga's eyes blazed. Such a direct accusation was a hair's breadth from insult, but it was also inarguably true. Blood Amacha had never been a ruling family, and they had always coveted the throne. He knew it well enough, so he could not take umbrage without weakening his own position. Anaïs, for her part, gazed coolly around the chamber. She did not glance at the representatives of Blood Gor, whom she had regrettably reminded of their past failures. Blood Othoro had thankfully dwindled long ago, and taken its madness with it. Her gaze passed across Barak Zahn and lingered there for a moment, but he was as impassive as before. His letter had unnerved her considerably; she had no idea if she could count on his support or not. The deal they had made could be in tatters if he suspected that Anaïs had tried to kill him or his Weaver . . . but why should he think such a thing? They were allies, weren't they?

An elderly Barak stood up then, his lean body draped in heavy robes.

'Barak Mamasi tu Nira,' the Speaker announced.

'I beg that you consider this matter well,' said Mamasi. He was a neutral, as far as Anaïs knew. He disliked getting his family involved in disputes of any kind if he could help it. 'To force a council vote on this matter can only bring ruin. Opinion among the Baraks is deeply divided: you know this. Abdicate, Empress, for the good of the land and for your daughter. If you stay, civil war must follow, and Lucia's life would be in great danger were you to lose.'

'Barakess Juun tu Lilira,' said the Speaker, as she stood and made a sign that she wished to speak in support of Mamasi.

'Now, of all times, we must remain united,' declared the ancient Barakess. "The very land turns against us. Evil things haunt the hills and forests, and grow bolder by the day. My villages are besieged by ill spirits; the earth sickens and crops fail. A civil war now would only add to our misery. Please, Empress, for the good of your people.'

'I say no!' Anaïs cried. 'I say my abdication would weaken the country more than Lucia ever could. There are at least three houses who hold power enough to challenge for the throne. I will name no names, and I do not presume to know their intentions, but a war of succession would follow should Blood Erinima relinquish their claim on the throne, and all of you know it!'

Silence again. She spoke the truth. Blood Batik claimed rights by marriage, but there was no way Anais would pass the responsibility for Saramyr into the hands of her wastrel, womanising husband. Blood Amacha claimed rights by sheer power; they owned the most land, and a large private army. And Blood Kerestyn were most powerful of all; they had been the ruling family before Erinima, and they had never lost the desire to reclaim the throne.

'I know the horror that the word "Aberrant" awakens in all of us,' she continued. 'But I know also that there are many interpretations of that word. Not all Aberration is bad; not all Aberrants are evil. It took the birth of my child to make me see that, but I see it now. And I would have all of you see it, too.'

She raised her hand to forestall another of her antagonists. 'I ask for the vote of the council in support of my daughter's claim to the throne.'

'The council will vote!' the Speaker called.

Anais stood where she was, her hands laid across each other, clammy with sweat. She could feel herself trembling inside. If the council approved by a majority, she could consider herself safe for a time. As the Barakess had said, nobody wanted a civil war now. But if her support was lacking, then she was in terrible danger. Would she truly abdicate, even for the sake of her child? At least, that way, Lucia might live . . .

'Blood Erinima, family of my heart. How do you say?' she asked.

'We support you as always, Empress,' said her great-aunt Milla. As eldest, she was the head of the family, even though her niece was Empress.

Anais looked about the chamber, scanning the grandiose tiers. She would have to ask each of the thirty families in turn, and the order that she chose them was crucial. Some families who were wavering might be swayed if a more powerful ally took the lead. Blood Erinima was easy. She asked then three other families, all certainties, who assured her of their support. A fourth one, whom she had thought she could rely on, decided to remain neutral.

Then, reasoning that it was best not to use up all her support this early in the vote, she chose an obvious enemy: Blood Amacha.

'We oppose you, Empress, with all our strength and vigour,' Barak Sonmaga replied, somewhat unnecessarily.

She asked several other families, receiving mixed reponses. The powerful Barak Koli voted against her; his daughter Mishani was noticeably absent. Blood Nabichi threw unexpected support behind the Empress. But there was one to whom many of the lesser families were looking: Blood Ikati. Anais took a breath; their support was vital for snaring in some of those who sat on the fence.

'Blood Ikati,' she said, her voice echoing across the chamber. 'How do you say?'

Barak Zahn tu Ikati unfolded his lean, rangy body from behind his stall. He regarded Anais carefully. Anais met his gaze with her own, unfaltering.

I have done him no wrong, she told herself. *I have nothing to fear.*

'Blood Ikati supports your daughter's claim, Anais tu Erinima,' the Barak said, and as he sat down Anais felt herself weaken at the knees.

The ritual of asking each family was a nerve-racking affair, and by the time it had concluded there was no clear majority. Her supporters and opponents were evenly matched, and there were few who abstained. The council was divided, split down the middle.

Anais felt a thrill of mixed relief and trepidation. If the council had voted heavily against her, she would have been tempted to consider abdication, whatever the cost to Blood Erinima. Her daughter's life would surely be forfeit if Anais tried to put her on the throne with no support. But now her course was set. Though it was risky, she had enough strength behind her to dare this, even if she was sorely tempting the prospect of civil war. When they left the chamber, Blood Amacha would be gathering their allies and Blood Kerestyn theirs. The only comfort she took was that the opposition was divided, whereas her support was as solid as she could hope for.

'My daughter sits the throne,' she said. 'I bid you all a safe journey.' And with that, she left, her composure threatening to break as she stepped from the dais; but she did not allow herself to cry until she was alone in her chambers.

It was perhaps an hour later when Barak Zahn tu Ikati came to her chambers.

Ordinarily, Anais would not have received visitors after council; but for him she made an exception. They had known each other long enough that formality was unnecessary, so she had Zahn shown into a room with plush chairs and gently smoking scented braziers, and she appeared wearing a simple dress and her hair, freshly brushed, worn loose. The décor was relaxed and homely, calculated to put him at his ease. Here some concession had been made to luxury over aesthetic beauty, and the room had a cosy air about it, with rugs on the *lach* floor and curtains of coloured beads hanging over the tall, narrow window arches.

'Zahn,' she said with a bright smile. 'I'm glad to see you.'

'You too, Anais,' he said. 'Though I wish the circumstances were somewhat different.'

She gestured him to a chair and sat opposite him. 'Troubled times indeed,' she said.

'I cannot stay, Anais,' said Zahn, scratching his neck with his thumb absently. 'The afternoon is drawing on, and I have to journey back to my estate. I came to bring you a warning.'

Anais adopted an attentive posture.

'A servant found my Weaver, Tabaxa, as he lay dying,'

Zahn said, frowning slightly. 'He was struck down very suddenly, it seems, and was bleeding from the ears and eyes; yet there was not a mark on him.'

'It sounds like another Weaver did it,' Anais said. 'Or perhaps poison.'

Zahn made a negative grunt. 'Not poison. The servant removed Tabaxa's mask, and he said a word before he died. Very clearly.'

Anais suddenly pieced together the puzzle: why Zahn had sent that letter; why he had seemed so cold in the council chamber. 'Vyrrch,' she said.

Zahn did not reply, but his eyes told her she was right.

'Then why . . . ?'

'Did you know of it, Anais?' Zahn demanded, suddenly lurching forward towards her.

'No!' she replied instantly.

Zahn paused, half out of his chair, and then sank back with a sigh. 'As I thought,' he said. 'A single word is a slim rope to hang so much weight on, Anais. But you must watch him, your Weave-lord. Perhaps he seeks to undermine you. Have you thought what it might mean for the Weavers if Lucia sits the throne and there *isn't* a revolution?'

Anais nodded grimly. 'She is a mockery of all their teachings about Aberrants. They have killed Aberrant children for so long, and so young . . . Lucia is living proof that they do not always turn out evil, if at all. If she becomes Empress, they fear what she will do.'

'Perhaps,' said Zahn, 'it is something that needs to be done.'

Anais nodded slightly, her gaze turning to the windows, where Nuki's eye watched benevolently over Axekami from behind the bead curtains.

'Why did you vote for me, Zahn, if you thought I had sent Vyrrch to spy on you?'

'Because I trust you,' he said. 'We have been allies and opponents by turns for a long time now, but you have never broken a deal with me. Also, I confess, I wanted to see how you reacted when you saw me; I would have been able to tell, I think, if you had been guilty.'

'Maybe you would,' said Anais with a faint smile. 'Still, I am grateful for your trust.'

'I must go now,' said Zahn, standing up. 'I shall see myself out. Please, Anais, take warning. Do not turn your back on Vyrrch. He is evil, and he will kill your child if he can.'

'And I can do nothing to him without proof,' she replied sadly. 'And perhaps not even then. Goodbye, Zahn. I hope we meet again soon.'

'Indeed,' said the Barak, and he left Anais alone in the muggy warmth of the afternoon, thinking.

ELEVEN

The morning sun dawned red as blood behind the barge as it lumbered westward into Axekami. They called it the Surananyi – the fury of Suran. Somewhere in the eastern deserts of Tchom Rin, great hurricanes were tearing across the desolate land, flinging the red dust into the sky to mar the light of Nuki's single eye.

Legend told how Panazu, god of rivers and rain, had been so besotted with Narisa, daughter of Naris, that he had asked a wise old apothecary to make him a potion that would cause her to fall in love with him. But the old apothecary was none other than Shintu the trickster in disguise, and Shintu put a feit on Panazu so that he would think the first woman he saw was his beloved Narisa. So it came to pass that he returned to his home, and the first to greet him was his sister Aspinis, goddess of trees and flowers. Panazu, thinking his sister was Narisa, chose the moment to slip his potion into Aspinis's drink, and she fell under its influence. And so they coupled, and when the morning came and their eyes were cleared they were horrified at what they had done.

But worse was to come; for they were the son and daughter of Enyu, goddess of nature and fertility, and from their coupling grew a child. They dared not tell their mother, for the child was not natural, conceived as it was of incest; and they knew well how their mother could not condone anything that was not complicit with her laws. Aspinis fled, hiding her shame. But she was beloved of the gods, and sorely missed; and so Ocha and Isisya ordered that all should search for her until she was found.

So began the Year of the Empty Temples, when the people

of Saramyr suffered greatly, for the gods turned their faces away from the land and hunted through the Golden Realm for their lost kin. Crops failed, cruel winds blew, famine struck the land. Even Nuki turned away from them, and the sun was dim that year. And though the people thronged to the temples to pray for deliverance, their gods were not present.

Then, joy. Aspinis returned from the wilderness, and all the Golden Realm celebrated. In Saramyr the crops flourished, the fish were plentiful and the livestock grew fat once again. Aspinis would not speak of where she had been; but Shintu, who had guessed what had happened, threatened to tell her mother Enyu unless she revealed to him where the baby was. Aspinis – who had no inkling of Shintu's hand in the affair – told him that the baby was in a cave deep in the desert, where she would have long died.

Shintu, eager to see the results of his meddling, travelled to the cave, and there he found the baby not dead, but very much alive. She was being fed by snakes and lizards who brought her morsels, and she was a wrinkled and ugly thing with long, tangled hair and odd eyes – one green and one blue. But Shintu was struck with pity then, and he took the baby to his own home and nurtured her in secret, and named her Suran. She became a bitter girl, for in the way of the gods she remembered what had been done to her as an infant, and when she was grown she left Shintu and went back to the desert to dwell among the lizards and the snakes, to become the antithesis of everything her hated parents stood for. Suran was the outcast, the goddess of deserts and drought and pestilence; and when she raged, the whole of Saramyr saw red.

Tane's heart felt heavy in his breast as he sat on the forecastle of the barge, feeling the slow surge of the ship beneath him as it bore him onward. It was a low, clumsy craft, laden heavy with ores and minerals from the mines in the Tchamil Mountains. The rough cries of the bargemen sounded in his ears, hollering in their jagged dialect; peeping birds banked and swirled high above, mistaking the barge for a fishing vessel and hoping for breakfast; hawsers creaked and timbers groaned. All around him, life; and yet he felt lifeless.

He looked down at the planks between his knees, their colour stained red by the bloody sun, and traced the grain of the wood with his gaze. How like himself those lines were, he thought. They travelled their solitary way, sometimes brushing near to another line but rarely touching. Sometimes they were swallowed by a whorl or knot, sucked into a tangle; but always they emerged on the other side, always returning to an aimless and lonely path. He felt himself flailing inwardly, scrabbling for a greased rope of purpose that eluded his grip. Of what worth was he, one among thousands, millions; what right had he to expect the forbidden happiness of belonging? The gods meted out their gifts and blessings as they chose, and there were certainly many more worthy than him. Though he was a priest, he was still lower than these simple bargemen; for he had taken the order to atone for his past, not out of nobility or generosity. To pay off his guilt and regain his innocence. How many lives, how many sacrifices would it take before the gods were satisfied?

He felt sorrow for the priests of the temple that he had left behind, but no real grief. He and Jin had returned to Tane's erstwhile home at daybreak, and found it in terrible disarray. The priests were scattered haphazardly about like discarded dolls. They scarcely seemed real to Tane as he identified each of them: effigies only, as if the faces he had known these past few years had been replaced by waxy sculptures with glazed, glassy eyes and dry mouths gaping and lolling purple tongues.

'They were looking for something,' Jin said.

'Or someone,' Tane added.

He took Jin's silence to mean she had guessed who he referred to.

Later, he brought the priests out of the temple and laid them on the grass. There, he named them silently in prayer to Noctu, that she might record their deaths and inform her husband Omecha. He said another prayer to Enyu while Jin waited patiently, and he was just finishing when Jin's sharp intake of breath warned him that something was amiss.

When he opened his eyes, he saw the bears. They waited at the edge of the clearing, massive black and brown shapes hidden in the foliage, watching and waiting. Tane bowed to them, and then led Jin away to the boat which the priests used to travel to the nearby settlement of Ban and back.

'Is there to be no burial?' she asked.

'That is not our way,' he replied. 'The forest beasts will have them. Their flesh will return to the cycle of nature; their souls to the Fields of Omecha.'

They had bought passage on a barge from Ban. During the six-day journey, Tane had been given plenty of time for introspection. He sought inside himself for the well of loss, but found nothing. He was confused by the absence. His home, all the faces he had known, his tutors and friends and even old Master Olec were gone in a single night. Yet he could not bring himself to grieve; and in fact, he felt a guilty excitement at the prospect of moving on. Maybe he had never belonged there at all, and he had simply not admitted it to himself until now. Maybe that was why he could never find the inner peace he sought.

Enyu has another path for me, he thought. *She has spared me the slaughter and set me on my way. I, the least worthy of her followers.*

The thought made him strangely happy.

The sun had risen high in the eastern sky by the time they reached Axekami, but it had still not cleared the veil of desert dust that hung before it, and the capital of Saramyr glowered angrily in brooding red. The approach to the city proper was through the sprawling shanties of the river nomads, whose stilt huts and rickety jetties crowded the river banks. Withered, wiry old men poled back and forth, seeming to take their lives in their hands as they cut into the path of the barge. The barge master did not slow or pay any attention. The nomads sat outside their wooden homes and shops, scraping leather or weaving, and their eyes were suspicious or indifferent as they passed over the hulking barge that plied past them down the Kerryn. Nomads only trusted their own kind, and likewise were mistrusted by all.

Jin came and sat by him as the shanties gave way to buildings, mostly warehouses and shipyards initially. She brushed her hair back over her shoulder and watched the wine-coloured water.

'I think you want to find this Kaiku tu Makaima for more reasons than simply helping me deliver my message,' she stated.

Tane looked at her sidelong. She was still gazing out over the gunwale. He studied her profile; it was flawless. She truly was beautiful; and the curious thing was she seemed to grow more beautiful by the day. If anything, she seemed *too* perfect in aspect. Even the great beauties had imperfections: a freckle, or a slight unevenness about the lip, or the colours of their irises mottled slightly. The imperfection heightened their beauty by contrast. But Jin had not even that.

She puzzled him. She had proved herself during their conversations these past six days to be luminously intelligent and well-travelled. Coupled with her appearance, she had the world in her lap. He found it hard to imagine anything she could not do, any position she could not attain with ease if she had the will. Why, then, an Imperial Messenger? Why choose a dangerous and dusty road, always on the move, never settling? Who *was* she, in truth?

She turned to him expectantly then, and he realised she wanted an answer. He gave her none. Let her speculate as she liked. Even he could not fathom why he was following Kaiku's trail; only that she was the last destination left to him after his home was gone.

'Do you think we can find her?' he said at length.

'I can find this Mishani you spoke of with ease. She is Mishani tu Koli, daughter of Barak Avun. If Kaiku is with her, our task is that much easier.'

Tane nodded. He hoped he had not made a mistake in revealing what he knew to Jin; but he could scarcely have done otherwise. They were companions, at least for a short while, and he had no idea how to find someone in a city the size of Axekami without her. Still, his suspicions about her had hardly been eased by the apparent knowledge she displayed of the shin-shin, and led him to wonder once again about that strange light he had seen in her eyes back in the forest.

'We are safe from them, at least for the moment,' she had told him. 'Whatever brought them to your temple, they cannot track us on the water. They may guess where we are heading, and possibly follow us downstream on the north bank, but once near Axekami they will not come any closer. The city is the place of men, where spirits do not belong.'

'And they'll stop tracking us then?' Tane had asked.

'Shin-shin are persistent, and they do not let their prey go easily. But if they are tracking us at all, they may give up when we reach the city. Or they may wait outside and hope to pick up our trail again when we leave.'

Tane had wanted to ask her how an Imperial Messenger had learned so much about spirits and demons, but in the end he decided that he would rather not know.

The vast capital swelled around them, domes and spires and temples crowding together, hugging in close to the Kerryn. To the north, the land sloped upwards and the buildings rose with it, until it became too steep to build on and rose almost sheer in a great bluff, upon which stood the mighty Imperial Keep, its skin burnishing red-gold in the dust-hazed sunlight. The city streets were a canvas of tinted whites, weathered greens, columns and fountains and parks. Here a clutter of warehouses in the worst state of dereliction; there a gallery, a bell tower, a library, all elegant sweeps of stone and wood and inscribed in fine metals across their entranceways. An enormous prayer gate lunged across the border of the Imperial Quarter, a tall ellipse of stone and gold, its edges dazzling even in the muted rays of Nuki's eye.

To the south was the famous River District, where there were no roads but only canals, a place both exquisitely fashionable and extremely dangerous. It was as chaotic and beautiful as the rest of the city, only concentrated in a smaller area, with buildings of extraordinary design crowding over each other on tiny, irregular islands. The people that walked to and fro or were poled along the canals by puntmen were swathed in extravagant and impractical fashions, such as would make respectable society blush; but in the River District, nothing was too extreme.

Tane took it all in with wonder. He had been to Axekami before on odd occasions, but it still held the power to awe him. His world had been the quiet of the forests, where the only loud noise was the sharp crack of a hunting rifle or snap of a fire. Already he could hear the pummelling blanket of sound that came from the city; many thousand voices jabbering, the rattle of carts, the lowing of manxthwa as they plodded through the streets. The city seemed to seethe on the shores of the river, waiting to consume him as soon as he stepped away from the sanctuary of the barge, an inescapable din that might drive a man mad. Tane was afraid of it and desired it all at once.

The same, he thought, could be said of his future.

Kaiku knelt before the mirror in the sparsely furnished guest bedroom, and looked at herself. The face that returned the gaze seemed unfamiliar now, though the red of her irises had long faded back to their natural brown. The world had turned but once since she had learned of her condition, and yet it seemed she had forever been this way, a stranger to her own perceptions.

Outside she could hear the sounds of the servants returning from the burial. Mishani would be with them. Kaiku had not thought it appropriate to go.

She had not cried. She would not. *Keep the tears to quench the flame,* she had thought in a fanciful moment; but the truth was, she felt no sadness. Sorrow had belaboured her past the point of tolerance, and still it had not broken her back. It held no power over her now. Instead, she felt a hard point of bitterness in her breast, a small stone forming in the chambers of her heart like a polluted pearl inside an oyster. She was sick of sorrow, sick of pain. How could she trust anything now, even the evidence of her eyes and ears, when twenty harvests of safety and happiness had come and gone in her life only to be smashed aside in a single day of tragedy? How could she rely on anything again? Weighed against that, grief and remorse were useless. All that was left was giving up, or going on.

She chose the latter.

Mishani had closed herself up like a fan since the fire of yesterday afternoon. The blaze was mercifully checked quickly and caused little damage to the house, but the damage it had done to their relationship was immeasurable. Her once-friend was cold to her now, an impassive veneer rigidly locked in place. And though she did speak, her words were robbed of feeling, and it seemed that it took great effort to converse.

'You died, Kaiku,' she had said the previous day, in the wake of her accusation. 'It is not uncommon for Aberration to lay dormant for years, until something . . . wakes it up. All this time, you have carried it inside you and not known it.'

'How can you tell?' she had demanded, desperate to refute her host. 'You are not a priest; how can you tell? How can you tell what is inside me is not a demon, a malevolent spirit?'

Mishani turned away. 'We learned little of Aberrants from our tutors, you and I. They taught us manners, calligraphy, elocution; but not about Aberrants. They were not fit for polite young noblewomen like ourselves. But I have learned much since I have come to court, Kaiku, and I know how they preoccupy even the greatest of the high families.' She spoke quietly, as if fearing someone would overhear; though the lack of doors in most Saramyr houses meant that eavesdropping was severely frowned upon, and repeating what one heard was tantamount to obscenity. 'Our catches in Mataxa Bay grow more befouled by the year. Each haul brings in more three-clawed crabs, more fish with extra fins, more eyeless lobsters. Aberrations.'

Her voice was taut, suppressing disgust. The fact that Kaiku could tell at all meant that Mishani wanted her to know how she felt about it. In the background, Kaiku could hear the sounds of the servants racing to put out the fire she had started; the creaking of bucket handles, the slosh of water, shouts of alarm. They seemed impossibly distant.

'I have seen a girl in a village on my family's land,' she continued, her back to her visitor. 'She was hideous to look at, a freak of melted skin and hair, blind and lame. Where her hands touched, flowers grew. Even on skin, Kaiku. Even on metal. We found her being kept in a pen. She had killed her mother as an infant, after the poor woman allowed her daughter to feel her face. The mother's eyes were bored through by flower roots, and she choked on blossoms that grew in her mouth.' She paused, reluctant to go on; but she did so anyway. 'I have never seen a person possessed by a spirit, but I have seen and heard of many Aberrants, and I have heard of several who brought flame simply by being in a room. Most burned themselves to death; the rest were executed by the Weavers. They had two things in common, though, the fire-bringers. All were female. All of them had your eyes when the flames came. Your red eyes.' She faced Kaiku at last, and her gaze was hard and grave. 'Aberrants are dangerous, Kaiku. *You* are dangerous. What if I had been in that room with you?'

That had been yesterday. Since then, she had been left alone, given the bare minimum of attention by her host, given time to think on her condition. She had done a lot of thinking.

She could hear the weeping of the servants as they neared the house. Yokada, the servant girl who had been the only witness to Kaiku's condition as she escaped the fiery room, had died. It had been said she left a brazier burning in Kaiku's room, sparking the blaze. She had drunk poison last night, a suicide to atone for her crime. Kaiku doubted that the suicide was voluntary. She wondered if Yokada had even known she was drinking poison at all.

Mishani had grown ruthless in her time at court.

Kaiku had no illusions. Being at her lowest ebb afforded her a wonderfully clear perspective on things. Mishani had not been protecting her; she had been protecting herself. Blood Koli's standing would suffer terribly if it was found that they were harbouring an Aberrant. Worse, that the heir to the family had been fast friends with that unclean creature all through childhood and adolescence. The taint would be on Mishani's family then; they would be shunned. Their goods would fall in price, and stories about the strange fish in Mataxa Bay might start circulating. Kaiku's presence in their home was enough to ruin Blood Koli. Mishani could not risk the loose tongue of a servant girl undoing generations of empire-building.

Mishani came into the room without ringing the chime. She found Kaiku still sitting before the mirror. Kaiku turned her gaze to Mishani's reflection.

'My servants tell me you did not eat this morning,' she said.

'I feared to find something deadly in my food,' Kaiku replied, her manner chilly and excessively formal, her mode of address altered so that she spoke as if to an adversary.

Mishani betrayed no reaction. She met Kaiku's eyes in the mirror levelly, her small, thin face in amid the mass of black hair.

'I am not so monstrous that I would order your death, Kaiku, no matter what you have become.'

'Perhaps,' Kaiku replied. 'Or perhaps you have changed much these past years. Perhaps I never really knew you.'

Mishani was perturbed by this shift in character. Kaiku was not properly and rightfully ashamed of what she was; instead, her tone condemned Mishani for her lack of friendship, her lack of faith. Kaiku had always been stubborn and wilful, but to be an Aberrant was surely indefensible?

Kaiku stood and faced Mishani. She was a few inches taller than the other, and looked down on her now.

'I will go,' she said. 'That is what you came to ask, is it not?'

'I was not intending to *ask*, Kaiku,' Mishani replied. 'I have told you what I know about the Mask. It is better if you go to Fo and seek answers for yourself. You understand, I am sure.'

'I understand many things,' said Kaiku. 'Some less palatable than others.'

There was a long silence between them.

'It is a measure of our friendship that I have not had you killed, Kaiku. You know how dangerous to my family you are. You know that, by revealing yourself as an Aberrant, you could hurt us badly.'

'And be executed by the Weavers,' Kaiku retorted. 'I would not throw my life away like that. It is precious. You thought so too, once.'

'Once,' Mishani agreed. 'But things have changed.'

'*I* have not changed, Mishani,' came the reply. 'If I was ill with bone fever, you would have sat by me and nursed me even though you might have caught it yourself. If I was hunted by assassins, you would have protected me and used all your family's powers to keep me safe, though you yourself would have been endangered. But this . . . this you cannot condone. I am afflicted, Mishani. I did not choose to be Aberrant; how, then, can I be blamed for it by you?'

'Because I see what you are now,' she replied. 'And you disgust me.'

Kaiku felt the blow of her words as an almost physical pain. There was nothing else that needed to be said.

'There are clothes in that chest,' Mishani said. 'Food in the kitchens. Take what you will. In return, I ask this courtesy. Leave after sunset, that you may not be seen.'

Kaiku tilted her chin proudly. 'I ask no favours of you, nor will I grant any. I want only what is mine: my father's Mask, and the clothes and pack I came with. I will leave as soon as I have them.'

'As you wish,' Mishani replied. She paused then, as if she wanted to say something else; but the moment passed, and she left.

Kaiku walked boldly out of the front gate once the servants had brought her belongings. Barak Avun – Mishani's father – was away, so she was spared the dilemma of whether to thank him for his hospitality and bid him goodbye. She could feel the servants watching her leave. The sight of their noble lady's friend departing in trousers and boots – travelling clothes – was odd enough. Perhaps some of them also blamed Yokada's suicide on her. She cared little. They knew nothing of her affairs. They were only servants.

I have a purpose, she thought. *A destination. I will go to the Isle of Fo. There I will learn of the ones who killed my family.*

The afternoon was sweltering and muggy now that the sun had climbed clear of the obscuring red dust of the Surananyi, and so bright that her eyes narrowed unconsciously. The Imperial District's streets were as clean and wide and beautiful as ever. She had money in her pack. Her first destination would be the docks. She would not think about Mishani, nor about what had been done to her, until she was far away from this place. She would not look back.

She left the compound of Blood Koli, turned a corner into a narrow side-street sheltered by overhanging trees, and almost walked into Tane, coming the other way with a woman at his side.

Surprise paralysed them both for a moment, before Kaiku found her voice. 'Tane,' she said at last. 'Daygreet. Shintu's

Luck, no?' The latter was a phrase expressing amazement at an unlikely coincidence – in this case, their meeting here.

'Not luck,' he replied. 'We have been searching for you. This is Jin, an Imperial Messenger.'

Kaiku turned to the woman who walked with him, and the colour drained out of her. The sound of the city birds chirruping in the trees lining the lane seemed to fade. She became aware that, in this narrow passageway, she was all but invisible to anyone on the main thoroughfare.

'Is something wrong?' Tane asked, putting a hand on her shoulder in concern. 'Are you ill?'

Kaiku's mind whirled in denial even as her senses bludgeoned her with their evidence. A subtle difference in the bone structure, in the hairline, the lips, the skin . . . but none of those mattered. She saw the eyes, and she recognised her. Impossible as it was, she recognised her.

'She is not ill,' said Jin, grabbing Kaiku by the front of the shirt and pulling her roughly so they were face to face, their noses almost touching. Tane was too startled to intervene. 'You know me, don't you, Kaiku?'

Kaiku nodded, suddenly terrified. 'Asara,' she breathed.

'Asara,' said the woman in agreement, and Kaiku felt the sharp prick of a blade at her belly.

TWELVE

The temple of Panazu towered over the River District of Axekami, its garish blue colliding with the greens and purples and whites and yellows of the surrounding buildings and overwhelming them with sheer grandeur. It rose tall, narrow in width but extending far back into the cluster of expensive and outrageously ostentatious dwellings that huddled on the small island of land. Steep, rounded shoulders of blue stone were swirled and crested like whirlpools and waves, and curved windows of sea-green and mottled silver glided elegantly across its façade. Panazu was the god of rain, storms and rivers, and so it made sense that here, where there were no roads but only canals, he should reign supreme.

The River District was an archipelago of buildings, sheared into irregular shapes by the passage of the canals that ran asymmetrically through the streets like cracks in a broken flagstone. It sat just south of the Kerryn, a florid clump of houses, gambling dens, theatres, shops and bars. Long ago it had been a simple heap of old warehouses and yards, convenient for storage of small items; but as Axekami grew and larger cargo barges began to arrive, the narrow canals and the small amount of space to build in the River District necessitated a move to larger, more accessible warehouses on the north side of the Kerryn. The River District became a haven for criminals and the lower-class element for many years, until a group of society nobles decided that the eccentricity of living in a place with no roads was too much to resist. The cheap land prices there triggered a sudden rush to buy, and within a decade large portions of the District had been swallowed by insane architectural projects, each newcomer trying to outdo his neighbours. The criminal element already present boomed with the new influx of wealthy customers; soon the drug hovels and seedy prostitution bars were replaced by exquisite dens and cathouses. The River District was for the young, rich and bored, the debauched and the purveyors of debauchery. It was a dangerous, cut-throat place; but the danger was the attraction, and so it flourished.

'I thought she was dead,' Kaiku said.

Tane looked over at her. Slats of light shining through the boards above drew bright stripes across her upturned face. The room was dark and swelteringly hot. It was the first thing she had said since Asara – the one he had called Jin – had left them here.

'Who is she?' Tane asked. He was sitting on a rough bench of stone, one of the square tiers that descended into a shallow pit at the centre of the room. This place had been a steam room, once. Now it was empty and the air tasted of disuse.

'I do not know,' Kaiku replied. She was standing on the tier below, on the other side of the pit. 'She was my handmaiden for two years, but I suppose I never knew who she was. She is something other than you see.'

'I had my suspicions,' Tane confessed. 'But she had the mark of the Imperial Messenger. It's death to wear that tattoo without Imperial sanction.'

'She was burned,' Kaiku said, hardly hearing him. 'I saw her face, burned and scarred. It is her and yet not her. She is . . . she is more beautiful than before. Different. I would say she was Asara's sister, or a cousin . . . if not for the eyes. But she was *burned*, Tane. How could she heal like that?'

Asara had been angry. Kaiku could still feel the press of her dagger against her skin, that first moment when they met outside Blood Koli's compound. For a fleeting instant, she had expected Asara to drive it home, thrust steel into muscle in revenge for what Kaiku had done to her.

But what *had* Kaiku done to her? Up until that moment, she had thought her uncontrollable curse had killed her saviour and handmaiden; now she found she had been mistaken. It was not an easy thing to accept.

'You left me to die there, Kaiku,' Asara said. 'I saved your life, and you left me to die.'

Tane had been too surprised to react until then, but at that moment he made a move to protest at Asara's handling of the one they had come to find.

'Stay there, Tane,' Asara hissed at him. 'I have given a lot to ensure this one stayed alive, and I will not kill her now. But I have no such compunctions about you, if you try and stop me. You would be dead before your hand reached your sword.'

Tane had believed her. He thought of the flash of light he had seen in her eyes back in the forest, and considered that he did not know who or what he was dealing with.

'I thought I had killed you,' Kaiku said, her voice calmer than she felt. 'I was scared. I ran.' She had considered adding an apology, then thought better of it. To apologise would be to admit culpability. She would not beg forgiveness for her actions, especially in the face of Asara's deceit.

'Yes, you ran,' Asara said. 'And were things otherwise I would hurt you for what you did to me. But I have a task, and you are part of it. Come with me.' She turned to Tane, her face still beautiful, even set hard as it was. 'You may accompany us, or go as you wish.'

'Where?' Tane replied, but he had already made up his mind. He would not abandon Kaiku like this.

'To the River District,' said Asara.

She had put her dagger away as they walked, warning both of them not to attempt escape. Neither had any intention of doing so. Though there was violence in her manner, they both sensed that Asara did not mean them actual harm. When Kaiku added up all she knew about Asara, she came to one conclusion: Asara had been trying to take her somewhere ever since the night her family died. If it had been kidnap she intended, she could have done it long ago. This was different.

Kaiku was part of Asara's task, and she guessed that the task involved getting her to the River District of her own will. She could not deny more than a little curiosity as to *why*.

They had crossed the Kerryn at the great Gilza Bridge into the gaudy paveways that fronted the houses of the District. The sudden profusion of extravagance was overwhelming, as if the bridge formed a barrier between the city proper and this nether-city populated by brightly plumed eccentrics and painted creatures. Manxthwa loped past, laden with bejewelled bridles and ridden by men and women who seemed to have escaped from some theatrical asylum. There were no wheeled vehicles allowed here, even if they had been practical on the narrow paveways that ran between the stores and the canals, but the punts and tiny rowboats more than made up for them, explosions of colour against the near-purple water.

Asara had taken them to an abandoned lot behind a strikingly painted shop that proclaimed itself as a purveyor of narcotics. The lot was almost bare but for a low wooden building that had apparently been a steam room in days gone by, and an empty pool. All else was dusty slabs and the remnants of other, grander buildings.

'Wait here,' said Asara, ushering them into the old steam room. 'Do not make me come and find you. You will regret it.'

With that, she was gone. They heard the rasp of a lock-chain on the door, to further ensure that they stayed. She had answered none of their questions as they walked, shed no light on their destination. She merely left them in ignorance, for hours, until the sun was sinking into the west.

They talked in that time, Tane and Kaiku. Tane recounted the fate of the priests at the temple; Kaiku told him what they had learned of the origin of her father's Mask. But though conversation between them was as easy as it had been when they first knew each other, their guard was undiminished, and each held back things they did not say. Kaiku made no mention of her affliction, nor why Mishani had sent her

131

away, nor what had passed between her and Asara back in the forest. Tane did not reveal how he felt about the death of the priests, the strange, growing excitement he was experiencing at being cast adrift and sent on some new destiny.

So they waited, and speculated, both curiously unafraid. Once Kaiku had surmounted the initial shock, she was happy to let these events unfold as they would. The worst that could happen was that she would be killed. Considering her condition, she wondered idly if that would not be for the best.

The beams of light coming through the overhead boards – once sealed with tar that had been stripped or decayed long ago – were slanted sharply, climbing the eastern wall, when the door opened and a stranger stepped into the hot shadows.

She was tall, a tower of darkness. Her dress was all in black, with a thick ruff of raven feathers across the shoulders. Twin crescents of dusk-red curved from her forehead, over her eyelids and down her cheeks; her lips were painted in red and black triangles, alternating like pointed teeth. Her hair, as dark as her clothes, flashed night-blue highlights in the shafts of sun, and was fashioned into two thick ponytails, side by side to spill down her back. A silver circlet adorned her brow, with a small red gem set into it.

She glided into the room, Asara following and closing the door behind them.

'Welcome,' she purred, her voice like cats' claws sheathed in velvet. 'I apologise for the venue, but secrecy is necessary here.'

'Who are you?' Tane demanded, studying her outlandish attire. 'A sorceress?'

'Sorcery is a superstition, Tane tu Jeribos,' she said. 'I am far more unpleasant. I am an Aberrant.'

Tane's eyes blazed, and he switched his wrath to Asara. 'Why have you brought her here?'

'Calm yourself, Tane,' Kaiku interceded, though she herself had felt a thrill of disgust at the mention of Aberrants, an ingrained reaction deeply at odds with her current position. 'Let us listen.'

Tane flashed a searing glare at the three women in the room, then snorted. 'I will not listen to the talk of one such as her.'

'Go, then,' Asara said simply. 'Nobody will stop you.'

Tane looked to the door, then back to Kaiku. 'Will you come?'

'She must stay,' said Asara. 'At least until she has heard what we have to say.'

'I will wait for you outside, then,' he said, and with that he stalked to the door and was gone.

'A friend of yours?' the tall lady asked Kaiku, with a faintly wry edge to her tone.

'It would seem so,' said Kaiku. 'Though who can say?'

The stranger smiled faintly in understanding. 'It is good that he has gone. I would have the things I am to discuss with you kept private, for your sake. He may come round, later.'

'Kaiku tu Makaima,' Kaiku said, introducing herself as a roundabout method of learning the name of the one she was addressing.

'I am Cailin tu Moritat, Sister of the Red Order,' came the reply. 'We have been watching you for quite some time.'

'So Asara told me,' Kaiku said, glancing at her former handmaiden. She had hinted as much in the forest, the morning after the shin-shin had come to their house, but Kaiku had not known who she meant until now. 'What do you want with me?'

Cailin did not answer directly. 'You are changing, Kaiku,' she said. 'I am sure you know that by now. Fires burn within you.'

Kaiku could not meet Asara's gaze, so she kept her eyes on Cailin. 'You know what they are?'

'I do,' she replied.

Kaiku ran a hand through her hair, suddenly nervous,

fearing to ask her next question. Both stood on the lowest of the stone tiers, on opposite sides. She faced Cailin across the gulf of the stifling steam pit, the two of them striped by dusklight from outside. Motes danced in the air between them.

'Am I an Aberrant, then?'

'You are,' Cailin replied. 'Like myself, and like Asara. But do not attach so much weight to a word, Kaiku. I have known Aberrants who have taken their own lives in shame, unable to bear the burden of their title.' She looked down on Kaiku from within the red crescents painted on her face. 'You, I believe, are stronger than that. And I can teach you not to be ashamed.'

Kaiku regarded her with a calculating eye. 'What else can you teach me?'

Asara noted with approval the difference in manner between this Kaiku and the one she had dragged out of the burning house. She had suffered much, and learned many unpleasant truths; yet she was unbowed. Perhaps Cailin's faith in this one had been well founded.

'You do not know how to control what you have,' Cailin said. 'At the moment, it manifests itself as fire, as destruction; childish tantrums. I can teach you to tame it. I can help you do things you would never have dreamed.'

'And what would you ask in return?'

'Nothing,' came the reply.

'I find that hard to believe.'

Cailin stood very still as she spoke, a thin statue wrapped in shadow. 'The Red Order are few. The Weavers get to most of our potential candidates before we do; that, or they unwittingly burn themselves to death, or kill themselves in horror at what they are or what they have done. We teach them how to cope with what they have before it consumes them. They then choose their own path. Each of us is free to leave and pursue what lives we may. Some become like me, and teach others. I would teach you, Kaiku, before your power kills you or those around you; whether you then decide to join us is up to you. I would take that risk.'

Kaiku was unconvinced. She could not marry the appearance and manner of this lady with such apparent altruism. What *did* lie behind this offer of assistance, then? Was it simple narcissism? A desire to mould another in her image? Or was it something more than that?

'Is *she* one of you, this Red Order you speak of?' Kaiku asked, inclining her head towards Asara.

'No,' said Asara, and elaborated no further.

Kaiku sighed and sat down on the stone tier. 'Explain yourself,' she said to Cailin.

Cailin obliged. 'The Red Order is made up of those who have a specific Aberration. You have the power within you that we call *kana*. It manifests itself in different ways, but only to women. It is a privilege of our gender. Aberrations are not always random, Kaiku. Some crop up again and again, recurring over and over. This is one such. It is not a handicap or a curse, Kaiku; it is a gift beyond measure. But it is dangerous to the untrained.

'In recent years we have become skilled at finding those who carry the power, even when it has not manifested itself. Some display the power early, in infancy; they are usually caught by the Weavers and executed. But some, like yourself, only find your talent when it is triggered, by trauma or extreme passion. You have great potential, Kaiku; we knew that some time ago.'

'You sent Asara to watch me,' Kaiku said, piecing the puzzle together. 'To wait until I manifested this . . . *kana*. And then she was to bring me to you.'

'Exactly. But events conspired against us, as you know.'

Kaiku let her head fall, her forearms crossed over her knees. A moment later, the short wings of brown hair began shaking as she laughed softly.

'Something is amusing you?' Cailin asked, her voice edged with a brittle frost.

'Forgive me,' she said around her mirth, raising her head. 'All this tragedy . . . all that has happened to me, and now you are offering me an *apprenticeship*?'

'I am offering to save your *life*,' Cailin snapped. She did not appear to appreciate the humour.

Kaiku's laughter trailed away. She cocked her head elfishly and regarded Cailin. 'Your offer intrigues me, have no doubt. There seems to be a great deal I do not know, and I am eager to learn. But I cannot accept.'

'Ah. Your father,' Cailin said, the chill in her voice deepening.

'I swore vengeance to Ocha himself. I cannot put aside my task for you. I will travel to Fo, and find the maker of my father's Mask.'

'You still have it?' Asara asked in surprise. Kaiku nodded.

'May I see it?' Cailin asked.

Kaiku was momentarily reluctant, but she drew it from her pack anyway. She walked around the tier and handed it to Cailin.

A breath of hot wind stirred the still air inside the abandoned steam room, shivering the feathers of Cailin's ruff as she studied it.

'Your power is dangerous,' she said, 'and it will either kill you or get you killed before long. I offer you the chance to save yourself. Turn away now, and you may not live to get a second chance.'

Kaiku gazed at her for a long time. 'Tell me about the Mask,' she said.

Cailin looked up. 'Did you not hear what I said?'

'I heard you,' Kaiku said. 'My life is my own to risk as I choose.'

Cailin sighed. 'I fear your intransigence will be the end of it, then,' she said. 'Allow me to offer you a proposal. I see you are set on this foolishness. I will tell you about this Mask, if you will promise to return to me afterwards and hear me out.'

Kaiku inclined her head in tacit agreement. 'That depends on what you can tell me.'

Cailin gave her a slow look, appraising her, taking the measure of her character, searching for deceit or trickery therein. If she found anything there, she did not show it; instead, she handed the Mask back to Kaiku.

'This Mask is like a map. A guide. Where it came from is a place that you cannot find, a place hidden from the sight of ordinary men and women. This will show you the way. Wear it when you are close to your destination, and it will take you to its home.'

'I see no profit in being cryptic, Cailin,' Kaiku said.

'It is the simple truth,' she replied. 'This Mask will breach an invisible barrier. The place you are seeking will be hidden. You will need this to find it. That is all I can tell you.'

'It is not enough.'

'Then perhaps this will help. There is a Weaver monastery somewhere in the northern mountains of Fo. The paths to it were lost long ago. It would have been considered to have disappeared, but for the supply carts that come regularly to the outpost village of Chaim. They deliver masks from the Edgefathers at the monastery, untreated masks for theatre, decoration and such. They trade them for food and other, more unusual items.' She gave a dismissive wave of her hand. 'Go to Chaim. You may find there what you are looking for.'

Kaiku considered for a moment. That jibed with Copanis's guess, at least. 'Very well,' she said. 'If what you say proves to be true, then I will return to you, and we can talk further.'

'I doubt you will live that long,' Cailin replied, and with that she stalked out, leaving Kaiku and Asara alone.

Asara was smiling faintly in the hot darkness. 'You know she could have made you stay.'

'I suspect she wants me willing,' Kaiku said.

'You have quite a stubborn streak, Kaiku.'

Kaiku did not bother to reply to that. 'Are we finished here?' she said instead.

'Not yet. I have a request,' Asara said. She brushed the long, red-streaked fall of her hair back behind her shoulder and set her chin in an arrogant tilt. 'Take me with you to Fo.'

Kaiku's brow furrowed. 'Tell me why I should, Asara.'

'Because you owe me that much, and you are a woman of honour.'

Kaiku was unconvinced, and it showed.

'I have deceived you, Kaiku, but never betrayed you,' she said. 'You need not be afraid of me. You and I have a common objective. The circumstances behind your family's death interest me as much as you. I would have died along with you if the shin-shin had been quicker, and I owe somebody a measure of revenge for that. And need I remind you that you would not even have that Mask if not for me, nor your life? The breath in your lungs is there because *I* put it there.'

Kaiku nodded peremptorily. 'I wonder that you are not telling me your true reasons. I do not trust you, Asara, but I do owe you,' she said. 'You may come with me. But you will not have my trust until you have earned it anew.'

'Good enough,' Asara replied. 'I care little for your trust.'

'And Tane?' Kaiku asked. 'You brought him here. What about him?'

'Tane?' Asara replied. 'I needed his boat. He is a little backward, but not unpleasant. He will come, if you let him, Kaiku. He seeks the same answers we do; for whoever sent the shin-shin to kill your family were also responsible for the slaughter at his temple.'

Kaiku looked at Asara. For a moment she felt overwhelmed, swept along by the pace of events as if on a wave, unable to stop herself from hurtling headlong into the unknown. She surrendered herself to it.

'Three of us, then,' she said. 'We will leave in the morning.'

The estates of Blood Amacha stood between the great tines of a fork in the River Kerryn, many miles east of Axekami. There the flow from the Tchamil Mountains divided, sawn in half by the inerodable rock formations that lanced from the earth in jagged rows. Passing to the north of them, as almost all traffic did, the Kerryn became smoother, fish more plentiful, and there was only a trouble-free glide downstream to the mighty capital of Axekami. To the south, however, the new tributary was rough and treacherous: the River Rahn, shallow and fast and little-travelled.

The Rahn flowed east of Blood Amacha's estates before curving into the broken lands of the Xarana Fault, and there shattering into a massive waterfall. Only the most adventurous travellers, in craft no bigger than a canoe, might be able to negotiate the falls by carrying their boat down the stony flanks to the less dangerous waters beneath; but the Xarana Fault had its own perils, and not many dared to enter that haunted place. The Fault effectively shut off all river travel between Axekami and the fertile lands to the south, forcing a lengthy coastal journey instead.

From the fork in the rivers, the rocky spines gentled into hills, tiered with earthen dams and flooded. Paddy fields of saltrice lapped down the hillside in dazzling scales. Cart trails ran between them, and enormous irrigation screws raised water from the river to supply the fields. Atop the highest hill sprawled the home of Blood Amacha, an imposing litter of buildings surrounding an irregularly shaped central keep. The keep had high walls built of grey stone, and was tipped with towers and sloping roofs of red slate. It was constructed to take advantage of the geography of the hilltop, with one wing dominating a rocky crag while another lay low against the decline of the land, where the wall that circumscribed the building did not need to be quite so high. The buildings clustered around it were almost uniformly roofed in red, and many were constructed using dark brown wood to follow the colours of the Amacha standard.

West of the keep, the hills flattened out somewhat, and here there were no paddy fields but great orchards, dark green swathes pocked with bright fruit: oranges, likiri, shadeberry, fat purple globes of kokomach. And beyond that . . . beyond that, the troops of Blood Amacha drilled on the plains, an immensity of brown and red armour and shining steel, five thousand strong.

They trained in formations, vast geometric assemblies of pikemen, riflemen, swordsmen, cavalry. In the sweltering heat of the Saramyr midday, they grunted and sweated through mock combats, false charges, retreats and regroups. Even in their light armour of cured, toughened leather, they performed admirably under the punishing glare of Nuki's eye, their formations fluid and swift. Metal armour was impractical for combat in Saramyr: the sun was too fierce for most of the year, and the heat inside a full suit of the stuff would kill a man on the battlefield. Saramyr soldiers fought without headgear; if they wore anything at all, it was a headband or bandanna to protect themselves from sunstroke. Their combat disciplines were based on speed and freedom of movement.

Elsewhere, swordsmasters led their divisions in going through the motions of swordplay, demonstrating sweeps, parries, strokes and maneouvres, and then chaining them all together into sequences of deadly grace, their bodies dancing sinuously around the flickering points of their blades. Fire-cannons were targeted at distant boulders, and their bellowing report rolled across the estates. Ballistae were tested and their capacities gauged.

Blood Amacha was gearing up for war.

Barak Sonmaga tu Amacha rode solemnly through the heat and dust of the drilling ground, his ears ringing to the rousing cries of battle all around him, the barked commands and the tumultuous responses of the training groups. The air smelt of sweat and damp leather, of horses and the sulphurous reek of fire-cannons and rifle discharges. He felt his chest swell, his pride a balloon that expanded inside him. Whatever his misgivings, whatever his fears for the land he loved, he could not help but feel overwhelmed by the knowledge that five thousand troops stood ready to give their lives at his command. Not that he appreciated their loyalty – after all, it was their duty, and duty along with tradition were the pillars on which their society was built – but the feeling of sheer *power* that it brought on made him feel close to the gods.

He had spent the morning making inspections, conferring with his ur-Baraks and generals, giving speeches to the troops. His decision to make them train without a break all through the hottest part of the day was heartily approved of by his subordinates, for the soldiers needed to be able to fight under any conditions. Not that the Barak had expected any dissent even if they had disagreed; the discipline of the Saramyr armies was legend, and Sonmaga was not accustomed to having his orders questioned.

Seized by a suddenly poetic mood, he spurred his horse and angled through the rows of soldiers towards the keep that sat distantly to the east, made pale and half real by graduated veils of sunlight. But it was not the keep that was his destination; instead, after a short ride, he reined in some way up the hillside that looked out over the dusty plains, and there he dismounted.

He was standing on a low bluff, where a short flap of rock had broken through the even swell of the hillside to provide level ground. Behind him and a little way upward were the first dry-stone walls that marked the edge of his orchards, and beyond that the grassy soil was subsumed in a mass of leaves and trunks and roots and fruit. He left his horse to crop the grass and walked out on to the bluff, and there he surveyed the arrayed masses of his troops.

The size of the spectacle took his breath away, but more humbling was the vastness of the plains that made even his army seem insignificant. The massive formations of men seemed antlike in comparison, their magnificence outshone by the world around them. The sky was a perfect jewel-blue, untroubled by cloud. The flow of the Kerryn was a blinding streak of maddening brightness, twinkling and winking in the fierce light of Nuki's eye, tracing its unstoppable path towards Axekami, which was hidden beneath the horizon. The plains were dotted with clusters of trees, dirt roads, the occasional settlement here and there; Sonmaga fancied he could see a herd of banathi making its slow way across the panorama, but heat haze made his vision uncertain.

Sonmaga offered a silent prayer of thanks to the gods. He was not a tender man, but what softness he had he reserved for moments like these. Nature awed him. This land awed him, and he loved it. His gaze swept over the tiny formations of his troops below, and he felt his doubts dissipate. Whatever came of this, he would know that he had done what his heart dictated. There were greater matters at play than thrones here.

He did not deny to himself that he wanted power. To elevate Blood Amacha to the ruling family would enshrine his name forever in history, and the honour would be immense. But a coup would be enacted on *his* terms, *his* way. He did not want a civil war, not now. The time was not right; it was too precipitate. Events had conspired to force his hand.

But there was a higher motive for victory than simple power. Sonmaga's deep, abiding love for the land made him sensitive to it, and the blight he saw creeping into the bones of the earth scarred him deeply. He saw the evidence even in his own orchards, the decline that was too gradual to spot until he compared tallies over the years and saw that more and more fruit was spoiling on the branch, more trees withering or coming up twisted. Though the blight had barely brushed his lands when compared to some other, less fortunate areas, he felt an unholy abhorrence of it, as if the corruption crept slowly into him as well as the soil. And then there were the Aberrants, children of the blight, born to peasants on his land; and he feared that if the time should come that he would marry and father a child, it might turn out like them, mewling and deformed and terrible. He would snap its neck himself if he saw a child of his born Aberrant.

And now, Lucia. The Heir-Empress, an Aberrant? There could be no greater affront to the gods, to nature, to simple *sense*. Now was not the time for *tolerance* of these creatures – a tolerance that would surely increase if Lucia reached the throne. They were symptoms of an evil that was killing Saramyr, and to encourage them to thrive was lunacy.

No, the desire for power would not have been enough to make Sonmaga war against his Empress, not at this juncture. But to arrest the progress of the poison in the land? For that, he would dare almost anything.

He brought out the letter in his pocket and read over it again, the letter that had been sealed with the stamp of Barak Avun tu Koli, and wondered if he might not be able to turn things around yet.

THIRTEEN

The isle of Fo lay off the sloping north-western coast of Saramyr, a day's travel across the red-tinged waves of the Camaran Channel. The wind had freshened as the afternoon wore on, and it cooed and whistled through the ratlines of the enormous junk, rippling the sails that sprouted from its back like the spined fins of some magnificent sea creature. The *Summer Tide* was a merchant vessel belonging to the wealthiest trading consortium in Jinka, and it showed. Her gunwale was moulded into the likeness of stormy waves, chasing each other from bow to stern, and in amongst them frolicked seals and whales, sea-spirits and imaginary beasts of the deep. The sails were a magnificent array, with polished wooden ribs holding great fans of beige canvas between them, and painted with the red sigil of the consortium. It was a thing of beauty, carrying a cargo of beautiful things: silks, perfumes, spices; and several passengers, two of whom were watching the desolate isle draw ever closer.

Kaiku was lounging against the thick oaken rail on the foremost deck, her feathered hair whipping restlessly against her tanned cheeks. It was not especially ladylike; but then, neither were her clothes, and she had ever been a tomboy. She wore trousers of heavy, baggy fabric and soft boots wound around with leather to keep them tight. In addition, she had on a light shirt of blue, wrapped right over left – men wore their shirts the opposite way – and belted around her waist with a sash of red. She felt the sun on her skin and flexed like a cat, luxuriating in the warmth. Tane, standing nearby, watched her with a hungry eye.

A week had passed since they had left Axekami and taken a

barge upriver to Jinka. Upriver travel was necessarily slower on craft that had no sails, but the Jabaza's current was not strong at this time of year, and the barge had plenty of wheelmen hired. These swarthy folk rarely came up on deck; their journey was spent in the treadmills at the hot heart of the barge, turning the massive paddle-wheels that powered the craft against the flow. For three days they had watched the flattened peak of Mount Makara rise slowly from the horizon, until it bulked vast among the surrounding mountains, a pale blue green, and they could see the wisps of smoke that issued from its volcanic maw.

That leg of the journey, from Axekami up the Jabaza, had been easy and pleasant, and the weather was good; yet Tane's recollection of it was polluted with disgust. For it had not been an entirely uneventful trip. Among the passengers on the *Summer Tide* had been a Weaver on his way to Jinka.

The Weaver had a separate cabin at the back of the boat, where he spent almost all his time. There was a cabin boy who saw to his needs, a fresh-faced lad of twelve years or so that brought in his food and took out his chamber-pot. His name was Runfey, and he was an ever-smiling presence aboard the barge, his high laugh often heard across the deck.

One day, as dusk approached, Kaiku was stricken with a sudden faintness. Tane was with her at the time; Asara was elsewhere, alone, as she usually preferred.

Kaiku had moaned aloud as her head went light; then she seemed to notice Tane, and fell quiet. Tane could not help feeling galled at the way she clammed up, hoarding whatever secret she kept. He did not pretend to understand her, but he sat with her until the faintness passed. Twenty minutes later, the noises began.

Kaiku had gone to lie down, and Tane was out alone, watching the moons rise as the darkness deepened. The river was a peacefully undulating abyss picked out in Iridima's light. The only sound was the sighing lap of the water against the hull of the barge, and the creak of her timbers. Tane had felt strangely peaceful then, calmer than he had been for a long time, even back in the forest when he had been trying to master his meditations.

The shrieking and raging started all of a sudden, coming from the Weaver's cabin. Tane moved closer, curious. The Weaver seemed to be in a fit of terrible anger, smashing things and throwing himself around inside. Two guards posted at his door made no attempt to disperse the small crowd of sailors that gathered at the noise, but they would let no one in. No one except Runfey.

He was brought by another guard, led by the arm to the Weaver's door. He was not struggling, but the naked fear in his eyes as they met Tane's would haunt him for a long time afterward. The guards opened the door, and all went quiet inside, a predatory kind of silence that made Tane cold. Then they put Runfey in there, and closed the door behind him.

Tane and six of the sailors stood there that night, and heard the screams of Runfey as the Weaver vented his anger on the boy. They heard him beg and plead as he was battered, heard him shriek and wail as other tortures were visited on him that Tane could only guess at, heard him cry out as he was raped repeatedly. Two hours they stood there as witnesses to the horrors that were carried out in that cabin, while their vile guest's post-Weaving rage exhausted itself. None would move, for it would be an unpardonable shame to turn their backs; and yet none dared intervene, either.

Only when silence fell did Tane leave to pray. He was still praying in the dead of night, when he heard the splash of something heavy tipped overboard. They saw no more of Runfey. Nobody spoke of it again. The next day it was business as usual, and Kaiku was still not even aware anything had happened. Tane had elected not to tell her; it would do no good to anyone.

After that, they had turned west into the Abanahn Canal. Tane felt an unfamiliar sweep of patriotic pride at the sight.

He had heard of it only in tales: a vast man-made waterway that connected the Jabaza with the coast, one of the mightiest feats of engineering in Saramyr. Enormous walls of white stone rose on either side, dotted with towers and gates and locks. Immense mechanisms with cogs that were half the size of their barge lay dormant, but Tane had heard how they could be used to raise impenetrable gates to prevent enemies sailing up the canal from the sea and reaching the interior of Saramyr. They passed beneath a curved prayer gate of monolithic size, arcing from one side of the canal to the other, its inscription offering the blessing of Zanya, goddess of travellers. In both directions sailed such a profusion of gaudy boats and barges that Tane spent all his daylight hours on the deck, watching them in amazement as a child watches a procession. Moments like this reminded him how painfully limited his life had been until now, spent almost exclusively in the Forest of Yuna.

What he saw of Jinka was even more hectic than the streets of Axekami. They disembarked at the docks amid the babble of hundreds of labourers, the creak and groan of pulleys and thick ropes as they unloaded crates and bales, the raucous laughter of sailors in the taverns. The Weaver had gone about his business elsewhere, while Asara took them to a boat master she professed to know. The boat master did not appear to remember her, but after a few words in private, he beamed and said he would be delighted to arrange them transport. Asara kept her silence.

And so they had stayed the night in a clean and respectable temple inn. Temple inns were resting places owned by the priesthood of one god or another, and the only place they were unlikely to be bothered by prostitutes or drunks or cut-throats while staying in the docks. Tane had fretted to himself about the shin-shin, unable to dispel their memory and remembering Asara's comment about how the demons might track them when they left the safety of the capital. But they had entered Axekami by water and left by water, and it seemed that their trail had gone cold. Nothing disturbed them that night.

When dawn came they were taken to the *Summer Wind*, and set sail for Fo.

Tane leaned against the railing now, next to Kaiku. She was radiant in the westering light. Not so beautiful as Jin – *Asara*, he corrected himself – but possessed of some different kind of attraction, and one that was stronger. Perhaps it was something to do with the way he had met her, her total vulnerability. She had appealed to his need to heal, and he had nursed her strength back. Perhaps it was their similarities: both had lost their families, both had their secrets. Or perhaps it was something altogether different.

Lucia dreamed.

Her dreams had always been strange, informed as they were by subconscious nonsense-whispers emanating from the life that surrounded her. When she dreamed, she heard the slow, childlike thoughts of the trees in the roof garden, the rapid and unintelligible gibber of the wind, the obsessively focused ravens and the impossibly ancient ruminations of the hill upon which the Keep stood, for whom the completion of a single thought would take longer than a human lifetime. It was never silent for Lucia, and the sounds all around her translated into strange images when she slept.

She had stopped dream-walking entirely of late. The unseen presence that had suddenly begun to stalk her was too frightening, and too dangerous. She felt its monstrous attention gnawing at the edges of her consciousness even now, however. It was ravenous, hungry, frustrated by her elusiveness. She would not let it catch her.

Over the year since she had begun exploring the Keep in her dreams, she had learned to control her abilities somewhat. Whereas at first she had no say over where she would find herself when she closed her eyes, and was only a spectator to her own wanderings, she had soon divined how to guide herself, and how to choose which places to visit. More importantly, she learned how *not* to dream-walk, so that she could suppress it if she wanted and sleep untroubled. She rarely felt rested after a night wandering the Keep's corridors in her mind; but in those early days, her curiosity about the world outside her prison kept her going back again and again. By day, she was a rumour among the folk of the Keep; by night, she was a ghost.

But other things had changed, too. Whatever it was that she had set in motion when she had given a lock of her hair to the man in the garden, it was gathering pace, and she felt it daily.

She dreamed that she stood on the edge of a high, rocky crag, a great promontory that dropped away hundreds of feet to jagged rocks below. The landscape spread out and away beneath her, an impossible chaos of ridges and shattered stone, tree-choked valleys and plateaux. It was thick with spirits down there, invisible in their hollows, and they cooed and whispered to each other in the night.

The night. The three moons hung before her in a velvet sky, so close that they were overlapping. Aurus seemed near enough to touch, looming immense in the star-pocked darkness. She was not in the least perturbed by the impossibility of the three moons being in such close proximity without the howling maelstrom of a moonstorm lashing the land. With the easy logic of sleep, she knew that it was simply not the right time yet.

She sensed the dream lady watching her before she turned to look. The sloping table of rock she stood on jutted out from a thick wood, and in the shadows of the treeline she could see the blurred, unclear shape of the mysterious stranger. She was a smear of black and white, a child's charcoal drawing, stretched thin and tall with a cloak folded close around her like a bat's wings. Always too far away to see clearly, always evading Lucia's sight. This one had found her when the unseen monster could not; but Lucia was not afraid of the dream lady. There was no malice there, only an unsettling intensity. Often she was simply present on the sidelines of Lucia's dreams, watching silently from some distant point, a rooftop or a cavern, her gaze unwavering as she followed the Heir-Empress. Sometimes she spoke, and though Lucia did not like her voice, her words were very clear and she told Lucia things about the world outside. Lucia, desperately curious, would converse whenever she could with the dream lady; but often the newcomer would not reply, would simply watch her disconcertingly, always from far away. Lucia did not know what to make of it all, but she had the impression that the dream lady told Lucia exactly as much as she wanted the young Heir-Empress to know, and nothing more.

Still, as time went on, she learned who and what the dream lady was, and she began to think of her as a strange kind of friend.

Tonight she was not talking, it seemed. She hung in the shadows, a half-seen haze, and stared. Lucia ignored her. She had learned by now that it was pointless doing anything else. Distractedly, she sensed the unseen malevolence, hunting for her again. It was far away, and no threat to her here.

There was no sound but the sigh of the cool wind and the calling of the spirits in the cracked landscape below. Lucia wandered to the edge and looked down, her blonde hair tumbling over her shoulder. When she turned back, the dream lady was gone.

It gave her a fright. She was quite accustomed to the dream lady's visits, but her sudden disappearances were always a surprise. Before, she had only ever vanished when the dark presence that stalked her had become too strong, got too close. She had told Lucia she must stay away from the presence, must not let herself be detected. Lucia had accepted that, but when she asked what the presence was, the dream lady would not say.

Now, however, the air seemed to become light, taking on a

coppery taste, and the fine hairs on Lucia's skin stood up. She felt as if she was being lifted, dragged upward towards the sky, though her feet remained firmly on the ground. The atmosphere had become charged, and the spirits hidden in the panorama beneath her had gone silent.

She felt a hand touch her on her shoulder, far bigger than any human hand, thin white fingers tipped with hooked nails. Her heart seemed to slow to a stop. She did not dare turn around. She could feel them, their presence making her consciousness crawl. Ageless, endless, mad things, the three sisters that stalked the earth when the three satellites shared space in the night sky. The Children of the Moons.

The touch was both dreadful and divine, filling her with terror and awe in equal measure. She squeezed her eyes shut, knowing that behind her there was no ground to stand on, that the spirits hung in the air over the precipice, massive and cold and fearful. She could not bear to look at them, could not face the depthless void of their eyes, where motivations boiled that were as alien to humanity as the gods were. And though some part of her knew this to be a dream, it brought her no comfort; for dreams were no refuge from beings such as these.

Words were spoken, but they came as an awful, thin, sawing noise, making Lucia shudder. She could not hope to comprehend them. She trembled, bowing her head, her lower lip shaking and her eyes screwed firmly closed.

Then they were before her instead of behind, the three of them looming, and though she could not see them she could *feel* their outlines through her eyelids. She felt something brush the side of her hair, and she shivered. A fingernail. It brushed her again, infusing her anew with panic and wonder, the strange current that passed into her from the contact. It took her a breathless moment to realise what the spirit was doing. It was stroking her, using only a single finger, as a person might do to a delicate animal, or a mother to a newborn baby. Gentling her. The voice came again, and once more it was horrible to the ear; but this time softer somehow, a tonal quality that transcended language and meaning.

Lucia did not know what they wanted. She did not even know if *wanting* was a concept that applied to them. But she said a tiny prayer to the moon sisters, and then opened her eyes, and looked upon their children.

The Imperial bedchamber was shadowy and quiet. Warm night breezes blew in through elegantly curved window arches, stirring the thin veils that hung before them. Against one wall, the enormous bed was a rolling landscape of opalescent sheets, gold and white and crimson. At each corner stood one of the Guardians of the Four Winds, carved in precious metals and reaching up to hold aloft the canopy that roofed the whole of the grand structure.

Anais tu Erinima, Blood Empress of Saramyr, stood by a dresser of finest wood, leaning gently against the wall with a silver cup of amber wine in her hand. Her light hair was loose, falling about her deceptively innocent face and over the shoulders of the black silk nightdress she wore. The jet-coloured *lach* of the floor was cold against her bare soles – apart from its reflective properties, *lach* was a stone valued for its reluctance to take up heat, and hence keep a room cool.

She sipped her wine and waited, nursing her fury.

How she hated him. As if the Emperor Durun had not been enough of a trial before, this business with Lucia had made him a hundred times worse. He seemed to be going out of his way to anger and humiliate her. His drunkenness, always apt to get a little out of hand, was appalling now. He caroused at feasts, bawling and vomiting until even his hunting companions seemed uneasy. The hunts themselves were a mercy, because they got him out of the Keep for a few days at a time; but he used them as an excuse to stand up important guests and often reeled home in a worse state than he had left.

She seethed as she thought on it. At least she had the small revenge that his family, Blood Batik, had thrown their support behind her at the council. But this in itself was a double-edged sword. If Blood Batik had declared against her, she would at least have had the comfort of annulling her marriage to Durun; now she was forced to suffer him, for she could not do without the support of his family. Durun was too stubborn and bullheaded to toe the family line in this matter, and his frustration was evident. He and his father Barak Mos – a firebrand to equal his son – had bellowed at each other often in the past weeks, but each confrontation only sent Durun away with a renewed desire to embarrass himself. After that, the Barak had come as near as he ever came to apologising to Anais, asking her to forgive his son's transgressions and promising to make up for them in the future. Anais knew how much it had taken for him to overcome his not inconsiderable pride to do this, and she was touched; but it did not abate her anger one bit.

Durun's indiscretions with the ladies of the Keep had been an open secret for years now. Usually he preferred the younger ones; impressionable daughters of minor nobles who were visiting court, too flattered by the Emperor's attentions to think of the consequences. Other times he laid with servants who dared not say no to him. Sometimes he brought whores from the cathouses into the Keep. At first it had only been on rare occasions, and Anais had tolerated it. This was not a marriage of passion, but of politics; she was happy to do anything to make it more endurable. But gradually he had become less discreet, and the rumours began.

Anais initially felt humiliated by the whole affair, bound by the notion that she should be good enough at bedplay to keep him on her pillow; but then, as always, she had not been in a position where she could do Blood Batik the grievous insult of divorcing their favourite son. The strength her marriage provided was what had got Blood Erinima to where it was, and she could not throw it away, not even when their vows were being so flagrantly abused.

Eventually, she ceased to care. Let him do as he would. In

the main, she was indifferent to him as a husband anyway. Sometimes, just sometimes, when he turned the bright flame of his passions on to something worthwhile – or more rarely, on to her – she saw a glimpse of the man he might have been, the marriage as it could be. But those moments were too brief and far between; only enough to frustrate her with possibilities. He wasted himself on idiot passions, fighting and drinking and whoring.

But now Durun had gone too far.

Tonight he had come back from a hunt, roaring drunk, and ordered a feast for himself and his companions. There in the hall they had made pigs of themselves and swilled wine. Durun, flushed with triumph at killing a boar single-handed, had been even more out of control than he usually was. When one of the servants had come to pour him another drink – a simple, slender and plain-faced girl whose lack of wit or beauty was made up for by a disproportionately large chest – he pulled her around him and on to the table, scattering greasy food and cups of wine, and had her there. Anais's handmaiden, whom she had charged with delivering a message to the Emperor when he returned from the hunt, walked in then. She found him between the legs of the servant girl, her breasts exposed between the torn halves of her shirt, gasping with each thrust while Durun's hunting companions gathered round and cheered. She had reported a slightly less graphic version of events to the Empress.

Anais was livid. Rumours were one thing; people could pretend to ignore them. But this was intolerable. The Emperor of Saramyr, rutting like an animal in a hall full of servants and the sons of nobles, flouting his infidelity for all to see. It was more than she could bear.

The heavy, unsteady footsteps that approached the bedroom door heralded the arrival of her wayward husband. He pushed the door open and lumbered through unsteadily. With his sharp, knifelike features, his bearing was proud and haughty even in such a state as he was. He saw Anais standing by the dresser, and shut the door behind him. Brushing back the long fall of fine black hair – spotted with grease and matted with wine now – he raised an eyebrow at her.

'Wife,' he said. 'You seem angry.'

She crossed the room in three strides and threw the cup of wine in his face.

'You disgusting excuse for a man!' she hissed.

He sputtered, instinctively backhanding the silver cup out of her grip. It clashed and clattered across the *lach* floor and rolled to a stop. She slapped him, hard. He recoiled, more surprised than hurt. She hit him again, more violently this time. A small part of her was telling her that an empress should not act this way, but the wine and her pent-up fury overrode it. She was seized by the need to hurt him, encouraged by her first assaults; and she hit him again, and again, pounding against him with her fists.

He shook off his initial bewilderment as the pain seeped through his drink-fogged brain. Anais's next blow was arrested by a black-gloved hand, seizing her wrist. Instinctively, she struck with the other one, but he caught that too, holding her arms apart. She struggled desperately against him, suddenly wanting to escape. She saw the blaze in his eyes and feared she had gone too far. He was much larger and stronger than her, and he held her with effortless ease.

'Let go of me!' she hissed. 'Bastard!'

His dark eyes threatened her with pain, and she twisted to be out of his grip; then suddenly he was lifting her up by her arms, slamming her against the wall hard enough to knock the breath from her.

'Heart's blood, Anais,' he husked. 'It's been too long since you've had this kind of fight in you.'

And then he was kissing her, hard and savagely, biting her lips and her tongue. She struggled against him, making sounds of protest through her nose; he slammed her against the wall again.

'Now will you behave?' he demanded.

She sagged. 'Bastard,' she said again, but there was no strength in it. He stepped back and let her go. She regarded him for a time in the shadows, her eyes baleful and wary all at once. Spirits, she truly hated him; but she wanted him as well. It was only his heart and mind that were weak and stupid; when he towered over her like this, when she was at bay before him, she could imagine that he was the powerful, dangerous man she had wished for a husband, instead of the indolent sluggard that she got.

Well, why shouldn't she take what pleasure she could from him? She got so little else. And she only needed his body . . .

Surging forward, she grabbed his head, her fingers like claws at the back of his skull, drawing him into a kiss as brutal as the one he had given her. She tasted wine on his breath, mingled with other things less pleasant, but it did nothing to dampen her suddenly awakened ardour. He shoved her against the wall again, and this time she saw the animal lust on his face. He did not want *her*, not specifically; he wanted woman, any woman. Well, that would suit her. She wanted a man, and he would do for now.

Grabbing the front of her nightdress, he tore it half away in one great swipe. She had braced herself against it, but she was still overwhelmed by his strength, pulled into him by the force. He pushed her back again, and with a second effort he rent it from her completely. She stood before him, her pale and slender form naked in the shadows, her small, hard breasts rising and falling with her breath. Then they fell to each other.

Their congress was rough and forceful, each using the other's body without thought of tenderness. Anaïs tore her husband's clothes away as eagerly as he had hers, running her hands over the taut muscles of his body and the thin covering of fat overlaying them, the legacy of too much drink and rich food. No quarter was asked, and none given; he impaled her over and again as they rolled across the bed, each seeking the dominant position. Finally she pinned him down and he relented. She drove herself against him faster and faster. For all that he was drunk, and all his many failings, he still possessed a certain endowment beyond that of most men, and Anaïs speared herself upon it mercilessly. In the morning they would be as they always were, argumentative and spiteful; but for now, with the weight of the realm on her shoulders and more worries than she could count, she took the passion she craved so desperately, and found her release therein.

She wanted to tell him that she hated him but the words, when they came in the throes of orgasm, were quite the opposite.

FOURTEEN

When the night came, Asara hunted.

They had arrived in the port of Pelis before sunset, the crossing made swift by favourable winds. The folded sails and rigging of the other junks that swayed in the harbour were silhouettes against the red-orange flamescape on the western horizon. Shadows were long, and the air was full of the bawdy sound of chikkikii as they cracked and rattled their wing-cases from invisible hiding places. Though the ubiquitous dockhands and sailors were present here as at every trading port, the work proceeded at a quieter, more leisurely pace, as if in reverence to the coming dusk. Lantern-lit bars and provincial-style shops idled lazily in the warmth of the dying day. It was a time for lovers to walk arm in arm, for seduction behind closed shutters.

Kaiku was plainly taken by the atmosphere of the place, even before the *Summer Wind* had creaked into its bay and the mooring lines were thrown to the men on the dock-side. Such a short divide from the mainland, and yet even a stranger could tell at a glance that things were done a different way here on Fo. Asara had been here many times before, and always disliked it for the very reasons that appealed to Kaiku. It was peaceful in Pelis, and peace meant boredom to Asara. She looked forward to moving on, into the wilder parts of Fo, where life was not so easy.

Once disembarked, Asara declared that she would find them passage north tonight, and they would leave in the morning if they could. She advised Kaiku to buy herself a rifle; she would need protection where they were going. Kaiku was excited at the thought. She had always been an excellent markswoman, and recent events had meant that she had slipped out of practice. She and Tane went off to buy supplies and weaponry.

Asara was left alone, as she liked it.

It was an easy matter to get them a ride on a trade caravan going to Chaim. Her previous visits had taught her who to go to, though she looked radically different now than she did then, and nobody recognised her. Only one caravan was departing in the morning, but it was well-guarded enough and suitable to their needs. She approached the caravan master as he was overseeing the loading of the cargo. He gave them a very good price for passage. It was so easy to manipulate men, looking as she did. She was coldly aware of the effect her beauty had on the male mind. She went through the motions of flirtatiousness, bored inside, executing a sequence of smiles, laughs, tilts of her body, small touches. Her victim's arousal was plain on his face. Sometimes the sequence took a little tailoring to suit the individual, but usually not. She sighed to herself as she walked away, the agreement done. What brainless animals men were: like dogs, simple to train, begging for treats, eager in heat and appetite. She had little enough respect for anyone – with a few notable exceptions – but at least most women had some modicum of dignity. Men were just embarrassing.

Her transaction done, she met up again with Tane and Kaiku, who informed her of the inn they had found where they would all be staying. Asara knew it well, and it was a safe choice. She told them to go back and rest; she had some business to conclude before retiring. They accepted her explanation, knowing better than to pry. There had been questions on their journey: where were the burns she had suffered; why did she look different? More gratifying was Tane's shock when she appeared on the deck of the barge with short sleeves, and he saw that the tattoo of the Messengers' Guild that had run the length of her inner arm was now only a dark smear like a bruise. The next day it was gone entirely. She gave them no answers. She was not a freak for their curiosity.

She walked the town while the inky shadows of night seeped through the narrow, picturesque streets. Aurus and Neryn shared the sky, the vast pearl moon and her tiny green sister. Iridima, the brightest, was not to be seen; her orbit took her elsewhere, it seemed. In the pale, green-hued glow, Asara wandered down lantern-lit lanes, killing time. She passed a street of bars and restaurants, silhouettes moving in the windows as conversation and laughter drifted out; but it all seemed alien to her, and made her feel unaccountably lonely. This place was possessed of a wonderfully historic charm, with its balconies and coiled-metal railings and uneven alleyways, but it did not have the power to touch Asara.

Gradually, the town of Pelis gentled itself to sleep. She waited, patient as a spider. She had already chosen her prey for the night, spotted him waddling home, puffing at the exertion of hauling his fat frame up the sloping cobble streets. Usually she preferred women – the sensuous curves of their bodies, their fragrance appealed to her – but her encounter with the caravan master had given her a perverse desire for someone bloated and disgusting. He was a fishmonger, by the smell of him, and he lived in an unremarkable corner house of a quiet street. Usually she would have spent more time studying him before she struck – ensuring that he lived alone, observing his habits – but tonight she would have to allow herself a little recklessness. There was no telling when she might next get a chance, and the need was pressing at her.

Her rifle she had stashed underneath a row of bushes; it would only get in her way here. She haunted the street until she was sure that nobody was observing her, and then crossed to the wall of the house and pressed herself flat against it. The ground floor was secure, but on the second storey the shutters were open to let the summer night breezes blow through the house. Asara tested the texture of the wall. It was of local stone, rough and weathered, and it provided more than enough handholds for her.

She took a final look about and then climbed. In four swift movements she had scaled up to the window-ledge, where she looked inside. The room beyond was bright with green-edged moonlight, and cluttered with the fishmonger's voluminous clothes, heaped untidily about the tiled floor. It was simple and sparse, built to be cool and airy to combat the heat. The fishmonger himself was a mountain of flesh on a mat in one corner, rolled on his side with his back to her, half covered by a thin sheet. His shoulders, dusted with curls of hair, rose and fell as he slept. She slipped inside, over the ledge and on to the floor without a sound.

She padded silently towards him, glancing warily at the dark, uncurtained doorway leading into the rest of the house. When she reached the edge of his sleeping-mat, she straightened and brushed her hair back behind her ear, looking down on him. She could smell the acrid night-sweat rising from his skin, pungent with the scent of the fish he had eaten and handled. And something else too, another faint smell: perfume, and coitus. Her eyes fell to the shallow depression in the mat next to his bulk, too small and light to have been made by him.

She whirled just as the woman appeared at the doorway, returning from whatever nocturnal desires had made her get up. She was dressed in a simple grey nightgown, her black hair tangled and her eyes muzzy with sleep. For the briefest of instants, she froze as she saw Asara standing over her lover; then she screamed.

Asara was on her in an eyeblink. She lashed a kick across the woman's face, sending her spinning in a whirl of hair and arms to crash into the wall and collapse. Whether dead, unconscious or only stunned, Asara had no more time to deal with her. The fishmonger was scrambling off the bed, crabbing away from her frantically on his heels and elbows, a small cry of bewilderment and alarm coming from his lips.

She pinned him down with a hand to his flabby throat and trapped his arms with her knees; he was too slow to resist, and by the time he realised what she had done, it was too late. She sat on the rise of his hairy belly, feeling his legs kick uselessly behind her, trying to get a knee up into her ribs but foiled by the gut in between. She took a glance over at the woman, still slumped against the wall, her face covered by her hair. Then she returned her attention to the fishmonger, who was flailing ineffectually beneath her even though he was easily double her weight. His faint cries were strangled by her grip. His eyes bulged in fear.

'Shh,' she said softly. 'I only want a kiss.'

She moved her lips to his as fast as a snake taking a mouse, and sucked.

The fishmonger went rigid as something seemed to tear inside him, something not physical, and gush out through his mouth and into hers. It glittered, this thing, and sparkled; a rushing, bright stream that flickered between their lips as she robbed it from him. For a few long seconds, he felt as a ghost must, fading in the rays of the dawn; and then the horror in his eyes waned, and his pupils grew dark and dim, and his body relaxed in death. Asara let him go with a gasp, wiping her mouth with the back of her hand. His head smacked hard against the tiled floor with a nauseating sound. She took a few heavy breaths in and out, relishing the swelling warmth inside her, and then she got off him.

She had no understanding of what it was in her body that made her this way. There was no anatomical comparison for her to draw against. Arbitrarily, she thought of it as a coil, a tight whorl of fleshy tubing nestled just behind her stomach and before her spine. When glutted, it was thick, and she could feel its warm presence there; when starved, it was flaccid and thin, and the space where it had shrunken from ached with an emptiness a hundred times worse than hunger. Using her talents drained it, like exercise promotes appetite. When she had no need of them, the hunger came on her only rarely; just enough for her body to keep at bay the onset of age. But recently, since her first encounter with the shin-shin, she had been forced to excessive use.

Healing herself after Kaiku had left her near death had almost been too much for her. She had been helped by two foresters who had come to investigate the blaze and found instead a scorched and disfigured handmaiden. The sustenance they provided restored her health more than any care they could offer. Sloughing off the burned skin of her face and hands, regrowing her hair: these took time and effort and strength, and that strength had to come from somewhere. Altering her features was more of a whim, executed after she had restored herself to her satisfaction. She had been careful not to seem outstandingly beautiful while posing as Kaiku's handmaiden, and settled for being merely pretty for two years. But she had a vain streak, and she decided that the time had come to indulge it once again. The slightest shift in aspect rendered her from pleasant-faced and demure to an object of lust. How awful it must be, she thought, for those who are condemned with the face they are born with.

But then, she reflected ruefully, she never knew hers.

Seized by a suddenly maudlin air, she walked over to the woman and pushed her head back. A black bruise was already forming on her cheek. She was unconscious, still breathing. Asara tilted her head first to one side, then to the other. She was not pretty, but possessed of a certain voluptuousness that Asara found faintly intoxicating. If she had not come in, had not seen Asara's face, then Asara would have let her live. But now, she could not.

Asara enfolded the woman in her arms and flicked her hair back over her head, then put her lips to the partly open mouth of her victim.

The Empress Anais tu Erinima stalked along the corridors of the Imperial Keep, in a foul mood. She had barely had time to get into her bath after a day of meetings, arguments and reports before she had received the news that Barak Mos, her husband's father and the power behind Blood Batik, had arrived with an important message for her. Anyone else she would have let wait – with the possible exception of Barak Zahn – but Mos was too important to take even the slightest risk of offending. Batik was the single strongest ally she had, and she needed all she could get right now.

Her route took her around the edges of the Keep, where sculpted arches looked out over the soft night beyond. Neryn was peeking out from behind her mighty sister Aurus, a pale green bubble on the edge of the mottled, pearl-skinned disc that loomed huge in the star-littered sky. Thin streamers of moon-limned cloud drifted in the lazy warmth of the summer darkness. Below, the city was a net of lantern lights, deceptively peaceful and quiet. She had wanted nothing more on this night than to relax on a balcony and sip wine, and let the cares of the past weeks ease out of her; but it was not to be, it seemed.

Every day was like this now. She had barely a moment to herself in daylight, and her nights were no longer sacrosanct either. Each morning brought a new crisis: a protest demonstration somewhere, news of the famed agitator Unger tu Torrhyc stirring trouble among the people, another noble who wanted to beg favour or make veiled threats, an allegiance changed, a suspicion of deceit, an appointment, a dismissal, an oath . . . everything was important now, everything had to be attended to. She had stirred up Saramyr, for better or worse. Now she was surrounded by enemies, and few of them wore their colours overtly.

The one positive aspect of all this chaos was a surprising one. Her relationship with her husband had smoothed somewhat; in truth, a part of her tiredness was due to the fact that she took out her frustrations on him in the bedchamber, vigorously and every night. With all the cares of the realm clamouring for attention, and each day more hectic than the last, her need for release manifested itself with increasing intensity. Durun matched her, which was more than she could say of most men. And though they still could not be said to *like* each other, Durun had at least ceased to be quite so antagonistic to her, and she noticed he had stopped finding excuses to be absent from the Keep so he could be in the bedchamber when she got there.

She should have realised it before. The best way to keep him on a leash was to keep him in her bed. It was a mutually beneficial arrangement, but no more than that. Not to her, anyway.

She was sweeping along the corridor, her shoes tapping on the veined *lach* of the floor, when she saw the Weave-lord Vyrrch emerge from a door ahead of her. A familiar worm of disgust twitched in her gut at the sight of the shambling, bent figure, buried under a robe of patchwork rags, mismatched material stitched haphazardly layer over layer. The hideous, immobile bronze face turned to her within the frame of his tattered hood.

'Ah, Empress Anais,' he croaked, with feigned surprise. She knew by his tone that this meeting was no accident, but she had no patience for it.

'Vyrrch,' she acknowledged, curt enough to be rude.

'We must talk, you and I,' he said.

She passed him by without slowing. 'I have little to say to one who desires the death of my child.'

Vyrrch wasted a moment on surprise, then followed her with his peculiar, broken gait. Twisted and corrupted his bones might have been, but he was not as slow as his appearance suggested.

'Wait!' he cried, outraged. 'You dare not walk away from me!'

She laughed at his bluster. 'The evidence points to the contrary,' she replied, relishing his discomfort as he hobbled along, falling behind her.

'You dare *not*!' he hissed, and Anais felt herself suddenly wrenched as if by some great force, an invisible hand that seized her and whirled her around to face him. She tottered, stunned for a moment; and then the hand was gone.

Vyrrch regarded her icily from behind his Mask.

'I should have you executed for that,' Anais said, her cheeks flushed with fury.

Vyrrch was not cowed. 'We are displeased with you, Anais. Very displeased. If you get rid of me, no Weaver will take my place. We are bound to Adderach above all other loyalties, and you are working against the interests of our kind. None of us will claim the title of Weave-lord if I am removed. Do you think you will survive the civil war you are bringing upon us all, without a Weaver to defend you?'

'My Weaver works to *betray* me,' she hissed. 'Do you think I am not aware of that? Perhaps I would be better with none.'

'Perhaps,' he replied. 'Though without any way to contact your far-flung interests – unless, of course, you care to revert to horse messengers or carrier birds – I cannot imagine you will make an effective empress any more.' She thought she could hear a smile in his withered and broken voice, and it angered her more; but she reined herself in, made her anger go cold and hard like new-forged metal plunged into ice water.

'Do not threaten me, Vyrrch. You know well that if the hand of the Weavers was suspected of meddling in the politics of the land, then my enemies and allies alike would destroy you. Your insane kind are an accessory to government, not a part of it; and you know as well as I that the high families would sooner see an Aberrant on the throne than a Weaver. You may have ingratiated yourself so much that we think we cannot do without you; but you are here on our sufferance, and you would do well to remember that. Like rebellious dogs, you will be put down if you try and bite your masters. And the Weavers grow altogether too bold.'

'Do you think so?' Vyrrch mocked. 'Perhaps, after you have persuaded the people to accept an Aberrant freak as their ruler, then you will persuade the high families to get rid of us? I don't think it likely, do you?'

'Do not speak of *freaks* to me, you vile thing. I have no interest in the Weavers' displeasure. You are not part of the government of this land, and you have no say in it. Now I am late for a meeting.'

She turned and stalked away, and Vyrrch did not call her again; but she felt his gaze burning into her back all the way along the corridor.

Barak Mos was a man of great presence, though physically he was not as tall as his son. He was broad-boned, with a wide chest and shoulders and thick arms, and there was a squatness about him – with his strong, bearded jaw, flat head and short limbs – that lent him an impression of impressive solidity. At just under six feet in height, he towered over Anais; but she had never faced him in anger, and she knew him to be gentle towards her. She had dealt with enough of the son's tempers to be able to field his father's, anyway.

She met him in a room of her chambers that she particularly liked, dominated by a massive ivory bas-relief of two rinji birds passing each other in flight, their long necks and white wings outstretched, their ungainly, sticklike legs curled up beneath them. The three-dimensional effect of one bird occupying the foreground as it flew between the viewer and the other bird had always appealed to Anais. It appealed to Mos too, apparently, for he was admiring it as she entered.

'Barak Mos,' she said. 'I apologise for keeping you waiting.'

'No trouble,' he replied, turning towards her. 'Rather, let me apologise for the inconvenient hour. I would not have come, but I have grave information.'

Anais gave him a curious look and then invited him to sit. For such a gruff man, he was being excessively polite. The apology was a pleasantry; to get Barak Mos genuinely to say sorry was like getting blood from a stone, which is why she had been so impressed when he had asked her forgiveness for his son's debauched ways.

Two elegant couches were arranged around a low table of black wood, looking out across the room through a partition to the open balcony beyond. On the table was a bowl of kama nuts, giving off a fragrance that was bitter and fruity and smoky all at once. It was the recent fashion among young ladies of the court to keep some kama seeds in their pockets to lend them this enticing fragrance, and Anais had grown to like the scent.

They settled themselves, Anais reclining and Mos sitting on the edge of his couch, leaning forward with his hands clasped before him. She noticed suddenly and with embarrassment the lack of refreshments in the room. Mos caught her gaze and waved absently.

'Your servants came,' he said. 'I sent them away. I won't be here long. Order something for yourself, if you like.'

That was more like the Mos she knew; tactless. As if she needed his permission to call for refreshments in her own home. She decided against it, more concerned with hearing the Barak's news.

'I don't have to tell you that this goes no further than us,' he said, giving her a serious gaze.

'Of course not,' she replied.

'I am only telling you this out of concern. For you, for my son, for my granddaughter.'

A small smile of surprised gratitude flicked over the Empress's face at the term. She had not expected to hear him acknowledge Lucia so.

'I understand,' she replied.

He seemed satisfied. 'Your Weaver, Vyrrch. Weave-lord, sorry. Why is that?'

'Why is what?'

'Why is he a Weave-lord?'

Anais was bewildered. She thought a man in Mos's position should know *that*, at least. 'It is the title bestowed upon the Emperor or Empress's Weaver. Usually it is also because they are the best at their craft.'

Mos harumphed, seeming to digest this. 'Do you trust him?'

'Vyrrch? Heart's blood, no. He would murder my daughter if he thought he could get away with it. But he knows what would happen if the high families thought a Weaver had slain the Heir-Empress. Aberrant or not.' She hesitated to use the word, but there was no other that fitted her purposes.

'That's true enough,' he said, shifting his broad bulk. 'Let me be blunt, then. I suspect that Weave-lord Vyrrch and Barak Sonmaga tu Amacha are working together against you.'

Anais raised an eyebrow. 'Indeed? It would not be a surprise to me.'

'This is bad business, Anais. I have spies, you know that. I don't much approve of them, but they're as necessary as Weavers are in the game we play. I sent them to find out what they could after this whole business began, and I suppose one of them struck lucky. We heard about a man named Purloch tu Irisi. He's a cat-burglar of some renown and great skill. I can vouch for that: he got into this Keep, and into the roof gardens, and he got to Lucia.'

Anais felt a jolt of terror. 'He got to Lucia?'

'Back when all this started. Weeks ago. He could have put a knife in her, Anais.'

The Empress was rigid on her couch. Why had Lucia said nothing? Of course, she should not have been surprised. A life of being hidden had made her secretive, and she was so unfathomably introverted at times. At those times, Anais did not understand her child at all. It made her sad to think of the gulf between them, that her daughter would not mention something so important. But that was just her way.

'Murder wasn't his mission, though,' Mos was continuing. 'He got a lock of hair instead. He wasn't after her; he didn't know anything more than what he was sent for.'

'Why? Why the hair?' Anais asked, her eyes darkening.

'His employer needed proof she was an Aberrant, so he could spread the news and stir up the nobles. The Weavers have some test, some way of telling. The gods only know the ins and outs of their science. But they need a part of the body: skin, hair, something like that.' He shrugged. 'Anyway, this Purloch was clever. He wouldn't take on a task like that without insurance. Too smart to be someone's pawn. He wanted to know who it was that hired him; so he traced the middlemen back to their source. Sonmaga.'

Anais nodded to herself. She had never solved the mystery of how this furore suddenly started, how the high families all seemed to know at once about her child being different. Sonmaga! It *would* be him.

'Do you have proof of any of it?'

Mos looked momentarily embarrassed. 'Purloch disappeared directly after he had completed his task. There is no testimony against Sonmaga, and if there were, it would be useless. A thief's word against a Barak's?'

'Did this . . . Purloch know about Vyrrch's involvement?'

'He knew nothing, or he said nothing,' said Mos. 'There is no link, or at least none that anyone but a Weaver could follow. But there was one thing that sat uneasily with me about the whole affair. Purloch's fee was huge. All that effort and expense on Sonmaga's part, just to hire a man to steal a lock of hair. Points to one conclusion.'

'Sonmaga must have suspected,' she said.

'He already knew she was Aberrant,' Mos agreed with a nod. He seemed to have no problem with the word, used in conjunction with the one he had called 'granddaughter' moments ago. She took heart in that.

'Because somebody told him so,' she concluded. 'Vyrrch.'

'He found out somehow,' Mos said. 'It's the only answer.'

'Not the only answer,' Anais replied cautiously. 'Others knew. Tutors, a few servants . . .'

'But none more likely than Vyrrch,' Mos countered. 'None with so much to lose by an Aberrant taking the throne. What if she *does* become Empress? She'll know the Weavers would have killed her at birth, given the chance. What if she stops the Weavers killing Aberrant children? What if she tries to undermine them, drive them out? The Weavers know they could not thrive in a realm where an Aberrant ruled. They would suddenly find they have to fear retaliation for over two hundred years of rooting out deviancy.'

'Maybe it's what we need,' Anais said, thinking over her conversation with Vyrrch. 'Gods-cursed parasites. We'd be better off without them. We should never have let it get this far, never have allowed them to become indispensible.'

'You'll find no stronger agreement than mine,' Mos said. 'I despise their slippery ways. But beware of setting yourself squarely against them, Anais. You walk a precarious edge.'

'Indeed,' said Anais, musing. 'Indeed.'

FIFTEEN

The compound of Blood Amacha was enormous, the largest in the Imperial Quarter of Axekami, larger even than that of the ruling family, Blood Erinima. It rested on a flat tabletop of land, a man-made dais of earth that raised it up above the surrounding compounds by a storey. Within its walls, a virtual paradise was wrought: lush tropical trees imported from distant continents, sculpted brooks and pools, wondrous glades and waterfalls. In contrast to the usual minimalism of Saramyr gardens, this place was abundant to the point of gaudiness; but even here, the tendency towards neatness was still in effect, and there were no fallen leaves on the paths, no chewed branches left on the trunks, no blighted leaf uncut. Unfamiliar fruits hung in the branches, and sprays of strange flowers nestled amid the bushes. There were even foreign animals here, chosen for their beauty and wonder – and their inability to harm those who wandered the gardens of the compound. It was like stepping into another land, a storybook realm of magic.

Mishani tu Koli sat on a wooden bench that was carved into the living root of an enormous chapapa tree, a slim book of war sonnets by the swordsman-poet Xalis in her hand. A kidney-shaped pool lay before her, fed by a trickling fall of water over red rocks, with exotic fish lazing within. The afternoon air hummed with the benevolent drone of insects.

She counted the ostentation of Blood Amacha's compound as faintly vulgar, considering it the highest arrogance to raise themselves above the other nobles in such a way; yet she could not deny the thrill of walking their gardens, nor the pleasure of knowing that she was sitting on a tree that was seeded on another continent entirely. Amacha's gardens had been growing for over three hundred years, and this tree had been here for most of that time, imported as a sapling from the jungles of Okhamba.

For all its breathtaking splendour, though, she could not find her ease here. Her mind would not stay on the verses on the page, and the tranquillity of the gardens did little to soothe her. She ached inside with a feeling of such loss and sadness that she wanted to weep, and worse was the knowledge that she had created her own misery.

She played the moment over and over in her memory, hearing her own voice come back to her, watching the reaction on the face of her friend.

Because I see what you are. And you disgust me.

With those words she had sawn through ties twenty harvests in the making. With those words, she had overcome the weakness of indecision, committed herself to the course she knew was right. By banishing Kaiku, she protected her family, protected her *father* from dishonour. It was a daughter's duty to do so, to hold her family above all else, sometimes even the Empress herself.

With those words, she had turned her back on her lifelong friend, and now she wanted to scream with the pain of it.

But she didn't scream. That was not her way. She showed outwardly no sign at all of her grief, nor of the warring forces of recrimination and justification that battled behind her calm, dark eyes.

Her father had had questions for her when he returned. News of the death of Kaiku's family had been slow in escaping the Forest of Yuna, but when it did it was all over the court. Barak Avun had been canny enough not to reveal to anyone that Kaiku was staying with his daughter until he had been given the opportunity to talk to her. He never got the chance. She was gone by the time he came back, and had effectively disappeared.

Mishani feigned shock, pretending that Kaiku had said nothing about the slaughter of her family. Barak Avun did not believe her, but he did not challenge her either. He knew his daughter well, knew how loyal she was. If he demanded, she would tell him; but the fact that she was not telling him meant it was something he would be better off not knowing. That, on top of the strange fire on the day of the council meeting and the curious deaths of Kaiku's family, had him mightily suspicious; but he trusted her, and let the falsehoods settle.

She was protecting his honour by risking her own. He allowed it, but the message between them was unspoken. Even though her intentions were good, even though it were better that she did not tell him, she was still neglecting a daughter's duty by lying to her father. She owed him greatly.

Mishani had tried to distract herself from her thoughts of Kaiku by burying herself in the family business and the intrigues of court. The Barak indulged her by confiding closely in her. The court was a hotbed of power-plays in the wake of the council meeting and the Empress's announcement that the Aberrant child would sit the throne. New alliances were being forged, uniting against the ruling family. Agitators had taken to the streets.

In particular, one man, Unger tu Torrhyc, was stirring up a storm with his fiery orations against the Heir-Empress. Mishani had attended one of his demonstrations in Speaker's Square, and been impressed. The anger in the city was rising to fever pitch. Violent protests had already been quelled by the Imperial Guards in the poorer districts. The Empress might have enough support among the nobles to keep a precarious hold on her throne, but she had made no overtures to the common folk, and they were solidly opposed to the idea of an Aberrant ruler. Whether oversight or arrogance, it could prove to be her downfall.

Yet all the rhetoric that flew about the streets and the court rang hollow to Mishani now. The cries that Aberrants were freaks, a blight, that they were *evil* by birth . . . what had previously made so much sense now seemed like the hysteria of foaming zealots. How could it apply to Kaiku? She was no more 'born evil' than Mishani was. She was no more evil *now* than Mishani was. And if it did not apply to her, then how many others did it also exclude? What evidence was there that Aberrants were evil at all?

And yet there was still the fear and disgust. That she could not deny. She had been repulsed by Kaiku, though her friend had not changed physically one bit beyond the colour of her eyes. It was the *knowledge* that repulsed her, the thought that Kaiku was Aberrant. But the more she thought on that, the more she found there was no weight to the reasoning. She was repulsed because Kaiku was Aberrant. But she could not come up with any other reason than that. The danger of being near her did not bother Mishani; as Kaiku had said, she would have stood by her if she had been suffering from an infectious disease. But Aberrancy was different.

Wherever she turned in the corridors of her mind, she came up against the same phrase: *because she is Aberrant.* It was phantom logic, a dead-end in the pathways of thought. So deeply ingrained in her was it that it required no more reason than it *was*, no evidence to back it up. If she was asked why the sun was in the sky, she could tell the story of how Ocha put his own son's eye out because two were too bright, and then set him to watch over the world; and how Nuki was chased round the planet by the three amorous moon-sisters, giving us night and day. She could explain why the birds sang, why the wind blew, why the sea rippled; but ask her why Aberrants were revolting and terrible, and she had only this answer: *because they are.*

Suddenly, it did not seem good enough.

A benefit of her father's strong opposition to the Empress was that Blood Koli found themselves in the favour of Blood Amacha. Blood Amacha and Blood Kerestyn were the only two families with the power to lay claim to the throne except for Blood Batik, the Emperor's family – but they had chosen to side with the Empress, despite the Emperor's obvious detestation of his daughter. Those who had voted against the

Empress at the council were being feted or bullied by the two claimants as they gathered their forces in anticipation of conflict; but Blood Koli and Blood Kerestyn had a history of antagonism, so the increased friendship between Barak Sonmaga tu Amacha and Barak Avun tu Koli seemed natural under the circumstances.

Her father and Barak Sonmaga had been in conference most of the day. She and Avun had joined their host for breakfast, enjoying a delicious meal on the porch of the sprawling wooden townhouse that hid among the exotic fauna. There they had watched strange deer as they ate, and heard the chirruping of hidden animals in the foliage. Afterward, the men had gone to talk. Usually Mishani would have been allowed to join them; but this meeting was of the gravest secrecy, and she was excluded. She did not mind. She was not in the mood for parley anyway.

Now she heard the soft tread of feet on the path behind her, and she put down her book, stood up and bowed to her father and the Barak Sonmaga, fingertips of one hand to her lips and the other arm folded across her waist. Sonmaga bowed slightly in return, put a hand on her father's shoulder with a meaningful glance, and then walked on, leaving them alone. Mishani noticed that her father was carrying something, securely tied in a canvas bag.

'Father,' she said, 'are we leaving now? Did all go well?'

'Soon,' he said. 'May I sit with you for a while?'

'Of course,' she said, moving her book and sitting back down, her ankle-length hair thrown over one slender shoulder.

Barak Avun sat, the bag put aside. He seemed nervous to be holding it. Like his daughter, he was fine-boned and lean. Sharp cheekbones stood out on a tanned and weathered face, and his hair had receded from his pate and now held out in a horseshoe shape from ear to ear. He gave the impression of being permanently tired and weary, though it was a misleading assumption to make. Mishani loved her father, but she respected him more. He was a ruthless and eminently successful player in the games of the court, and she could not have asked for a better tutor.

'Daughter, there are things we must speak of,' he said. 'You know that the discovery of the Heir-Empress's secret has come at a bad time for Saramyr. The harvest promises to be lean this year, despite the weather, as the blight in the earth takes hold. The wild places are more dangerous than ever. We cannot afford a civil war now.'

'Agreed,' Mishani said. 'But since the Empress is determined to see her child on the throne, it seems unlikely that any other option is available. Even if we conceded to her, I doubt that the people would. Axekami is tipping towards revolt.'

'There is another way,' he said. 'The Empress is sterile. Birthing that spawn of hers has made her barren. If the Heir-Empress were removed, then Blood Erinima would have no choice but to forfeit their position as ruling family once Anais died. And probably before.'

'If Lucia were . . . removed,' Mishani said carefully. She did not like the way this conversation was going. 'Then the Empress would stop at nothing to hunt down whoever was responsible, and civil war would likely ensue anyway.'

'Not if she had nobody to blame. No target on which to vent her wrath.' Barak Avun grew sly. 'Not if it was the work of the gods.'

'Speak plainly, Father,' she said, her thin face set. 'What have you in mind?'

'The Empress is wooing the nobles as well as she can, by introducing them to the Aberrant child so that they may see she is not deformed or freakish. Reports say she is, on the contrary, quite pretty if a little . . . odd. But pretty or not, she must be removed if the stability of the country is to be maintained.'

'Am I to take it from this,' Mishani suggested daringly, 'that Blood Amacha is not quite prepared for civil war yet, and finds the thought of revolution unappealing at the moment? I would think they would prefer to bide their time and strike when they are assured of their ability to beat Blood Kerestyn to the throne.'

Barak Avun regarded his daughter with eyes gone dull as a lizard's. 'You are clever, daughter, and you fill me with pride. But be obedient now. You have a task.'

Mishani bowed her head a little in submission, letting her black hair fall across her face.

The Barak settled back, satisfied. 'You will go to see the Heir-Empress, and give her a gift.' He motioned to the canvas bag next to him, but Mishani noted that he was still chary of being near it. 'You were absent at council; Anais does not know whether you are opposed to her or not. She will welcome the chance to change your mind. Go see the child, and offer her a present.'

'What is in the bag, Father?' Mishani asked, feeling her blood begin to run cold. She knew what the Barak was asking her, and knew equally that she could not refuse him. He had not mentioned her absence at council by accident; he was making another point of her recent disobedience.

'A nightdress,' he said. 'Beautifully embroidered; a work of art. It is infected with bone fever.'

Mishani had expected as much, and made no reaction.

'The Heir-Empress will sicken within a week, die a few weeks later. Perhaps a few others in her chambers will catch it too. Bone fever strikes at random; nobody will suspect the gift. And even if they do, it cannot be detected, and thus cannot be traced to you or me,' he said.

Or Sonmaga, Mishani thought sourly, knowing him to be the author of this plot. She wondered what he had promised Avun for using his daughter this way. The use of poison was still counted an acceptable, if not honourable, method of assassination. But use of disease was abhorrent, and rarely even considered. Only barbarians would do such. What depths her father and Sonmaga had stooped to; and what depths they would condemn her to, if they made her their accomplice.

No, she thought. *Not accomplice. Scapegoat.*

She looked hard into her father's eyes. She believed he thought it would work, and he thought he was doing what was good for the country. But she knew also that if she were somehow caught, he would cut her loose like an anchor from a ship to save his family. She had seen moves like this a hundred times in court, but she had never been the subject of them before. Never had she felt so cheapened, never so much a pawn as now; and the one who wounded her this way was the one she trusted most in the world. She felt fundamentally betrayed, and in that she felt the love she bore for her father curl up and die. She was shocked at how fragile a thing it must have been.

Mishani gazed at the stranger on the bench next to her a moment longer, then dropped her eyes to the pool before them. Sun glittered in the edges of the ripples.

'I will do as you say,' she said. She could scarcely do otherwise.

At the foot of Mount Aon, the great monastery of Adderach crouched and glowered, a testament to the insanity of its architects. Its form was bewildering to the eye, the sand-coloured stone of its skin moulded so that it seemed to melt from one form to another: here a narrow walkway, terminating over a drop; here a sculpture of howling demons; there a redundant minaret, a half-constructed window, a corkscrewing spire. One wall of an entirely disused wing was crafted in the shape of a screaming face, thirty feet high, teeth bared and eyes wild. Statues stalked the desolate surroundings, the delirious babblings of mad minds scoured by cold winds from the upper altitudes. Lonely walls stood, guarding nothing. Inside, staircases went nowhere, whole wings were inaccessible because nobody had thought to build a door, cavernous halls vied with tiny rooms too small to stand up in.

It was a masterpiece or an atrocity, born of a thousand projects of whim and caprice that somehow fused together seamlessly into one; and it was such a place that the Weavers had made their cradle of power, from which they watched over the land of Saramyr and made their plans.

The Weavers had no recognisable hierarchy. Their structure was anarchic, random and operating under uncertain values; but there was one overarching principle that united them all, and that was the good of the whole. Though individually their motives were saturated in dementia, they each worked together towards the same goal at any given time. None questioned this strange group consciousness; nobody asked who set the goals, who directed their efforts, whether it was a majority decision or the determination of a select few. It simply *was*. The force that kept them coherent was a web that bound them all together, like the sublime threads of the Weave.

The monastery was built over a vast, labyrinthine mine. It had lain disused for over two hundred years now, but still it stood, and creatures of a foulness beyond imagining roamed its tunnels in the blackness. The mine had been the site where the first of the witchstones had been found, two and a half centuries ago, buried deep beneath the earth, and from there the Weavers had sprung.

At first the miners had no idea what they had found. They were simple, tough and honest folk, working a seam of iron deep in the Tchamil Mountains, far from civilisation; at that time, the mine was new, and nothing Aberrant stalked the dark passageways as they did today. Living as remotely as they did, the miners had built settlements, and among them were stoneworkers and carpenters and the like: artisans. They came to view the thing that the miners had found, and it was they that gave the substance its name.

It was plain from the first that this was no ordinary stone. For one thing, a man could sense it just by being close. The hairs on his arm would stand on end, his skin would crawl, his teeth tingle. Not in fear, but because he stood in the presence of energy. The air felt charged around the stone, like it was before a moonstorm, and even the most pragmatic of those hardy folk were forced to admit that.

The second odd thing was the state in which it was found. It was a vast, uneven hulk of black, grainy stone, like an outcrop of volcanic rock; except that it was discovered deep underground, whole and unattached, inside a small cave. The surrounding stone had been melted to glass by unimaginable heat, and no matter how they mined, there was no evidence of a seam anywhere. It was impossible that it could have formed naturally. Which begged the question: how did it get there? Could it have been a relic of the Ugati, the native folk who had lived in Saramyr for uncountable years before the first Emperor drove them out?

The history of the Weavers was not clear on exactly what happened next. All that was certain was that the artisans began rubbing dust from the surface of the witchstone and infusing it into their crafts. Perhaps it was the strange properties of the stone that attracted them, or the novelty of an entirely unheard-of substance integrated into their work. Carpenters rubbed the dust into the grain of benches, stonemasons mixed it in with mortar. It was an odd craze, but no odder than a hundred thousand others across the land. The empire in general knew this much about the origin of the Weavers only because some of the folk from the settlement made the trek across the mountains to try and sell their wares, confident that their new edge would appeal to the markets in the west. Their samples were well received; the raw sense of energy they gave out amazed buyers. During that time, the folk of the settlement told people about their strange discovery. When they had sold their samples, they returned home to fulfil the orders that eager customers had made. They never came back.

The settlement was silent for years. Remote as it was, buried in the trackless mountains, it faded into memory. The initial flurry of excitement in the markets diminished and the witchstone artefacts were forgotten.

What happened during that time is a matter of speculation.

At some point, the decision was made to introduce witchstone dust to the craft of mask-making, and during that period some experimenter must have discovered the other powers of witchstone dust. There is no telling how the process began, or how it went on. Perhaps, at first, they used it as a narcotic, for long-term exposure to witchstone caused disorientation and euphoria. Later they discovered that having it close to the face – and hence the brain – was the most effective method of attaining that feeling. From there, small and rudimentary effects in the physical world were noticed. While under the delirium of the witchstone, a cup would be moved without anyone touching it; a flame would flare or gutter; a man might know the thoughts of his friend and be suddenly aware of his innermost secrets. It can only be guessed how arduous the path was from simple addiction to an unknown substance to gaining control of it. How many of them stumbled unwittingly into the full light of the Weave, and lost their minds and souls to its glory? How many atrocities of rape and murder and mutilation were committed in the agonies of post-Weaving withdrawal? History does not recall. But when they emerged again from that settlement after their long silence, no women and children were left.

Two centuries ago, the first Weavers appeared in the towns and cities of Saramyr. Their powers were weaker then, and cruder; but they already moved with one purpose, operating to a master plan. Subtly, they infiltrated the homes of the noble classes, making themselves invaluable. In those days, the people of Saramyr were naïve to the Weavers, and those that proved an obstacle to them were simply *influenced*, their minds and opinions changed to suit the plan. In a matter of a decade, they were integrated; and from there they began to grow, and build, and scheme.

In a firelit chamber somewhere in the depths of Adderach's convoluted arteries, an apparition of Weave-lord Vyrrch hung in the air. It was a dim and blurred ghost, a mottled smear of brown and grey and orange, approximating the colours of his patchwork robe. Curiously, the form seemed to gain definition the closer it came to his Mask, as if the Mask was the focus of the phantom. It was the only thing sharply defined, a translucent bronze face amid the ether of Vyrrch's body.

The three Weavers that Vyrrch faced were different to the last three, and they had been different to the three before. Lacking a hierarchy, the Weave-lord had no superiors to report to; instead the three Weavers present would disseminate the information throughout the network using the Weave. They, in turn, spoke for the others.

'The Empress is being less than cooperative,' observed one, whose name was Kakre. His Mask was of cured skin stretched over a wooden frame, and made him look like a corpse.

'I expected no less,' said Vyrrch, his croaking voice seeming to come from the walls around them. 'But the situation turns to our advantage. It would be . . . inconvenient if she abdicated now.'

'Explain yourself,' demanded Kakre. 'Is not the Heir-Empress's claim to the throne a great threat to the Weavers?'

'Indeed,' Vyrrch replied. 'And as things stand, the forces on either side are evenly matched. But I have not been idle in the Imperial Keep. The Baraks dance to my tune.'

'And what advantage for us?' whispered a fat Weaver, his face a blank oval of wood with a long, braided beard of animal hair depending from it.

Vyrrch turned his gaze to that one. 'Brother, I have plans in hand to rid us of the Empress and her troublesome brood. I have struck a pact with the most powerful player in this game; and when he becomes Blood Emperor, we will be raised up with him. We will no longer be merely an accessory to government; we will be the power behind the throne!'

'Be careful, Vyrrch,' warned Kakre. 'They do not trust us, do not want us here. They will turn on us if they can. Even your Barak.'

'They suspect,' added the third weaver, whose black wooden Mask wore a snarl. 'They suspect what we are about.'

'Then let them suspect,' Vyrrch replied. 'By the time they realise the truth, it will be too late.'

'Perhaps,' said Kakre, 'you had better explain to us your intentions.'

Vyrrch returned to himself shortly afterward, his consciousness flitting down the synapses of the Weave to arrive back at his physical body. His breathing fluttered, and his eyes, which had been open and glazed, focused sharply. He was sitting in his usual place, amid the stench and rank squalor of his chambers. For a time he composed himself, awaiting the backlash of withdrawing himself from the sheer bliss of the Weave. Recollection slotted into place around the usual patches of amnesia, and he looked around quizzically. He vaguely remembered having a girl brought to him yesterday, a particularly spirited little thing as it turned out. He'd had her trussed up, like a spider with a fly, intending to keep her and feed her and use her as necessary. The motive behind it eluded him; perhaps he had wanted instant relief for his next post-Weaving psychosis rather than having to wait for the servants to bring him what he needed on request. The clever bitch had slipped her bonds somehow and was loose in his chambers, hiding. She was trapped in here with him, for he wore the only key to the heavy door that would give her freedom, and he never took it off. He liked that. A little game.

He felt no desire for her now, though. Instead, he felt a sudden and overwhelming compulsion to rearrange his surroundings. An alien and quite dazzling logic had settled on him, a way things should be done, and he saw as if in a vision from the gods how he should alter his living space. He got up to do so, knowing it to be just another form of mania, but powerless to prevent it anyway. The girl could wait. Everyone could wait.

Then when he was ready, he'd have them all.

SIXTEEN

They travelled north along the great Dust Road that curved from the south-east to the north-west of Fo, terminating in the mining town of Cmorn on the far coast. The sun was barely up in the east as they set off, and Neryn was still doggedly high in the sky and would have remained visible until the afternoon, clouds permitting. They did not. By midday, what had begun as a few wisps of cirrus had marshalled into a humped blanket that muted the sun, slowly cruising overhead. The heat did not diminish in proportion to the light, but Tane found himself glad of the shade anyway. Life under a forest canopy had not prepared him for the exposure of recent days, and he still found himself becoming woozy if he stood in the glare of Nuki's eye for too long.

Their caravan was pulled by a pair of manxthwa, whose enormous strength powered a train of seven carts. The hindmost five were covered with tarpaulin and lashed down, packed with a wide variety of supplies for the isolated village of Chaim. The foremost two were for passengers, fitted with a narrow bench on the inner lip of each side so that six people could sit in each cart. A further seat was provided at the front for the driver, a withered, crotchety-looking old man who wore a thin shirt over his ropy frame, and the fat caravan master. Kaiku, Asara and Tane sat in the front passenger cart; the one behind them was full of guards, muttering between themselves and leaning on their rifles.

Tane studied the manxthwa idly as they travelled the Dust Road. They were seven feet high at the shoulder, with short back legs and long front ones in the manner of apes. Their knees crooked backwards, and ended in spatulate black hooves to take the weight of their immense frame. Their bodies were covered in a thick and shaggy fur of a dull red-orange, a legacy of their arctic origins; and yet the heat of Saramyr seemed not to bother them one bit. Their wide faces were drooping and sad and wrinkled, lending them a mis-leading impression of aged wisdom, and two stubby tusks protruded from beneath their lower lips, jutting out from squared chins.

What odd creatures they were, Tane thought; and yet perfect. Enyu's creations were each a wonder, even those things that preyed on man. A shadow seemed to settle on his heart as he thought of the Aberrant lady they had met in Axekami. She may have been outwardly unblemished, but inside she was a corruption of Enyu's mould, a horror. The goddess of nature created her children each for a reason, and Aberrants were a mockery of that.

Towards the end of the day, they turned off the thorough-fare, leaving behind the traffic of rickety carts and painted carriages to head northward. The Dust Road had been aptly named, for each step of the manxthwa stirred up the stuff, powdered stone blown off the surrounding land. Most of Fo was a vast, flat waste of rock and scree, with little vegetation but the hardiest, thorny scrubs. It was high above sea level, higher than the mainland, and its soil was unforgiving. Its bones had been bared by millennia of wind and rain, and made it stark and bleak.

Once the Dust Road was behind them, they travelled on rougher paths, barely more than shallow ruts worn into the ground by the passage of caravans like theirs. They had not gone more than a mile along that way when the driver turned them off the track and circled the caravan.

The caravan master bustled round to help Asara down from the passenger cart. He was bald and rubber-lipped, with tiny eyes and a nose buried in a mass of corpulent, blubbery features. There was a slightly fish-like aspect to his face. His name was Ottin.

'Why are we stopping?' she asked, as she accepted his hand. His skin was clammy and cold.

'It's best not to travel too near the mountains at night,' he replied. 'Dangerous. We will reach Chaim tomorrow, you'll see.'

A fire was made, and Kaiku was surprised to feel the temperature begin to drop hard as the sun fled the sky. The guards took shifts in walking the perimeter of the circle of caravans, while the others sat in the restless light of the blaze. The unfamiliarity of this land, the strangers surrounding her and the promise of danger had combined to make Kaiku feel quite intrepid. She relaxed and listened to the talk at the fireside, and a strange contentment took her.

'There's a blight on the isle, no doubt of that,' the driver was saying. It was a common complaint in Saramyr, but they had never heard it applied to Fo. 'Cancer in the bones of the earth.'

'It's the same on the mainland,' Tane said. 'A malaise for which we can't find a source. Once the forests were safe to walk; now we know better than to be caught out at night. The wild beasts are becoming more aggressive; and the spirits that haunt the trees are cold and unfamiliar.'

'I don't know from forests, but I can tell you the source all right. Up in the mountains. That's where it's coming from.'

'Such superstitious nonsense!' declared Ottin, glancing at Asara to see if she approved of his outburst.

'Is it?' the driver replied sharply, fixing him with a wrinkly squint. 'You tell me if we don't start to see it in the land, the further north we go. North is the mountains. Makes sense to me.'

About that, at least, the driver was right. By midday it was difficult not to notice. Bare trees thrust out of the soil, their limbs crooked and misshapen, oozing sap from some places where the bark was thin as human skin, and in others bowed down by a tumescent surplus of it. They saw one whose branches grew in loops, straggling out of the trunk at one

point only to curve back and bury themselves into it elsewhere. Thin, hooked leaves stood out like spines along the
tangle of boughs.

The guards were more alert now. Kaiku noted how they
faced outwards from their cart with their rifles ready, and
never stopped scanning. She began to pick up on their
wariness, and fiddled with her hair nervously. Ottin, apparently oblivious to it all, continued his inane attempts at
banter with Asara. She bore it with remarkable patience. It
seemed that the discounted fare the caravan master had
offered came with a hidden price: taken with Asara's beauty,
he tried ceaselessly to insinuate himself into her affections.
Kaiku and Tane exchanged glances and smiled in amusement.

But Tane's amusement was only fleeting. Nowhere in the
Forest of Yuna had he ever seen the signs of the corruption in
the earth as obviously as here. His tanned brow furrowed as he
looked out over the empty landscape towards the ghostly peaks
of the Lakmar Mountains in the distance. A sudden flurry of
movement among the guards drew his attention to their right,
where something darted among an outcrop of rocks, making a
throaty cackling sound that echoed in the still air. They kept
their rifles ready, but it made no further appearances.

'See?' said the driver suddenly, pointing up. 'Those things
are so common, they even have their own name. Gristle-
crows, we call them.'

The passengers looked, and saw above them a trio of black
birds, swooping and turning. Indeed, they did seem like
crows at first glance, but it was only when Tane asserted his
perspective that he realised they were much higher than he
thought, and therefore larger.

'How big are they?' he asked, unable to credit the evidence
of his senses.

'Six feet wing-tip to wing-tip,' the driver croaked back.

Kaiku swore under her breath, an old habit borrowed from
her brother and one she had often been reprimanded for as
unladylike. It scarcely seemed to matter out here.

Tane peered up into the clouded sky at them. It was difficult to make out details, but the more he looked the more he reconsidered their likeness to their namesakes. Their beaks were thick and malformed, more like keratinous muzzles with a hooked lip at the front. Their wings were sharply kinked in the middle, in the manner of bats' wings, though they were thickly shagged with untidy black feathers. He grimaced and looked away, hoping never to be any closer to them than he was now.

'Interesting,' said Asara. When she said nothing else, Kaiku took the bait.

'What is interesting?'

'This is not the first type of Aberrant that has become so common as to constitute a species,' she said, gazing pointedly at Tane, who ignored her. 'In amongst all the freaks of nature produced by this . . . *corruption* in the land, there are many that have flourished. For every hundred useless aberrations there may be one that is useful, that provides its bearer an advantage over its kin. And if that one survives to breed, and pass on its—'

'There's nothing new in what you're saying, Asara,' Tane snapped. 'Those ideas have been part of Jujanchi's teachings for decades.'

'Yes,' said Asara. 'He was one of Enyu's priests, wasn't he? A great thinker, by all accounts. He used his theories to explain diversity in animals. Strange how his teachings apply to Aberrants, then, when your creed dictates that they are not children of Enyu.'

'Aberrants follow the *laws* of nature,' Tane replied, 'because they are corruptions of the same basic root. It doesn't make them natural, or any less foul.'

What about me, Tane? Kaiku thought. *What would you think of me, if you knew what I was?* In truth, she wondered that Tane did not suspect Asara of being an Aberrant, but it seemed that he would rather not know.

'But perhaps this corruption is not corruption at all,' Asara posited. 'Maybe it is only accelerated change. Those things up there may be foul to your eyes, but as big as they are they will rule the skies. Does that not make them a superior breed? Consider, Tane: more new species have probably arisen in the last fifty years than in the last five hundred.'

'Change in nature is slow,' Tane countered angrily. 'It is that way for a reason: so that everything around it can adapt. And besides, this is not just a matter of animal speciation. Crops are dying, *people* are dying. Not only that, but the spirits are changing, Asara. They grow hostile. The guardians of natural places are fading, being overrun by things like . . . like the *shin-shin*.'

'The shin-shin were summoned,' Asara replied. 'To get back that Mask. Or to get Kaiku. That was not the random anger of the spirits that killed your priests. They followed the trail to your temple. If they could get across the Camaran Channel, they would follow it here too; but I suspect we lost them in the city, and the trail is cold now.'

'Then whoever summoned the shin-shin knows how to treat with the dark spirits,' Tane said, suddenly calming and becoming contemplative. 'Could it be that they're also responsible for the sickness in the land?'

The reply that Asara was about to give was swallowed in a sudden riot of movement and noise. Kaiku yelped in surprise as she saw a blur of black lunging out from the stony soil of the roadside, and then their cart was tipped violently and they were flung to one side of it. Tane and Asara were thrown into Kaiku, and the three of them pitched over on to the road as the cart toppled with a loud splintering of wood. Tane rolled away out of instinct as the cart was dragged towards them, but mercifully it did not tip again, or it might have crushed the passengers beneath it. They scrambled clear amongst the shouts and chaos of the guards, who had been similarly surprised, and there they saw what had befallen them.

The Aberrant thing was huge, an ungodly fusion of teeth and limbs that had lain in a burrow by the roadside, disguised by a thin covering of shale, until it had sensed their approach. It was still half in the burrow, with only the foremost part of its body visible. Kaiku caught a horrified impression of a blind, eyeless face that was all jaw and teeth, a mouth stuffed with yellowed, crooked fangs amid a multitude of spiderlike legs that had crammed out of the burrow and enwrapped one of the manxthwa at the lead of the caravan. Both the manxthwa were lowing and bellowing in fear. Ottin had pulled himself clear, but the driver was screaming, trapped and entangled in the tethering ropes that served as bridles for the great beasts.

'Heart's blood, *shoot it*!' Ottin shrieked at the guards, but they already had their rifles up and ready. A volley of gunfire tore into the Aberrant creature and it squawked in fury, but it would not let go of its prize. It was dragging the manxthwa closer to its burrow, with the driver and the rest of the caravan pulled in by the force. Those spider limbs that were not engaged with the manxthwa waved tremulously in the air, seeming poised to strike at anything that came near.

The driver screamed again, begging incoherently as the Aberrant made another effort and dragged its prey another foot closer.

Kaiku reacted suddenly and without thinking. She ran back to the passenger cart, which was still on its side, and clambered on to it. Tane shouted at her to come back, but she barely heard him. The Aberrant thing gave another great pull, and the whole caravan shifted. Kaiku grabbed on and rode the lurch, praying that the cart would not tip further. It didn't. Heart thumping, she edged along it to where the manxthwa were bridled.

Ottin was yelling orders at the guards as they reloaded, though nobody was listening to him. He had backed away to the other side of the road, keeping the caravan between him and the horror that attacked them. As he saw Kaiku climbing towards where the driver was trapped, he shrieked something at her too. Whether he was encouraging her or otherwise, she never knew; for as she looked up at him, the second Aberrant creature burst out of its burrow behind Ottin and enfolded him in its vile arachnid legs. The scream that tore from his throat then was like nothing Kaiku had ever heard or wanted to again, but it was quickly silenced as he was stuffed into the creature's toothy maw with a cracking of bones and a flood of gore.

She scrambled onward, breathing hard in horror. Tane and Asara were firing on the first Aberrant creature, trying to dissuade it from the panicking manxthwa, but it held fast. Kaiku reached the front of the caravan, wedging herself into a corner formed by the overturned driver's seat. The terrified driver was gibbering at her, spittle bubbles flecking his lips. She saw that he was lashed tight to the flank of the manx-thwa by the tautened tethering ropes. The spider legs of the Aberrant flexed within a few feet of her, each as thick as her arm, encircling the heaving flanks of the thrashing beast.

And then suddenly the fire was there, leaping into life inside her. She felt it stir with a flood of panic, which only seemed to double its intensity. It wanted out of her, wanted escape from the confines of her body, awakened by the spark of fear and excitement. She grabbed on to the tethering ropes and shut her eyes.

No, she willed it. *No, you will stay where you are.*

For the first time, she realised what she had done when she turned down Cailin tu Moritat's offer to help her control her power. In one moment she saw clearly what her recklessness had achieved, the price of her impatience, her eagerness to avenge her family. If she let it go here, they would all die.

'Kaiku!' It was Tane, calling her name. He could see that something was wrong with her, but the air was awash with rifle fire, and she could not hear him.

She tried to forget the cries of the driver; deafened herself to the report of the rifles. Peripherally, she realised that some of the guards had noticed the second Aberrant beast and were rushing around to the other side of the caravan to deal with it. She turned her thoughts inward, forcing the heat back into her abdomen as if trying to keep down vomit or bile. The driver howled at her to help him, unable to understand why she had suddenly frozen. She ignored him.

And now it faded, reluctantly receding, defeated by the barrier of her will. Her eyes flicked open, bloodshot and tear-reddened, and she gasped and panted hard. The physical effort had been immense. But she had won out, for now.

The Aberrant beast hauled on the manxthwa again, bringing her roughly back to reality as the caravan was wrenched another few feet closer to the burrow. The manxthwa in its grip was apoplectic with fear, almost within biting distance of the thing. Kaiku cringed as the thing's chitinous limbs stroked the air above her.

She pulled a knife from her belt. It had been with her ever since the Forest of Yuna, when Asara had given her travel clothes to change into; she had scarcely noticed it until now. It was a good forest knife, adapted to skin animals or cut wood with equal ease. Swiftly, she began to saw at the tethering ropes that held the driver. He squirmed, attempting to break free before she had even got through the first one.

'Stay still!' she hissed, and he did so.

Tane and Asara fired, and fired again. The creature that had hold of the manxthwa was by no means immune to the bullets, for they could see the dark splashes of blood that spattered its black body; but it seemed possessed of a suicidal persistence, and would not release the bucking manxthwa from its grip. Tane's weapon fired dry, and he broke it open to put new ignition powder in the chamber, glancing at Kaiku as he did so. She was frantically working on the ropes, her arm pumping as she cut, her face red and sweaty.

The creature braced and hauled with a greater effort than before, desperate to get its meal and get away from the stinging rifle balls. It could not understand why the manxthwa was so heavy, for it had not the brain to realise it was tethered. The puzzle frustrated it mightily. It applied brute strength.

Kaiku cried out as the entire caravan shifted a metre across the road. Asara and Tane had to scatter as the passenger cart finally toppled upside down. Kaiku was pitched over with it, landing heavily on the stony dirt of the road and rolling to a stop a short way distant. The driver gave a strangled shriek, and then the tethering ropes, weakened by Kaiku's efforts, finally gave way. With a triumphant squawk, the Aberrant monstrosity bundled the manxthwa into its burrow and dragged it underground.

Tane scrambled to Kaiku's side, but she was already levering herself up on her elbows. Asara stood over the two of them, framed against the clouded sky, her rifle trained towards the Aberrant burrow.

'Are you hurt?' Tane asked, almost touching her and then thinking better of it.

Kaiku shook her head. 'I do not think so.' She stood up. 'Bruised,' she elaborated. 'Why have the guns stopped?'

Tane and Asara noticed it at the same time. The guards on their side of the caravan pricked up their ears. The train of carts that was snarled and corkscrewed along the centre of the road formed a barrier that prevented them seeing to the other side.

'Ho! Is all well over there?' one of the guards called.

'All's well,' came the reply.

They hurried around the end of the caravan, and there they saw the remainder of the guards clustered around the grotesque corpse of the second Aberrant creature. Its massive jaw lay on the road, its legs limp around it, half out of its burrow.

'It must have been a lucky shot,' said one, prodding it with the barrel of his rifle. 'We got the brain.'

'We should move out of here,' said a short, grizzled guard, evidently the leader. 'Take the remaining manxthwa, and two carts for passengers. Leave the rest.'

'Leave the goods?' another protested.

'There's no caravan master to sell them. We're not paid to deliver goods.' The leader jerked a hand at the approximate location of the other burrow. 'And that thing is still alive, and it will be out again as soon as it's finished its meal.'

All of them began to untangle the carts and right those that could be righted. Three guards stood near the burrow entrance, from which the sounds of crunching bone could be heard as the unfortunate manxthwa was devoured. The driver was disentangled from the ropes, but it was too late for him. His neck had been broken, and he stared glassy-eyed towards the earth.

'What was his name? The driver?' Tane asked as he lent his back to the effort of tipping a cart back on to its wheels.

'Why?' one of the guards replied.

'He should be named,' Tane grunted. 'To Noctu, recorder of lives.'

But nobody knew his name.

They managed to get two carts tethered to the remaining manxthwa, who could smell the blood of its departed companion and was snorting skittishly. The Aberrant beast did not emerge again, even after the sounds of feeding had ceased. Leaving the train of goods on the road, they took the body of the driver, wrapped in a tarpaulin, and bundled it in with them. In that manner, they drove on towards Chaim.

'Those monsters are your Aberrants, Asara,' Tane said as they set off, dejected and shocked and tired. 'Those are your *superior breed.*'

Overhead, the gristle-crows circled and swooped.

SEVENTEEN

Chaim had little to offer the traveller. It was a skeletal, sparse mountain village, with low houses of wood or stone scattered around a few rocky trails that wound haphazardly through the village. Everywhere the eye roamed it struck a hard plane; there was no softness of foliage, no sprinkle of mountain flowers or grass. Even the people seemed hard, squat and compact with narrow, dull eyes and brown, wind-chapped skin. It could not have been more different from the quaint, provincial charm of Pelis; this place seemed to have been scratched from the mountainside and built out of grudging necessity, and it loured in a stew of its own bleak misery.

It was not a place that welcomed strangers, but neither was it hostile to them. Kaiku, Asara and Tane found themselves simply ignored, their questions responded to with unhelpful grunts. Kaiku tried asking about for anyone who might remember her father passing through, but what began as a slim hope petered to nothing in the face of the villagers' stoic rudeness. In this place, a person either lived here or they didn't, and outsiders got short shrift from the natives.

They arrived in Chaim in the late afternoon. The caravan guards bade them a peremptory farewell, and they were left to themselves. Wandering through the simple streets of the village, buffeted by occasional gusts of cold wind and frowned upon by the rising peaks all around them, they felt curiously alone.

Asara's talents for procuring aid failed them in this desolate place. Their inquiries after a guide were met with ignorance and surliness, and her striking beauty appeared to have no effect on the men here. It piqued her mightily, Kaiku was amused to note.

'Probably they find their relief with their pack animals,' she muttered.

Eventually it was a guide who found them, as night gathered and lanterns were lit.

They were sitting in what passed for a bar here, merely the downstairs portion of someone's house that sold a raw local liquor. It was devoid of joy or atmosphere, a simple scattering of low, round tables cut from rough wood and a few threadbare mats for patrons to sit on. A stone-faced woman meted out measures of the liquor from behind a counter in the corner. Lanterns half-heartedly held back the gloom, while simultaneously contributing to it by the fumes from the cheap, smoky oil they were filled with. Despite being so small, and half-full with villagers who muttered to each other over their tumblers, the place still managed to feel cold and hollow. Kaiku could scarcely believe that a place like this existed. She had no illusions about the state of many bars in the Poor Quarter of Axekami, but she had always imagined them to be at least raucous, if not exactly brimming with celebration. This place seemed like a gathering of the condemned.

The three companions were contemplating their next move when a short, scrawny figure sat down with them. He was buried in a mound of furs that dwarfed his bald head, making him seem like a vulture. By the condition and tone of his skin, he was a mountain man like the rest of them, but when he talked it was in a rapid chatter that seemed quite at odds with his kinsfolk.

'I'm told you're looking for the mask-makers, that right?' he said, before any of them could wonder who he was. 'Well I'm here to tell you that it can't be done, but if you still want to try I'm your guide. Mamak!'

'Mamak,' Kaiku repeated, unsure if that was his name or some local exclamation that they did not understand. 'You will take us, then?'

'What do you mean, it can't be done?' Tane interrupted.

'As I said. The paths have been lost, and not even the greatest of mountain men have ever found them.'

'We knew that,' Kaiku said to Tane, laying a hand on his arm. 'Do not be discouraged.' She knew him well enough by now to see the signs of an impending mood swing, and Tane had been overdue for a plunge into miserable despair for hours, beleaguered as they had been by the events of the day. Apart from the frustration they had experienced since their arrival in Chaim, Tane had been dwelling on the fate of the driver of their caravan. The lessons of his apprenticeship to the priesthood were gnawing at his conscience. Nobody should die without being named to Noctu, he said; and yet it was only the caravan master who hired him who must have known the driver's name, and he was gone.

'If you cannot take us there,' said Asara coolly, resting her elbows on the table, 'then why do we need you?'

'Because you'd be lost within an hour,' he said with a quick grin, showing long teeth narrowed into crooked, browned columns by decay and neglect. 'And up in the mountains there's creatures so warped that you'd never be able to guess what kind of animal they originally came from. Like the thing that nearly had your lives on the way here.'

Asara did not trouble to ask how he knew about that. The guards had been talking, it seemed.

'Listen,' he said. 'It's not my way to pry into your business. You say you knew you were looking for a place that couldn't be found, and you still want to look. I'd guess you know something I don't. Or you think you do.' He sat back, splayed his fingers on the coarse wood of the table before him. 'I can take you to where the monastery *ought* to be. It still shows up on old maps, and nobody knows the mountains better than me. But when we get near, you'll see what I mean when I say it can't be found. You'll be walking down a trail, heading north, and all of a sudden you realise you've ended up a mile south, though you could've sworn you were checking your bearings every step of the way. There's something there, clouds a man's mind, turns you around, and no amount of care can get through it. Believe me, people have tried.' He tipped them a conspiratorial wink. 'Still want to go?'

'How much?'

'Five hundred poc. No, round it up to ten shirets.'

'You can have it in coins. I do not have paper money,' Kaiku lied. Her grandmother had always warned her about showing money in public, especially in places like this. Presumably Mamak thought he was overcharging, but it was still cheap by city standards.

Mamak shrugged. 'Five-seventy poc, then,' he said. 'In advance.'

'Three hundred now,' Asara said. 'The rest when we are up in the mountains.'

'As you'll have it,' he said.

'Good. When do we leave?'

'Have you booked into the inn yet?'

Asara made a sound to the negative.

'Then we can leave right now.'

'It's dark,' Tane pointed out.

Mamak rolled his eyes. 'The first stretch is a trail as big as a road. It'll take a few hours. We camp at the end of that, and in the morning we tackle the rough stuff. I suppose you have some kind of warm clothing?'

Asara showed him what they had brought. He tutted. 'You'll need more. This isn't the mainland. The nights up there aren't so warm, and the weather's a beast even in summer.' He stood. 'I have a man we can see. Best to get going.'

The next few days were hard.

Both Tane and Kaiku were quite used to the physical exertions of long journeys. Both had hunted in the forests, chased down deer and travelled far to lay traps or find a picturesque spot to fish or bathe. Tane, for his part, had often made forays for rare herbs into the lesser teeth of the Tchamil

Mountains, which blended into the Forest of Yuna on its eastern edge until the soil gave way to rock and the trees disappeared. But neither of them was quite prepared for the sense of wilderness that overtook them as they ascended into the Lakmar Mountains that dominated the northern half of Fo.

The mountains seemed to exude a sense of something that was like death but yet not: the absence of life. The unforgiving rock shouldered all around them in great, flattened slopes, yet there was rarely more than a fringe of tough grass or hardy weeds to be seen. What trees there were served only to remind them of the caravan driver's warnings of blight in the mountains; they were gnarled and crooked, sometimes with several scrawny trunks sharing the same withered branches, joined seamlessly together. Jagged peaks reared across the horizon, made bluish by distance; but the world around them was grey and hard. The silence was oppressive, and seemed to stunt conversation. The only one who seemed unaffected was Mamak, who chatted away as he walked, telling them old legends and stories of the mountains, many of which were variations of ones they knew from the mainland.

Kaiku, at least, was glad of his talk, for it distracted her from fatigue. The paths had become progressively steeper and harder as they travelled onward, and they were forced to climb often. This was the first serious exercise she had undertaken since her convalescence in the temple of Enyu, and her muscles ached. Tane seemed to be doing better, though his pride would not let him show fatigue; Asara was tireless.

Given time to contemplate, Kaiku found herself wondering more and more about Asara. During her time as Kaiku's handmaiden, they had been good friends, and shared many secrets. They had talked about boys, made fun of her father's foibles, teased the cook and picked on Karia, Kaiku's other handmaiden. And even though she knew it now to be a charade, and that Karia had ended unwillingly giving her life to resurrect her dead mistress, she missed that person Asara had been. This new Asara – presumably the real one, though how could she be sure? – was colder and harder, fiercely asserting her independence from everybody. She did not need reassurance or company, it seemed; she had no interest in talking about herself, nor did she appear to care about Kaiku or Tane. Tane accepted this as the way she was, but Kaiku was not so certain. Sometimes she caught glimpses of a stubborn child in Asara, balling its fists and scrunching its brow and protesting that it *didn't* want to talk to anyone. She was an Aberrant, that much Kaiku knew; but beyond that, her beautiful companion was still a mystery.

She thought about Tane, too. Before she had left the temple, he had made some small overtures to her in his awkward way about staying with him. She had been forced to deny him then, because she had to move on. He had followed her and joined her instead. He had told her of how the shin-shin had destroyed his temple, and how he was seeking the ones who had summoned them to exact his revenge; but Kaiku knew there was more to it than that, and she felt something . . . unfamiliar in response. Yet whenever she allowed herself to dwell on it, whenever her eyes roamed across his back and imagined the taut play of lean muscles beneath, her thoughts became soured. For Tane was a priest of nature, and she was an Aberrant. It was in his blood to hate her. And sooner or later, inevitably, he would find her out. Like Mishani.

She clamped down on her sorrow as soon as it bunched to spring. Mishani. That was a name forever in her past now. If she must live on, she must prepare herself to be shunned and despised, even by the ones she held most dear. Perhaps she was merely being obtuse, unwilling to accept what seemed the obvious truth: that Cailin tu Moritat and her Red Order were the only ones who would accept her now, the only ones who *wanted* her. Though she suspected their motives, she could not deny that. To everyone else, she was simply an Aberrant, and no different from the foul things which attacked their caravan.

Mamak seemed a capable guide, and they felt as safe in his hands as it was possible to feel in such an alien place. Many times he made them backtrack to avoid a bluff, or to take advantage of an overhang. Rarely did he explain why – one of the few things he was not overly vocal about – but whenever they wondered about the absence of the dangerous creatures they had been warned of, they thought of these detours and suspected it was thanks to him they had not met any. They did see smaller breeds, however: some whole and strange, and some malformed. These latter flopped inefficiently about, searching for food. They were usually cubs or chicks, for they would not survive to adulthood before becoming a meal for some superior predator. The evidence of these predators came at night, when the whistling wind was joined by eerie baying and yelping from unnatural throats. On the second night they had stayed awake, listening to the cries come closer and finally encircle them. But Mamak had not allowed a fire that night, and though they shivered, the creatures passed them by.

On the third day, the weather worsened.

They were caught out on a long, slanted table of bare rock when the storm hit, seemingly out of nowhere. Kaiku was shocked at the speed that the cloud cover darkened to glowering black, and the ferocity with which it unloaded on them. She was used to the slow, ponderous buildup of humidity on the mainland, when it was possible to sense precisely when a storm was about to break; here, there were no such indications. Mamak cursed and increased the pace, leading them up the exposed tilt of the rock towards shelter; but it would take several hours to traverse the open ground, and they feared the storm would overwhelm them by then.

Kaiku had never felt anything like it. The rain, icily cold, battered and smashed at her with such force that it stung the skin of her face. Lightning flashed and tore the air, and thunder blasted them and rolled through the creases of the mountains. It seemed that by being this high they were disproportionately closer to the cloud, and the violence of the storm's roar was enough to make them cringe. The wind picked up steadily until it pushed at them with rough shoulders, snapping from different directions in an attempt to tip them and send them tumbling away. As Mamak had advised, they had bought heavy coats for the journey, and they were never more glad than now; but even with their hoods pulled over their heads, the wind and rain slashed them with brutal force.

They bowed to the fury of the elements, forging on with their packs tugging at their backs. Their teeth chattered and their lips and cheeks were numb, but they wearily forced one foot in front of the other and hurried up the rocky slope, slick with rain. And each time Kaiku thought she could take no more, that she must somehow stop this assault immediately or just curl up and collapse, she looked up at the steep cliff they were heading towards and moaned in misery at how little ground they seemed to have made.

Eventually, the unendurable ended, and they stumbled into a cave, frozen and soaking and shivering. It was a good size for the four of them, its walls a ragged mess of black stone, shot through with scrappy veins of quartz which glistened as if moist. The floor was tilted slightly upward from the mouth, so it had mercifully stayed dry, even though they would still have taken shelter there if it had been inches deep. Mamak stalked to the back of the cave and angrily pronounced it unoccupied. Then he shouted and swore and stamped, profanities echoing off the uneven walls, cursing the gods in general and Panazu specifically for the storm.

'He seems annoyed,' Asara deadpanned, and Kaiku was so surprised that she started laughing, despite it all.

'I'm glad you two are in such good spirits,' Tane said morosely, and by his tone Kaiku guessed that the black mood which had been hovering over him of late had finally descended.

Mamak was leaning against the cave wall, his head rested on his forearm, breathing hard to relax himself. 'Warm yourselves as best you can,' he said. 'I'll make a fire.'

'With what?' Tane snapped, depression making him thorny. 'There's no wood on this damned mountain!'

It was not strictly true, but Mamak did not bother to correct him. 'There are other ways of making fire in the mountains,' he said. 'I have done this before, you know.'

Tane flashed him a sullen glare and marched to the entrance of the cave, where he sat alone, looking out at the lashing rain, with the fur lining of his hood rippling as stray gusts found their way in. Kaiku sat dripping against one of the walls, hugging her coat close around her, her jaw juddering from the cold. Asara sat down next to her. Kaiku gave her a look of vague puzzlement, for she had expected the other to sit alone; then Asara opened her coat, and put one arm around Kaiku, gathering her into the voluminous furred folds. Kaiku hesitated a moment, then relented, curling up into Asara with her hooded head on her companion's breast. Asara's damp coat enfolded her completely, like a wing, and Kaiku burrowed into the warmth of her body. In the hot, dark place that Asara had provided for her, she felt the shivering recede to the rhythm of Asara's heartbeat in her ear, and before she drowsed and slept she felt safer and more content than she had for a long time.

When she awoke, it was to a new heat. A fire was burning in the cave. Asara sensed her stirring and unfolded her wing; Kaiku blinked muzzily and relinquished Asara's body with some reluctance. She sat upright, meeting Asara's gaze, and gave her an awkward smile of thanks. Asara inclined her head in acceptance. Tane was watching them from the other side of the blaze, with undisguised disapproval in his eyes and something that he was loathe to admit as jealousy. Outside, the sky boomed and the storm raged unabated, but here in the cave there was a pocket of warmth and light that robbed its thunderous threats of potency.

'Awake then?' Mamak said cheerily. 'Good. We're going to have to sit this out. No telling how long it will be.'

Kaiku squinted at the flames. The fire burned with an amber hue, and at its base was not wood but a black, crinkly skeleton of thin fibres like spun sugar.

'Fire-moss,' Mamak said, anticipating her question. He held up a handful of the stuff; it was a black, soggy puffball. 'Weighs almost nothing, burns for hours. It secretes an inflammable residue, but its structure is extremely tough and takes a lot of heat to burn through. Useful tip if you don't have any wood to hand, and extremely portable.'

Inevitably, they talked. The storm showed no sign of abating, and so Mamak produced a jar of a sharp, murky liquor and passed it around to them. They had brought provisions for two weeks' travel, and so there were plenty of ingredients for a pot of vegetables and cured meat. Once their stomachs were full and their tongues loosened, they discussed and laughed and argued over a range of subjects. But it was Asara who introduced the one that occupied them most of the night: the affair of the Heir-Empress and the rising unrest in Axekami. The argument that ensued was not new to them, pitched between Asara, who was intent on challenging Tane's religious prejudice, and Tane, who was intent on defending it. Kaiku stayed out of it, unsure of her own feelings on the subject, and Mamak didn't care one way or another about Aberrants as long as they didn't try and eat him. Tane was in the midst of an assertion that the Heir-Empress could not possibly be good for the country because the country would never have an Aberrant as leader when Asara stopped him dead with a single question.

'Do any of you know what the Heir-Empress can actually do?'

There was silence. Tane fought for an answer, and found none. The fire was eerily silent, for there was no snapping of wood. Outside, the storm raged on, and if there were any Aberrants brave enough to venture out in it, they heard none.

'I thought not. Let me educate you, then, for you may find this very interesting. You especially, Tane. Have you heard of the Libera Dramach?' Before any of them could answer, she went on, 'No, you won't have. Their name is known among the people of Axekami, but they are only a rumour at present. That will soon change, I think.'

'What are they, then?' Kaiku asked, the shadows of her face wavering in the light of the burning fire-moss.

'In the simplest terms, they are an organisation dedicated to seeing the Heir-Empress take the throne.'

Tane snorted, making a dismissive motion with one hand. 'It's been scarcely a month since anyone even knew the Heir-Empress was an Aberrant at all.'

'We have known for years,' Asara replied levelly.

'We?' Mamak inquired, passing her the jar of liquor.

Asara sipped. 'I belong to no master or mistress,' she said. 'But as much as I can be said to be part of something, I am part of the Libera Dramach. Their aims and mine coincide, and have from the start.'

'And what are their aims?' Tane demanded.

'To see the Heir-Empress on the throne,' she repeated. 'To see the power of the Weavers destroyed. To stop the slaughter of Aberrant children. And to stop the blight that encroaches on the land.'

'How will the Heir-Empress's succession have any bearing on the malaise in our soil?' Tane asked. This had caught his interest.

Asara leaned forward so that her face was underlit in orange flame. 'She can talk to spirits, Tane. That is her gift. Spirits, animals . . . she is an element of nature, closer to Enyu than any human could be.'

'That's blasphemy,' Tane said, but not angrily. 'An Aberrant can't be *anything* to Enyu. And besides, her priests can talk to spirits. *I* can, to some degree.'

'No,' Asara corrected. 'You can listen. You can feel the spirits of nature, sense their mood; even the greatest among you has little more that a rudimentary understanding of them. They are to humans like the gods are: distant, unfathomable, and impossible to influence. But she can *talk* to them. She is eight harvests of age, yet already she can converse with a skill far beyond the best of Enyu's priests. And she gets better ever day. This is not something she has learned, it is something she was born with that she is learning to *use*. It is her Aberrant ability, Tane.'

Tane was silent for a time, head bowed. Mamak and Kaiku, sensing that this was between Asara and the acolyte, stayed out of it and waited to see what his reaction would be. Presently he stirred. 'You're suggesting that she could be a bridge to the spirits? Between us and them?'

'Exactly,' Asara said. 'For now, she is kept at the Imperial Keep, in the city, where men and women rule. But you know and I know that there are places in our land where the great spirits dwell, places where people such as us dare not go. But *she* could go. She is an ambassador, don't you see? A link between our world and theirs. If there is any hope of turning back the tide that is slowly swallowing us, then she is it.'

'How do you know?' Tane asked. He sounded . . . *over-whelmed*. Rather than the stoic denial Kaiku had expected from him, he seemed to be listening. Truly, he was an unpredictable soul. 'How did you know of it, before the rest of us?'

'That, I cannot tell you,' said Asara, with a soft sigh. 'I wish I could do so, to make you believe me. But lives are at risk, and loose talk can still undo what has been done.'

Tane nodded slightly. 'I think I understand,' he replied. He said nothing further for the rest of the night, merely stared into the fire, meditating on what he had been told.

The storm did not abate by the morning, nor the morning after that. They did not speak again of the Heir-Empress or the Libera Dramach; in fact, they spoke little of anything at all. Kaiku was becoming worried; she had never seen a storm that lasted so long, never imagined the sky could sustain such fury. And despite Mamak's assurance that such storms were not unheard of, the atmosphere in the cave became strained. When Tane suggested that Mamak might have been unwise to curse Panazu, god of storms, the two men nearly came to blows. Asara cleaned her rifle for the twentieth time and watched them owlishly.

As the day waned on the third night in the cave, Mamak announced that they had to turn back.

'This storm can't hold much longer,' he said, throwing another wad of fire-moss from their diminishing supply on to the small blaze they had going. 'But it's a good two days' journey yet to the site of the monastery, and that makes five to return to Chaim. If everything went perfectly to plan, if we left tomorrow and we found the monastery immediately and came right back, we would still only have a day's margin of food. You don't take risks like that in the mountains. I don't, anyway.'

'We cannot turn back!' Kaiku protested. 'I swore an oath to Ocha. We have to go on.'

'The gods are patient, Kaiku,' said Asara. 'You will not forget your oath, and nor will Ocha; but you cannot rush blindly at this. We retreat, and try again.'

'You'll die if you don't, besides,' Mamak put in.

Kaiku's brow was scored with a line of frustration. 'I cannot turn back!' she reiterated. Asara was puzzled at the desperation in her voice.

'But we must,' she said. 'We have no choice.'

Tane awoke several hours later. The storm howled and boomed outside, its tumult now a background noise. Kaiku was sitting at the fire, staring into its heart. She had been banking it up with fire-moss. Tane, still lying on his side, blinked at her and frowned. He had been withdrawn since his conversation with Asara, fiercely preoccupied with his own thoughts; now he noticed that Kaiku had lapsed into a similar attitude.

She jumped slightly when he spoke.

'Kaiku?' he observed. 'Why aren't you asleep?'

'When I sleep, I dream of boars,' she replied.

'Boars?'

'You turn back so easily, Tane,' she said, her voice soft and contemplative. 'I swore to the Emperor of the gods, yet you turn back so easily.'

He was still barely awake, and his eyes drowsed heavy. 'We will try again,' he mumbled. 'Not giving up.'

'Perhaps this was not your path to take after all,' she murmured to herself. 'Perhaps it is mine alone.'

If she said anything else Tane did not hear it, for he was drawn back into oblivion once more.

The next morning, Kaiku was gone. She had walked into the storm with only her pack and her rifle. And with her went the Mask.

EIGHTEEN

Mishani wore a robe of dark green for her audience with Lucia, and a wide sash of blue around her slender waist. The sash was more than decorative, for pressed against her lower back was the gift she had been charged to deliver. The slight bulge it made was hidden by her thick, ankle-length hair, which she had bound with blue strips of leather. A flat square of elegant wrapping paper, and within it the nightdress that would be the Heir-Empress's death.

It took every ounce of her carefully cultivated self-control to keep herself calm as she was escorted into the presence of the Empress. Quite aside from anything else, the prospect of having a garment riddled with bone fever pressed close to her skin was terrifying. Her father had assured her that the package was sealed tight, and its wrapping treated with odourless antiseptics to keep the disease inside; and besides, it was a very low-grade infection, and it would only take effect if breathed in over a period of time, such as in sleep. Mishani sneered inside at his words; it was bitterly obvious that he knew nothing about bone fever, that he was merely parroting the blithe assurances of Sonmaga. What had the Barak of Blood Amacha promised, that had turned her father into his lapdog, and *her* into his cat's-paw?

She was taken aback by her own vehemence. Before all this, she would never have allowed herself to think so uncharitably about her father. But as she was shown into the room where Anais was waiting, she was still certain that everything she felt was justified. He knew she could not refuse him, and he betrayed her by using that assurance for his own ends. She did not want to be party to murder; and to make her an assassin of the lowest kind, the sort of filth who would use *disease* as a weapon . . . The raw shame if she was caught would drive her to suicide.

And what of the shame if I succeed?

Her father was full of meaningless words: she would be averting a civil war, saving many lives, doing a great service for Saramyr. She heard none of them, knew them for the empty platitudes they were. She wanted to weep, to hug him and then shout in his face: *Do not do this, Father! Can you not see what will happen to us? It is not too late; if you change your mind now, I can still be your daughter.*

But he had not changed his mind. And she felt the bonds between them sawn apart so brutally that she could barely look at him. Suddenly she saw every annoying tic, every blemish on his face, every unpleasant quirk of his character. She did not respect him any longer, and that was a terrible thing for a daughter to admit.

She would murder for him, because she must. But after that, she was no longer his. She suspected he knew that, but he sent her anyway.

Sonmaga. Her hatred for him knew no bounds.

Mishani talked with Anais for some time, though afterward she hardly remembered what was said. The Empress was trying to divine Mishani's standpoint on Lucia's accession to the throne, but Mishani revealed nothing in her pleasant responses. Anais inquired after her father also, obviously hoping to learn why Mishani had come when the Barak was such a staunch opponent to her. Mishani said enough to assure Anais that she was approaching the situation with an open mind, and she did not believe in judging somebody she had never met.

But a cold dread was settling slowly on to Mishani as she spoke to the Empress. Was her mask slipping, and her own fear and trepidation showing through? Certainly it seemed as if the Empress was procrastinating, unwilling to show Mishani through to Lucia's chambers. She seemed frankly nervous. The package pressed against Mishani's lower back burned with the heat of the shame it bore. Could the mother sense she meant harm to the child? She felt perspiration prickle her scalp.

Then Anais was inviting her through, up to the gardens that nestled among the confusing maze of the Imperial Keep's top level. The temple to Ocha that was the centre point of the roof rose magnificently against the midday sky, and the four thin needles at each corner of the Keep reached higher still. The uppermost level of the sloping edifice was a labyrinth of gardens, small buildings, waterways and stony trenches which served as thoroughfares between them, like sunken streets. From below it was impossible to see there was anything up here, and Mishani had always borne the assumption that the roof was flat and featureless apart from the temple which was easily visible from anywhere in Axekami. Now she realised she was wrong; it was like a miniature district of the city. Mishani noticed also several squat guard towers around the gardens, and soldiers with rifles watching within.

'I apologise for all the guards,' Anais said as they came out into the blinding sunlight. She had noticed Mishani's furtive glance. 'The security of Lucia is paramount, especially now.'

'I understand,' Mishani said, feeling her throat tighten. She had hidden her package because she had little knowledge of how closely Lucia was guarded, and did not want to risk it being opened and checked. Though it would be a grave insult to imply that she meant the Heir-Empress harm, she did not dare take the chance. She wanted to give her gift to Lucia in secret if possible; but she doubted now that the opportunity would arise.

Anais seemed about to speak, thought better of it, then changed her mind again. 'I learned that someone had . . . got close to Lucia recently,' she intimated. 'Someone who could have done her harm.'

'How awful,' Mishani said, but inside she felt the tension slacken like an exhaled breath. So that was why she was nervous. She did not suspect Mishani.

They came across Lucia in the company of a tall, robed man

with a close-cropped white beard. They were standing in a small square that formed a junction between several paths, and were playing some kind of learning game that involved arranging black and white bead-bags in different formations on the flagstones. Trees rustled around them with the activity of squirrels and the stirring of the hot, sluggish air. As the Empress and Mishani arrived, they looked up and bowed in greeting.

'This is Mishani tu Koli,' she said to the group at large. 'And here is Lucia, and Zaelis tu Unterlyn, one of her tutors.'

Zaelis bowed. 'It's an honour to meet you, Mistress,' he said in a throaty bass.

Mishani acknowledged him with a nod, but she had barely taken her eyes off the Heir-Empress since she arrived. Lucia, in turn, was regarding her steadily with her pale blue, dreamy gaze, an almost fey expression on her face. Her blonde hair stirred in a soft gust of warm wind.

'Come and walk with me, Mishani,' Lucia said suddenly, holding her hand up.

'Lucia!' Anais exclaimed. She had never behaved in such a way before with guests; usually she was the model of politeness. Such an imperative request from a child to an adult was nothing short of impertinent.

'Lucia, remember your manners,' Zaelis cautioned.

'No, it's quite all right,' Mishani said. She looked to Anais. 'May I?'

Anais hesitated a moment, caught between her desire to have the child where she could see her and winning over Mishani. In the end, she did the only thing she really could. 'Of course,' she smiled.

Mishani took Lucia's hand, and it was as if some spark passed between them, a minute current that trembled up Mishani's arm. Her face creased slightly in puzzlement, but Lucia beamed innocently and led her away from the others down a paved path, across an immaculate lawn bordered by a dense row of tumisi trees, hemmed in from the rest of the gardens.

They walked in silence a short way. Mishani felt a creeping

nausea in her stomach. The child next to her seemed only that: a child. Like Kaiku, she was physically unmarred by her Aberrance.

I am to murder a child, she thought. *And by the foulest means imaginable.* It was what she had been thinking ever since her father asked her to do this, but now the reality of the situation crowded in on her and she began to suffocate.

'You must get tired of seeing people like me,' she said, feeling the sudden need to talk to distract herself. 'I expect you have met a lot of nobles over these past weeks.' It was an inanity, but she felt disarmed and it was all she could find to say.

'They think I'm a monster,' Lucia said, her eyes placid. 'Most of them, anyway.'

Mishani was taken aback to hear such words from an eight-harvest child's mouth.

'You don't, though,' she said, turning her face up to Mishani's.

She was right. It was different with her than it had been with Kaiku. She could not even consider this child as being Aberrant; not in the sense that she knew it, anyway. She felt the nausea in her gut become painful.

Spirits, I cannot do this.

They turned from the lawn into a shaded nook, where there was a simple wooden bench. Lucia turned them into it and sat down. Mishani sat next to her, smoothing her robe into her lap. They were away from the sight of anyone, but for a single raven perched on a distant wall of the garden, watching them with disconcerting interest.

I cannot . . . cannot . . .

Mishani felt her control teetering. She had almost hoped the Empress would stay with them, that the opportunity to give Lucia the parcel would not present itself; but the child was unwittingly making it easy for her.

'I have a gift for you,' she heard herself say, and her voice sounded distant over the blood in her ears. She felt the package slide free from her sash as she tugged it out, and then it was in her hands. Flat and square, gold-embroidered paper and a deep blue bow.

Lucia looked at it, and then at her. A sudden surge of emotion welled inside Mishani, too fast for her to suppress; she felt her lip quiver as she took a shuddering breath, as if she were about to weep. She forced it down, but it had been an unforgivable breach in her façade. Two years she had been practising the stillness and poise of court, two years of building her mask; but now she felt as a young girl again, and her confidence and poise had fled. She was not as strong as she had thought she was. She flinched and railed at her responsibility.

'Why are you sad?' Lucia asked.

'I am sad . . .' Mishani said. 'I am sad because of the games we play.'

'Some games are more fun than others,' Lucia said.

'And some are more serious than you imagine,' Mishani answered. She gave the child a strange smile. 'Do you like your father, the Emperor?'

'No,' Lucia replied. 'He scares me.'

'So does mine,' Mishani said quietly.

Lucia was silent for a time. 'Will you give me my gift?' she asked.

Mishani's blood froze. The moment that followed seemed to stretch out agonisingly. A sudden realisation had hit her: that she was no more prepared now to kill the child than she ever had been. She thought of her father, how proud she had always made him, how he had taught her and how she had loved him.

She shook her head, the tiniest movement. 'Forgive me,' she said. 'I made a mistake. This gift is not for you.' She slid it back into her belt.

Lucia gazed at her blankly with her strange, ethereal gaze. Then she slid along the bench and laid her head on Mishani's shoulder. Mishani, surprised, put her arm around the child.

Do not trust me so, she thought, burning with shame, *for you do not know what kind of creature I am.*

'Thank you,' Lucia whispered, and that destroyed the last of her composure. She felt the swell of tears expand behind her eyes, and then she wept, as she had not wept for years. She cried for Kaiku, and for her father, and for herself and what she had become. She had been so sure, so certain of everything, and yet all the certainties had been shattered. And here was the daughter of the Empress thanking Mishani for choosing not to murder her, and—

She looked up and into Lucia's eyes, her weeping suddenly arrested. It hit her then. She knew. The child *knew*. And yet Mishani wondered if she would not have taken the gift anyway, and worn it, and died if it were offered. She had the sudden prescience of being at the fulcrum of some terrible balance, that uncounted futures had depended on that single instant of decision.

Lucia gave her a shy smile. 'You should go and see the dream lady,' she said. 'I think you would like her.'

The crowd in Speaker's Square that evening was immense.

The square was a great flagged quad, bordered by tall rows of grand buildings. Its western side was almost entirely taken up by the enormous Temple of Isisya, the façade a mass of swooping balconies, mosaics and carvings, its lowest storey shaded by an ornamental stone awning that encroached on to the square, supported by vast pillars. The other buildings were similarly impressive: the city library – ostensibly public, but whose volumes were illegible to the peasantry, written as they were in High Saramyrrhic; the central administrative complex, where much of the day-to-day running of Axekami took place; and a huge bathhouse, with a bronze statue of a catfish resting on a plinth set into its broad steps, the earthly aspect of Panazu.

In the very centre of the square was a raised platform over which a carven henge was raised, its two upright pillars elegantly curving up to support the bowed crossbeam, on which was written in languid pictograms a legendary – and historically dubious – quote from the Blood Emperor Torus tu Vinaxis: *As painting or sculpture is art, so too the spoken word.*

The crowd crammed around the speaker's podium and spread all the way to the edges of the square, clogging the doorways of the surrounding buildings and spilling out into the tributary streets. Its mood was ugly, and it told in the scowls on people's faces and the frequent scuffles that erupted as patience ran out and fuses burned down. Its cheers in support of the speaker – and these were often and heartfelt – had a savage edge to them. Most of the crowd knew what they felt about the matter of the Heir-Empress already; they had come to hear someone who could articulate the rage and frustration and revulsion they nursed in their breasts, and agree with him. That someone was Unger tu Torrhyc.

Zaelis watched from beside one of the marble pillars of the city library, scanning the throng. They milled in the slowly declining heat of the evening, when the sun's light had reddened and the shadows of the buildings to the west stretched across the convocation, a sharp border dividing them into light and darkness. As Unger delivered a particularly barbed comment about the Heir-Empress, the crowd erupted in a roar, and Zaelis saw the glimmer of primal fury in the city folk's eyes, age-old hatred rooted so deep that they did not even remember its origins. Barely any of them knew that it was the Weavers who had planted that seed, the Weavers who had instigated and encouraged humankind's natural fear of Aberrants, and had been doing so for two centuries or more.

On the central platform of the square, Unger stalked between the red wooden pillars of the henge, prowling here and there while he orated, his voice carrying to all corners of the gathering as his hands waved and his wild hair flapped. He was not a handsome man, a little too short for his frame and his features large and blocky; but he had charisma, nobody could deny that. The passion was plainly evident in his voice as he harangued the multitude of the dangers that would beset Saramyr with an Aberrant on the throne. He used the stage like a master theatre player, and his tone and manner rode the swell of the crowd, becoming louder and louder until he was almost screaming, whipping his audience to fever pitch. What he was saying was nothing new, but the way in which he said it was so persuasive, the arguments he posited so unassailable, that he was impossible to ignore. And as his fame had grown over these past weeks, so his listeners had multiplied.

Zaelis felt a cold foreboding as he looked out over the crowd. The tension in the air was palpable. Axekami teetered on a knife-edge, and its Empress appeared to be doing nothing about it. Zaelis wondered in despair if Anais had even listened to her advisors as they explained the growing discontent in the streets of the capital, or if she had still been thinking of ways to win the high families round to her side. She was so preoccupied by the reports of Blood Amacha and Blood Kerestyn massing their forces that she had no time to consider anything else; and as much as he respected and admired her, he had to admit that she was guilty of the arrogance of nobility. Deep down, she did not believe that the underclasses were capable of organising themselves enough to hurt her. She saw Axekami as a creche, swarming with unaccountably wilful children who had to be kept in line to prevent them from harming themselves. The idea that they might throw off their loyalty to her over this matter had occurred to her on a superficial level, but no more. She suffered from a lack of empathy; she could not understand the level of hatred they bore for her beloved child. She underestimated the dread the word *Aberrant* still evoked in the common man.

But Zaelis's real concern was for Lucia. With two factions already building their forces against her, Anais could not afford to fight on a third front, this one *inside* the walls of her city. If any of the forces opposed to her won the victory, then

Lucia's life would be forfeit. No matter that she was not the monster they imagined her to be – though he had to admit she frightened even him at times, and the gods only knew what kind of power she would wield in adulthood if she continued developing at the rate she was going. She would have to be killed because of what she represented.

Zaelis thought about that for a time, ignoring the rhetoric that Unger tu Torrhyc threw out to the crowd like bloody bones to baying hounds. Then he left, his thoughts dark, pushing his way through the throng and back towards the Imperial Quarter.

He did not notice the man in grubby baker's clothes as he passed by on the outskirts of the gathering. Nor would he have troubled himself about it if he *had* noticed; he had more important things on his mind than that. Perhaps he would have puzzled over the man's odd expression – a combination of furtiveness, defiance and feverishness. He might have noticed the heavy pack the baker carried, triple-strapped shut. And if he had waited long enough, he might have seen the second man arrive, also carrying a heavy pack, and the grim mutual recognition passing between them, as of two soldiers meeting on a battlefield over the carnage of their dead companions.

None of that would have meant anything to Zaelis, had he not simply walked on by. And besides, it was only one of many similar meetings across the city that had been going on ever since the news of the Heir-Empress broke. Only a seed, another small part of one of Axekami's endless intrigues.

The baker and his new companion – neither of whom had met before – slipped away from the crowd without a word, towards a place that both of them knew but neither had ever been to. A place where others of their kind were gathering, each carrying another deadly load in their packs.

NINETEEN

In the mountains, the snow fell thick, carried on a wind that blew down from the peaks and whipped the air into a whirling chaos of white, a blizzard that wailed and blustered along the troughs and passes.

A solitary woman walked in the maelstrom wearing a red and black Mask, using her rifle as a staff to support her exhausted body. She staggered through the knee-deep crust, beneath a skeletal cluster of trees that rattled their snow-laden branches violently at her. She slipped and fell often, partly from the treacherous, uneven floor of stone under the crust, but more because her legs were failing, her strength eroded with every gust of wind that buffeted her. Yet each time she fell, she rose again and forged onward. There was little else she could do. It was that, or lie down and die there.

The mountains had become one endless, featureless ascent; a blanket of white delineated only by the lines, ridges and slopes where the black rock of the mountains poked through. Some distant part of her told her it was unwise to be trudging up this shallow trench, a wide furrow in the mountainside with stone banks rising to shoulder-height on either side. Something about snowdrifts. But the voice was fractured, and she could not piece it together enough to make sense of it.

Kaiku barely knew where she was any more. The cold had numbed her so much that she had lost sensation in her extremities. Exhaustion and incipient hypothermia had reduced her to a zombie-like state, slack-jawed and clumsy, pushing herself mechanically onwards with no clear idea of where she was going. She was a being entirely of instinct now, and that instinct told her to *survive*.

She had lost count of the days since she had left the cave where she had sheltered with Tane, Asara and Mamak. Five? Six? Surely not a week! A miserable week spent in this forsaken wilderness, starving, frightened and alone. Each night huddled and shivering in some hole, each day a torture of frustration and terror, searching for paths while cringing at every sound, and hoping that whatever made it might be something she could catch and eat rather than something that would catch and eat *her*.

How much longer would Ocha test her so?

Back in the cave, she had been visited by the same dream every time she closed her eyes. In it she saw a boar, and nothing more. It was huge, its skin warty and ancient, its tusks chipped and yellowed and massive. The boar said nothing, merely sat before her and looked at her, but in those animal eyes was an eternity, and she knew she was looking at no mere beast but an envoy of Ocha. She was struck by awe, filled with an ache and a wonder more potent than any meditation she had ever been able to achieve, a vast sorrow mingled with a beauty so enormous, so overwhelming and fragile that she could not help but weep. But there was something else in the boar's eyes, in its doleful face. It *expected* something of her, and it mourned because she was not doing it, and its grief tore her heart apart.

She woke each time with tears running down her cheeks, and the sadness lingered long into the morning. She did not speak of it to the others. They would not have understood. Nor did she understand, then. It was only in that moment of perfect clarity, when she had stared into the fire after all were asleep, that she knew. Ocha had heard her oath made in the Forest of Yuna. She was to avenge her family. He would not brook delay or retreat; he demanded action and strength of heart.

And so she did the only thing she could do: she took the Mask, and walked into the storm. Though the wind tore at her and the rain lashed her with freezing darts, she knew at that moment what she was doing was the will of the Emperor of the gods.

After that, things deteriorated.

For a day she stumbled through the furious wind and rain and lightning. The pain of endurance seemed nothing to her at first, for she knew it was not without purpose. But soon it began to wear at her resolve, as her teeth chattered and her skin prickled with freezing droplets. She pulled her hood tighter to her head and staggered on, not knowing where she was going, trusting to Ocha to guide her.

How she survived that first day, she did not know; her existence had degenerated into a nightmare in which the very air was against her, trying to push her over with great gusts and whipping her exposed skin mercilessly. Her lips were cracked and her eyes bloodshot, her cheeks tender and raw.

She found herself an overhang for shelter, little more than a scoop of rock in a sheer, broken face. It kept off the rain from above, but water still ran along the ground from upslope and the wind howled through her niche. At some point during the day, unnoticed by Kaiku, the thunder had passed on, and this was her first glimmer of hope; for though she believed she could not make another day in this storm, she knew she would be moving on whatever the weather at dawn. She prayed to Panazu for an end to the downpour.

Somehow, she slept, exhaustion overcoming the excruciating discomfort of her meagre shelter. That night, she dreamt nothing.

She awoke to the splash and patter of water, and the dazzling light of a cold, clear sky turning the flat planes of wet stone to sparkling brightness. The storm had passed.

Painfully, she pulled herself from her shelter and tried to stand up in the glare of Nuki's single eye. A crippling cramp put her back down on to her knees, the legacy of sleeping on freezing rock. One of her arms and one thigh were numb, and she could not curl her fingers more than a feeble twitching.

But soon the blood returned to her body, and she flexed her hand into a fist; and though she ached, she felt an inner rejoicing, and sent thanks to Panazu for answering her prayer.

She stood up then, and looked about. The mountains seemed so different when she was standing on them than they did from a distance. From afar, their immensity rendered them simple, vast ridges of rock that tapered towards a peak. But once among the folds and crevices and slopes and bluffs that formed their skin, it was suddenly more complex, for stone reared high all around and it was difficult to imagine a world outside, where the land was flat and not circumscribed by frowning buttresses of grey and black. Perspective became skewed, and navigation ceased to be as easy as it seemed from a vantage outside the mountains.

She took the Mask from her pack and looked at it. It leered back at her, an insouciant, disrespectful smirk frozen on its red and black face. For this, her family had died. For this a temple of Enyu had been destroyed, its priests slaughtered. She turned it over and examined it. She held in her hands a True Mask, and if she believed what she had been told, it would show her the path to the place where it was made. The hidden monastery where the Weavers lived.

She had been putting the moment off as long as she could, fearful of that small margin Mishani had warned her about, the slim chance that she might slide through the seams in the wood into insanity and death. But really, she had made her choice when she decided to walk out of the cave, and procrastination felt false now.

The time had come. She put it to her face.

The effect, if anything, was something of an anticlimax. She did not die, nor go insane. She felt a certain strangeness, a sensation of being detached from the world she saw through the carven eyepieces; and the wood of the Mask seemed to warm and soften against her face, feeling more like a new layer of thick skin than something rigid. Then there was an overwhelming contentment, like sinking into the plush folds of a soft bed. After a time this faded as well, and she felt only faintly foolish for having been so worried.

She set off again. She had not known what kind of guidance she might expect from the Mask, and for a time she doubted it was guiding her at all. Then she remembered what Cailin had told her, that the Mask would only work once they neared the monastery. But how far was that, and in what direction? It could be on the other side of the mountains!

She shook herself mentally. Such thoughts brought her no profit. She had taken this journey as an act of faith, and faith was needed to sustain her. She believed that Ocha would not abandon her so, when it was he who had set her on this path. But then, who knew the ways of the gods, and what mortal pieces they might discard or forget in whimsy or caprice?

The next few days were progressively worse. Her meagre rations dwindled to nothing; most of the food had been in Mamak's pack. She wandered higher and higher into the mountains, taking no direction, choosing instead that the gods should determine her way.

She came across small Aberrant creatures time and again, often so malformed that they were slow enough to catch with her hands, or pick off with her rifle. But she would not eat Aberrant flesh; she mistrusted it abominably. Out of desperation, she tried a fleshy root that poked from cracks in the stone at the base of rivulets and small waterfalls, feeding tough, thorny weeds. It made her gag and retch, but it was subsistence. She dared not try others she saw, for the trees and plants they supported seemed warped by blight, and she feared poisoning herself. She broke away bundles of brittle twigs from the crooked trees for firewood, but they were near-impossible to burn, and she could only ever manage a small blaze after an hour of effort, by which time it seemed scarcely worth it.

By the next day the fleshy root disappeared entirely, and

she was forced to spend most of her day foraging for food, which slowed her further. The temperature dropped sharply. Her route was taking her higher into the peaks, and frost dusted the ground, even in the sunlight. She wrapped her coat tight around her, but the cold seemed to seep in anyway, and her teeth chattered whenever she stood still for more than a few minutes. She stuffed the coat with grass and whatever bitter foliage she could find and used it as insulation.

The terrain became hard, and she found herself climbing. Twice she escaped death by pure chance, when some instinct warned her a handhold was about to crumble or a ledge was unstable. Other times she hid in fear as great, shaggy manthings lumbered past her, or stood in grey silhouette, haunting the horizon. The Aberrants bayed at night, when she froze in hollows or crevices she had squeezed herself into for shelter; but miraculously, though it seemed they were all around, she did not come across a single one at close quarters. They were distant things, suggested shapes that moved in valleys far below or lurked in shadows. Gristlecrows glided overhead now and again, but they did not seem interested in the stumbling figure beneath them. Perhaps they recognised her purpose, and kept away.

This is my test, she repeated to herself, a mantra that kept her walking and putting one foot in front of the other. *This is my test*. But at some point her mind wandered, and when it came back to her the mantra had changed. *This is what I deserve. This is what I deserve.*

And she knew then the real reason why she had walked out into the storm that night. Starvation and exhaustion had chased the clutter from her mind. Here, though she sweated and reeked and felt like an animal rather than a woman, though she had scrabbled in the dirt for foul roots to abate the ache in her stomach, she had found self-knowledge and clarity.

She hated herself.

I am Aberrant, she thought. *And I will pay for it, and pay again, until my debt is met.*

And then the blizzard came, howling out of nowhere and catching her unawares. There was no shelter for her, no respite from the maelstrom. She felt the cold of death settle into her marrow. Her lips were tinged blue, her tanned skin pale, her muscles cramped and aching. Tiny crystals of ice hid in her eyelashes, having found their way through the eye-pieces of the Mask. She shivered uncontrollably as if palsied. Such weather would have tested the hardiest of mountaineers, but Kaiku was starving, tired, and under-equipped. Soon the cold seemed to seep away, and she began to feel the heaviness of sleep upon her, dragging her down, dulling her mind.

When I sleep, I die, she said to herself, and some force inside her kept her walking, powered by will alone. She had something she had to do, something she was meant to . . . something . . . something . . .

Then, a light. She blinked away snow, disbelieving. There was fire, burning within a cave, bright with warmth. Heedless of danger and bereft of thought, she staggered towards it, knowing only that warmth meant life. Her rifle, which she had been using as a walking staff, still trailed in her numb hand, cutting trenches in the snow behind her. Now she could smell cooking meat, and her hunger quickened her pace. She tripped and stumbled the last few feet, almost falling into the cave, a small avalanche of snow around her boots.

There was something sitting at the fire, a shape confusing enough that her bewildered and deadened brain could not at first pick it out. Then it shifted, and a long sickle gleamed in a hand. None of this really registered with Kaiku, until she heard a shriek and saw a flurry of movement come racing towards her; then instinct took over, and she brought up her rifle to protect herself. There was a chime of metal, and her rifle was jarred in her hand by the sickle; then the report of the weapon, deafening at such close range, as something warm and heavy crashed into her. They went down together in silence, landing in the snow, Kaiku still too confused and stunned by the noise of the rifle to understand what was happening. She did not even realise it had been primed.

They lay there, still, the musty smell of the thing atop her slowly pervading Kaiku's senses.

This was strange, she thought.

Then she felt the liquid warmth spreading across her collarbone and throat and down her chest. Blessed warmth! The feeling brought back the memory of the fire, suddenly like a beacon to her. Slowly and by degrees, she shifted the bulk of the thing that had attacked her, not even caring what it was or why it had stopped moving. She crawled to the fire, and the heat of the blaze made her skin sear and itch; but she endured it long enough to pull the roasting creature from the spit before she retreated to a less painful warmth. The gods knew what it was, but it was the size of a small rabbit. She tore off her Mask. Aberrant or not, she no longer cared. Greedily, she ate the meat half-cooked, blood running down her chin to meet the blood that soaked her neck and breast, but before she got past halfway she had fallen asleep, sitting cross-legged with her head hanging inside its furred hood.

She awoke several times throughout the next few days, though she remembered virtually nothing of them afterwards. There was a small hoard of firewood stacked at the back of the cave, and a pack with delights such as bread, rice and a jar of sweet fried locusts, hunks of dried meat and even a smoked fish. Like a dream-walker, Kaiku rose periodically, motivated by bodily needs too primal to bother her conscious mind. Somehow the fire kept going, even though it almost burned out twice; Kaiku automatically dumped firewood on it when her precious source of warmth seemed ailing. She ate, too, mechanically dipping into the pack and eating the food therein with no preparation; she did not cut the meat, nor the bread, but bit mouthfuls of both off and then fell asleep again.

Finally, she returned to true wakefulness and realised that she was still alive. It was night, but the fire was burning low, and the blizzard had stopped. Shadows shifted disconcertingly across the rock walls with the capricious sway of the flames. The whimpering cry of an Aberrant beast sounded distantly, echoing across the peaks. For a time she lay where she was, trying to remember. She could not think how long she had slept, or even recall how she came to be here. The last thing she remembered was the blizzard.

She put fresh firewood on the blaze, thanking providence for this haven but still utterly confused, and it was then that she saw the thing at the mouth of the cave. Puzzled, she walked over to it. At first it seemed like a heap of discarded cloth in a tailor's store. Looking closer, she saw that it was a robe, a heavy garment patched together from a multitude of different hides and materials with no sense of order or symmetry. With her boot she pushed the corpse over on to its back.

The robe was indeed heavy, with a cowl that was far too big, threatening to swallow the face it sheltered. But it was not a face; it was a Mask. A strange, blank thing, white, its brow quirked as if curious, with a carven nose but no mouth. The right side, from cheek to chin, was bored with small holes such as might be found on a musical pipe or a horn, set in no particular pattern. The left side was cracked and shattered by a rifle ball, and its ivory colour stained and bloody. The furs around the stranger's neck were flaky red with dried gore.

She looked down at the figure for a long while before gingerly removing the Mask. The face beneath was pale and hairless, with bulbous eyes frozen wide in death and narrow, white lips. A little freakish in appearance, perhaps, but definitely a man. A Weaver. She had killed a Weaver.

The stranger's coat looked warm. Kaiku set about stripping it off the corpse. Suddenly energised, as if in reaction to the days of inactivity in the cave, she took snow in her hands and scrubbed out as much of the blood as she could, then set it to dry by the fire.

When she was done, she stripped the corpse's underclothes – even the soiled and wet leggings that felt like sealskin – and washed them too. Her fear of the cold was greater than her disgust at the voiding of the man's bladder and bowels in death. With those set to dry, she rested by the fire.

Later she dressed herself anew, stuffing her own clothes into her pack. The leggings and hide vest fit snugly, and the heavy robe of patchwork fur was extremely warm. She began to sweat in the heat of the fire, and relished the discomfort for its novelty.

Whoever this Weaver was, he had been on a journey when he was caught in the blizzard. He had provisions for several days' travel, and he had gathered firewood before the snows became too bad. He was digging in to wait for the snowstorm to pass. It was this stranger's foresight – and the fact that he had conveniently managed to die – that had saved Kaiku's life.

This man came from somewhere, Kaiku thought. She wondered how far away that somewhere was.

She ate, slept, and woke with the sun. It was a new dawn, fresh snow was on the ground, and the sky was a clear blue. Today was the day she would leave.

She picked up her father's Mask and looked at it, as she had done many times before. Its vacant gaze held no answers. She put it on, and once again it gave her nothing.

'I am not done yet, Father,' she mumbled to herself, and set forth into the snow again.

TWENTY

The Barak Avun's rage knew no limit.

'You had her alone, you offered her the gift, and then you *took it back*?' he cried.

Mishani looked at her father, all glacial calm and studied poise. Her hands were tucked into the sleeves of her robe and held before her; her hair fell in black curtains to either side of her thin face. They were in his study, a small, neat room with dark brown furniture and a matching wooden floor. Fingers of evening light reached through the leaves of the trees outside and in through the shutters, tickling bright motes and making them bob and dance.

'I did, Father,' she replied.

'Ungrateful child!' he spat. 'Do you know what we were promised for your service? Do you know what your family would have gained?'

'Since you saw fit to exclude me from your dealings with Sonmaga,' she said icily, 'I do not.'

Mishani was really quite surprised by the vehemence of her father's reaction to her news that the Heir-Empress had not received the infected nightdress. He seemed to have abandoned all dignity, red-faced and shaking with anger in a way that she had not seen him before. The remnants of the old Mishani wanted to comfort her father, or at least fear his wrath; but in her heart, she was scorning him. How easily she had torn away his façade of unflappability. She had told him the honest truth about what had happened in the roof gardens of the Imperial Keep. She could have lied, told him that Lucia was too well guarded or that they had intercepted the gift she brought; but she would not degrade herself so.

She held herself with pride in the face of her father's fury. If not for years of conditioning, she would not even have troubled to maintain the formal mode of Saramyrrhic used to address a parent.

'Where did I fail with you, Mishani? Where is your loyalty to your family?' He paced around the room, unable to stand still. 'Do you know how many lives would have been saved if you had done what I asked?'

'If I had murdered an eight-harvest child?' Mishani replied. Her father glared at her. 'Say it, then, Father. Do not hide behind euphemisms and evasive language. You are quite willing to have me bear the burden of your actions; at least have the courage to admit them to yourself.'

'You have never spoken to me this way, Mishani!'

'I have never had cause to until now,' she said. Her voice was perfectly level, chilling in its rigidity. 'You dishonour yourself, Father, and you dishonour me. I do not care to know what Sonmaga promised you. Even if it were the keys to the Golden Realm itself, it would not have been worth what you asked me to do. You made yourself his pawn for a reward; that I could understand. But you made me your pawn because you knew I could not refuse. You took advantage of me, Father. I would have done anything you asked if I could have done it with honour, no matter how hard it was. I have killed to protect you before!' His eyes widened at this; though he had suspected the death of Yokada to be no accident, the admission was still a surprise. 'But *this*? To give an infected nightdress to a child, and have her die a lingering death? I will not stoop so low, Father. Not even for you.'

Avun was almost choking with rage. 'How dare you suggest that your honour is greater than mine in this matter?'

'I suggest nothing,' said Mishani. 'You went through with this deed. I, at the last, did not.'

'She is an Aberrant!' Avun cried. 'An Aberrant, you understand? She is no *child*. She should have been killed at birth.'

Mishani thought of Kaiku, and the words came from her

mouth before she could stop them. 'Perhaps that is not the way things should be, then.'

Her vision exploded in a blaze of white, and she was on the floor, her hair like a black wing over her fallen body. It took a few seconds to realise that she had been struck, hard, across the face. Surprise and pain threatened tears, but she swallowed them back and quelled any reaction on her face. She looked up at her father with infuriating calm. His bald pate was sweating, his eyes bulged. He looked ridiculous.

'Viperous girl!' he said. 'To turn on your own family this way! You will go back to Mataxa Bay tomorrow, and there you will stay for the season, and when winter comes we may see if you are my daughter again.'

He glared at her a moment longer, waiting to see if she dared to offer a rejoinder that he could punish her for. She would not give him the satisfaction. With a snort, he stalked out of the study.

She went to the servants' yard almost immediately, detouring past her room on the way to apply a face powder that would hide the bruise on her jaw. It did an adequate job, though it made her look a little sickly. Well, it would have to do. If she was leaving for Mataxa Bay tomorrow – and she could scarcely stay with things as they were – then she had business to attend to this evening.

She found Gomi currying the horses in the stables. He was a short, stocky man with a shaven head and flat features, managing to combine an impression of wisdom, earthiness and reliability in their assemblage. He bowed low when he saw her silhouetted in the light at the stable door, but Mishani fancied she saw something unpleasant in his eyes as he did so. Yokada, the servant girl Mishani had poisoned to protect her family's reputation, had been his niece.

'Bring the horses and prepare the carriage,' she said. 'I wish to go out.'

A short time later they were travelling through the streets

of the Imperial Quarter, heading down the hill towards where the burnished ribbon of the River Kerryn slid through the city. Gomi was driving, sitting at the front with the reins of the two black mares in his hands. The carriage was as black as the horses, chased with elegant reliefs of blue lacquer and edged in gold around its spokes, a testament to the wealth of Blood Koli.

Mishani sat inside, looking out of the window. The clean, well-maintained thoroughfares of the Imperial Quarter seemed bland now, where before she had always enjoyed the sight of the ancient trees, fountains and carvings that beautified the richest district in the city. Vibrant mosaics had lost their colour; the play of shadow and reddening sunlight across the plazas was no longer attractive. Where once the wide streets and narrow alleys that sprawled up the contours of the hill had seemed to harbour intrigue and whisper of secrets, now they were just streets, robbed of mystery. She felt washed-out somehow, a lifetime of assumptions and conditioned responses turning to driftwood in the current of events. Her mind strayed to Kaiku again and again, and a single question weighed on her heart like a tombstone.

Was I wrong to do what I did?

The streets of the Imperial Quarter gave way to the Market District, and traffic thickened around them. Though Nuki was fleeing westward and the ravenous moons would soon come chasing into the night, the markets did not sleep until long after dark. They clustered together in an interlinked series of squares, set at uneven angles to each other and connected by winding sandstone alleys. The city here had a rougher edge, less well maintained than the Imperial District, but it was possessed of a comforting vibrancy. The squares were thick with noisy stalls, multicoloured awnings of all shapes and sizes piling on top of each other for space. The air smelled of a dozen kinds of food: fried squid, potato cakes, sweetnuts, saltrice, all mingling amongst the jostle of cityfolk that milled to and fro.

But even the steadily growing babble and ruckus ahead did little to lift her spirits; where once it had seemed a thriving hive of life, now she heard only a senseless cacophony of meaningless cries, like the voices of madmen.

She thought of her destination, and wondered if she herself was entirely rational. *You should go and see the dream lady,* the Heir-Empress had said; and when she left the Imperial Keep, Mishani had realised that she knew where the dream lady was, without a word on the subject being spoken between them. She knew, as if something had touched her heart and shown her.

The child both terrified and fascinated her. There was no questioning that she was special; but was she evil? *Could* an eight-harvest child be evil? She thought of the malformed infant who made flowers grow wherever her fingers touched. Had *she* been evil, or just dangerous? The difference was important, but it had never seemed to matter until now.

And here she was, on her way to see Lucia's dream lady. What she might expect, she had no idea; but she knew that she had to find out before she was sent away from the city. For Kaiku, for Yokada, for her father, she wanted to be shown a truth.

Gomi, perhaps out of spite, had chosen a route that skirted the edge of the busiest market square in the district, and they were soon slowing as they forced their way through roads crowded with lowing animals and jabbering cityfolk who darted between the carriages and carts that choked the road-way, carrying with them baskets of fruit and bread or hurrying furtively away to their homes.

Mishani frowned. Even preoccupied, she noticed the atmosphere that prevailed here. The sounds of the Market District *were* different, and not only to her ears. She saw other passengers and drivers looking about in confusion. Stalls were packing up and being deserted. Customers were fleeing the square. It was not happening all at once, but rather an unevenly spread phenomenon. Everywhere Mishani looked, she saw people locked in intense discussion before hurrying to their friends to pass on what they had heard. The traffic had choked almost to a halt now, and Gomi scratched the thin rolls of fat at the back of his neck and shrugged to himself.

Mishani leaned out of her carriage door a little way and called to a boy coming up to his twelfth harvest. It was undignified to do so, but she had a creeping concern that there was something happening she should know about. The boy hesitated, then came over to her, subservient to her obvious status as a noble.

'What is going on here?' she asked.

'The Empress has arrested Unger tu Torrhyc,' the boy said. 'Over at the Speaker's Square. Imperial Guards took him away.'

Mishani felt a shadow of dread climb into the carriage with her. She did not need to, but she gave the boy a few coins anyway. He took them gratefully and ran. She sensed the air of impending panic, and feared it. The people knew as well as her what would come of arresting the most popular and outspoken opponent to the Empress among the common people. Mishani cursed silently. She had thought the Empress arrogant before in the way she ignored the cityfolk and concentrated only on the nobles; now she was staggered by her foolishness. To inflame an already enraged populace by publicly arresting their figurehead was nothing short of an incitement to riot.

'Gomi!' she called, leaning out of the window again. 'Can you get us away from here?'

She saw him turn around to reply, his mouth opening in an O, and then the world exploded around her.

The carriage was lifted from the road in an ear-shattering tumult and a flash of light. She felt herself thrown heavily back inside the carriage as it was swatted aside by the force, and a split second later the door where her head had been punched inward, smashing into splinters. The whole side of the carriage crumpled in on her, splitting into wooden daggers, but she had neither the time nor the purchase to react, and instead she could only watch in shock as the confining wooden box she rode gathered in to crush her life away.

Suddenly, overwhelmingly, there came a single picture in her mind, strong enough to be a vision. Time seemed to freeze outside, and Mishani was once again on the beach at Mataxa Bay, with the summer sun sparkling on the rippling waves. She was perhaps ten harvests old, and laughing, running breathlessly through the surf. Behind her came Kaiku, holding a sand-crab the size of a dinner plate before her, laughing also as she pursued her friend. And there was nothing in Mishani's heart at that moment but joy, and carelessness, and freedom.

Then: reality. She blinked.

The side of the carriage had crumpled and splintered, and the broken blades of wood had stopped mere inches from her.

She began to breathe again. Sounds from outside filtered in. Screams arose; first a single one, then many. She heard the hungry growl of flame, running feet, cries for help. Stunned, she could not piece together the evidence of her senses to determine what had happened. Instead, she concentrated on freeing herself from the coffin that her carriage had become. She had been thrown up against one door when the other one caved in, but it had been buckled by the impact and would not open when she tried it. Twisting herself within the dark confines of the carriage, she elbowed the shutters open – which had been closed by the force of the explosion – and mercifully they gave easily. She clambered out, her hair snagging on loose bits of wood as she emerged into the evening light.

It took only moments to see what had happened. The epicentre of the blast was clearly visible by soot marks. Something – perhaps a cart, for it was now impossible to tell – had exploded by the side of the road, destroying the fascia of a money-house. Shattered wreckage of carriages and horses reduced to smoking meat surrounded the epicentre; they had absorbed the blast that would have otherwise killed Mishani. Instead, her carriage had been thrown against the side of another carriage to her right; the two of them had merged into a mess of wreckage.

All around, the carnage was horrific. Men, women and children lay still on the road, or hung impaled where they had been flung against a heap of jagged debris. The wounded moaned and writhed or staggered among them, some newly bereft of a limb. The air tasted of blood and sulphur and acrid smoke. Plaintive wails issued from a noble lady who was kneeling by the scorched corpse of her husband. Gomi lay next to the dead horses that had drawn her carriage, his brains dashed out on the road. A fire was burning some-where, and outside the blast area people were shrieking and fleeing in headlong panic. Mishani flinched as another explo-sion tore through the air nearby, and a hail of pebbles and splinters pattered across her head. The screams were silenced, only to begin anew.

She gazed at the mayhem with the dull, slack face of a sleepwalker. Then, slowly, she began to walk, not hearing the cries for help or seeing the bloodied hands that reached out in supplication. There was no sense in returning home, back to the protection of a father who had betrayed her. She was heading for the River District, and the dream lady.

The Guard Commander was thrown to his knees before his Empress in a clatter of armour.

'You gave the order,' she accused.

The throne room of the Imperial Keep was less ostentati-ous than some of the state rooms, but its décor was heavy and grave, befitting the business that was conducted there. Arched windows were set high in the walls, slanting light down on to thick hangings of purple and white, the colours of the Blood

Erinima standard. Braziers smoked gently with incense, set on high, thin poles, corkscrews of silver that stood on either side of the dais where the thrones rested. The thrones themselves were an elaborate fusion of supple, varnished wood and precious metals, coils of bronze and gold interweaving across its surface in seamless unity.

Anais rarely came in here except during times of crisis or meetings of extreme importance; the air of intimidation that the throne lent her was an edge she did not usually need. She had been receiving report after hurried report for an hour now, but it all came down to one thing: Unger tu Torrhyc had been arrested by Imperial Guards. But she had not told them to do any such thing.

'Empress, I did give the order,' the man replied, his head bowed.

'Why?' Anais demanded. Her tone was cold. This man's admission had already signed his own death warrant.

The Guard Commander was silent.

'*Why?*' she repeated.

'I cannot say, Empress.'

'Cannot? Or will not? Be aware that you are already dead, Guard Commander, but the lives of your wife and children depend on your answer.'

He raised his head then, and she saw the terror and confusion on his face. 'I gave the order . . . but I do not know why. I know full well the consequences of my action, and yet, at that moment . . . I thought of nothing, Empress. I cannot explain it. Never before has . . .' He faltered. 'It was an act of madness,' he concluded.

Anais's anger was only fuelled by his unsatisfactory answer, but she kept her passions well reined. She flicked her gaze to the Guards that stood at the kneeling man's shoulder.

'Take him away. Execute him.'

He was pulled to his feet.

'Empress, I beg of you the lives of my family!' he cried.

'Concern yourself with the last moments of your own life,'

she replied cruelly, dismissing him. He wept in fear and shame as he was led away. She had no intention of punishing his family, but he would go to his death not knowing that. For a man who had jeopardised her position with such gross stupidity, she was in no mood for mercy.

She motioned to a robed advisor who stood near her throne, an old academic named Hule with a long white beard and bald head.

'Go to the donjon and bring Unger tu Torrhyc to me. See he is not mistreated.'

Hule nodded and departed.

The Empress settled back on her throne. Her brow ached. She felt besieged, conspired against by events. The chain of explosions that had ripped across the city in the last hour had happened too fast and were too well coordinated. They had already been in place, awaiting the spark to ignite them. Torrhyc's arrest threw that spark. There seemed to be no specific targets in mind; they occurred in crowded streets, on ships at the docks, even outside temples. Whoever was behind them, she suspected that their intention was to sow mayhem. Their method was effective. She had already been forced to send over half her Imperial Guards to quell riots in different districts of the city, but the sight of their white and blue armour only seemed to agitate the crowds.

The Guard Commander's idiocy had put her in a dire position, but it was not irretrievable yet. Unger tu Torrhyc's influence was evidently greater than she had first imagined. She knew he was an agitator and an orator of great skill; now it seemed apparent that he had a subversive army working for him. It was not hard to see how a man of his charisma could inspire that kind of loyalty in his followers.

Someone had planted those bombs. She suspected that Unger tu Torrhyc could tell her who.

At that very moment, the subject of the Empress's thoughts brooded in a cell, deep in the bowels of the Keep.

The prisons of the Imperial Keep were clean, if a little dark and bare. His cell was unremarkable, the same as every other cell he had been put in. And he would be released with his head held high, just like every other time. Noble lords, land-owners, even local councils had incarcerated him before. His calling made him many enemies. The rich and powerful did not like to be brought to account for the injustices and evils they brought upon the common folk.

He had begun to view being arrested as part of the process of negotiation now. He had become too dangerous, a threat to the safety of the city. Stirring up trouble, inciting revol-ution. He had expected arrest; it was a mere flexing of muscle, to show that they were still the ones in power. Afterwards, they would talk to him. He would bring them the people's demands. They would agree to some, but not all. He would be released, hailed as a hero by the people, and use that status to resume haranguing the Imperial Family until the people's remaining demands were met.

This time the people's demands were simple, and not open to negotiation. The Aberrant child must not sit the throne.

Anais had been a good ruler, as far as the frankly despotic system of Imperial rule went. Even Unger would admit that. But she was blind, and arrogant. She was so high up on her hill, in this mighty Keep, that she did not see what was hap-pening in the streets below. Furthermore, she did not appear even to be interested. She dallied with politicians and nobles, winning the support of armies here and signing treaties there, and all the time forgetting that the people she ruled were crying out in an almost unanimous voice: *We will not have her!*

Did she think her Imperial Guards could keep the people of Axekami in line? Did she plan to rule them by force? Unacceptable! Unacceptable!

The people would be heard, and Unger tu Torrhyc was their mouthpiece.

He had been placed far away from other prisoners, so that he could not spread his sedition among them. A high, oval window beamed a grille of dusk light on the centre of the stone floor. There was a heavy wooden door, banded with iron, with a slat for guards to look in that was now closed. Otherwise, the cell was absolutely bare, hot and gloomy. Unger sat in a corner, his legs crossed, his eyes closed, and thought. He was a plain man, plain of dress and plain of speech, but he questioned all and everything. That made him a threat to those who relied on tradition for their advantage. And whatever his feelings on Aberrants were, the Empress could not be allowed to foist upon the people a ruler that they so vehemently did not want.

His eyes flickered open, and his heart lurched in his chest. There was someone in the cell with him.

He scrambled to his feet. The cell had darkened suddenly, as though a bank of cloud had swallowed the last of the day's light. Yet, by the dim rays coming through the window, he saw the faintest shape in the far corner of the room. It filled him with an unwholesome dread, emanating malevolence. There had been nothing in here before, and the door had not opened. Only a spectre or a spirit could have come to him this way.

It did not move, and yet he never for a moment doubted the shrieking report of his senses. The air seemed to whine in his ear.

'What are you?' he breathed.

The shape moved then, shifting slightly, an indistinct form that brightness seemed to shy from.

'Are you a spirit? A demon? Why have you come?' Unger demanded.

It walked slowly towards him. He took a breath to cry for help, to rouse the guard outside; but a gnarled and withered hand flashed into the shaft of dusk from the window, one long finger pointing at him, and his throat locked into silence. His body locked also, every muscle tensing at once and staying there, rendering him painfully immobile. Panic sparkled in his brain.

The intruder moved into the dim light. He stood hunched there, his small body buried in a mountain of ragged robes and hung with all manner of beads and ornaments. He wore a Mask of bronze, contorted into an expression of insanity; and as Unger watched, he slowly unfastened the latch strap and removed it.

He was like a man, but small and withered and grotesque, his skin white and parchment-dry. And his face . . . oh, there was ugliness such as Unger had never seen. His aspect was twisted so far out of true that the prisoner would have shut his eyes if he could. One side of the sallow face seemed to have melted, the skin becoming like wax and sliding off the skull to gather in folds of jowl and chop, a flabby dewlap depending from his scrawny neck. His eye on that side laboured to see from beneath the overhanging brow; his upper lip flopped over his lower one. But his right side was no less repulsive: there, his lips had skinned back as if they had simply rotted away, exposing teeth and gum in a skeletal rictus; and his right eye was huge and blind, an orb that bulged from the socket, milky with cataract.

'Unger tu Torrhyc,' croaked the intruder, his malformed lip flapping. 'I am the Weave-lord Vyrrch. How pleasant to meet face to face.'

Unger could not reply. He would not have had the words anyway. He felt a scream rise inside him, but there was nowhere for it to go.

'You've served me well these past weeks, Unger, though you didn't know it,' the foul thing continued. 'Your efforts have accelerated my plans tenfold. I had expected it would take so much more than this to set Axekami on its way to ruin. I had to tread carefully, to keep my hand hidden, but you . . .' Vyrrch wagged a finger in admiration. 'You stir the people. Your arrest has angered them mightily. I never would have thought it so simple.'

Unger was too terrified to think where Vyrrch was leading this; the sensation of having bodily control robbed from him was overwhelming his reason.

'It was quite a risk, even the little push it took to make the Guard Commander do what I needed. I had thought there would be outrage, *counted* on it . . . but even I had under-estimated the effectiveness of your secret army of bombers, Unger. I would hate to see them stop the good work they are doing.'

'Not . . . not . . .' Unger managed, forcing the words in a squeak past his throat.

'Oh, of course they're not yours. They're *mine*. But the people and the Empress alike assume you are responsible, so let us not disabuse them of that notion.'

The creature was close enough to touch him now, and Unger could see that it was not wholly real, but faintly trans-parent. A spectre, after all. It ran a finger down his cheek, and the sensation was like freezing water.

'Your cause needs a martyr, Unger.'

The spectre seized him savagely by the back of the head, and despite its apparent intangibility, Unger felt its massive strength. His muscles loosened, and he screamed as it prop-elled him against the wall of the cell, smashing his skull like a jakma nut on a rock, leaving a dark wodge of blood and hair above his corpse.

The gates to the temple of Panazu in the River District of Axekami stood open as dusk set in. Mishani stood beneath them, looking up at the tall, narrow façade that towered over her, its shoulders pulled in tight and sculpted into the form of rolling whirlpools. She was bedraggled, exhausted and suffer-ing from shock, and yet she was here, at the abode of the dream lady. The sounds of Axekami beginning to tear itself apart were audible across the Kerryn. New explosions could be heard, and bright flames rose against the gathering dark. Voices were raised in clamour, mob roars made weak and thin by distance. This night would be an evil one for all concerned.

She walked up the steps to the temple, through the great gates and into the cool sanctuary of the congregation chamber. The interior of the temple was breathtaking. Pillars vaulted up to domed ceilings, painted with frescoes of Panazu's exploits and teachings. The walls were chased with reliefs of river creatures. The vast curved windows of blue, green and silver in the face of the building dappled the temple in shades of the sea floor, and seemed to stir the light restfully to heighten the illusion. The sound of water was all around: splashing, trickling, tinkling, for the altar was a fountain from which many gutters ran, directing the crystal liquid into artful designs carved into the blue-green *lach* on the floor. The congregation area, where the oblates came to kneel and pray, was surrounded by a thick trench of water in which swam catfish, the earthly aspect of Panazu, and bridged by short arcs of *lach*.

There was nobody here. The place was peaceful and deserted. Mishani shuffled in, and did not even turn around when the gates closed behind her of their own accord. She walked listlessly down the central aisle, her mind and body still numb from the tragedy she had witnessed in the Market District.

'Mishani tu Koli,' a soft voice purred, echoing around the temple. Mishani looked to the source of the sound, and found her standing to one side of the chamber. The dream lady. She looked more like something in a nightmare, a tall, slender tower of elegant black, her face painted with crescents of red that ran over her eyelids from forehead to cheek. Her lips were marked with alternating triangles of red and black, like teeth. A ruff of raven feathers grew from her shoulders, and a silver circlet with a red gem was set on her forehead.

She crossed the chamber to the central aisle, emerging between the pillars to stand before Mishani. She took in Mishani's unkempt appearance without a flicker of an expression.

'My name is Cailin tu Moritat. Lucia calls me the dream lady. She told me you would be coming.' Cailin took her by the elbow. 'Come. Rest, and bathe. Your journey has not been easy, I see.'

Mishani allowed herself to be led. She had nowhere else to go.

TWENTY-ONE

Time did not pass in Chaim. Rather, it elongated, stretching itself flat and thin, sacrificing substance for length. Tane had ceased counting the days; they had merged into one great nothing, a relentless, frowning wall of boredom and increasing despair.

The disappearance of Kaiku had hit them hard. At first there was something akin to mild panic. Had something been into the cave and taken her while they slept? Mamak searched and found no sign. It took a short while before Tane remembered the strange things Kaiku had been saying to him while he drowsed:

Perhaps this was not your path to take after all. Perhaps it is mine alone.

The storm kept them in the cave another day. Mamak flatly refused to let them search.

'If she's out there, the fool is dead already. When this storm breaks, I go home. You can come with me, or stay in this cave if you wish.'

Tane begged him, offered him triple his fee if he would find her. He told her that Kaiku had money, and lots of it. Mamak's eyes lit at the prospect, and for a moment Tane saw greed war with sense on his face; but in the end, his experience of mountain travel tipped the balance, and he refused. Asara shook her head and tutted at Tane for his loss of dignity in desperation.

'I want her back!' he snapped in his defence.

Asara shrugged insouciantly. 'But she is gone, Tane. Time for a new plan.'

When the storm gave up the next morning, they accepted

the inevitable and returned to Chaim. Tane talked of raising an expedition to search the mountains for Kaiku – or her body – so that they might at least retrieve the Mask. Tane had not forgotten that without that Mask he had no hope of discovering who had sent the shin-shin that had massacred the priests of his temple. But the plan was unsound, and everyone knew it. Even Tane knew it. There was not a prayer of finding her in all the vastness of northern Fo, with her tracks erased by rain and wind. By the time they came down out of the mountains and were back on the path to Chaim, he had stopped talking about it.

Tane and Asara found themselves rooms in Chaim's single lodging house, a bare and draughty construction that catered for the few outside visitors the town received. Neither intended to leave, or even spoke of such.

'She decided to go on alone,' Tane said. 'If she makes it, she'll come back here.'

'You are chasing false hope,' Asara told him, but she did not argue further, nor make any move to depart herself.

There was nothing to do in Chaim. The unfaltering rudeness of the locals began to wear on them after a time, and they talked to nobody but each other. At first, there was little for them to speak of. Too many barriers existed between them, too many deceptions. It was just like it had been with Kaiku.

Gods, do we ever take our masks off, even for a moment? Tane thought in exasperation.

But gradually their enforced solitude bred conversation, as the slow trickle of water through a holed dam will erode the surrounding stone till it cracks. After what might have been a week of waiting and wondering, they found themselves back in the makeshift bar where they had first met Mamak.

'You know what I am, Tane,' Asara said.

The statement, put casually in the midst of the conversation, brought the young acolyte up short. 'What do you mean?' he asked.

'No games,' she said. 'The time has come for honesty. If you are to walk the same paths as I, as seems increasingly to be the case, then you should face up to what you already know.'

Tane glanced around the bar to ensure they were not being overheard, but it was almost empty. A bleak, wooden, chilly room with a few locals in a corner minding their own business. A scatter of low, rough-cut tables and worn mats to sit on. A grouch-faced barmaid serving shots of rank liquor. Spirits, he hated this town.

'You are Aberrant,' he said quietly.

'Well done,' she replied, with a hint of mockery in her voice. 'At last you admit it to yourself. But you are a strange one, Tane. You listen. You are ready to learn. That is why I will tell you this, for you may one day come to my way of seeing. So swallow your disgust for a moment, and hear what I have to say.'

Tane leaned forward over the table, his cheeks flushed. With the lack of anything to do in the town, Chaim's inhabitants had a lot to drink about, and the potency of the liquor attested to that. Asara was dead sober, as always; her Aberrant metabolism neutralised alcohol before it could affect her, and she did not know how it felt to be drunk.

'I am old, Tane,' she said. 'You cannot guess how old by looking at me. I have seen much, and I have done much. Some memories bring pride, others disgust.' She turned the wooden tumbler of liquor inside the cradle of her fingers, looking down into it. 'Do you know what experience is? Experience is when you have handled something so much that the shine wears off it. Experience is when you begin to see how relentlessly predictable people are, how generation after generation they follow the same simple, ugly pattern. They dream of living forever, but they do not know what they ask. I have passed my eightieth harvest, though it does not show on me. Since I reached adulthood, I have not aged. My body repairs itself faster than time can ravage it. That is my curse. I have already lived the span of a normal lifetime, and I am bored.'

It seemed such bathos that Tane almost laughed, a bitter hysteria welling within him; but the tone of Asara's voice warned him against it. '*Bored?*' he repeated.

'You do not understand,' Asara said patiently. 'Nor, I think, will you ever. But when so much has become jaded, all that is left is the search for something new, something that will fire the blood again, if only for a short while. I was purposeless for a long time before I met Cailin tu Moritat, seeking only new thrills and finding each less satisfying than the last. When I found her, I saw something I had never seen before. I had thought I was a freak, a random thing; but in her I saw a mirror to me, and I saw a purpose again.'

'What did you see?' asked Tane.

'A superior being,' Asara replied. 'A creature that was human and yet *better* than human. An Aberrant whose Aberration made her better than those who despised her.'

Tane blinked, wanting to shake his head and refute her. He restrained himself. Her words were preposterous, but he would listen. He had learned her opinions on the subject of Aberrancy over the weeks they had spent together, and while he did not agree with much of what she said, it had enough validity to make him think.

'I saw then the new order of things,' Asara continued. 'A world where Aberrants were not hated and hunted but respected. I saw that Aberrancy was not a fouling of the body, but merely a changing. An evolution. And as with all evolution, many must fall by the way for one to emerge triumphant. If I am to live in this world for a long time to come, I will do all I can to make it a more pleasant experience for myself. And that means I must work towards that new order.'

'I think I see,' he said, recalling other snatches of conversation they had shared over the period of their self-induced confinement in Chaim. 'You help the Red Order because they represent Aberrants whose abilities make them greater than human. And the Libera Dramach . . . they work for the same thing you want; so you help them too.'

'But the Red Order and the Libera Dramach are working together for the time being, with one common goal in mind,' Asara said, enmeshing her fingers before her.

'To see the Heir-Empress take the throne,' Tane concluded.

'Exactly. She is the key. She is the only one that can reverse the blight on our land. She is the bridge between us and the spirits, between the common folk and the Aberrants.' Asara grabbed Tane's wrists and fixed him with an iron gaze. 'It *must* be this way. And we must do what we can to make it so.'

Tane held the gaze for a moment, then countered with a question. 'Why did you watch over Kaiku for so many years?'

He regretted it almost immediately. It had come out without thought, seeming to trip from his subconscious to his tongue without routing through his brain; and yet he knew by some terrible prescience what would be Asara's reply.

Asara smiled faintly and released him. She sat back and took a sip of liquor. 'I became her handmaiden at the behest of the Red Order. Her previous one met with an accident.'

Tane let this one pass. When he did not react, Asara continued.

'They found her through whatever method they have; their ways are a mystery to me. They knew she would manifest . . . powers sooner or later, and they asked me to watch her until she did. There was no way she would be coerced to join until she had her first burning. Who in their right mind would believe they were an Aberrant without any evidence?'

Asara's words dropped into Tane's consciousness like a stone into thick honey. The world seemed to slow around him, the whispering of the other denizens of the bar becoming a meaningless susurrus in the background. Across the coarse wooden table he could see Asara's beautiful eyes watching his face, evaluating the effect of what she had just told him.

'But you knew that, didn't you?' she asked.

Tane nodded mutely, his gaze falling. She relished it, he realised. He had asked her a question he already had the answer to, and she was amused that he still felt her response like a pikestaff in the ribs.

'Small things,' he murmured, when he could bear her wry silence no longer. 'When first I met her, she was raving about a woman named Asara. She told me you had been killed by a demon in the forest. Later you reappeared. No explanation was given, and I didn't ask for one.'

'You thought it was not your place to enquire,' said Asara scornfully. 'How like a man.'

'No,' he said. 'No, I suppose I didn't want to know. I was cowardly. Then there was you. I suspected you from the start. Add to that the lengths you went to to bring her to the Aberrant woman Cailin, the secrets you held between you that I was not privy to, the way you seemed to change . . .' He sighed, a strange noise of resignation. 'I'm not feeble-minded, Asara. I've been walking with Aberrants since my journey began.'

'Yet you believe your journey was ordained by your goddess, that you were spared for a purpose; but there is no greater foulness to Enyu than an Aberrant. Reconcile these things, if you can.'

Tane bowed his head, his shaved skull limned in dim lantern light. 'I can't. That's why I've been avoiding them.'

'Here it is in the open, then,' said Asara, brushing back the red-streaked fall of her hair behind one sculpted ear and leaning forward. 'She is Aberrant, gifted with the ability to mould the Weave as the Weavers do. But she is dangerous to herself and others; she needs schooling. I came to Fo for several reasons, but one was to stop her committing suicide. Every day she spends here increases the risk that her powers will break their boundaries again. Eventually, she will either burn herself or be killed by those that fear her.' She relaxed back, her gaze never leaving Tane, never ceasing to calculate him. 'I told Cailin I would bring her into the fold, and I will. Assuming she still lives, of course. I will wait in this spirit-blasted wasteland until hope is gone. That may be weeks, it may be months; but age has a way of foreshortening time, Tane, and I am a patient woman.'

Tane was silent. The sensation of drunkenness felt suddenly unpleasant, having soured within him.

'Join us, Tane,' said Asara. 'You and I share the same goals. You may hate Aberrants, but you would see the blight on this land stopped. And the Heir-Empress is the only chance we have.'

'I do not . . .' Tane began, feeling the words stall and clutter in his mouth. 'I do not *hate* Aberrants,' he said.

'Indeed not,' Asara said, raising one eyebrow slightly. 'For you love one of them, I suspect.'

Tane flashed her a hot glare, forming a retort that died before it could be born. Instead, he became sullen, and did not reply.

'Poor Tane,' Asara said. 'Caught between your faith and your heart. I'd pity you, if I had not seen it endless times before. Humankind really is a pathetically predictable animal.'

Tane slammed his hands on the table, spilling their liquor. He arrested himself just as he was about to lunge at her. She had not moved a muscle, staying relaxed on her mat, watching him with that infuriating amusement on her face. The others in the bar had their eyes on him now. He wanted to strangle her, to hit her, to slap her hard and show her that she could *not* speak to him that way.

Like father, like son, he thought, and suddenly he went cold, the rage in him flickering and dying out. He slammed his hands on the table again in one last, impotent display of frustration, got up and stalked out of the bar and into the night.

The chill air and knife-edge wind sawed through him eagerly. He welcomed the discomfort, hurrying away from the bar, away from the lights in the windows, seeking only to distance himself from Asara and all she had said. But he could no longer avoid it now. There was no question, no element of doubt any more. He had been treasuring that margin of uncertainty, for in that small space he could still stay with Kaiku and not offend his goddess, could still protest that he was never certain she was Aberrant. Now it was gone, and he was forced into a quandary.

There were few people on the rough trails that passed for streets in Chaim. No lanterns burned except through grimy windows. The moons were absent tonight, and the darkness was louring and hungry. He let himself be swallowed by it.

After a time, he came to a sloping, craggy rock atop a slope that looked out over the faint lights of the grim village, and there he sat. It was bitterly cold, but he had his coat on and his hood pulled tight. He meditated for a time, but it was hopeless. No enlightenment could come to a heart in such turmoil. Instead he prayed, asking Enyu for guidance. How could she have sent him on this way to ally himself with Aberrants, if Aberrants were corruptions of her plan? What was he supposed to do? So many uncertainties, so many un-answered questions, and he was left scrabbling for purpose once again. How could something as simple as faith be so contradictory?

It is my punishment, he thought. *I must endure.*

And there it was: his answer. This agony of indecision was only part of his penance. He must accept it gladly, and act as he thought best, and bear the consequences of that.

I owe the gods a life, he told himself. It was a phrase he had been using to account for his suffering ever since he was sixteen harvests of age, and he had murdered his own father.

He had no clear recollection of anything before the age of eight or nine, except of the fearful dark shape that lumbered through his embryonic memories, and the crushing inevit-ability of the pain that was to follow. Pain was a part of the jigsaw of Tane's childhood as much as joy, hunger, triumph, disappointment. In some form or another it visited him daily, whether it were a sharp cuff on the ear while he ate his oats or a thrashing in the corner for some real or imagined mischief. Pain was a part of the cycle of things: random and illogical and unfair, but only in the way that illness was or any other misfortune.

His father, Eris tu Jeribos, was a member of the town council of Amada, deep in the Forest of Yuna. Politics had always been his ambition, but while he was shrewd and clever enough to make headway time and again, he was forever dragged back by those facets of his personality that alienated him from his fellows.

He was pious, and nobody could fault him for that; but his extreme and puritanical views met with little favour among the other councillors. He made them uneasy, and they feared to let him gain any more power than he had in the council; yet though he knew this, he was a man of such conviction that he could do nothing but continue to expound his beliefs. And so he was always frustrated, and each time a little more of the humanity inside him shrivelled to a bitter char.

But there was something other than his obvious piety: an almost indefinable quality that he projected to only the most subtle of senses, so that his peers shrank from him without knowing why. He was cruel. And though he took pains never to show a hint of it in public, somehow it seemed to emanate from him and put people on edge. Perhaps it was the flat bleakness of his hooded eyes, or the curl on the edge of his voice, or his thin, gaunt, stooped body; but whatever it was, the things he did in private carried themselves to his public life whether he wanted them to or not.

Tane had been taught to hunt by his father when he was ten harvests old. He was a remarkably adept pupil, and he applied himself vigorously, having finally found something that pleased the strict patriarch. And if he noticed the gleam in Eris's eyes was a little too bright as he watched a rabbit thrashing in a snare, or that he took a fraction too much pleasure in snapping a wounded bird's neck, then he counted himself lucky that his father was happy, and less likely to turn on him without warning as he usually was.

When he was twelve, he was out walking in the woods and he came across his father skinning a jeadh – a long-muzzled, hairless variety of the wild dogs that haunted the northern end of the Forest of Yuna. The jeadh was still very much alive, staked to the ground with its legs forced apart. The spirits knew how Eris had subdued it like that. Tane had been attracted by the muffled whimpers and yelps that it forced through the crude muzzle Eris had formed when he tied his belt around its mouth.

He stood and watched, unnoticed by Eris, who was too engrossed in what he was doing to pay attention to anything else. He watched the slow, careful way his father parted the layers of skin and subcutaneous fat with his knife, drawing back a bloody flap to expose the glistening striations of pink muscle beneath. For half an hour he was motionless, standing in full view in the clearing, but his father never saw him as he meticulously took the beast apart, piece by piece, unpeeling it like an orange until he could see its heart beating in terror between its ribs. Tane looked from the animal to his father's face and back, and for the first time he truly understood that he was the son of a monster.

Tane's mother Kenda was a pale, mousy woman, small and shy and grey and quiet. It had occurred to him in later life that her marriage to Eris might have made her this way, but strangely Eris's cruelty never extended to his wife, and he never beat her as he did Tane. At most, he snapped at her, and she would scuttle away like a startled shrew; but then, since she seemed to possess no will of her own and dared not accomplish the smallest task without being told to do so by Eris, she never gave him a reason to be displeased with her. Tane remembered his mother as something of a nonentity, a pallid extension of his father's wishes, a menial thing that swept and scampered and was wholly ineffectual on her own.

Kenda had bore Eris two children. Each had brought her close to death, for her weak body could barely stand the trials of pregnancy; but Tane doubted that she had even considered herself or her health in the equation. Tane's sister Isya was six harvests younger than him, and he loved her dearly. She was the one anchor of humanity in their household. Somehow she grew up unsullied by the parents who raised her, taking on none of their traits as most children are wont to do. Instead, it was as if her personality were formed in the womb, crystalline, rejecting any possibility of absorbing outside influences.

She was a happy child where Tane was serious, a dreamer, a creature of imagination and boundless energy, who would cry when she found a broken chick that had fallen from its nest, or laugh and dance when it rained. Tane envied her passion for life, her carefree joy; and he treasured it also, for just to be near her was to feel the warmth she gave off, and the world seemed better for her being in it. She endured the bumps and scrapes of childhood like any other, but he was always there for her, to bandage a skinned knee or soothe her tears. It was through learning to care for her that he first realised the healing properties of herbs, and began to apply them to his own bruises too. For her part, Isya adored her older brother; but then she adored everyone, and not even the stern manner of their father – who was careful never to beat Tane within her earshot – or the nervous shyness of their mother were enough to deflect her affection.

It was Isya and Isya only that made life bearable for Tane as he grew into adolescence. It was as if his father had somehow sensed the disgust his son now felt for him, after seeing him torture the jeadh in the forest. This, coupled with his increasing frustration at the town council, led to the regular beatings that Tane suffered suddenly intensifying. He would be set impossible tasks of learning, told to go to the library in Amada and memorise entire chapters of Saramyr history to recite word for word. If he failed, as he inevitably did, he was thrashed until his body was bruised black and his lungs rattled for breath.

He took to retreating into the deeper forest for days at a time. His father's lessons in hunting and survival served him well during these periods when he was away, and he began to yearn more and more to stay on his own, surrounded by the animals and trees, none of whom could possibly be as cruel to him as the lean ogre who waited at home. But there was one thing that always drew him back: Isya. Though his father's casual violence had been hitherto directed only at Tane, he did not dare leave his sister to Eris's mercies, in case one day he might seek a new target to vent himself on.

When he was sixteen harvests and Isya was ten, that day came.

He had been away for a week, searching the stream sides and rocky nooks for a particular shrub called iritisima, whose roots were a powerful febrifuge, used to bring down fevers. By now most of the time he was not away he was at the library, learning the intricacies of herblore alongside the futile task of keeping up with his father's lessons. Isya missed him, but he was faintly dismayed to see that she got along fine in her own company, and did not need her older brother half as much as he liked to think. She had cultivated friends in the village, too; real friends, not the acquaintances Tane had. He could never begin a true friendship while he still had to hide the bruises and mysterious convalescences that were part of his routine.

When he returned home to the cabin, sitting beneath the shade of the overhanging oaks that leaned over the low cliff at its back, he found it silent. The day was warm and humid, and his shirt was damp with sweat. Using his bolt rifle as a walking staff – the way his father had warned him never to do – he made his tired way to the door and peered inside. A quiet house usually meant Eris was away, but this time there was a certain malevolence about the peace, something that prickled at his intuition.

'Mother?' he called as he propped his rifle inside the porch. Her face appeared in the doorway to the kitchen, a flash of fright, and then she disappeared. He felt something cold trickle into his chest. Striding quickly, he went to Isya's door and opened it without waiting to knock.

She was huddled in a corner by her simple pallet bed, curled up like a foetus, her hair a straggle and her face puffy with tears. In that moment, in one terrible second, he knew what had happened – hadn't he always feared it, secretly? His breath stopped, as if to plug whatever it was that was rising from his belly to his throat. Seemingly in a dream, he crossed the room and crouched next to her, and she threw herself into his arms and hugged him tight, desperately, as if she could crush him into her and he could take away the pain as he had always done before. The veins on his neck throbbed as she screamed into his shoulder; his eyes fell to the spatters of dark, dark blood on her pallet, the bruises on her thin arms where Eris's hands had gripped. Her saffron-yellow dress was a dull rust-brown where she had gathered it between her knees.

He remembered holding her. He remembered brewing her a strong infusion of skullcap and valerian that put her to sleep. And then he went out, into the forest, and did not return till the next morning.

His father was back by then, sitting at the round table in the kitchen. Tane went in to check on Isya, who was still asleep, and then sat down opposite Eris. He swung a half-full bottle of liquor on to the table. His father watched him stonily, as if this were a day like any ordinary day, as if he hadn't ruined and dirtied the one precious thing he had ever created, forever destroyed the fragile innocence of a creature more beautiful that the rest of her family combined.

'Where did you get that?' he asked, his voice low, as it always was before he struck.

'It's yours,' Tane said. 'I took it.'

His mother, who had been hovering by the stove, began to scuttle out quickly, sensing the rising conflict.

'Get us two cups, Mother,' Tane said. She stopped. He had never *ordered* her to do anything before. She looked to his father. He nodded, and she did as she was bade before retreating.

'You're drunk.'

'That's right,' said Tane, filling the two cups. Eris rarely drank, but when he did it was always this: abaxia, a smooth spirit from the mountains.

Eris looked steadily at Tane. Ordinarily, Tane would be rolling and pleading beneath his fists or the buckle of his belt by this point. But Eris had sensed he had gone too far this time, crossed some invisible line, and Tane was strong enough now to stand up to his father. There was a belligerence about his manner, and beneath that a look in Tane's eyes that he had never seen before. A kind of emptiness, like something had died inside him and left only a void. For the first time in his life, he secretly feared his son.

'What do you think you're doing?' he asked slowly, warily.

'You and I are going to take a drink,' Tane replied, pushing his cup towards him. 'And then we're going to talk.'

'I'll not be told what to do by you,' Eris said, rising.

'You'll sit *down!*' Tane roared, slamming his fist on the table. Eris froze. His son glared at him with raw hatred in his eyes. 'You'll sit down, and you'll take a drink, or the gods help me I'll do worse to you than you did to Isya.'

Eris sat, and with that the last of his authority was gone. For so many years he was used to his word being unchallenged in his own home that he simply did not know how to react when it was. His hands were trembling as Tane composed himself again, brushing a flick of dark hair back from his forehead. His skull was unshaven then.

'A toast,' Tane said, raising his cup. Shakily, Eris did the same. 'To family.'

With that, he drained his cup in a single swallow, and his father followed him.

'She was all I had, Father,' Tane said. 'She was the only good thing you ever did, and you've ruined her.'

Eris's eyes would not meet Tane's.

'*Why?*' he whispered.

His father did not reply for a long time, but Tane waited.

'Because you weren't here,' Eris said quietly.

Tane let out a bitter laugh.

Eris looked at him then. 'What are you going to do?'

Tane tapped the bottle of abaxia with a fingernail. 'I've already done it.'

His father opened his mouth to speak, but no words came out. The expression of horror on his face was something Tane had never seen before.

'Tasslewood root,' he said. 'First it paralyses your vocal cords, then robs the strength from your limbs. After that it gets to work on your insides. It takes up to fifteen minutes to die, so the books say. And best of all, it's practically undetectable and the cadaver is unmarked, so it seems like a simple heart failure.'

'You . . . but you drank . . .' Eris gasped. He could already feel the numbness at the base of his throat, his larynx swelling.

'It's quite a plant, really, the tasslewood,' Tane said conversationally. 'The leaves and aerial parts provide the antidote to the poison in the roots.' He opened his mouth, displaying a wad of bitter green mush that he had kept concealed under his tongue. He swallowed it.

His father tried to reply, to plead or beg; but instead he slumped off his chair and fell to the floor. Tane got down and crouched next to him, watching him twitch as he lost control of his limbs. His father's eyes rolled and teared, and Tane listened dispassionately to the soft bleats of agony that were all Eris could force from his body.

'Look what you made me, Father,' Tane whispered. 'I'm a murderer now.'

He took the cups and the bottle when he left. They were the

only evidence that could be used in accusation against him for his father's death. Not that he believed he would be accused. His mother did not have the initiative. He walked into the woods with the sound of her rising scream coming from the cabin behind him, as she discovered the body of her husband.

That day he roamed the woods, half mad with grief and self-loathing. He had no idea what would come afterwards, how they would keep going, what would become of them. He knew only that he would look after Isya, protect her, and never let a man such as Eris harm her again. He only hoped she would emerge from her ordeal as the same girl he had known before.

He returned to the cabin at night, and it was once again silent. He found his father still lying in the kitchen. Of his mother and Isya, there was no sign. At first he felt a flood of panic; but then reason calmed him. They had gone to a friend's house, or to have Isya seen to by the physician in Amada. Whatever else, his mother did not have the strength of character to leave her home permanently. He took the corpse away and buried it in the darkness, and settled to wait for their return.

After a week it became apparent that they were not coming back. He had underestimated his mother. Perhaps her need to run had overcome her fear of facing the outside world without her husband. Perhaps she truly loathed her son for what he had done. Perhaps she was terrified that he would come back and kill them, too. He would never know. She had gone, and taken his sister with her. He had lost the one he meant to protect, and now there was no one and nothing. Only him.

Towards dawn, he returned to the lodging house briefly to collect his possessions. He avoided Asara's room, not wishing to face her. There was much he had to think on, insoluble questions he had to find answers to. He could not do it here in Chaim, and he could not do it in company. He would leave Asara to watch out for Kaiku's return for the time being. He trusted her that far, at least.

He had gathered everything from his draughty, rickety wooden room and was about to leave when he saw a note on his bed, signed in Asara's flowing hand. Hesitantly, he picked it up.

Should you change your mind, he read, *take this note to the priests at the Temple of Panazu in Axekami. Tell them you wish to come to the fold. They will understand.*

A ghost of a frown crossed his tanned brow, and then he pocketed the note and left. There would be trader carts going south with the sunrise. He intended to be on one of them.

TWENTY-TWO

The snow crunched beneath her heavy boots as Kaiku forged her way westward through the high peaks of the mountains. From a distance, she looked like a shambling mound of fur, buried as she was in the patchwork coat she had taken from the dead man in the cave three days ago. Her voluminous cowl flapped over the smooth red and black Mask that she wore on her face, and she walked with the aid of a tall staff, her rifle slung across her back.

Heart's blood, she thought to herself. *When does it end?*

The last of her stolen rations had been consumed yesterday, and she was once again faint from hunger. Some inner voice had told her to push on with all her strength, to travel through the night and make good time while she still had something more than snow in her belly. That voice had told her that the peaks must give up their secrets soon, that she could not be more than an overnight trek from the monastery. Now, at mid-afternoon of the next day, the voice was conspicuously silent.

She rested for a moment, leaning on her staff like a crutch. There was no chance of catching anything to eat out here, and the snow had buried any plants or roots beneath three-foot drifts. The wilderness was a bleak, empty maze of white, and the only signs of life were the distant cawing of gristle-crows and the occasional howl of the Aberrants at night. Once again, she was facing starvation, and all she could do was keep going.

The Mask felt natural on her now, as if it had moulded itself subtly to the contours of her face. She remembered the fear and trepidation she had felt at the thought of putting it on, her worries of insanity or addiction. How ridiculous that seemed now. The Mask was not her enemy. In fact, it was perhaps her only hope of survival out here. She trusted the Mask, took comfort in it; and though it had proved remarkably ineffective thus far, her faith had seemed to grow still. And it was here, after many days, that her faith was finally rewarded.

She raised her head and saw a gorge she recognised.

Crossing to it, she stood at its snowy lip and puzzled over it for a time. She was certain she had been here before, and yet she would have remembered coming across such a vast rent in the landscape, and she could not recall seeing it on her journey. At its southern end was a path that led in between two of the more foreboding peaks; she knew that, too, with a certainty that seemed strangely groundless, as she was equally certain that she had not passed it since she began her trek into the mountains.

When she investigated, she did indeed find a path, and she took it.

As the day wore on, she found more and more landmarks she knew: an enormous, twisted tree that raked out of the snow and held crooked fingers to the sky; a flat, glassy plain of ice that was passable by following a rocky spine of black stone through its midst; a forked mountain peak, split asunder by some great and ancient disaster. Each sight triggered a memory that was not hers, but which belonged to one of the previous wearers of the Mask, and which had been absorbed into its wooden fibres by some incomprehensible osmosis.

Father, she thought. She could feel tears threatening. It seemed as if the wood smelled of Ruito, a cosy, musky smell of old books and fatherly affection, the scent she got when she sat in his lap as a child and burrowed into his chest to sleep there. She sensed him as a ghost in her mind, frustratingly elusive but present nonetheless, and she felt as that child again.

The next day, hungrier and weaker, she came across a strange phenomenon. Walking along an unremarkable curve of rock, an insect in the snowy waste, she felt the Mask grow suddenly warm. Her head began to feel light. The sensation was not unpleasant, but a little worrying. As she moved onward, the heat grew greater; experimentally, she tried backtracking, and to her surprise the heat faded.

There is something there, she thought.

There was nothing to do but go on. She walked slowly, feeling the presence of something vast and invisible before her. Instinctively, she put out a hand, fearing to walk into something, though there was nothing that any of her five primary senses could tell her.

Her hand brushed the barrier, and the glittering Weave opened up to her.

It was breathtaking: a vast, sweeping band of golden threads, stretching from horizon to horizon. It lacked the definition a wall would have; rather, it was a thickly clustered mass of whorls and loops, slowly revolving, turning inside out, swallowing each other and regenerating once again. The shining threads of the Weave were thrown into turmoil here, as if the stitching of the world had caught and snarled into a seething mess. And yet the barrier followed the contours of the land, always staying at approximately six metres high and six deep. Chaos within an ordered framework. This was no accident, nor some freak of nature. This was placed here on purpose, and by beings who knew how to manipulate the world beyond human sight with great skill.

With a gasp, she drew her hand back, and the barrier faded from sight. The Mask was radiating in response, making her dizzy. This was how the monastery had stayed hidden all this time. The barrier turned an unprotected mind around, misdirecting it, disorientating. Only with the Mask could someone hope to break through.

More firmly now, Kaiku put her hand out to the barrier. A slight pressure, and the stirring fibres slid apart to admit her.

She closed her eyes, took a breath and said a short prayer to the gods, then stepped into it.

She was engulfed in light, swallowed by the womb of the Weave. The fibres surrounded her, a gently swirling sea of wonder, and she felt she could simply let herself be swept away by it and never have another care again. But she was not so unguarded against the dangers of the Masks that she would surrender herself to her desire. This was how it felt when she had died, this beauty, this perfection of ecstasy; and so she knew there would be no coming back if she yielded. She remembered that this was how the world appeared to her when the burning came upon her, when her irises turned to red and she saw the Weave that sewed its way beneath the skin of human sight. She feared that, and held on to that fear, for it kept her anchored to reality. She pushed onward, through the sublime paradise, and broke through to the ugly and harsh light of the world on the other side.

It felt as if she had been robbed of something beautiful, like a lover's betrayal. She looked over her shoulder, but the barrier had receded into invisibility again. For a moment, she wanted nothing more than to be back there, enfolded in the light instead of this cruelty of cold and hunger. Then she turned her head, and walked on, the Mask cooling on her face.

Over time, she had developed a tendency to mutter to herself, an unconscious reaction to the oppressive loneliness of her journey. Most of her monologue was random and meaningless, but a lot of it involved her condition, a rambling and repetitive confession that she was an Aberrant and a danger to others, that she should stay out here in the wilderness where there was nobody to harm and nobody to shun her. Sometimes she talked to her father and brother as if they were beside her. Sometimes she imagined a huge boar was walking with her, just out of sight on the edge of her vision, and its presence comforted her.

Delirium and hunger had lent these fantasies strength, and

they had taken hold of her weakened mind and fastened there. They were what kept her going when her endurance flagged, and they would have kept her walking till she dropped and died, had she not come across the monastery when she did.

She saw it first through a gap between two mountain slopes to the south. It was a clear day, or she might have missed it entirely; but the air was cold and sharp as crystal, and her eyes were still keen. It was buried in the mountainside a mile or two away, a great façade hewn out of the surrounding rock, massive and stolid. She found it hard to make out any detail at this distance, but she could see the narrow stone bridge that arced from the entrance to the other side of a deep gorge, and presumed that it was there she should be heading if she wanted access.

It took her most of the day to find the way up to the monastery, which was a set of wide, steep steps carved out of the mountain's stony skin. The sheer scale of it provoked a vague awe through the haze of exhaustion. The steps had been carved centuries ago, their edges weathered to curves and crumbling; if the Weavers truly lived at the top, then they must have occupied the monastery rather than built it, for the stairway was older than the Weavers were. Snow-buried statues guarded it from pedestals set to either side, but when Kaiku cleared away the snow she found them moss-covered and worn smooth by the elements, so she could not tell what they were. The seemingly endless stairway sapped what little stamina she had remaining, and she was asleep on her feet by the time it ended.

The change in the rhythm of her steps woke her out of her shallow drowse, and she found herself on a narrow path, part of a small outpost that clung precariously to the flanks of the mountain. There were several buildings of brick and stone, linked by curving paths that went where the shape of the mountain would allow. The dwellings were old and looked abandoned, waiting silently with their shutters creaking in the freezing breeze. They were ugly and simplistic, like the houses in Chaim but more sturdy. A little further up, she saw where the bridge began, a stout and unornamented span of stone that leaped across the massive divide, where only a snowy murk drifted below. There was no sign of life.

By now exhaustion had claimed her, and she knew she would soon be unable to go no further. Stumbling towards the nearest building, she pushed open the wooden gate and found that it was a chicken barn, long empty but still retaining some mouldy hay in the pens. She clambered into one, gathered the hay about her, and was instantly asleep.

Cramps in her stomach woke her rudely from slumber, and she was dragged unwillingly into awareness again. She lay with her eyes closed for what seemed a long while, until the scuffing of someone's feet in the hay next to her made her jerk in alarm.

Someone was leaning over her. For one terrifying moment, she thought it was the ghost of the man she had slain in the cave; but though the clothes were similar, they were not identical. This one's ragged robes were of different kinds of fur, and the Mask that peered at her was pale blue, and made of wood rather than bone. It was a portrait of idiot curiosity, a fat moon-face with a pooching lower lip and wide, dark eyes set in an expression of surprise. Kaiku scrambled back, but her progress was impeded by the stone wall behind her. Her rifle lay nearby, though not near enough so she could easily lunge for it.

The moon-face tipped its head to one side, then bobbed closer, peering intently. It was like being sniffed by some wild animal who was trying to decide whether she was food or not. Kaiku did not move.

Silently, the blue moon-face withdrew and lost interest. The Weaver turned and climbed out of the chicken pen, pausing to examine a few other things on the way. Then he left, closing the gate behind him.

Kaiku's heart was pounding. What did this mean? In the days since she had left the cave in the mountains, she had never once considered that the death of the man whose robes she wore might have repercussions. Now she knew it had been a foolish oversight. What if they recognised each other by their robes as much as their Masks? What if the Weaver who had worn this red and black Mask was known to them? Kaiku's father might have killed him as Kaiku had killed the Weaver in the cave. If they found that the one wearing these blood-spotted robes, this leering Mask was not the man they knew . . .

. . . the man . . .

It hit her then, something so obvious that she had overlooked it in her delirium. The Weavers were exclusively male. No women were allowed in their order. It was only by grace of their heavy, disfiguring garments that her body shape was not recognisable; yet even then the slope of her breasts could be faintly determined, unless she hunched her shoulders forward. If she so much as spoke, she would be discovered.

Feeling sudden panic welling within her, she grabbed her rifle and hurried to the door of the building. Opening the gate a little, she feared to see Moon-face running towards the monastery to raise the alarm; but instead she saw the shambling figure wandering about a little way down the path, idly poking and pushing things or picking up stones for closer scrutiny.

She stepped out warily. It was morning, bitterly cold and damp. The snow-dusted flanks of the gorge were hidden by white mists, churning far below. The bridge hung in the air nearby, spanning the chasm. It seemed impossibly fragile, the worse because its lack of ornamentation made it feel temporary, incongruous with the carven façade on the other side. Kaiku looked at it, and at the mouth of the monastery beyond. She was suddenly afraid. What had she been hoping for when she climbed up here? Why had she not considered the danger? Why had she not held back and observed?

A pang in her stomach reminded her. She could not afford the time to wait and spy out the land, for she was starving. To return to the wilderness far below meant certain death.

There was no choice.

A quick search of the outpost – carefully avoiding the attentions of Moon-face – revealed nothing but deserted buildings, and yielded no morsel to eat. So it was that Kaiku found herself crossing the narrow stone bridge to the monastery, leaning on her staff like an old man, and hoping only that whatever was within would not question her disguise.

The monastery façade was stern and simple. Great pillars held up a roof that sloped back to merge with the rock of the mountainside, and beneath it there crouched four mighty statues, four creatures all haunch and scale and fang. As Kaiku approached, she saw that the pillars were decorated with thousands of tiny, intricate glyphs and pictograms, and that the statues were not weathered like their inferior counterparts on the stairway she had climbed yesterday. These were so carefully carven that it was almost possible to believe they breathed. The portal to the monastery had heavy stone gates, but they were open and inside it was dark.

Kaiku hesitated. The statues made her skin crawl. She had a notion that their eyes were on her, a sensation too strong to be put down to nerves. She looked back across the bridge and saw Moon-face watching her from the other side of the gorge. The fear of discovery assailed her anew; but she could not turn back. Steeling herself, she walked onward and into the stone throat of the monastery.

The corridor she came into bore torch brackets but no torches. By the morning light that shone in through the square portal, she could see hints of statues to either side, deformed beasts that pawed at her or gathered themselves to leap. Beyond that, all was black. She went forward, her shadow preceding her, gradually merging with the darkness until she was swallowed by it.

Her eyes adjusted slowly as she went, tapping her staff

before her. This place seemed as deserted as the outpost, and yet Moon-face had come from *somewhere*. Though she was weak and fragile, her hunger drove her onward, even after the light from the entrance had disappeared with the turn of a corner.

And then she saw new light, and became aware of someone coming towards her from below. She stopped still at the top of a staircase she had been about to tumble down. The flickering torch came nearer, until she could see that it was held by another creature of motley and rags, this one with a face like a grinning skull, made of blackened bone. The newcomer came up the stairs and halted a few steps below Kaiku. She was stooped so that her robes buried her, the better to conceal her femininity; but she felt her heart begin to accelerate as the Weaver regarded her. Was he waiting for her to speak? She could not: to open her mouth would be to give herself away. After a short pause that seemed to stretch agonisingly, he grunted and handed Kaiku his torch, then walked past her, without fear of the darkness. Kaiku let out a pent-up breath.

The steps took her down to a new corridor, and as she progressed along this one she found that the torch brackets were occupied more often than not, and smoky flames cast warm reddish light about the pathways of the monastery. The walls, ceiling and floor were built of massive bricks of a sandy-coloured stone, and decorations were strewn haphazardly about: here a little votive alcove, there a hanging, chiming talisman. Sometimes there were tiny carven idols standing on shelves, and sometimes Kaiku had to duck beneath hanging streamers. She could discern no pattern to the imagery; it was as if someone had hoarded the detritus of a dozen religions together. There were icons from far-off lands, heathen dolls from the jungle continent of Okhamba, ancient Ugati carvings, depictions of the Saramyr pantheon including some of those gods who had been all but forgotten. She even saw a graven fountain, now dry, that had the three aspects of Misamcha set into its pedestal in the classical Vinaxan style, from the very beginning of the Saramyr Empire.

The corridor split off into two, and that into four, and soon Kaiku was hopelessly lost within the subterranean maze of the monastery. She wandered through chamber after chamber, finding them arranged utterly without order or direction, as if planned by some madman. She passed other masked Weavers several times, but all of them ignored her, and she began to relax a little, content that her disguise hid her gender well enough.

Presently, after walking for some time down deserted ways, she came across an area which she took for some kind of prison. There was no light burning and nobody present, but the sound of shuffling and scraping from the dark recesses of the cells told her that at least some of them were occupied.

Curiosity overcame hunger, and she crept inwards. What kind of prisoners did the Weavers keep? The chamber was little more than a short, wide corridor between two rows of barred cell doors. The silence as she stepped inside became total; even the shuffling stopped. Her torch showed her only the bars, and did nothing to illuminate what was behind them.

She stood indecisive for a time. Then, slowly, she stepped over to one of the cells, holding her torch up. There was something pressed back there in the shadows, something . . .

It sprang at her without warning, crashing into the bars and lunging with one clawed arm. She yelled and pulled herself away, the claws missing her by centimetres. The torch fell from her hand to the floor, rolling back a little way, out of the creature's reach.

An Aberrant. She had seen its kin many times in the mountains, but never one like this. This one was a true grotesquerie, a malformed abomination of muscle and tooth. It had four arms, but all were different sizes, ranging from withered to massively swollen. A single eye blinked balefully from a face that was black and wizened, and its lower portions were a terrible tangle of half-grown limbs and tentacles, wrapped around each other, some crooked and broken. Its back was a shiver of spines and fins. It looked like the collision of several different types of creature, all fighting to represent themselves by a limb or a feature and resulting only in a horrible clutter of nauseating aspect.

'. . . *kkilll yoooou* . . .' the thing gurgled in Saramyrrhic, and Kaiku's heart froze.

Suddenly, all around her, the cells were alive, things rattling the bars of their cages or reaching out of the darkness for her. Roars and bleatings became mangled words from deformed mouths, pleadings, curses, even some awful noise that sounded like weeping. Kaiku recoiled in terror, snatching up the torch, but she dared not take her eyes off the thing that had spoken first. It retreated slowly out of the light, letting the darkness take it once more, and as it did so it spoke again.

'. . . *lookkk wwwhatt yoou've ddooone ttto ussss* . . .'

She fled the prison, horror making her blood cold as she ran, and she did not stop until she was beyond the reach of the clamour. There she leaned against a wall, panting, listening to her heart slow. The shock of having that thing attack her had been bad enough, but to hear it speak . . . it was almost more than she could bear, in her weakened state. They were *full-grown* Aberrants in the midst of a Weaver monastery. Intelligent, aware, and imprisoned. What could it mean?

Seeking to distract herself from the memories, she stumbled onward, thoroughly lost. The possibility had occurred to her several times that she might be unable to escape this maze before she starved, but for the moment her hunger was forgotten. Instead, she pressed onward, knowing no direction but away from that prison.

After a time, she became aware of a dull hum coming from somewhere ahead of her. By now she had passed into unlit corridors that were little more than crude tunnels, and there were no torch brackets here. She had seen nobody for some while, and had resigned herself to the fact that she had strayed far from the beaten path. She had been about to turn back to where there was a greater likelihood of finding food, but the hum intrigued her enough to keep her going.

A light further up the tunnel drew her to it, and she found a wide rent in the side of the corridor which let out on to a broad ledge in a vast chamber. The hum was coming from the chamber, and the light from within shone on her, a strangely uneasy glow of an indefinable hue.

The ledge blocked her view of the chamber below, so she wriggled through the rent and crawled to the lip, and there she looked over and saw what was beneath.

The chamber was more ornate than anything she had seen so far in this place. It was possessed of a powerful, stony grandeur, its sandy walls curved into pillars or gliding into mighty stone lintels above the gold-etched gates at floor level. Kaiku was very high up, her ledge only a little below the flat ceiling. On either side of her, a cluster of enormous gargoyle-like creatures leered over the proceedings below, smaller cousins to the vast statue that dominated the far end of the chamber. That one was fully fifty feet high, its shoulders scraping the ceiling as it squatted in the unnatural light. The creatures were foul beyond imagining, eyeless things with gaping maws whose proportions seemed to defy sense. They were monstrously malformed, just humanoid enough to be recognisable as such but twisted so far out of true that Kaiku could not help but doubt the sanity of the mind behind them. They were lit from below, their hideous features made more menacing by shadow.

But it was what was happening in the centre of the chamber that drew Kaiku's attention. There was the source of the light: a massive rock, perhaps forty feet in length and half that in height. It was not like any rock Kaiku had ever seen.

The shape of the thing was utterly irregular, and doubly so for a mineral. It seemed to have *sprouted*, like a plant or a coral reef, so that great roots and lumpen antlers of stone reached out from its core and buried themselves in the floor, walls and ceiling of the chamber. It seethed with an unnatural glow. Kaiku narrowed her eyes behind her Mask and felt a sickness creep into her belly. It made her feel ill just to look upon it.

I know of these, she thought to herself, the memory of the Mask coming to her. *This is a witchstone.*

She was gazing on the source of the Weavers' power, and their most jealously guarded treasure.

There were twelve Weavers surrounding the rock, attired as Kaiku was in patchwork robes and odd Masks. There was a thirteenth person as well, but this one was naked: a thin, emaciated man struggling weakly in the clutches of two of the robed figues. Kaiku watched as they dragged him up a set of steps and pulled him on to the jagged back of the witchstone. She guessed what was going to happen even before one of them drew his sickle and cut the unfortunate man's throat.

The man slumped forward on his face. One of the robed figures retreated while the other turned him over and cut him from chin to manhood, opening him up to expose his insides. These he roughly began to hack at, pulling them out one by one without finesse, laying them aside on the rock when they were free. Heart, kidneys, liver, intestines . . . in moments, he was surrounded by the man's organs.

Kaiku had been watching this with no particular horror. The fate of that man did not concern her, nor the method in which he was despatched. But there was something wrong with what she was seeing, and it took her a little time to understand what it was.

There was no blood. Oh, certainly, the man *bled*, and the Weaver's garments were sprayed with gore; but the rock, where almost all the blood had eventually fallen, was spotless. Where the heart had been taken out and laid aside, it lay as clean and dry as an apple. Where the intestines should have rested in a pool of red, they were rubbery and blue and immaculate. The blood was coming out, all right, but where was it going? It was as if the rock absorbed it somehow.

Or *drank* it.

Kaiku frowned at the thought, but she could see now that the witchstone was beginning to darken, the foul glow fading and being drawn inwards, until the cavern was almost pitch black. The only source of light was within the rock, and the rock was full of veins, a network of glowing lines hanging in the pure darkness, as if its skin had become transparent and its own innards were exposed. And at its core, a pulsing chamber like a human heart, pushing the bright white blood around it.

By the spirits, Kaiku thought. *The witchstone. It is alive.*

The memories hit her then, a sudden rush of understanding that flooded into her brain, triggered by the realisation. Connections that she had never considered before became suddenly obvious, each one sparking another and another until the circuit was complete and she saw the whole of the grand design, as her father had seen it. Kaiku knew, in a flash, what Ruito tu Makaima had found out, why he had run, and why they had killed him for that knowledge.

The witchstones were alive. And just as the dust of the witchstones in the Weaver's Masks corrupted and warped their bodies, so the witchstones were corrupting and warping the earth in which they lay.

It opened up to her then as a vision. Ruito in his study, in a hired apartment in Axekami, poring over a map and a heap of charts and scrolls. A project he had been working on in secret for years, a passion, a suspicion. In her vision, Kaiku stood with him at the moment of realisation – though she had not been present in real life – when all the facts and figures and distances fell into place. There was a correlation between the reports of Aberrant births and their proximity to Weavers. He saw that the epicentre of Aberrancy always lay at the site of a Weaver monastery, and the monasteries were always built around the witchstones. How could nobody have

seen this before? How many people had been killed or
dissuaded, to keep their silence? But Ruito saw, and determined to investigate, to gain the proof he needed to confront
the nobles with. So he had come here, and seen this, and then
he had run.

But they had known. Somehow, they had known, by some
carelessness that even Ruito was not aware of. An invisible
trigger, a misplaced word . . . who could say? By the time he
returned to the mainland, it was hopeless. Only in secrecy
could a man such as he hope to overcome the Weavers. Once
they were forewarned, he would never be able to so much as
get a message to the nobles. They would not even let him
leave his house, watching his every move like vultures.
Perhaps if he had gone straight to Axekami, tried to spread
the knowledge to others, they would have killed only him.
But he had come home, shattered by what he had seen, to
think and recuperate; and they had been following him all the
way. It was only then they had let themselves be seen, let him
know they were on him like a shadow. They allowed him to
come all the way home, back to his family, and then they
showed themselves.

And Ruito knew that his life was at an end; he had
discovered too much.

Kaiku felt she would choke on sorrow as she felt him make
his choice. There was no escape, and no way to unknow what
he knew. He would be killed, and so would his family. But
they could at least leave the player's table with honour,
instead of at the foul hands of whatever creatures the Weavers
would employ. He would not let his family be subject to
tortures or interrogation, to have their minds laid bare and
flayed by the monsters he had stirred up.

It was no assassin who poisoned the evening meal that day,
no agent of the Weavers who killed Kaiku that first time. It
was her father.

When they were assured of his impotency, once they had
scoured his apartment in Axekami and removed all his work,

the Weavers sent the shin-shin. But the shin-shin were too late to do anything but clean up the evidence, and it was only through the strength of Asara that anyone was left to tell of it at all.

Kaiku's eyes flooded with tears. She felt all the despair, all the loss, the terrible realisation that her father had borne. No wonder he had seemed haunted when last he returned to their home; he had been broken by the scale of the conspiracy he had uncovered, shattered by the knowledge that neither he nor his family would be allowed to live. Destroyed by the choice he had to make, to poison his loved ones or leave them to a far worse fate.

The Weavers had killed Aberrants for two hundred years, preached hatred towards them, used their positions of power to ingrain it into the consciousness of the people of Saramyr. But they were not doing it out of the desire to keep the human race pure, nor for any religious reason. They were cleaning up their own mess, covering their tracks, destroying the evidence.

The source of the Weavers' power was also the source of the blight that was wasting the land.

This final realisation was too much for her. Starving, exhausted and frightened, she slid back through the crack in the wall and away from the ledge. She did not know how long she stumbled until she fainted, but she welcomed oblivion with open arms.

TWENTY-THREE

Anais tu Erinima, Blood Empress of Saramyr, stood at the top of the Imperial Keep and looked over the city below. A pall of smoke was drifting up from the north bank of the Kerryn, joined by several thinner cousins nearby, polluting the evening sky. The air was as dry and hot as the inside of a clay oven. Behind her and to her left, Nuki's eye was a westering ball of sullen orange, setting the horizon afire behind the grand bulk of the temple to Ocha that lay in the centre of the Keep's roof. Beneath the walkway that supported her lay the Keep's sculpture garden, a frozen forest of artistic shapes and constructions, open to the sky. The strange forms that inhabited the garden cast long, warped shadows across their neighbours. Narrow white paths wound through carefully tended lawns, gliding between the pedestals that the sculptures rested on.

She laid her pale, elegant fingers on the low wall that protected her from a dizzying drop, and let her head bow. An Imperial Guard in white and blue armour stood at his post further along the walkway, pretending not to notice.

She wanted to scream, to throw herself from this height and tumble to her death below. Wouldn't that make an ending? Wouldn't that be worth a song, or a poem? If the war poet Xalis was still alive today, he would make a good fist of it, describing her sharp and sudden finale in his equally sharp and sudden verse, the words like the cut and thrust of a sword.

The city was tearing itself apart. Most of the nobles had fled by now, back to their estates where they gathered what armies they had and waited to see which way the wind was blowing. The court had scattered, and that made the Weavers more important than ever; civil war was in the offing, and every house was scrambling to ensure they would keep their heads above water when the conflict came. In her heart, Anais knew that the author of her misery was within her own Keep: Vyrrch. And yet the alternative to him was to blind and cripple herself, to leave herself without a Weaver in the face of her enemies. Vyrrch may have dared to act in secret, but he could not overtly refuse to defend her or keep messages from her, or he would reveal his hand and the power of the Weavers would be jeopardised. If it was once proved that Vyrrch had meddled, then the nobles would retaliate. But not, she suspected, until after they had done their level best to kill her child.

The frustration was abominable. Even her supposed allies within her camp were against her. Why could none of them see? Did her years of sound rule count for nothing? By the spirits, it was her *child*! Her only child, and the only one she could ever have. Lucia was supposed to rule. She was blood-line!

But what price for a mother's love? How many would die for her pride in her daughter? How many would lose their lives before the people saw that Lucia was no freak, not a thing to be loathed, but a thing of beauty?

The unfairness of it rankled. She had been coping with the disorder until that idiot Guard Commander had ruined everything by arresting Unger tu Torrhyc. And then, when she was prepared to release him and show the people the generosity of their ruler, Unger was found dead, having smashed his own brains out against the wall of his cell. The stories circulated in the streets already, of how he bravely sacrificed himself before the Empress's torturers could make him retract his words.

And at the centre of the web, Vyrrch. She knew it was him. But she had no way to prove it.

'Anais!' came the cry from below. She stirred from her

maudlin reverie and looked down into the sculpture garden, where Barak Zahn tu Ikati was hailing her. She raised a hand in greeting and made her way down to him. He met her at the bottom of the steps. For a moment they regarded each other awkwardly; then Zahn put his arms around the Empress and hugged her, and she, surprised, returned the embrace.

'To what do I owe this undue affection?' she murmured.

'You look like you need it, Anais,' he replied.

He released her, and she smiled wearily. 'Does it show so much?'

'Only to one who knows you such as I,' Zahn replied.

Anais inclined her head in gratitude. 'Walk with me,' she said, and she took his arm as they strolled through the sculpture garden.

The sculptures of the Imperial Keep dated back to pre-Empire days, monuments to the acquisitive instincts of the second Blood Emperor, Torus tu Vinaxis. Only good fortune had made him decide to choose Axekami as the place to keep his treasures, for the first capital of Gobinda was swallowed by cataclysm shortly after his reign ended, and much would have been lost. He was responsible for starting most of the art collections in the current capital; a man too sensitive and creative to be a good ruler, as history told when he was usurped by the now-dead bloodline of Cho. Anais found some of them restful, others interesting, but few inspiring. She had not the heart of an artist, which was why – she told herself – she had been such an effective Blood Empress.

'Things are turning for the worse, Zahn,' Anais said, as they ambled past a curving mock-organic whirl of ivory. 'The people are becoming uncontrollable. My Imperial Guards are already stretched to the limit, and their presence only seems to incite the people more. Every riot put down breeds two smaller ones. The Poor Quarter is burning. Unger tu Tor-rhyc's cursed band of followers are causing untold damage in the streets of my city.' Her eyes dimmed. 'Things are turning for the worse,' she said again.

'Then what I have to tell you will not improve your mood, Anais,' said Zahn, rubbing his bearded cheek with a knuckle.

'I already know,' she replied. 'Blood Kerestyn have marshalled their forces to the west. They are marching on the capital.'

'Did you also know that Barak Sonmaga and the forces of Blood Amacha are marching from the south to meet them?'

Anais looked up at him, and for a moment there was the aspect of something hunted in her eyes. 'To join with Kerestyn?'

'Doubtful,' said Zahn. 'At least, there has been no intelligence to that effect. No, I believe Sonmaga intends to block Kerestyn from entering the city.'

'At least until he can march in himself,' Anais scowled.

'Indeed,' Zahn said ruefully. There was a silence between them, as they walked through the looming aisles of sculpture, their shoes crunching on the gravel path.

'Say it, Zahn,' Anais prompted at length. 'You came here for more important reasons than to deliver a message.'

Zahn did not look at her as he spoke, but fixed his eyes on an imaginary point in the middle distance. 'I came here to beg you to reconsider your decision to keep the throne.'

'You are saying I should abdicate?' Anais's voice hardened to stone.

'Take Lucia with you,' Zahn said, his tone flat and devoid of emotion. 'Leave the throne to those who desire it so much. Choose your child's life over your family's power. You can live in peace and prosperity the rest of your days, and Lucia will be safe. But your position is worsening, Empress, and you know what will happen if Blood Amacha or Blood Kerestyn have to take this city by force.'

Anais was furiously silent.

'Then I will say it, if you won't,' Zahn continued. 'You, they may well allow to live. But they will execute Lucia. They cannot risk her being a threat to their power, and the people will want their blood.'

'And if I abdicate?' Anais spat. 'They will get to her, Zahn. She is still a threat even if I give up all claim to the throne. As many people who hate Aberrants, there are some who don't and she will become a focus for their discontent, an icon for them to rally behind. Whether Kerestyn or Amacha become the ruling family, whether I abdicate or not, they will kill Lucia. They will send assassins. She is *too dangerous to live*, don't you see that? The only way I can keep my child alive is to stay Empress and *beat* them!'

She was aware suddenly that she was shouting. Zahn put his hands on her shoulders to calm her, but she swatted him away.

'Don't touch me, Zahn. You have no right any more.'

'Ah,' the Barak said bitterly. 'Yes, I have heard that you have taken to sharing your bed again with your wastrel husband. I remember when you—'

'That is *not* your business!' Anais snapped, her pale skin flushing.

Zahn held up his palms placatingly. 'Forgive me,' he said. 'I forget myself. Do not let us argue; there are more important things at stake here.'

Anais searched his eyes for hints of mockery, but she found him honest. She relaxed. When Zahn saw she was ready to listen, he spoke again.

'If you are adamant on staying, Anais, at least let your allies help you,' he said. 'There could be a thousand troops here in two days, ten times that in a week. You could put down the uprising, keep the people safe, and once within the city we would be unassailable. Amacha or Kerestyn would not dare enter.'

'Zahn,' Anais said wearily. 'I trust you. But you know I cannot allow a force like that into Axekami. There are too many families involved, too many political uncertainties.'

'Word has reached me that Barak Mos of Blood Batik has offered his troops, and that you accepted.'

'Your spies are inept, my Barak,' Anais said without

rancour. 'Mos has offered me troops, but I have not accepted yet. He is a different matter, anyway. My defence is in his interest: he has his son and granddaughter to protect. Durun would just as likely be killed as I if either Blood Amacha or Blood Kerestyn took Axekami.'

'Mos is also the head of the only other family strong enough to take the throne,' Zahn reminded her.

'His son already *has* the throne,' Anais replied. 'I have not annulled our marriage through these years despite the obvious unsuitability of my husband. He has no reason to think I might now.'

'Do you believe you can hold Axekami against your enemies, with the very people of the city against you?' Zahn asked.

'The people will learn to accept Lucia,' said Anais. 'Or I will *make* them learn. As to now, they are like children in a tantrum, and must be punished. I will keep them in order.'

They turned a corner, into the long shadow of a rearing thing that might have been a stone cobra, or perhaps a man and woman entwined. The evening sun shone through the gaps in the sculpture, reddening imperceptibly as dusk came on. Zahn gave it barely a glance. They walked on for a time in the sultry heat of the Saramyr summer before Anais spoke again.

'I owe you an apology,' she said.

Zahn was surprised. 'For what?'

'I have been presumptuous. I have been so busy trying to win my opponents over that I have not considered one of my greatest allies. For weeks I have been introducing Lucia to the high families in an attempt to dispel the myths that have arisen about her; but you have supported me from the start in this, and I have never once invited you to see the cause you fight for.'

Zahn inclined his head. She knew as well as him why he was on her side. 'You are right, of course. I never have met her. I would be honoured if I might do so now.'

*

The Heir-Empress Lucia had finished her lessons for the day, so she went up to the roof gardens to enjoy the last of the evening light. Zaelis had stayed with her. She liked the tall, white-bearded tutor. He indulged her relentlessly, and his deep, molten voice was comforting. She knew – in the unique way that she knew things – that he had her best interests at heart. She also enjoyed the freedom she felt when she was alone with him. He was the only one around whom she could use her talents overtly.

They were sitting together on a bench, a picturesque arbour within a shaggy fringe of exotic trees. Berries hung in colourful chains amid the deep, tropical green of the leaves. Insects droned and clicked from a hundred different hiding places, occasionally swooping past them in languid curves or hurried, darting rushes. Ravens perched all around them. The ravens of the Keep had learned to accept Zaelis, and he had learned to relax in their presence. They were fiercely protective of the young Heir-Empress. Saramyr ravens had a strong territorial instinct, and it bred in them a desire to guard and protect. They watched over Lucia as if she was an errant chick, motivated by parental drives they were not intelligent enough to understand.

'Are you worried, Lucia?' Zaelis asked.

She nodded. He had become adept at reading her moods, even though they rarely showed in the dreamlike expression she always wore.

'About what is happening in the city?'

She nodded again. Nobody had told her anything – the tutors and guards had been instructed to keep outside matters secret after Durun's outburst in front of the child – but Lucia knew anyway. How could you keep something like that from a girl who could speak to birds? Zaelis had ignored the edict and elaborated on the situation for her. Lucia had not told him that the dream lady had informed her of most of it anyway.

'This was my fault,' she said quietly. 'I started this.'

'I know you did,' Zaelis replied, in the casual mode of address used for – and by – children, even the Heir-Empress. 'But we've been waiting for you to start it for a very long time.'

Lucia looked up at him. 'You'll look after me, won't you?'

'Of course.'

'And my mother?'

Zaelis hesitated. There was no point lying to her; she saw right through him. 'We'll try,' he said. 'But she won't see things the way we do.'

'Who is "we"?' Lucia asked.

'You know who *we* are.'

'I've never heard you say it.'

'You don't need to.'

Lucia thought about that. 'Do you think I'm wicked?' she said after a time.

'I think you were inevitable,' Zaelis replied.

She seemed to understand; but then, with Lucia, who could say?

'Mother's coming,' she murmured, and almost simultaneously the ravens took wing, disappearing in a raucous flutter of black feathers, rising into the red sky.

A moment later, the Blood Empress came into view, walking with Zahn along a tiled path between a stand of narrow trees. She glanced once at the departing ravens, but no other reaction crossed her face. Zaelis got to his feet, ushering Lucia up with him.

'Barak Zahn tu Ikati, allow me to present my daughter Lucia,' the Empress said.

But her words seemed scarcely heeded by either the Barak or the child. The two of them were staring at each other with something like amazement on their faces. Anais and Zaelis exchanged a puzzled glance as the moment became awkward; and then Lucia's eyes filled with tears, and she flung herself at the Barak and hugged him around the waist, burying her head in his stomach.

'Lucia!' the Empress exclaimed.

Zahn folded his hands over the little Heir-Empress's blonde tresses, a strange look in his eyes, a mix of bewilderment and shock. Lucia pulled herself away suddenly, glaring at him through her tears; then with a sob she turned and fled, disappearing into the leafy folds of the garden.

All three were dumbstruck for a moment before Anais found her voice.

'Zahn, I cannot apologise enough. She never—'

'It's quite all right, Anais,' Zahn said, his voice sounding distant and distracted. 'Quite all right. I think I should go now; I seem to have upset her.'

Without waiting for her leave, Zahn turned and began to walk slowly to the entrance of the garden. Anais went with him, leaving Zaelis alone on the path. He sat back down on the bench.

'Well, well, well,' he murmured to himself, and an odd smile creased his face.

TWENTY-FOUR

Asara killed again in Chaim. It was an unwise risk, for she had no need to feed; but she sought diversion, and there was no other in the bleak, empty trading village to interest her. She chose a man this time, because she had less respect for them than for women, and she was less likely to suffer something like guilt for robbing their life as a source of amusement. This one was drunk, a leathery, tough brawler who had no fear of the short, dark route from the bar to his house, where no lights burned. Asara taught him otherwise.

Afterward, when she had hidden the body far away where it would not be discovered for days, she returned to her room. She was not worried about being caught. There was not a mark on him, nothing to link them. He had simply got lost on his way home in the dark, and fallen victim to exposure. Or perhaps his heart just stopped. He was a drinker, after all, and well-known for it.

She sat in her room, alone. As she preferred it. As it always was.

Her room at the lodging house was as spartan as everything else in Chaim. There was a double bed in the centre, its woollen covers dark with age and moth-ragged. There was a lantern on the wall, and bare, ill-fitting floorboards. Beyond that, there was nothing. The mountain winds cooed outside, sending chilly fingers in through the cracks in the wall to brush across her skin. The lantern was unlit, which made little difference to Asara – her night vision was near-perfect, like a cat's. It was freezing, as always, for the winds cut to the bone here even in summer. She listened to the night, and the sudden, sharp gusts that whipped around the rickety lodging house.

The bliss of feeding was short-lived, and when it left her she was maudlin. She sat cross-legged on the tatty bed and looked at the empty room. Alone, ever alone. She did not know any other way. For there were none like her, not even the other Aberrants. She was a reflection, a cypher, without identity or cause. She was nothing, not even herself.

There was no memory of her childhood. There had been a time when she had wished she could gaze upon herself at the moment of her birth, thinking that if she could see her first face, even if it was the scrunched-up red ball of a newborn, then she might have a fix on her identity, a base line from which all her other selves grew. But it was fancy. She suspected anyway that she would not like what she saw there.

Her mother died in the pregnancy. During her early years, in her lonely quest for herself, she had tracked down the place where she had been born. She learned of a woman there who had become pregnant, and within three months had wasted away to the point of death. Yet the woman's belly was so swollen that the physicians of the village cut her open, and they found a fully grown babe within. Asara had no doubt that it was her. She had sucked her mother dry from inside the womb.

What happened to the baby, nobody knew. Perhaps it was given away, perhaps lost and found. It was remarkably hard to trace her own trail, when with each new location she was a different person.

She remembered several mothers and fathers, foster parents who took her in. She was irresistible to them. With a child's eagerness to please, she unconsciously changed herself, day by day, to accommodate her new parents' vision of the perfect offspring. She bewitched them by fulfilling their heart's desire. But always, sooner or later, the time came to leave. When a relative marked the drastic alterations since they had visited last year, too gradual for her parents to see but obvious to one who had been away for a while; when her cravings and appetites had claimed too many lives; when people began to question where she had come from: that was her time to move on, leaving only the memory of a curious ailment known as the Sleeping Death behind her, a disease that struck at random and left not a mark on the victim's body. As if their life had simply left them.

She grew fast. When she was six harvests old, the craving began, and instinct taught her how to sate it in the same way it taught babes to suckle or adolescents to kiss. She was clever even then, and careful never to be caught, though there were times when she had come close. In the early days, the hunger was worse, for she was growing as well as changing. By the time she was thirteen harvests of age she had the form and understanding of an eighteen-harvest girl. In those days, she seemed to absorb something of her victims, shreds of understanding and knowledge that kept her mind apace with her body; that talent she had lost with the passing of childhood, and never regained. To her, it was simply a part of growing up.

Her uncanny growth meant that she was forced to move on frequently, and learn hard lessons in life; but she was a good pupil, and an attentive one, and she survived the fate that most Aberrants suffered. She avoided the Weavers and the hatred of those around her, until she had mastered herself enough to disguise her condition.

As time went on, she grew bitter and resentful. She searched for her past and found fragments, each as unsatisfying as the last. In the end, she gave up. And yet the feeling remained, even now, eighty harvests after her birth. She had no core. She was a mirrored shell, reflecting other people's ideas of beauty, but under it all there was nothing. A void that sucked in life, and was never quite filled. It demanded that she prey on the things she imitated, desperately drawn to their light like a moth to a candle. She was an effigy, a parasite . . . anything but a person.

Time had given her ample opportunity to change, both in conviction and form. She had spent a few years as a man before deciding that it did not suit her. She had briefly tried to struggle against her need to feed and liberate herself from it, but in the end she could not convince herself of the worth of human beings, and she still saw most of them as a brand of cattle only slightly more unpredictable than oxen or cows. The rest were dangerous to her: the Weavers and the nobles, those who would hunt her down and slay her because she was a threat to them. No, she owed humanity no favours, and though she still hung on to a vestigial semblance of guilt and regret at sacrificing a particularly pretty life to her hungers, it was more in the manner of having been forced to break a beautiful vase.

But all changes led back to the same void, the same boredom and emptiness. And so she sat, alone, in her room in Chaim, and wondered when it might ever end.

Asara awoke at mid-morning, a moment before there came a knock at her door. She dressed hurriedly, already alert, and opened it.

The owner of the lodging house was there, a thin, grizzled, wiry man with few teeth. She dismissed him from her gaze, shifting it immediately to the one who stood next to him. Their eyes met, and the other managed a smile so weak that it told all the story it needed to tell.

Kaiku.

'This one wanted you,' the owner said. 'Was asking around.'

Kaiku stepped into the room. She looked half the weight she had been when they set off into the mountains, three weeks ago. Asara embraced her gently; she felt frail and thin, all bone.

'Bring us food,' she said to the owner. 'Meat, fish.'

'She'll be staying in this room, then?' the owner queried, a note of disapproval in his voice.

'Yes,' Asara replied bluntly. 'She will.'

By the time she had turned back, Kaiku was lying on the bed, asleep.

They did not leave the room for three days. Kaiku slept most of that time, and Asara watched over her. She seemed withdrawn, hollowed-out, and by the look in her eyes Asara knew it was something more than a physical trial she had suffered. She barely talked the first day, and only a little more on the second. Asara did not press her, not even to ask whether she had found the monastery or not. She knew Kaiku had, anyway. Her father had borne that same look about him when he returned to their house in the Forest of Yuna, shortly before the shin-shin came. Instead Asara simply waited, and guarded her while she recovered.

At Asara's behest, the owner knocked and brought them food at intervals. He was well paid for his trouble. The wealth that Asara and Kaiku carried between them, while not impressive by city standards, was a small fortune in Chaim. Kaiku ate, at first a little and then a lot as her shrunken stomach stretched to the prospect of life-giving energy. She was ravenous. At night, they slept huddled together. Asara had the owner bring extra blankets, but Kaiku shivered anyway.

By the third day, Kaiku's strength had returned somewhat. Without prompting, she suddenly began to talk.

'I imagine you are curious to know where I have been,' she said to Asara, who was sitting on the edge of the bed combing her hair.

'The thought had crossed my mind, yes,' she replied dryly.

'Forgive me my silence,' Kaiku said. 'I have had much to think about.'

Asara finished her combing and twisted to face Kaiku, who was wrapped in a blanket, hugging her knees. 'You have suffered,' she observed as a way of excusing her.

'No more than I deserve,' she replied. Then she told Asara about what she had seen and done, of her journey across the mountains and the slaying of the Weaver whose robes she stole, of the Mask and the crossing of the barrier that hid the

Weavers from the world. She talked of the monastery and the strange things within, of the foul prison full of Aberrants and the creature's accusation: *Look what you've done to us* . . .

Asara's eyes widened as Kaiku recounted what she had seen in the chamber of the witchstone, and the vision the Mask had given her. She did not weep as she spoke of her father and his fate; but tears stood in her eyes, marshalling behind her lashes. Finally, she told Asara of the true nature of the witchstones. The jealously guarded source of the Weaver's power was also the despoiler of the land. Kaiku, Asara, Cailin, the Heir-Empress Lucia . . . all the Aberrants were merely a side-effect of the witchstones' energy that the Weavers harnessed in their Masks.

As she spoke, Asara found herself breathless with wonder. Each word seemed to increase the sensation of incredulity. The witchstones were the *source* of the blight? The Weavers were responsible for the very Aberrants they murdered? For the first time in longer than she cared to remember, she felt she was on the cusp of something truly worthwhile. All she had been working for these last years, with the Red Order and the Libera Dramach, in her time as Kaiku's handmaiden . . . all of it flexed into focus at this moment, and she felt the pounding of blood through her body and was *alive*.

'Do you know what you have discovered?' Asara managed. 'Do you know what you have *found*?' She grabbed Kaiku's arm. 'Are you sure? Are you sure it was no delirium you saw, but your father's memories?'

'As sure as I can be,' Kaiku said wearily. 'But Father's notes burned with the house, and if there were any left in his apartment in Axekami, I doubt there is any trace now.'

'But this could topple the Weavers!' Asara enthused. 'If the nobles knew, if we could *prove* it . . . the rage at being deceived would be . . . spirits, even if we *cannot*, we can plant the seed, help them ask the right questions! Why has nobody thought of it before?'

'They have,' Kaiku said. 'But most scholars are patronised

by a noble, who in turn has a Weaver. They usually met with accidents before they could get far into their research, I imagine. My father was independent, and he kept his research secret, and even then he was discovered.'

Asara was barely listening. 'How did you get away, Kaiku? From the monastery?'

Kaiku shrugged minutely. 'It was easy.'

She told the rest of her story then. When she had woken from the faint induced by stress and hunger, she had forced herself to her feet and attempted to find her way back to the more central areas of the monastery, where food would be. Whether the Mask was helping her or not she could not divine, but she found a kitchen not long after, populated by short, scurrying servants whom she had not encountered until now. They were almost dwarfish in stature, wiry and swarthy, and their bunched-up faces revealed nothing about their thoughts, if indeed they thought at all. They seemed a simple, servile breed.

By pointing to a bone plate and to the stove, Kaiku procured herself a meal of root vegetables, a curious kind of rice-potato hybrid, and chunks of dark red meat swimming in an oily sauce. She retreated to solitude to eat, tipping her Mask up and spooning the food beneath, afraid in case anyone should see her face. It was surprisingly delicious, but the relief of putting food in her belly again made it seem all the more wonderful. She returned for more and the servants filled her plate unquestioningly. From then on, Kaiku navigated by that kitchen, using it as her base point so she always knew where to return to after she had done wandering.

It took her several tries to find her way out of the monastery, by which time she had become confident enough that her disguise would not be seen through. The Weavers kept themselves to themselves, and they were an eccentric breed. She came across some of them squatting in corners, rocking themselves gently and muttering gibberish; others sprang shrieking out of hiding at her and then fled. Most just passed her by. She soon realised that a Weaver who did not speak was a minor oddity among the insanity of the monastery, and she took comfort in that.

She had not known what plan she had in mind for when she found her way to the open air once again. Perhaps she had thought to walk back into the wilderness and trust to Shintu's luck to get her through. But Shintu smiled on her in other ways.

When she did emerge into the harsh, snow-crisp light, there was some kind of activity going on in the tiny settlement that clung to the mountainside opposite the monastery. She crossed the bridge that spanned the chasm and investigated. Several dozen of the dwarfish servants were hauling sacks and boxes down the immense stone stairway that led to the foot of the mountain. She watched them for a while before guessing what they were about. They were loading up carts! Suddenly excited, she made her way past them and began her descent of the stairway. It was no short trip, but she had a sense that if she missed this opportunity she may never get another.

At the bottom, she saw her efforts had not been in vain. Three large carts with great wheels wrapped in chains sat there, and manxthwa were being tethered to them. Several Weavers were bustling around. A moment's consideration led her to discard the idea of hiding in the carts, so she did the only thing she could think to do. The driver's bench was wide enough for three, and there only appeared to be one driver for each cart. She clambered on to one of the carts and waited.

It seemed like hours before the servants had finished loading, during which time Kaiku sat still, praying that nobody would question her. She was trusting to the shield of the Weaver's insanity to let her get away with this; she had seen many far more random acts in the short time she had spent wandering the monastery. After a time, one of the dwarf servants clambered into the seat next to her. He looked at her incuriously for a moment, and then snapped the reins, and the manxthwa hauled away. Kaiku let out a breath; the Weavers were staying behind.

It took them several days by cart-trails to get back to Chaim. The servants spoke between themselves in an incomprehensible dialect, but never to Kaiku. They did not remark on how she always took her food away to eat, or how she disappeared to make toilet. At some point, they passed through the Weave-sewn barrier that surrounded the monastery again, but the servants seemed unaffected by its disorientating effects and drove right through. Kaiku was exposed to the momentary surge of bliss that accompanied that golden world of waving threads, and then it was snatched from her again with enough force to make her heart ache afresh. She settled into quiet misery, and endured. Over the entire length of the journey, she did not speak a word, and when they arrived at Chaim she could have wept with relief at the sight of the grim, squalid little town.

'When we reached here,' she concluded. 'I found a place to hide and changed back into my clothes. The Mask and robes are in my pack.' She motioned with her head towards the bulging bag in the corner of the room. 'I hoped you would have waited for me. One of you, at least.'

Asara let the unspoken question about Tane go unanswered, and that was all the answer Kaiku needed. She did not ask again.

'Kaiku, what you have done . . . it is a wondrous thing,' she said, as some sort of consolation.

'Wondrous?' Kaiku queried, and her eyes fell to her blanketed knees. 'No. I am condemned over again. Don't you see? I swore to the Emperor of the gods to avenge my father's death. The Weavers are responsible for that. Not just one, acting alone. *All* of them. How can I . . . how can one person face the Weavers? How can I destroy creatures that can kill with a thought, that can read a person's mind? My task is impossible, but my oath still stands.'

'Then you should come back to the mainland with me. To the Red Order. You have done enough here, Kaiku . . . more than enough. One person cannot destroy the Weavers; but you have done more with your strength of heart than dozens who have gone before you. And you have allies.'

Kaiku nodded, though there was no conviction in her. 'You are right. I promised Cailin I would be back. There is nothing more to be done here. We will leave tomorrow.'

Night fell, the cold, bleak night of the mountains. They ate again, then slipped into their nightclothes and into the bed with a practised rapidity. The thought of leaving this place was on both of their minds, but there was still that question lingering unsaid, and so it was no surprise to Asara when Kaiku began to weep softly. She did not need to ask what it was that troubled her; she knew well enough.

'He is gone,' she whispered, and there was a shift of blankets as she moved closer and buried her head in Asara's shoulder.

Asara made a noise of confirmation. 'I told him. About you, about me. It was right that he should know.'

'Father, Mother, Grandmother Chomi, Machim . . . even Mishani. And now Tane,' Kaiku whispered. 'They all leave me, one way or another. How much more of this am I to endure, Asara?'

'Everyone you become close to will leave you, Kaiku,' Asara said softly, feeling an uncomfortable welling of emotion herself, 'until you accept what you are. Would you rather Tane left us now . . . or when he saw your eyes after a burning? He has many contradictions he needs to resolve, Kaiku. Do not lose heart. He may find you again.'

The words gave new strength to Kaiku's tears. 'Do you think he will?'

'Maybe,' Asara said, her breath stirring Kaiku's fine hair as her lips lay close. 'Maybe not. He was learning, and accepting. Perhaps there was more to him than I guessed.' She placed a hand on Kaiku's head, stroking it gently. 'You are not alone.

But you must choose to be Aberrant, Kaiku. Stop thinking of yourself as one of *them*. *They* hate you now. *They* are like Mishani: even the most trusted will turn their back on you. You have nobody but your own kind. For now at least, you have me.'

Kaiku drew away from Asara's shoulder, and wiped her eyes with the back of her wrist. She could sense Asara's gaze in the darkness, through she could see only the faintest glitter of light from her unnatural, night-seeing eyes.

No, she caught herself. *Not unnatural. Beautiful. She need never fear the darkness, as I must.*

'You are beyond them,' Asara said quietly. 'Forget the restrictions, all the rules you have learned. They do not apply to you; use them only when necessary to disguise yourself among them. Why should you submit to what you have been taught, when your teachers would have you executed if they could? Listen no longer. Disobey. Fight back.'

'Fight back,' Kaiku breathed, her fingertips touching Asara's cheek. She was overwhelmed, her heart seeming to swell to bursting at Asara's words, and she tasted a cocktail of fear and terror and excitement and freedom such as she had never known before. There was a moment in which something seemed to shift between them, when the sharing of their body heat became suddenly magnetic, a moment in which all things seemed possible and thus became so. And in that moment, Kaiku put her lips to Asara's, who was already meeting her halfway, caught in the same tide.

They melted into one, soft skin pressing together. Their lips were dry from the wind, but they moistened swiftly in the fervour, tongues touching and sliding as they tasted each other. Kaiku's hand slid along the curve of Asara's waist and the swell of her hip, feeling the taut muscle beneath. Asara gripped the back of her neck, rolling her weight so that Kaiku was underneath her, the sound of her breath quickening in the darkness. She sat astride Kaiku's hips, and Kaiku felt Asara's hot palms on her face, running down across her shoulders, over the swell of her breasts and the apex of her nipples, across her flat stomach.

Asara's breathing was rapid now, almost panting; Kaiku experienced a moment of doubt, that something was wrong, that she had become too excited too quickly.

'You shouldn't . . .' Asara sighed. 'Don't make me . . .'

But Kaiku, swept up in the rush, ignored her. She raised herself up to kneel on the bed and brought her lips to Asara's again, kissing her hard, all warmth and sensation and darkness. Asara's hair fell across Kaiku's uptilted face; she was straddling Kaiku's knees now, and she pulled herself closer, their bellies and breasts pressed together with only the twin layers of silken nightrobes separating skin from skin. Kaiku's nails raked down her back, as if they could slice through the barrier to what was beneath.

'You don't . . . you don't know what you do . . .' Asara murmured in protest, but Kaiku had slid one strap from her shoulder, pulling it down to her elbow, and her mouth had found Asara's nipple and was sucking it gently. She shuddered in involuntary pleasure, sweeping her hair back from her face, her hips rocking against Kaiku, her breath shallow gasps.

She seized Kaiku then, roughly, and pushed her down to the bed. Her fingers gripped clawlike on either side of the younger woman's skull, and she brought her lips to Kaiku's with a predatory lunge that she had practised a thousand times before. Something inside her was warning her to stop, to stop, but her hunger and desire had been maddened by Kaiku's passion, and the voice was weak and unheeded. Suddenly, she desperately wanted what was inside Kaiku, wanted to take back the life *she* had given, to suck out the part of herself that had gone into Kaiku when she stole the handmaiden Karia's breath and blew it into her dead mistress's lungs. A piece of Asara had gone with that breath, a sliver of her life had lodged in Kaiku's heart, and Asara knew in a flash that that was the true reason why she had returned to Kaiku after Kaiku had almost killed her in the Forest of Yuna.

Kaiku sensed something in Asara's urgency, but in her heat she did not know whether it was passion or anger or something altogether different, and her senses were too overloaded to rely on. Asara kissed her hard, harder, and Kaiku felt a pain inside her, as if some organ in her breast were about to rip free, her heart about to tear from its aortal mooring. Asara sucked, powerless to stop herself, wanting only to sate herself in the most complete way she knew how.

The door to the room burst inwards.

Asara tore herself away, and Kaiku flung herself across to the other side of the bed, gasping like one who had been an inch from drowning. Her body had sensed the proximity of death although her mind had not, and she felt the terror and panic crash in on her even as Mamak and three other heavyset men rushed into the room, wielding picks and shovels. They stopped at the sight that met them: the two women, one with her nightrobe hanging from her shoulder and her right breast exposed, breathing hard and caught in surprise. A leer began to spread across Mamak's face, and then Kaiku screamed, and he exploded.

The surge of *kana* ripped through her like a stampede. The world switched from reality to the infinity of golden threads, warp and weft, a diorama of beautiful light that burned her from within like molten metal in her veins. Her irises darkened to a deep red, and she lashed out in reaction to the fear, the passion, the surprise. She saw the bright pulse of Mamak's heart as a rushing junction of threads, the stream of his blood as it passed beneath his transparent skin, and she rent it apart with a thought. He burst in a shower of flaming gore, spattering his stunned companions and spraying the bed with shards of charred bone and brain. Asara shrieked and threw herself backwards, her instincts reminding her of what had happened the last time she had seen Kaiku like this.

But this time it was tighter, more focused. This time there was no surprise in its coming, and Kaiku managed to steer the rush, to force it away and direct it. With a sweep of her hand, she blasted the other men in the room, shredding through their fibres; and where the threads snapped, flame followed, an explosive release of energy. Mamak's companions became blazing pillars of fire, their howls silenced in seconds as their lungs and throats charred, their eyes bubbled, cooking from inside and out. One of them lunged at Kaiku in a last, idiot attempt for revenge or supplication, but he only slumped on to the bed and ignited it.

Kaiku felt the *kana* blow itself out like a candle in a gale, and her vision seemed to fade back to normality, the golden threads disappearing beneath solid forms and the light from the blaze that lit the shadowy room.

The blaze.

The room was afire.

It took her a moment to assimilate her surroundings again. Asara was already up, her nightrobe pulled back into place to preserve her modesty, eyeing Kaiku warily. She seemed unable to decide which was more dangerous – the flames, or the one who had brought them. The air was filling with a choking, sickly reek of burning flesh, and black smoke gathered on the ceiling.

Kaiku swayed, feeling her head grow light. The effort of corralling the *kana* so as not to incinerate the entire room had brought her to the brink of fainting. Asara saw her weaken, and was on the bed with her in a moment, grabbing her arm.

'Come on,' she hissed. 'We have to go.'

Kaiku allowed herself to be pulled, her head lolling on her neck like a marionette's, her red eyes drowsing. Asara gathered up their clothes in a single scoop and threw them over the burning corpses, through the open doorway and out into the corridor. Then she slung both packs and rifles on her back and propelled Kaiku off the burning bed. The flames were licking up the walls now. Mamak's charred remains lay across the doorway, still ablaze, blocking their exit.

'We have to jump him.'

'I cannot jump,' Kaiku murmured.

Asara slapped her, hard. She recoiled, her eyes focusing.

'Jump,' she hissed.

Kaiku took a two-step run and sprang over Mamak's corpse, too fast for the flames to find purchase on her gown. The corridor outside seemed freezing in comparison to the room she had escaped from. She could hear voices and footsteps downstairs, but she was already grabbing her trousers and tugging them on over her nightrobe. Asara burst through the doorway then, following Kaiku's lead. She pulled on her travel clothes just as the owner of the lodging house and several tenants with water pails came up the stairs and into the corridor, and a moment later they found themselves staring at the barrel of a rifle.

'I assure you, I am a very good shot,' Asara said, her eye to the sight.

'What happened?' the owner demanded.

'Our erstwhile guide decided he was tired of waiting for us to rehire him and intended to liberate us of our money,' Asara replied. She had surmised as much by their entrance, and by the unwise way Tane had flaunted their money on the trip down from the mountains.

'Get out of the way!' one of the men behind him cried. 'The place is burning, by the spirits.'

'Pick up the packs,' she said quietly over her shoulder. Kaiku obeyed wearily. The burning of the *kana* was already causing her to spasm in pain, jolts of agony pulsing through her body.

'What do you want?' the owner cried. 'Let me put out the fire! This is my livelihood!'

'Two horses, from your stables,' Asara said. 'We can buy them from you, or we can take them by force. Choose.'

'Heart's blood,' breathed another man suddenly. 'Look at her eyes!'

It was Kaiku he was referring to.

'Aberrant!' somebody hissed.

'Yes, Aberrant,' Asara replied. 'And she will do to you what she has done to that room if you get in our way. The horses, *now*, or we stay here until this whole place burns down.'

'I'll take you,' the owner snapped. 'You men, put out that fire!'

With Kaiku in tow, Asara edged down the corridor. The men rushed past her, shying back from Kaiku with mingled disgust and fear, carrying their buckets to the blaze.

'Good horses,' said Asara, 'and we'll pay you the worth of this place.'

The owner looked at her hatefully, but he knew what it might mean. A new start, in a new place, where life was not so hard and grim. 'You have the money now?'

Asara nodded.

'Then let the place burn. Come with me,' he said.

They rode that night, driving their horses, heading south through the biting wind across Fo, putting as much distance as they could between themselves and Chaim. Kaiku slept lashed to the saddle, for her *kana* had burned her out from within, and Asara kept by her side to guide her mount.

How strange the ways that the gods take us, Asara thought, and rode on as dawn lightened the east.

TWENTY-FIVE

The Xarana Fault lay far to the south of Axekami, bracketed at its east and west end by the rivers Rahn and Zan. It was a place of dark legend, a vast swathe of shattered land haunted by the ghosts of ill memory and stalked by restless spirits, who had been shaken awake in the tumult of its formation and never quite settled again.

The histories told of how Jaan tu Vinaxis, venerated founder of the Saramyr Empire, had built the first Saramyr city of Gobinda in that place as a commemoration of the defeat of the aboriginal Ugati folk. At that time the land was flat and green, and Gobinda prospered and became a great city on the banks of the Zan. But Torus, Jaan's son, was usurped by the third Blood Emperor, Bizak tu Cho. Stories speak of the debauchery that Bizak entertained, orgies of god-lessness and excess. Then came Winterfall, the day on which all men must give praise to Ocha for the beginning of a new cycle of the year. Bizak, after a three-day celebration, was too exhausted to attend. He sent his daughter in his stead.

At that, Ocha was angered. The histories tell that wise men dreamed of a great boar that night, with breath of fire and smoke and jagged tusks, who stamped the earth and split it asunder. They warned the Emperor to make amends to Ocha, reminding him that he was only Emperor of men, and Ocha was Emperor of the gods. But Bizak in his hubris would not listen, and so they fled.

There were few survivors of Ocha's mighty retribution, but those who escaped painted a terrifying picture. The ground roared and bucked and split, breaking into sections like stone hit with a hammer and pitching the people of Gobinda howling into the yawning chasms. Magma spewed from the earth, belching ash into the sky and blackening the sun, turning the world to a seething cauldron of fiery red light. Huge sections of the land plummeted suddenly hundreds of feet; rock shattered; lightning flashed; and over it all was a bellowing and screeching, as of a vast, enraged boar. Gobinda fell into the earth and was swallowed, and Bizak tu Cho, his daughter and all his bloodline went with it.

When the destruction was over, the land was buckled and ruined. The Rahn and the Zan, which had previously flowed true, were now kinked with immense waterfalls as they dropped to the newly sunken landscape. The Xarana Fault – as it came to be known, when more was understood of tectonics and the ways of the inner earth – was a maze of folds, juts, plateaux, valleys, moraines and promontories: a landscape of utter chaos. In the many hundred years since the cataclysm, it had grown new grass and trees that smoothed over its edges somewhat; but its lessons had never been forgotten. It was still a place of bad luck and ill fortune, and was seldom visited by the honest folk of the city. Spirits were abundant there; some benevolent, most of them not.

But some dared to make their home in the hard lands of the Xarana Fault. Those who sought solitude, or needed to hide; those who would risk the dangers for the rewards of precious metals and gems unearthed by the ancient upheaval; those who had found nothing for them in the cities and the fields, and wanted a new start. There were as many reasons as there were people living in the lands of the Fault, and amid the turbulent landscape dozens of small communities lived side by side, some in harmony and some in hostility. But all had the single understanding: the business of the Fault stayed in the Fault, and was not the outside world's to know.

Cailin tu Moritat sat high in the saddle of a black mare, framed against the hot mid-morning sky. Beneath her, the ground fell in massive semicircular steps, irregular plateaux that piled haphazardly on top of each other. On the backs of these plates of earth was built a small town: dense clusters of houses, supply stores, an occasional bar and a smattering of tiny shrines nestling off the dirt tracks that passed as streets. Bridges and stairways linked the disparate levels together. It was a jumble, an accretion of a hundred different styles of architecture; this place had not been planned, but built as necessity dictated, and by many different hands. The angular, three-storey houses of the Southern Prefectures rose out of a clutter of low, broad Tchom Rin dwellings; balconied and ornamented houses that would not have looked out of place in Axekami's River District were shamed by the crafty austerity of their neighbours. Some of the dwellings had been here twenty years or more – a long time in the turbulent environment of the Fault – whereas others were still being built, wooden ribs and angle joists bristling from the wounds in their exteriors. Most of the building had been done around six years ago, when the Libera Dramach had engulfed the existing dwellings and begun to draw in people from all over Axekami, some of whom were construction engineers of no mean skill.

At the top, where the steps ran up against a mighty flank of stone, there were caves that went far into the hillside, their entrances decorated with whimsical etchings, blessings for those who entered and supplications to the gods. There, hidden within, a labyrinth of chambers lay, a secret network enshrouded in impenetrable rock.

From her vantage point on a nearby ridge, overlooking all, Cailin could see the scale of the industry that went on here. Everywhere there was movement. Workers scuttled back and forth with orders for this and that. Foremen hollered at their men. Towers were being erected, their skeletons aswarm. On one plateau, a score of men and women were being trained in the sword, jabbing and thrusting in unison to their master's barked commands. The steps were littered with wooden cranes, lifts and bamboo scaffolding. Stacks of crates and bundled supplies were being hauled to and fro by carts that ran on curving tracks. Outposts were perched on the lips of the plateau, and sentries watched within, their eyes ranging out beyond the broken slopes to the short expanse of flat earth that surrounded them and the frowning walls of grim rock beyond. The rise of the neighbouring land sheltered this place from view so efficiently that it was only possible to see it from the edge of the valley that cradled it. There was no kind of organised army here, but the Xarana Fault was a brutal place, and any settlement that did not think and act as a fortress would soon find itself overrun.

Cailin allowed herself a tiny smile, the red and black triangles painted on her lips curving slightly. This was the Fold, the home of the Libera Dramach and, for the time being, also home to a small sisterhood of the Red Order. She could not help but admire the realisation of their leader's vision. Few even knew of the existence of the Fold. For years now the Libera Dramach had been recruiting and gathering in secret, drawing from all sources equally. Bandit gangs had been offered the chance to end their hand-to-mouth existence and join; scholars had been persuaded of the rightness of their cause; common folk who had a grudge against the Weavers – and these were legion – came in search of a way of striking back at those who had hurt them. With them came physicians, apothecaries, disenchanted soldiers, wives who had been turned out of home, vagrants, debtors. All found a place here. All were brought into the Fold. At the core were the Libera Dramach themselves, those sworn to the organisation, picked from among the hundreds who came. As to the rest, some believed in the cause, and some did not; but all found themselves a part of a community, self-governed and free of the laws of nobility or the Weavers; and that was a precious thing to many.

She still found it faintly surprising that such a disparate group of individuals might have kept a secret so large for so long, especially as most of the Libera Dramach spent their time away from the Fold, in the cities, going about their daily business. These were the spies, the suppliers, the network. But, though it was a potent rumour among common folk, word of the Fold had yet to reach the nobility – or, which was more likely, they had ignored it. The Xarana Fault was a place of secrets; there were vast illegal farms of amaxa root that supplied the cities without paying their taxes, whole enclaves of people who worshipped forbidden gods, monasteries where contact with the outside world was utterly shunned. Mention of the Fold would scarcely merit the attention of a noble. At least, not one who was not already part of the organisation. For the Libera Dramach had eyes even in the courts of the Empress, and there were many who believed as they did. Aberrants were not evil. The Heir-Empress should sit the throne.

A tribute to the skill and learning of their leader, then, that they had got this far, and were ready when the long-expected crisis came. The Heir-Empress had been discovered by the world at large. Now was the time for the Libera Dramach to take action.

Cailin turned her mount and headed down the grassy ridge towards the Fold. There had been several new arrivals of late, and the moment had come to bring them all together.

'I can scarcely believe it all,' Kaiku said. She stood fearlessly at the lip of one of the uppermost plateaux of the Fold, above the main mass of the buildings, and gazed in wonder at the landscape tumbling away from her below, the maze of different-shaped rooftops an overlapping and multi-layered jigsaw. The packed-dirt streets were seething with people from all over Axekami, a collision of makeshift fashions such as Kaiku had never seen. The afternoon sun beat down on her skin, warming her with its rays; birds winged and jagged through the sky overhead. She tilted her face up, closed her eyes, and felt Nuki's eye looking down on her, a red glow behind her lids. 'It is perfect.'

Asara sat on a large, smooth rock that towered aslant out of

the grassy plateau. She did not know what Kaiku was referring to as perfect: the Fold, the sunlight, or a more general
expression of contentment? She dismissed it, anyway. Kaiku's
spirits had been restored with a vengeance since leaving
Fo and taking the River Jabaza back towards Axekami.
They had disembarked some way north, warned by sailors
coming upriver that Axekami was in turmoil and no
boats were getting in. Taking the horses they had gained in
Chaim, they rode south, crossed the Kerryn by ferry east of
Axekami, and then made good time to the Xarana Fault.
There, Asara had taken them by one of the few relatively
safe routes through the maze of broken land, and thence to
the Fold.

The journey had been a strange one. Kaiku appeared to
have surmounted her loathing of herself, perhaps because
there was nobody left that she cared much about who could
leave her or hurt her. Her family were dead; Mishani and
Tane had betrayed her by their reactions to the news that she
was Aberrant. Rock bottom was a wonderful place in which
to re-examine oneself, and she seemed finally to have accepted what she was and made the decision to live with it.
Her initial despair at the impossibility of the oath she had
sworn to Ocha had warmed and turned to determination, a
rigid focus, an unswerving direction she could cling to. By
the end of their journey, Kaiku had been urging Asara on,
desperate to get to the Fold as quickly as possible and begin to
assess what chances she had of avenging her family against the
unassailable might of the Weavers.

And yet, though there was this general lightening of heart
about her, she had closed up to Asara again, just when she
was beginning to feel something like trust in her former
handmaiden. Asara told herself that the release of passion in
that cold, draughty room in Chaim was a demonstration of
Kaiku's decision to discard the old rules that no longer
applied to her as an Aberrant, proof to herself that she had
no boundaries left; only that, and nothing more. But she had

stirred something between them that refused to go away, and it hid in glances and loaded comments and darted out unexpectedly to sting the other. Kaiku was wary of Asara for another reason as well. She had never asked what had happened in that room, when Asara's kiss turned to something more than lips and tongues, and she sought to suck the breath from Kaiku's body; but she had sensed the danger on an instinctive level, and now she would not allow her guard down again.

Still, she was here, in the Fold. Asara had discharged her duty, an agreement taken on more than two years ago now. She felt something of a satisfaction in herself. She lounged on the warm rock, observing Kaiku's back as she admired the vista before her and soaked in the simple glory of a summer day.

'You have my deepest thanks, Asara,' Cailin purred next to her. Asara was quick enough to prevent herself starting and giving away her surprise at the dark lady's appearance. 'You have kept her safe. She is quite a precious asset to me.'

'I am afraid I did not do quite the job of keeping her safe that I could have done,' Asara replied, not looking up. 'But we have such things to tell you, Cailin.'

Cailin arched an eyebrow at her tone. 'Really? These I must hear.'

'Later. In private,' Asara said. She would pick the time and place. 'She has already started to get her *kana* under control,' Asara added. 'It is still wild, but not untameable. That is a rare thing, I understand.'

'Rare indeed,' Cailin replied, never taking her eyes off Kaiku. 'But then, we knew she would be strong. And you have put yourself in great danger for my sake. Once again, I thank you.'

'Not for your sake,' Asara corrected. 'For mine. She interests me. I have watched her lose everything, and become the thing she most despised; and I have watched her fight back and regain herself again. In my time in this world, I have seen the same loves, hates and struggles played over and again in endless monotony; but hers is a rarer story than most, and she still surprises me even now. I almost feel guilty for bringing her into your sphere of influence. You may fool her with your altruism, but not me. What are you planning, Cailin?'

'I believe you are fond of her, Asara,' said Cailin, a smile in her voice as she avoided the question. 'And I thought you too cynical for such fancies.'

'My heart and soul are not dead yet,' Asara replied, 'only dusty and jaded from lack of interest.'

Cailin laughed, and the sound made Kaiku turn and notice them for the first time. She walked over to them, away from the precipice.

'I am glad to see you are a woman of your word,' Cailin said, inclining her head in greeting. 'Did you find what it what it was you were looking for?'

'In a manner of speaking,' Kaiku said, and did not elaborate.

'The time approaches for action,' Cailin said, studying Kaiku from within the painted red crescents over her eyes. 'That is partly why I asked to meet you here.'

'What kind of action?' Kaiku demanded.

'Soon,' Cailin promised. 'But first, I have some people you might like to meet.' She waved a hand at where two newcomers were approaching along the plateau.

Mishani and Tane.

For a moment, Kaiku could not find the words to say, nor dare to think what this might mean. But then Mishani approached her, seeming strangely smaller now than before, her immense length of hair tied in a loose knot at her back. She hesitated for an instant, and then put her arms around Kaiku, and Kaiku embraced her in return. She sobbed a laugh, clutching Mishani tight to her. 'I'm so happy you're here,' she said; but the last of the sentence was incomprehensible with the tightening of her throat, and the tears that fell freely from her. Cailin flashed a triumphant look at Asara, who quirked her mouth in a smile.

The two of them held each other for a long time, there in the sun. Kaiku had no idea why she had come, or what had turned her around, but she knew Mishani well enough to realise what it meant. Eventually they released each other, and Kaiku looked to Tane, who smiled awkwardly.

'I had a little time to think,' he said, and that was all, for Kaiku embraced him too. He looked faintly abashed by the contact, but he held her also, and was a little disappointed when she withdrew much sooner than she had with Mishani.

Kaiku wiped her eyes and smiled at Cailin, who was watching her benevolently with her deep green gaze.

'People have a way of turning up when you least expect them to, Kaiku,' the tall lady told her. 'The four of you walk a braided path; your routes are intertwined, and they will cross again and again until they are done.'

'How can you know that?' Kaiku asked.

'You will learn how I know,' said Cailin. 'If you choose to take the way of the Red Order.'

'Is there a choice for me?'

'Not if you want to live to see the next harvest,' Cailin answered simply.

Kaiku demurred with a shrug. 'So, then.'

Cailin laughed once again, throwing her head back, her white teeth flashing between the red and black of her lips. 'I have never had an offer accepted with such poor grace. Do not be afraid, Kaiku; this is not a lifetime commitment you are making. A Sister of the Red Order is nothing if she is unwilling. All I ask is that you let me teach you; after that, you may choose your own way. Is that acceptable?'

Kaiku bowed slightly. 'I would be honoured.'

'Then we shall begin as soon as you are ready,' she said.

There were three Sisters in the room apart from Cailin. All of them wore the accoutrements of their order: the black dress, the red crescents painted over their eyes, the red and black triangles on their lips like teeth. Asara found their poise uncanny, but not unnerving.

In the conference chamber of the house of the Red Order, lanterns glowed against the night, placed in free-standing brackets in the corners. The red and black motif was mirrored in the surroundings: the room was dark, its walls painted black but hung with crimson pennants and assorted other arcana. Its centrepiece was a low, round table of the same colour on which a brazier breathed scented smoke into the room. The Sisters all stood, but Asara lounged in a chair. She had digested the importance of the news she brought long ago; it amused her to watch the reactions of the Sisters now.

'Do you trust her?' one of the Sisters asked, a slender creature with blonde hair.

'Implicitly,' Asara replied. 'I have known her for years. She would not lie; certainly not about this.'

'And yet there is no proof,' another pointed out.

'Not unless any remains in her father's apartment in Axekami,' Asara said. 'But I doubt that.'

Cailin bowed her head thoughtfully. 'This bears research of our own, dear Sisters. If a single scholar can assemble enough evidence to convince himself to travel all the way to Fo for proof, to risk himself and his family . . .' She trailed away.

'We must contact our Sisters further afield,' suggested another.

Asara raised an eyebrow. The Red Order had their ladles in more pots than anyone knew, she suspected. Though she had no clear idea of their membership, they were careful never to gather in one place in any great number. Indeed, four was the most she had ever seen together. She had gathered hints from Cailin that the Sisters were scattered all over Saramyr and beyond, engaged in hunting for new recruits like Kaiku or inveigling themselves into other organisations; but she believed there was another reason why they never congregated. They were paranoid. They knew well how fragile they were, how small their Sisterhood, and they feared extinction. While they were all connected by the Weave, there was no need to gather together, and hence no way the whole could be destroyed. Oh, she did not doubt that each of them was using their powers to further the Sisterhood, but she suspected fear was at the root. They were selfish, and sought power to stabilise themselves. The Red Order and the Weavers were not as different as Cailin would like to think.

'There is another matter,' Cailin pointed out. 'The caged Aberrants Kaiku came across. What do they mean?'

'Perhaps they are studying the effects of the witchstones on living beings. Perhaps they are searching for a cure to Aberrancy.'

'Perhaps,' Cailin replied. 'Perhaps it was merely a product of their insanity. Or maybe it is a clue to something much greater.'

'We should think on this,' agreed one of the other Sisters.

'But this changes nothing,' Cailin said, her voice rising decisively. 'Kaiku's discovery is only a first step, a breakthrough that demands our attention. But we have other, more pressing concerns now. This can wait. We must disseminate the information and ensure it becomes spread so wide that it cannot be suppressed, we must plan and research and investigate . . . but all that is for the future.' She made a sweeping gesture as if to clear it from their minds. 'For now, we have another task. Axekami is falling apart; the city is in the midst of revolution. The Imperial Guards cannot contain it. The armies of Blood Amacha and Blood Kerestyn squabble just outside the city. The Weave-lord Vyrrch works from within to undermine the Empress and kill her child.' She paused, and her eyes flicked to each of them in turn. 'This must not be allowed to happen. She is the only hope we have of turning the people of Saramyr away from the Weavers' teachings, making them understand that Aberrants are not the evil they imagine us to be. I do not care who takes the reins of the Empire if Blood Erinima is overthrown, but I will not lose the Heir-Empress. I have met her in her dreams, and I know something of what she can do. She is too rare and powerful a creature to die on the end of some ignorant foot soldier's blade. Perhaps Blood Erinima will emerge triumphant, but I count the chances as slim. The Empress has set herself squarely against the world. If she loses, Lucia dies.'

'Then what do you propose to do?' Asara asked.

'The plans are in place, between ourselves and the Libera Dramach, to ensure the Heir-Empress's safety the only way we can,' Cailin replied. 'We propose to kidnap her.'

TWENTY-SIX

The door crashed inward, wrenched off its hinges with one swing of the short, heavy battering ram that two of the Imperial Guards held between them. Guard Commander Jalis led the way inside, clambering over the fallen obstacle, passing from bright daylight into the gloomy murk of the narrow stone stairway. Already a hue and cry was being raised somewhere beneath. He raced downward, the tarnished white and blue plates of his armour clinking as he descended headlong towards the basement of the tannery. The stench of the place was even worse down here than it had been in the open air, and it crowded him in and almost made him gag. He swallowed the reflex. His heart was pounding, his blood up. Behind him two cohorts of Guards were cramming down the stairway, their rifles and swords clattering. Running blind into who knew what, and none of them cared. They had found the bastards at last, and they were in no mood to go easy on them.

Jalis burst out of the stairwell and into the wide, low-ceilinged basement. He had no time to register the details of the room; there was only a flash impression of space, and gloom, and the blur of metal swinging towards him. His sword swept up to meet another man's blade with a ringing of steel. He parried, parried again, then put his weight to his sword and struck, knocking his opponent back as he fended the blow weakly aside. Jalis forced his way into the room, clearing a path for the others to break through and join the combat. Swords clashed in a metallic cacophony, and bodies heaved against each other as battle was joined.

Jalis threw back his attacker with a second push and

stabbed. Until that point he had barely seen who it was he was fighting, but now he registered that it was a young man, wearing no armour and plainly no warrior, with his face contorted in an ugly grimace of hate. The unfair odds concerned him not one bit. He ran the young man through, and had his blade out and was fighting with someone else before his enemy's impaled body had hit the floor.

There were dozens of them, outnumbering the Guards in the room; but they were pitifully matched against trained, armoured soldiers. Jalis's arm juddered as he buried his blade in another man's neck, this one no more than eighteen harvests, little more than a boy. The Guards pushed outward from the stairway, allowing more of their number in behind them, and the ferocity of the initial onslaught diminished as more swords arrived to take the strain.

Jalis took a second to sweep the room with his eyes. The basement was massive, and poorly lit, but it took only one glance to realise that their information had been good. Everywhere, tables were laden with tubes of coiled brass, distillation bulbs, disassembled clockwork timers and fuses. All about lay kegs of ignition powder, stacked up against the round pillars that supported the ceiling, secreted in corners behind piles of crates. It was a disorderly clutter at the edges, where odd shapes bulked in the shadows, but the central section was lethally precise, its tables laid in stringent rows so that completed components could be passed along the line to the next worker.

This was the heart of Unger tu Torrhyc's secret army: the bomb factory. Dozens had died at the hands of these fanatics, and hundreds more from the chaos their bombs had sown. He had no pity for them. They were a threat to Blood Erinima, and to the Empire. Each one that fell to his blade made Axekami a better place.

And yet the frenzy with which they threw themselves on to the swords of the Guardsmen surprised even him. These were not fighters, yet not a one of them cowered, or tried to run.

Instead they had taken up arms and raced to the attack, and they were hewn down like wheat. Jalis grimaced as a spray of blood gave him a warm slap across the jaw, and wondered what misplaced loyalty possessed them to such fervour.

A moment later, the crack of a rifle jolted his attention, and a Guard to his left fell with a sigh to the ground. It was followed by another, and again. Jalis picked out the source; two men against the far wall, where there was a rack of rifles and ignition powder. Several more had arrived and were taking their choice of weapons. A Guard just behind Jalis was already unslinging his own rifle from his back, but Jalis grabbed his arm roughly.

'Don't be a fool!' he cried. 'Retreat! Get out!'

It had been a risky gamble, to plough blindly into the enemy as they had done, but there was only one way into or out of the basement and they had had no other choice. Now Jalis saw he had underestimated the zeal of the bomb-makers, and it might cost them dearly. Gods, they should know better than to fire rifles down here! The entire place was one enormous bomb waiting to explode! It was suicide!

But perhaps that was exactly their plan.

The Guards pulled back towards the stairway, but the bomb-makers had redoubled the fury of their attack, throwing themselves at the intruders with no heed at all for their safety, choking the passage to freedom. More rifles joined the firefight, shooting friend and foe alike with indiscriminate aim. Jalis tried to push his way back through the ranks, the cloying stench of the tannery suffocating him, sudden panic swelling within; but there was nowhere he could go. He felt a sinking, draining feeling in his chest, and the world slowed to a crawl, and a sinister prescience whispered in his ear that the end was upon him.

He did not hear the rifle ball that ricocheted into a powder keg, nor see the flash. The tannery exploded in a blast that smashed the surrounding streets to rubble, annihilating everything within and sending bricks and flaming timbers looping through the air to hiss and steam as they landed in the river, or to smash through walls and shutters. The earth shook, rattling even the fixtures of the Imperial Keep, and a great dark column of smoke belched upwards from the smouldering remains, to climb skyward and pollute the perfect summer's day.

'You know that my words make sense, Anais.'

The Empress glared at Barak Mos across the low table. They sat on pillows in one of the western rooms of the Keep, an informal meal set before them of fish and rice and crabs from Mataxa Bay. Durun paced back and forth before the pillared arch that let out on to a wide balcony for catching the afternoon sun in spring and autumn. As summer ascended to its zenith, they stayed in the shade; the humidity was hard to bear even there, and scarcely a breath of wind came to relieve them.

'Gods, wife, why don't you listen to him?' Durun cried, his long black hair sweeping as he came to a halt and gestured in exasperation at his spouse. 'It's the only way.'

'Durun, stay out of this!' his father commanded. 'You aren't helping.'

Anais used her tiny silver finger-forks to spear a morsel of slitherfish from her plate, making them wait while she ate it thoughtfully. Durun seethed in the background like a leashed dog in sight of a rabbit. Mos watched her.

'I am not sure I see the need. The single greatest cause of the disruption in Axekami is gone,' she said. 'The threat of Unger tu Torrhyc's army has been removed.'

'Indeed,' Mos agreed. 'But at the cost of two cohorts of your Imperial Guards. You were overstretched already, Anais; now you are worse off. Riots tear through the city; fires rage unchecked. The forces of Blood Amacha and Blood Kerestyn have arrived outside the city, and are squaring up to each other within sight of the walls. Chaos breeds chaos, my Empress; the city is falling apart, and it's beyond the strength of your forces to quell it. Should Amacha or Kerestyn strike at Axekami now, your men would be too busy dealing with the populace to put up any resistance.'

Anais raised an eyebrow. From the usually taciturn Barak, this validation sounded rehearsed. He had obviously been thinking about it for some time.

'Please,' Durun said, unable to resist interrupting again. 'We are next to defenceless here. I won't let our thrones be taken because we were too busy mopping up after the ungrateful cattle down in those streets. Let my family's men do that!'

'Ah,' said Anais. 'So you propose that the forces of Blood Batik will only be deployed for the duties of policing the city?'

Mos cast a furious glance at his son, who was too haughty to have the decency to blush. Instead, he snorted and turned his head away to look out on to the balcony, feigning indifference. He had just given away a potent concession that Mos no doubt had intended to use as his *coup de grâce* in this argument.

'Yes,' Mos grated. 'I'm aware of your caution in allowing any force into Axekami that is not blood-bound to your will, though it puzzles me that you don't seem to see we have the same interests. I have as much to lose as you if Axekami falls to an invader.' He took a breath. 'In order that you don't feel threatened, I propose you withdraw your Imperial Guards to their usual duties of guarding the Keep and securing the walls of Axekami; my troops will be used only in putting down the riots and restoring order to the city, unless you wish other-wise.'

'I may wish to use them in the defence of Axekami in the event of Blood Amacha or Kerestyn making an assault upon the walls. Is that acceptable?'

'Of course,' Mos said. 'My son and granddaughter are here.' Durun snorted again at this, making clear what he thought of Mos calling Lucia his granddaughter. Mos gave him a sharp look, which he ignored, before continuing: 'I would hardly let an invader storm the city while I had any power to prevent it. In fact, to prove my dedication in this matter, I'll stay in the Keep myself, with your permission. Whatever befalls you or Durun or Lucia will befall me as well.'

'This is not a small risk,' Anais replied evenly, her food forgotten before her. 'There would be few of your bloodline left if we were to lose.'

'Ah, but Anais, with my forces and yours combined, and the walls of Axekami protecting us, we *won't* lose. Amacha and Kerestyn *together* would have scarcely a chance of beating us. Squabbling and divided as they are, there is no hope of victory for them.'

Anais thought on it for a moment, returning to her food. He made a convincing argument, and she was aware that her situation was worsening with every passing day. In truth, she already knew in her heart what she would do; she had decided before Mos had called on her. She had to agree; she had no other choice. Yet no matter how trusted the ally, to invite a foreign force into the heart of the capital was dangerous. There were always angles she could not see, vested interests she was not aware of, even with men as plain-speaking and guileless as Mos and Durun.

It was a risk she had to take.

'Very well,' she said. Mos broke into a broad smile. 'But not one of your men shall set foot in the grounds of the Imperial Keep,' she added. 'Not even a retinue for yourself. Are we understood?'

His smile faded a little at the edges, but he nodded. 'Agreed. I will send for my men immediately.'

'You will have to use Vyrrch to contact your Weaver,' Anais said with a wrinkle of distaste. 'Be careful what you say to him.'

'I speak to Weavers as little as I possibly can,' Mos replied.

'I will make the necessary arrangements with my men,' Anais said. She looked at Durun, who looked back at her blandly, his dark eyes piercing on either side of his hawk nose. Typical of him: he had got what he wanted, and yet he acted as if it was his due rather than something granted by his wife. She dismissed him from her mind. She had him under control, anyway. His thoughts and loyalty were dictated by one organ alone, and it was not his brain.

'I'll talk to Vyrrch now,' said Mos, getting to his feet. 'Better to get it over with.'

'And what of the Bloods Amacha and Kerestyn?' Durun asked. The question indicated who was the mind behind this meeting, as if Anais could not have guessed.

Mos flexed his shoulders in the manner of a man relaxing at home, not in the presence of his Empress. Anais almost smiled at his lack of grace. 'Leave them be,' he said. 'Barak Sonmaga tu Amacha will never let the Barak Grigi tu Kerestyn approach the city; and he has not the strength to assault it himself, for that would mean turning his back on the armies of Kerestyn. Let us see if the arrival of a few thousand of our men from the other side of Axekami won't take some of the enthusiasm out of them. My intelligence tells me Sonmaga's ill-equipped for civil war anyway; not enough time to gather troops. And Grigi must know he can beat Sonmaga, but the losses he'd take would mean he'd have no chance of taking Axekami. They're at a stalemate. This might be just the thing to make them cut their losses and go home, and that would be one less problem to deal with.'

Durun stalked over to stand by his father's side. Anais got up from the table and saw them to the doorway of the chamber. 'Then may Ocha bless us and keep us all safe.'

Mos bowed deeply. 'You are wise, Anais, to choose as you have chosen today. The country is in good hands.'

'We shall see,' she replied. 'We shall see.'

The Heir-Empress Lucia tu Erinima knelt on a mat before her pattern-board, her shadow long behind her in the low, bright sun of the evening. She had been there since midday, on the upper terraces of the gardens. There she had settled herself amid the sun-warm beige stones that tiled the floor of this, one of the many tranquil resting places and walkways curving through the greenery. Before her the terraces dropped away in steps until they came to the high perimeter wall of the roof gardens; hidden beyond that was the city of Axekami, the sweltering sprawl of streets surrounded by an even higher wall to separate it from the vast grassy expanses of the plains.

Nuki's eye was descending through the thin streamers of cloud that haunted the distant horizon, and Lucia's eyes flickered periodically from the spectacle before her to the pattern-board and back again. Taking a wide-spaced, soft-bristled circular brush, she dipped it into one of the china bowls of heavy water that rested on the stone next to her and eased it across the pattern-board, leaving a faint mist of pink suspended there in the picture.

The pattern-board was an old art form, practised since before the time of many of the newer bloodlines. It involved the use of a coloured blend of water and paint and sap, thickened to a certain consistency, called 'heavy' water. This was applied to a pattern-board, a three-dimensional wooden cage that held within it a flattened oblong of transparent gel. The gel was part-baked into shape, after which it would always return to its oblong shape no matter what was done to it. This allowed artists to part the gel and paint inside the oblong, in the third dimension. The use of heavy water gave the pictures a curiously feathery, ethereal quality. When the painting was finished, the gel was baked further, becoming a substance like glass, and then displayed in ornate cradles that allowed the picture within to be viewed from all sides.

'Daygreet, Lucia,' came a voice from next to her, deep and smooth. She sat back on her heels, shading her eyes with one hand as she looked up.

'Daygreet, Zaelis,' she said, smiling.

Her tutor crouched down next to her, his lean frame draped in thin silk of black and gold. 'You've nearly finished, then,' he observed, making a languid motion towards the pattern-board.

'Another day and I'll be done, I think,' she said, returning her gaze to the floating swirls of colour before her.

'It's very good,' Zaelis commented.

'It's all right,' she said.

There was silence for a moment.

'Are you angry?' she asked.

'You've been here in the sun all day,' he said. 'And I've spent most of it trying to find you. You know how protective your mother is, Lucia. You should know better than to disappear like that, and you should *really* know better than to sit out in the full glare of Nuki's eye on a day like this.'

Lucia exhaled slowly in what was not quite a sigh. His tone and mode of address showed that he was not angry, but she was chastened all the same. 'I just had to get away,' she said. 'For a little while.'

'Even from me?' Zaelis sounded hurt.

Lucia nodded. She looked back at the sunset, then to the pattern-board, then pushed her fingers a little way into the top of it and pulled open a thin gash in the gel. She made a few quick strokes with a narrow brush, lining the pink of the clouds with red, then withdrew her fingers and let the rift seal itself.

Zaelis watched her, his face impassive. Of course she needed escape. To a girl as sensitive as Lucia was, the tension in the corridors of the Keep bled through even to here. And though he had kept his own concerns to himself regarding her safety, he was sure that even his best efforts at secrecy were useless against her. She knew full well that all the discord, all the deaths, were down to her in one way or another. Zaelis did his best to dissuade her from feeling guilty, but he was not even sure if she *felt* guilty. She had talked before of how she had set all this in motion, and wondered how it might have gone if she had tried to stop it instead of embracing the change. But whether there was regret there, Zaelis could not tell. Lucia's moods were like the deepest oceans, unfathomable to him.

Her head snapped up suddenly, with an urgency that made Zaelis jump. He followed her gaze, not dreamy and unfocused as it usually was but sharp and intense. She was looking to the north, where the white rim of Aurus was just cresting the horizon, foreshadowing the coming night. Her brow creased into a frown, and it trembled there for a moment. The fierceness of her glare shocked him; he had never seen such a look upon her face. Then she tore herself away, staring back into the heart of her painting, seeming to smoulder sullenly.

'What is it?' Zaelis asked. When she did not reply, he repeated: 'Lucia, what is it?' This second question was phrased in a more authoritative mode. He did not usually push her this way, but what he had witnessed a moment ago concerned him enough to try.

'I heard something,' she said reluctantly, still not meeting his eyes.

'Heard something?' Zaelis prompted. He looked back to the northern horizon. 'From whom?'

'No, not like that,' Lucia said, rubbing the back of her neck in agitation. 'Just an echo, a whisper. A reminder. It's gone now.'

Zaelis was staring at the edge of Aurus as it glided infinitesimally higher in the distance. 'A reminder of *what*?'

'A dream!' she snapped. 'I had a dream. I met the Children of the Moons. They were trying to tell me something, but I didn't understand. Not at first. Then . . .' She sagged a little. 'Then I think I did. They tried to show me . . . I don't know if it was a warning, or a threat . . . I don't . . .'

Zaelis was horrified. 'What did they tell you, Lucia?'

She turned to face him.

'Something's going to happen,' she whispered. 'Something bad. To me.'

'You don't know that, Lucia,' Zaelis protested automatically. 'Don't say that.'

She hugged herself to him in a rush, clutching herself close, taking him by surprise. He hugged her back, hard.

'It was just a dream,' he said soothingly. 'You don't need to be scared of a dream.'

But over her shoulder, he was looking to the northern horizon and the cold arc of Aurus's edge, and his eyes were afraid.

Weave-lord Vyrrch rested, his scabrous white flank heaving, the ribs showing through like a washboard. He was naked, his grotesque, withered body pathetic and repulsive to the eye. His scrawny, misshapen arms were gloved in blood; it spattered the melted skin of his face, his thin chest, pot-belly and atrophied genitalia. He looked like something recently born, curled amid the soiled sheets of his broken bed, panting and gasping.

For the object of his recent attention, however, there was no breath to be had. She was an old lady, chosen for the sake of variety in a fit of whimsy after he had sent Barak Mos's requested message to his Weaver. It had vaguely crossed his mind that he was murdering altogether too many people of late; most Weavers only reached that state of frenzy rarely. But then, wherever his servants procured his victims from, they were obviously not being missed. A servant's life was their master's or mistress's to take in Saramyr, and this one lady could not have been anything more than a cook or a cleaner, a servant of the Keep and hence of the Empress. He was sure Anais would not mind, even if she knew. She was aware of the deal when she took on Vyrrch as her Weave-lord; in doing so, she put the low folk of the Keep at his disposal, to satisfy his whims. A small price to pay for a Weave-lord's powers.

The old lady lay in a pool of viscous red, her simple clothes plastered to her body with her own vital fluids. He had been in the mood for the knife today, intending to take his time; but when she had arrived, he had flown into an unaccountable rage and stabbed her, hacking and plunging again and again. She died almost instantly, killed by the shock. It had only increased his fury, and he attacked the corpse over and over until it was almost unrecognisable as human.

Yes, perhaps he had been killing a little too much recently. But he was the spider at the centre of the web, and he needed feeding often.

The Guard Commander who had arrested Unger tu Tor-rhyc had been a tough one to crack, but Vyrrch had given himself time. As skilled as he was, he dared not simply seize the mind of a man and take control of him. That would require all his concentration, and confine him to his rooms; and there was every possibility that the Guard Commander might realise he had been meddled with once Vyrrch released him. Hasty operations like that were dangerous; he thought back to his recent attempt to sway Barak Zahn, when he was foiled by Zahn's Weaver, and wondered why he had not better considered the risk then.

You're slipping, Vyrrch, he told himself.

With the Guard Commander he had been forced to take a subtler route, implanting small, hypnotic suggestions in his dreams night after night, poisoning him against Unger, convincing him of the rewards he would gain for arresting the thorn in the Empress's side. When Unger tu Torrhyc was taken, Vyrrch had made sure he was with the Empress; that way, she could not accuse him of influencing the Guard Commander. How little she knew of the Weavers' ways.

The bomb-makers were a labour of months. He had been assembling them ever since his first suspicions about Lucia, long before he had persuaded Sonmaga tu Amacha to send the cat-burglar Purloch to confirm the rumour. Steadily wearing at them, turning them in their dreams, ordinary men and women gradually becoming fanatical. More and more time they began to spend in the study of explosives, more and more they became indoctrinated to the idea that any amount of lives was worth a belief. And all the while, they waited for the subliminal trigger: the discovery that the Heir-Empress was an Aberrant. At that signal, they abandoned jobs, homes, families, and became the single-minded bombers Vyrrch had envisioned. They gathered, and began to assemble their instruments of destruction. And when the preparation was done, Vyrrch gave them a new trigger, one that would set them on their destructive course. The arrest of Unger tu Torrhyc.

It was a master stroke. The world at large saw the logic in a man of Unger's charisma and outspoken political views being the leader of a subversive army. Vyrrch had killed Unger himself so he could not contradict the assumption, and that also provided a convenient martyr for the disgruntled citizens of Axekami. Now his own bomb-makers were dead, killing themselves rather than letting themselves be captured, and the circle was closed. There was no evidence to link him to any of it. Axekami was enraged, frightened, maddened; the Empress's eyes were turned outward to the city, and the stage was set for the final part of his plan.

There were more bombs yet to come.

But it had not all been seamless. There was still the niggling itch in the back of his mind that was Ruito tu Makaima, hidden away in some spot where he could not quite scratch it. That the scholar had managed to get into the Lakmar Monastery on Fo was achievement enough. Vyrrch still had no idea how he got hold of a Mask that would get him through the barrier; but he was unlucky enough to trip through one of the invisible triggers on his way out, little Weave-sewn traps that jangled alarm bells in the world beyond human sight. Their agents had shadowed him home, the better to see what his intentions were; but he seemed broken, holed up in the forest, and so they were content merely to keep him there while they decided what to do with him. And so it passed to Vyrrch, as many things did.

He had intended to capture and interrogate Ruito. If he had been able to do that, then he would not be fretting now.

But the scholar had outwitted him. The very night Vyrrch struck, he put poison in his family's evening meal, and when they drifted to sleep they did not wake again. Ruito had eluded him.

The shin-shin were hard to entice and harder to control, but it was necessary to ensure no survivors, and no evidence. Human agents were not reliable enough. He needed them to return the Mask without being tempted to use it, and demons told no tales – they could never be traced to him. The employment of such creatures was risky, even for a Weaver of his calibre; but the shin-shin were low demons, and weak, and they had proliferated in the wake of the witchstones' corruption of the land. They felt the power of the witchstones as some kind of benevolent entity, and when the time came they were content to do as Vyrrch asked them. Not that it was as simple as *asking*. With demons, as with any other spirits, communication was muddy and uncertain, passed on in impressions and vague emotions. Without the bridging influence of the witchstones, Vyrrch would not have been able to get through at all.

And then had come the day when the Makaima bloodline met its end. Except, of course, that something went wrong.

He knew there were a thousand reasons why he should not worry about it, and only one why he should. The Mask had gone.

The shin-shin were unable to identify who it was that had escaped; their demon minds worked in ways other than humankind. Their perception did not work on the principles of sight, but rather on ethereal scent-trails and auras beyond the register of mammalian creatures. It made them excellent trackers, but it also made them limited. They could no more differentiate between humans by sight than humans could tell a gull apart from a million other gulls. When Vyrrch had demanded to know who had slipped their grasp, they responded with a confusing identification of impossible markers that meant nothing to him. He was left frustrated.

Who had taken the Mask was yet a mystery, but it had been stolen by two humans. They told him that much. The bodies in the house had been burned to blackened skeletons – making a process of elimination a worthless endeavour – and there were too many servants about the place to make an accurate count, even if Vyrrch had the will to. The shin-shin, at least, had found Ruito's body before the house fell, so Vyrrch could breathe that bit easier. But still, someone had taken the Mask, and he had no idea who. They had chased the trail to Axekami, but the city was no place for demons, and even the shin-shin dared not set foot in that hive of men. There, they lost it.

Yes, a thousand reasons not to worry. What were the chances of anyone realising what they had, or knowing how and where to use it if they did? Most likely it had already been sold to some theatre merchant, his eyes gleaming as he bought what the owners thought was simply an exquisite mask. Scenario after scenario ran through Vyrrch's head, but only one kept coming back to him.

What if they had realised what the Mask was, and used it for its purpose?

No matter, he thought resolutely. In days, a fortnight at most, the jaws of the trap he had set around the Imperial Keep would snap shut. A new power would be ascendant, ruling in conjunction with the Weavers instead of over them. An unprecedented alliance, in which the Weavers would truly be the power behind the throne.

Their time was coming.

TWENTY-SEVEN

'The first step . . .' said Cailin softly. 'The first step is the most important. And the most dangerous.'

The small cave that enclosed them shifted and stirred in the light of a single torch that burned fitfully in its bracket. It was cool here in the bones of the earth, despite the warm summer night outside. Kaiku felt a curiously detached sensation, as if she and Cailin had been cut off from the rest of existence, with this hemisphere of rock forming the limits of their world. The cave was bare and empty, merely a bubble of air within the crushing mantle of stone that pressed in on them. The narrow tunnel that connected this tiny, secluded chamber to the rest of the caves of the Fold was a depthless void, and she wondered what might happen if she were to walk into that blackness, where she might emerge.

She sat cross-legged on a wicker mat in the centre of the chamber, her feathered brown hair damp and inelegantly ruffled, her eyes closed. Cailin walked slowly around her, looming high overhead, almost touching the ceiling. Her boots tapped hollow on the stone of the cave floor. She was talking, but her voice was somehow hypnotic, and Kaiku barely heard the words, absorbing instead the meaning and instruction within.

'Your *kana* is like any wild beast. It is uncontrollable, primal, apt to lash out when angered. Before you can begin to train it, you must first muzzle it, leash it, render it harmless. Or at least as harmless as you can make it.'

Kaiku felt a thrill of unease. For the last week she had been rigorously prepared for this by Cailin; yet now the moment was here, she was afraid. Afraid of what was inside her, of what it might do; afraid of the agony it brought when it boiled up through her veins. Cailin had schooled her in mantras that would calm her mind, warned her of the things she might see and feel, taught her the many things she *must not do* when the procedure was underway.

You will be tempted to resist. Every instinct will tell you to attack me, as if I were an invader. If you do so, I will kill you.

It was not a threat, merely a fact.

'I will sew myself into you, Kaiku,' she was saying, her low voice moving around behind as she walked. 'Were you not talented in the ways of the Weave, you would not even know I was doing it. But you have . . . defences. I am a foreign element, and your mind and body will try and expel me. You must not let it. You must remain passive, and calm, and let me do my work. I will muzzle the beast within you, but I cannot do so while you resist.'

She had heard it a dozen times before now, but it was all theoretical. Nothing would truly prepare her for the plunge. There was no precedent for this, even in her deepest memories. What if she could not do it?

She knew the answer to that. And yet it never crossed her mind to turn back and give up.

Cailin rested her slim, pale hands on Kaiku's shoulders. 'Are you composed?'

Kaiku took a deep breath and let it out, her eyelids fluttering. 'I am ready,' she lied.

'Then we will begin.'

The beast tore free from its lair with a ferocity and suddenness that was overwhelming. It roared and scorched its way up into her breast like a demon, raging and burning. Her eyes stayed shut, but inside the world exploded into an incomprehensible sea of golden threads, an endless, dazzling vista with no sky, no ground, no boundaries at all. For an instant, she knew nothing but terror as pain racked her, the searing wake of her *kana* fighting to be free.

Then, suddenly, she reorientated. By what instinct she

navigated, she could not guess; but in a moment the unearthly complexity of the dazzling junctions and infinite lengths seemed to make sense to her, to *fit* in some indescribable way. These were *her* threads, she recognised. This was herself, her territory within the Weave, the space occupied by her body and mind. She felt the rushing stream of golden blood pumping from the thick knot of her heart, saw it disseminate gradually out through capillaries to feed her flesh. She felt the anxious pre-awareness of incipient life in her ovaries, a cluster of mindless hopes, swarming with potential. She sensed the tide of the air sucking into her lungs, a curling muddle of fine fibres tugged in and spewed out again.

But there was something terribly wrong. A foul, cancerous unknown, a sickening, creeping blight that was seeping into her like blood into a rag, fast, fast, an invasion and violation of the most horrible kind . . .

She saw it then, in her mind's eye, coiling along the golden threads towards her heart, tentacles of light sliding into her territory, into the very fibres of her body, the striations of her muscles. Everything in her wanted to be rid of it, to expel this vileness from her. Her *kana* blazed in response, threading out towards the invader, to burn it out with cleansing fire . . .

No!

It was Cailin. She willed her *kana* to stop, to accept the invader even though every one of her senses screamed against it; and somehow it responded, stalling in its assault. It railed at her attempt to hobble it, but this was different to when it had been unleashed before. This time, the *kana* was still within her body, and had not broken free of the boundaries of her territory. Here, she could master the fire.

She let herself go mentally limp, beginning a mantra over and over. The onslaught continued through her, creeping in towards her core like the paralysing bite of a spider. She felt panic rising within her. What did she know, truly, of Cailin tu Moritat? She was opening herself up to this woman in a way more intimate than making love, giving her the freedom to do *anything* to her, to turn her lungs inside out or burst her heart or rearrange her thoughts so she was a willing slave to Cailin's whims. How could she trust *anyone* that much, let alone this enigmatic Aberrant who was more of a stranger to her than Tane or Asara?

She forced the thoughts down, concentrating on her mantra. Too late now, she told herself. Too late. And yet still the urge grew, to lash out, to expel this invader and be whole and unsullied again. The presence of Cailin was abhorrent, as Cailin had told her it would be. *Your mind will see me as a disease,* she said, and it did; it took all her willpower to stay still while the foulness consumed her.

But the alien threads were quick, slipping into her heart where they were pumped around her body, and with them came a strange, soothing sensation, as of ice put on a burn. Her *kana* quailed, but she sensed that the worst was over. The calm spread through her, swamping her inexorably, its touch bringing peace to the fibres of her body. No longer did it seem a disease that had swallowed her, but a benediction, and distantly, subtly, she felt Cailin begin her work . . .

The Fold was ever ready for battle, a fortress against the dangers of the Xarana Fault. Though there was no true army here, there was a hard core of military expertise culled from the populace, a combination of Libera Dramach and those who had been recruited or drifted their way in. Bandit leaders and strategists for the nobility sat side by side in war councils, the organisational brain behind the defence network of the Fold. And though there were few professional soldiers here, there was no shortage of volunteers to safeguard the new-found freedom that this isolated community offered. Everyone within the valley was expected to hold their own when the time came, and a man who could not shoot a rifle or use a sword or crank a ballista was dead weight. Training was informal, for most of these people were not warriors by nature, and the Fault's terrain was better suited for guerilla tactics anyway; but there were not many here who would be unable or unwilling to fight when the time came. And in the Fault, the time *would* come sooner or later.

Even as night settled into the creases of the world, the work went on by the glow of paper lanterns and bonfires. Fire-cannons were rolled out and cleaned. Ballistae stood silhouetted imposingly on the ridges, backlit by the flames. Mine-carts full of ammunition were rolled along the system of tracks that ran along bridges between the biggest plateaux. Scouting parties slipped quietly back into the Fold, barely noticed. Lifts squeaked and creaked as their pulleys strained against guide wheels and cogs.

Tane sat on the grassy side of the wide, shallow valley that cradled the Fold and hid it from sight. The folk here had warned him not to go out alone at night, but he was unable to reflect and meditate amid all the activity on the steps, so he took the risk and retreated to the darkness. Now he was glad he had.

He looked out over the cascade of the land, a hundred lanterns in bright points tumbling down the dark platforms and plateaux into the valley, pools of light hanging in the deep, abyssal darkness. The windows of the buildings that crowded the steps of the Fold speckled the black with yellow twinkles like grounded stars. High above, only Aurus rode the sky tonight, her vast face looking down on him, the dim white of her skin blotched with patches of pale blue. It was beautiful, to be here, to see this. He gave thanks to Enyu, and felt a strange contentment within.

These last weeks had been a turbulent time for him. It seemed that he had been running to catch up with himself ever since he had first found Kaiku, unconscious and fevered in the Forest of Yuna. It had taken her arrival – and the events that came in her wake – to knock him out of the life he had settled into ever since his mother and sister had left him alone.

His apprenticeship at the temple was a refuge, a restoration for the crime he had committed. He regretted less the fact that he had murdered his own father, but more that his actions had driven away the rest of his family. His mother was ineffectual without her husband's control, incapable of initiative. His sister had been recently raped. The misfortunes that could have assailed them were legion, and he would never know. For weeks he had tried to track them, to find word of them in nearby towns; but they had vanished, like smoke in the wind. Then the guilt had set in, the terrible weight of what he had done. Despair took him, and he languished in his empty home for weeks. After that, he had gone to the temple and offered himself to Enyu. If he could not heal himself, perhaps he could heal others. Grief-stricken, he was not thinking as clearly as he might have been; but the priests accepted him, and there he found order, a routine, and time to piece his life back together.

But it was the wrong life, and he had taken it for the wrong reasons. He had not the temperament nor the discipline nor – he sickened to admit – the raw faith to dedicate his life to serving Enyu in a temple. Kaiku had been the catalyst that had shown him that. He still believed Enyu had spared him from the slaughter at the temple for a reason, but it was not the reason he had first envisaged. She had sent him to walk among the Aberrants.

When he had left Asara in Chaim and gone south, he had sought only to get away from her. He could not bear the thought of Asara's mocking gaze, or what he might say to Kaiku if she ever returned from the mountains. He needed to be alone, to think things through. He had ever been a solitary child, and he was used to his own counsel; now he needed the peace to listen to it.

You believe your journey was ordained by your goddess, that you were spared for a purpose; but there is no greater foulness to Enyu than an Aberrant. Reconcile these things, if you can.

Asara's words haunted him as he took a ship from Pelis,

back to Jinka and the mainland. He could not reconcile them. Was this a test of his faith? Was he supposed to help them, or thwart them? Were they not all working towards the same goal: finding the hand behind the shin-shin? Was there a lesson to be learned here, or was he simply not seeing it? Whichever way he turned, he came up against the same block: Aberrants, whether they were inherently evil or not, were perversions of nature, products of the blight that had stricken the land. How could he believe that any path that Enyu set him would coincide with theirs?

He thought about it all the way back to Axekami, where he found the city in turmoil. It was only then that he realised he had given himself no plan, no destination, and that he had nowhere to go. What money he had with him was fast running out, and there was no prospect of getting any more. He had relied on Kaiku and Asara's charity since he had joined them, and payment for the journey back from Fo had sapped the little he had taken from his temple when he left. He thought to find another temple of Enyu, who would not turn away one of their own. Not in Axekami, for it was evident the capital was a seething boil of anger at the moment; but there were others elsewhere, where he could find calm and meditate on his quandary.

Yet he did not go to a temple. That would be going backwards, settling himself into the life that Kaiku had torn him from. And whatever else had come of it, he had not forgotten the feeling of *rightness* he had experienced as he and Asara sailed out of the Forest of Yuna towards Axekami. That feeling told him now that the temple of Enyu was not the answer. Instead, he went to the temple of Panazu.

Getting into the city was not easy, but Axekami had not closed itself off completely. Many folk were leaving in terror as martial law gripped the interior, and a way out was a way in. Tane had not forgotten the note Asara had left him. He was still no closer to an answer than he ever had been, but he had learned that he would never find the truth by leaving the path he had taken. All he could do was follow it and hope things became clearer. That was his reasoning, anyway. He resolutely refused to recognise the tug of his heart in the matter, and he would not think of Kaiku at all.

Now she had returned to him. The news she brought staggered them all, revealing the full extent of the Weavers' evil, showing them finally the source of the sickness in the land. Alone, she had walked into the wilderness, and come back bearing something more precious than all the jewels in the world.

It came to him then as a revelation. In his arrogance, he had always imagined that *he* was the one ordained by Enyu for great things. There had always been beneath his reasoning a selfish centre, considering all events in relation to him. But it was Kaiku who had found the source of the blight, picking up a thread woven by her father and following it to its end. Who knew how far back into time that thread stretched, the accretion of knowledge by scholar after scholar, building into wisdom? It took the courage and guile of one man to find the secret; but it took the strength of his daughter to bring it back. It was not Tane's path that was important, but Kaiku's. All that the priests of Enyu's temples had been working for these past decades, with their prayers and meditation, had been unravelled by an Aberrant, the most cursed of nature.

Then why was he there? As a witness? As one who should guard her? As a representative of Enyu's will? He had not been particularly successful at any of these tasks.

Perhaps you are just here, Tane, he thought. *Perhaps there is no greater plan, or if there is, it is too great for you to see it. You always were too introspective. That is why you never made a good priest. Too many questions, not enough blind faith.*

It was not satisfying, but it would do for now. Whatever the real answers, he had no doubts about Kaiku now. He would follow her where she went. As if his traitor heart would allow him otherwise . . .

*

'Out of the question,' Cailin snapped. 'She's too valuable.'

'Nobody knows that more than me,' Mishani replied. 'But if you want me to go, she goes too.'

Mishani and Cailin faced each other, locking eyes and wills. Cailin was almost a head taller than the diminutive noble-woman, but Mishani was not in the least cowed by her opponent's size or fearsome appearance. They stood in one of the upper rooms of the house of the Red Order, a long building with a curving, peaked roof which overhung the balconies running around its first floor. In contrast to the somewhat ramshackle nature of its surrounding buildings, this one was tidy and precise, with pennants of red and black hanging from the balcony rail before the entrance.

'You would willingly put your friend in danger, Mishani,' Cailin accused.

'No,' said Kaiku, from where she leaned against a wall boyishly. 'I asked her. I demand to go.'

'So do I,' put in Tane, who was watching from the other side of the room. Asara stood near him, a faint smirk on her face.

'Why?' Cailin asked, her voice cold. 'You are no warrior. Have you killed before? Have you, Kaiku?'

'I made an oath to Ocha,' said Kaiku calmly, ignoring the question. 'My enemy are the Weavers. The Weavers want Lucia dead. I wish to be part of any effort to thwart them.'

'You will be!' Cailin said, anger creeping into her tone. 'You will learn to be a more powerful force than you can imagine. Dying in the Imperial Keep before you grow into your strength is futile.'

'Cailin, she speaks sense,' Asara said. 'The Keep guards will expect warriors, much as those you have already chosen to go. They will not suspect women and priests.'

'She is dangerous still!' Cailin hissed, flinging out a finger at Kaiku. 'She has only begun to learn how to suppress her *kana*. If she should unleash it within the Keep, we would all be killed.'

CHRIS WOODING

'Don't be melodramatic,' Asara said. 'You merely wish to protect your investment.'

Anger blazed in Cailin's eyes, but Asara met her gaze with an insouciant stare.

'It is only two more, Cailin,' Mishani said. 'You have asked Asara and I to go because you need us. I am the only noble you have who is willing to set foot in Axekami again; Asara is an experienced handmaiden. But I will not go unless Kaiku goes. And Tane, if he wishes. You said yourself that we four trod a braided path. Perhaps it is braided more tightly than you think.'

Cailin framed a retort, then swallowed it. She rounded on Kaiku. 'Is your mind made up in this?'

Kaiku shrugged, an imitation of her brother from long ago. 'I have no choice. I made an oath.'

'Oaths can be interpreted any way you see fit,' Cailin pointed out archly. 'Very well then. We leave for Axekami tomorrow. All of us. If we do not move soon, we may lose our chance. The danger to Lucia grows daily, and we have little time remaining, if my sources tell me true.' She swept around and stalked out of the room, her black dress trailing behind her. 'We will steal the Heir-Empress from under their noses,' she declared as she left.

Kaiku gave a smile of thanks to Mishani, and wondered what she had let herself in for.

TWENTY-EIGHT

The armies of Blood Kerestyn and Blood Amacha faced each other across the grassy plain to the west of Axekami. The morning sun beat down on them, already cruelly hot and not even close to its zenith. It glinted off swords and rifles, sheening down the edges of pike blades and making men shade their eyes and squint. To the west, Blood Kerestyn, their gold and green standards limp in the windless humidity. To the east, Blood Amacha, a swathe of brown and red mingled with the colours of other, lesser families. Fire-cannons brooded in the swelter, their barrels fashioned into the likenesses of demons and spirits, their mouths open to belch flame. Between the armies was the killing ground, a great strip of untrampled grass where they would meet if it came to conflict.

The sheer weight of numbers was immense. Amacha's army had been swelled to over ten thousand, and Kerestyn had more than that, a wave of soldiers that had washed over the land and now teetered on the edge of breaking. From the city walls, they melted into two huge pools of blades and guns and armour. The front ranks were foot soldiers, horses pawing at the dirt and manxthwa loping back and forth, the soldiers standing ready, hair damp with perspiration. Behind them were riflemen, most in rows but some gathered in little clusters, cleaning and checking their weaponry. Further from the front ranks, the tents began, angular polygons of colour ranging from simple and utilitarian to complex and grandiose. Where the battle lines were still, the rear of the armies was a swarm of activity, a constant shifting of supplies, troops, and information. Tents were being erected; cannons were being repaired; armour was fixed or handed out. To the east, the enormous beige walls of Axekami were a frowning barrier that dwarfed them all to insignificance, stretching to either side of the battlefield and curving out of sight, a bristling mass of guard-towers behind which the jumble of the city's streets could be seen cluttering their way up the hill towards the Imperial Keep, its gold walls paled by distance.

The two vast forces shimmered in the heat haze, waiting.

The armies of Blood Kerestyn had begun their march on the capital some days ago, but they were slow, detouring to amalgamate with other, smaller forces on the way, minor families who had allied themselves with the Kerestyn cause. A further delay was caused by the need to skirt Blood Koli's lands around Mataxa Bay. The Barak Koli had firmly allied himself with Sonmaga, for better or worse.

Blood Kerestyn had been ousted from the throne by Blood Erinima over a matter of dishonour, not warfare. The last Kerestyn Blood Emperor, Mamis, had lied to the council of nobles over a matter of great importance and been discovered. He had done the sensible thing and abdicated, for the council had given a unanimous vote of no-confidence in their ruler after that; Anais's father had filled the void. But though Kerestyn had lost the might of the Imperial Guards, which were sworn to protect the Blood Emperor or Empress regardless of their family, they had retained the vast strength which had won them the throne in the first place. And they had bided their time, waiting for an opportunity just such as this.

Sonmaga tu Amacha was no less ambitious, but his ambition outstripped his means somewhat in this matter. He believed passionately that the Heir-Empress should be removed from the line of succession, even if Anais stayed as Empress. If only that cursed Mishani woman had done what she was supposed to, then all this could have been averted. He didn't want a civil war, principally because he suspected he would lose it. In ten years, when he had enough support, when his plans had come to fruition . . . maybe then would be the time to strike. But getting rid of the Aberrant Heir-Empress would solve all their problems. Kerestyn would no longer have a righteous cause motivating them, and their support would swiftly peel away if they chose to press their suit upon the capital. He wished he'd just had Purloch kill the little bitch when he had the chance, instead of settling for a lock of her hair; but Purloch had disappeared the moment he was paid, and had not been found since.

Sonmaga's tent bulked out of the sea of armour, an island of brown and red surrounded by other smaller, lesser islands. The constant convection of soldiers and horses flowed around them in a grubby tide, relaying messages, reporting from the front line. The smell of rank sweat was over powering, and the din was a constant background babble, so loud that it was only when people shouted at each other to be heard that they realised how their ears had adjusted to block it out. Sonmaga's tent was near the rear of his forces, his back towards Axekami. He had crossed the Zan and placed himself squarely between the forces of Kerestyn and the capital. He didn't want a civil war, but he'd be gods-damned if he'd let Blood Kerestyn walk into the capital without a fight.

The emissaries from Blood Koli came at mid-morning, twenty soldiers with the hardened leather of their armour dyed black and white. The newcomers arrived on horseback, their eyes narrow beneath the black sashes tied around their heads to avert sunstroke. Heading them was the Barak Avun tu Koli himself, his balding head held high as he rode, his omnipresent expression of weariness temporarily banished for the benefit of appearances.

The forces of Blood Amacha parted to let them through. That he had come out personally spoke of a matter of great importance. They passed through the ranks to the tent of the Barak Sonmaga, and there Avun dismounted and was shown inside.

Barak Sonmaga stood as Avun entered. He had been sitting

on one of the woven mats placed around the centre of the tent, studying a map. At the edges were low tables of refreshments, chests of clothes and charts, and a rack where Sonmaga's battle armour hung. It was stiflingly hot in here, but being out of the direct gaze of Nuki's eye was a blessing, and the tent walls somehow managed to muffle the worst of the noise from outside.

'Avun,' Sonmaga said. 'What news?' It was almost insultingly informal, but neither was much concerned with ritual greetings at a time like this.

Avun looked him over, the tired cast returning to his hooded eyes. 'You already know,' he stated.

Sonmaga raised a black eyebrow, impressed at Avun's reading of him. 'Yes, I do. Sit down, please.'

Avun joined him in sitting on another of the floor mats. Sonmaga poured cups of dark red wine for them both. Avun waited until Sonmaga had drank from his before taking a sip.

'The forces of Blood Batik approach the city from the east,' Avun said. 'If they had set out from Batik lands north of Axekami and gone directly south, we would have spotted them long ago. But they crossed the Jabaza and circled round so we would not detect their movement. Now they are almost at the city gates.'

Sonmaga let none of the faint disdain he felt for this man show on his face. Excuses, always excuses. He could not even control his daughter, his own blood; in fact, if his accounts were to be believed, she had fled and was missing even now. For such an allegedly brilliant player of the court, he seemed remarkably inept. His desperation for trade concessions with Sonmaga had revealed the sorry state of affairs at Mataxa Bay; he had even let slip about how ill-maintained the boats of his fishing fleet were, and how they were apt to sink at any time. He had always thought of Blood Koli as one of the most noble of families, an unassailable trading empire; but since circumstances had brought Avun and Sonmaga together, he had seen how hollow that assumption was. Avun was weak, and easily

dominated. Sonmaga was content to let it be so. The troops
Avun brought to this standoff were a valuable portion of Blood
Amacha's army. And if the price he had to pay was to listen to
this man's fawning agreement as they discussed their battle
plans and strategies, even letting Sonmaga dictate the movements of Avun's soldiers, then it was a small price indeed.

'Do you suppose Grigi knows about it?' Avun asked
banally.

'Undoubtedly,' Sonmaga replied. 'They will be at the city
tomorrow afternoon. The Empress has evidently decided to
let them in. I cannot imagine they are marching on the capital
to invade; not with Durun and Mos still in the Keep.'

'You have spies there?'

'It is there for all to see,' Sonmaga said, unable to stop a
hint of exasperation. Did this man have no eyes working for
him in the most important building in the Empire? 'Everyone
in the Keep knows it. If the forces of Blood Batik tried to take
Axekami by force, the Imperial Guards would kill Mos and
Durun in a moment. Their allegiance is to the *Blood* Empress,
not her husband. So we must assume they are approaching
with the Empress's consent.'

Avun nodded in understanding. Sonmaga watched him
over the rim of his cup as he sipped his wine. 'It appears we
remain in a stalemate,' Avun said at length, stating what
Sonmaga already knew.

'My only concern is what Grigi might do,' Sonmaga said.
'He must know he'll never get past the walls of Axekami with
Blood Batik inside. His only hope is to get inside before they
do. That means going through us.'

'Then why not get out of his way?' Avun said. Sonmaga's
eyes widened in disbelief. Avun floundered. 'Well, that is to
say, isn't what we wanted that the Heir-Empress be dis-
inherited? If we stand in Blood Kerestyn's way, then all we
are doing is keeping the capital safe until Blood Batik can
move in. Blood Erinima will keep the throne, and the Heir
Empress will come to power.'

'Do you think I am not aware of the situation?' Sonmaga barked. 'Do you think, all this time, I have not been seeking a way to get to the Heir-Empress, to do what your daughter should have done?' Avun cowered before the larger man, whose bulk seemed twice that of Avun's slender frame. 'I do not want Kerestyn on the throne; I want Erinima there, for when Anais's daughter dies – and make no mistake, I *will* get to her, or the people of Axekami will – then I have many more years to prepare before Anais's time is up. And when the Empress dies, childless and barren, then Blood Amacha will be ready to face even the strongest of enemies and claim the throne we have never had! If Kerestyn march into Axekami, with the forces they command, they will rule Saramyr for many decades to come. I cannot rely on another foolish mistake such as had them deposed before. I can only keep them out, and wait. Blood Batik may strengthen the capital now, but a thousand men cannot protect Lucia for ever. I play for time, Avun, for now is not the moment for me to strike.'

Avun's gaze dropped, shamed that he had offended Sonmaga. Sonmaga gave a curt grunt and got to his feet. Avun stayed where he was, head bowed like a servant. Sonmaga rolled his eyes. 'Get up, Avun. We should not quarrel. You know as well as I that we cannot withdraw now. I am committed, as are you. Do not let your courage falter.'

Avun's answer, whatever it was to be, was cut off by a sudden explosion somewhere nearby, a roar and a flare of flame that brightened the thin canvas of the tent. Sonmaga swore a vile oath in surprise, and the world was suddenly a clamour of voices as thousands of men began to shout at once. Another explosion followed, and another, the dull boom of fire-cannon artillery, incendiary bombs that sprayed a burning jelly across a wide area where they hit.

'By the gods, he's attacking us, the bastard!' Sonmaga bellowed. He could hear the distant battle-cry of the Kerestyn forces as they ran as one towards their waiting enemy, an avalanche of swords and pikes and howling throats, as massive and inexorable as the tide. They were joined by the cries of the troops of Blood Amacha, much louder and closer to hand. The generals were sending the front line to engage.

'I didn't think he'd dare,' Sonmaga raged to himself, crossing the tent to pick up his armour. 'The idiot! Doesn't he know this will ruin us both? I didn't think he'd dare!'

He felt suddenly a strong grip on his arm, and he was pulled around to face Avun, who had got to his feet as quick as a snake.

'There were a lot of things you did not think of,' Avun said. A long dagger flashed in his hand, thrusting up below Sonmaga's bearded jaw and ramming through his brain. The larger man gaped in shock. His eyes bulged, reddening with blood; but his life had already left him, cut away by that single stab, and the eyes were sightless. His body went limp, the once-powerful muscles robbed of their strength, and Avun stepped back and released the dagger as Sonmaga fell forward on to his face, smashing his nose to a pulp on the floor.

Avun looked down at the fallen Barak. Spirits, he was gullible. So ready to believe that Blood Koli were willing to be subordinate to him, simply because they had a history of antagonism with Blood Kerestyn. Sonmaga was a man of limited vision, who did not apparently realise that a political ally was most potent when it was kept secret. The façade of enmity between Kerestyn and Koli had fooled all but a clever few. Sonmaga was not one of those few.

He strode out of the tent. Leaderless, the forces of Blood Amacha would be in confusion. The troops of Blood Koli would turn against them when the moment was right, attacking them from within. Grigi tu Kerestyn already knew all Sonmaga's battle plans – which he had been good enough to share with Avun – and it was too late to change them now, as his generals already had their orders. The appearance of Blood Batik had meant time was suddenly short. Sonmaga and his men were an obstacle that had to be removed. With what Grigi knew of Sonmaga's movements, it would be a massacre.

He swept the fold of the tent open and stepped out into the sweltering heat and brightness. All around was a chaos of jostling men, the sound of swords being drawn, horses jockeying for space amid the crush. Flames licked the air nearby, sending choking columns of smoke up towards the sky. A distant crashing, slow and drawn out and immense, heralded the coming together of the two armies on the plains, thousands of blades meeting in a cacophonous mess. He shoved his way to his waiting horse, held by one of his men. Swiftly, he mounted. He saw a soldier entering Sonmaga's tent as he put his heels to the horse, but it was already too late to catch him. Oh, they'd know who the culprit was; but by then the forces of Blood Koli would have turned on them, and they'd be caught in a pincer, like the claws of the crabs of Mataxa Bay that had made his fortune. He thought he heard the cry of outrage as he rode away, and a smile touched his lips.

His only regret in all this was Mishani. If only she had trusted him, as a good daughter should. He had no intention of killing the Heir-Empress. That would have lost him and Blood Kerestyn much of the support they had gained. He had switched the infected nightdress for a harmless one before she had set off for the Keep. He would not risk his daughter and his family's reputation for Sonmaga; he would have simply told the Barak that the illness did not take in Lucia. After all, who knew what an Aberrant's immunities were? But Mishani failed him, turned on him . . . and finally left him. Dead or alive, he cared little. She had proved herself to be without conviction, and disloyal. She was no longer any concern of his. He had bigger plans.

The sound of rising death surrounded him as he rode, and the smile on his lean face widened. How he loved to play these games . . .

TWENTY-NINE

Night fell, but it brought no respite to the people of Axekami. Instead, the darkness bore fear on its back, and panic rode alongside. The western walls of the city were under attack from the forces led by Blood Kerestyn. The air boomed with the sound of fire-cannons, and the ground shook. Men ran back and forth in flaming silhouette along the mighty walls of Saramyr's capital. Guard towers swarmed. Rifle reports punctuated the constant, low roar of battle. Boiling oil was tipped down on to the invaders in a ponderous deluge, followed by agonised howls from below. Ladders clattered on to the battlements and were flung back again, shedding screaming soldiers as they toppled. Distant voices carried on the hot wind, disembodied barks of command or wails of pain.

In the streets of the city, gangs of men roamed with torches in their hands and makeshift weapons sheening dully in the light of the three moons. All the sisters had come out tonight: massive Aurus, bright Iridima, green Neryn. They occupied different positions in the sky, but it would not be for long. Their next few orbits would bring them into dangerous proximity. A moonstorm was coming.

Nobody slept tonight.

The gates of Axekami were closed, both to keep out intruders and to pen in the frantic populace. Many had taken to the walls themselves, their desire to defend their territory greater than their disgust for their Empress and the monster she intended to rule her people. The white and blue armour of the Imperial Guards mixed and mingled with a thousand different fashions, as men brought their old bows and rifles to bear on the forces of Kerestyn. The weeks of unrest and violence on the streets had heated the blood of the folk of Axekami, and while half of them willingly united against a common foe which was trying to force its way into their city, the other half rioted and looted in protest, demanding that Kerestyn be let in and the Empress give up her throne.

The guards at the eastern gate had been turning away people all day, and continued to do so after nightfall. Traders, frantic relatives, people desperate to salvage or defend their homes; everyone was refused. A small camp of rejected travellers had grown by the side of the road. Only nobles and people of importance were allowed inside the city, and then only after approval from the Keep.

When a simple covered cart rolled up, pulled by a pair of loping manxthwa and driven by a grizzle-jawed young man and his elegant wife, the commander on duty made ready to send them on their way like the others. But when he began to say the words, they came out not quite as intended. And he could not on his life think why he had ordered the gate guard to open up, Keep approval or not; nor why he had not thought to even search the cart. Afterward, he could hardly credit that he had not been dreaming; but the only thing he could really remember with any clarity was the lady's green eyes inside her hooded robe, and how they had suddenly darkened to red.

The tarpaulin was pulled from the cart a little while later, slung back by the young man to uncover the stowaways hidden beneath. They had stopped in a short dead-end alley just inside the city's eastern gates, with tall, deserted buildings rising over them on three sides, blocking out the green-tinted moonlight. They slipped out silently, flexing cramped and numb limbs, and assembled around the cart before the young man and the lady. She was Cailin tu Moritat, surprisingly beautiful without the fearsome makeup of her Order. Her hair was drawn back into a long braid, and her features were sharp-cheeked and catlike. The man was Yugi, the leader of this expedition: a roguish-looking bandit in his late twenties with a devilish smile and dirty brown-blond hair held back from his eyes by a grimy red sash. Despite Cailin's presence, it was quite obvious who was in command. Yugi represented the Libera Dramach, and it was they that held the loyalty of the multitude at the Fold. The Red Order were few in number and, powerful as they were, they were not the driving force here.

Mishani smoothed down her expensive robe and arranged her hair swiftly with the help of Asara. Kaiku glanced at Tane, who raised an eyebrow at Mishani as if to say: *How vain!* Kaiku could not suppress a smile. It was a joke; they both knew that Mishani's appearance was of paramount importance. She had an audience with the Empress in the morning.

'That was the easy part,' said Yugi, addressing them all. 'From here on in you must be on your guard at every moment. Mishani, Asara: in the next street waits a carriage that will take you to a safe house. In the morning, you make your way to the Keep at the arranged time.'

Mishani and Asara nodded their understanding.

'The rest of us have an altogether less pleasant way to spend the night,' Yugi said with a grin. 'We go on foot from here. We have a rendezvous to make.'

Nine of them set out into the city after Mishani and Asara had gone. Along with Kaiku, Tane, Yugi and Cailin were five other men of the Libera Dramach, chosen for their skill at stealth and combat. Just walking the streets was dangerous in Axekami at the moment; strength lay in numbers.

Yugi took them down narrow alleys and through a dizzying maze of back-streets, heading away from the Kerryn. The sounds of the assault on the western wall reached them even here, and the night was full of strange cries and unsettling noises. More than once they heard running footsteps, multiplying suddenly and married with cries of rage as a chase began. The mobs were out tonight, and there was nobody on the streets not looking for violence. Those they passed in side-alleys or huddled in dark doorways – the destitute and vagrant – cowered away from them. Yugi paid them no mind. He was leading them deep into the Poor Quarter.

The buildings seemed to pile up on one another around them, leaning in closer, groaning and warping under their own weight. Timbers bent dangerously, and the labyrinthine streets became cluttered with debris. Shutters hung askew from dark windows. Fire-gutted buildings displayed blackened ribs. Makeshift bridges spanned the diminishing width of the streets, ladders that went from window-ledges to adjacent rooftops. Here it was deserted, but Kaiku felt the unshakeable sensation of being watched. She glimpsed faces retreating from windows as she looked up at them, candles hastily snuffed at the approach of footsteps. Yugi was deliberately keeping them off the main thoroughfares to avoid meeting anyone, but into what danger was he taking them? They had been kept largely in the dark about the details of the plan to kidnap the Heir-Empress, for reasons of security; but it served only to make Kaiku more nervous when she had no idea what lay ahead. She felt the reassuring weight of her rifle against her back, and the sword at her hip, but even they offered her little comfort.

'In here,' Yugi said suddenly, stopping before a doorway in a derelict building that had been covered over with planking and then broken again. He ushered them within, following last after he had seen the coast was clear. This, then, was their destination, Kaiku thought with mingled relief and trepidation. They had been lucky to get this far through the city without coming across any of the mobs; but where were they to go now, from the heart of the Poor Quarter?

Inside, the darkness was deeper still. The green-edged luminescence of the three moons beamed in through chinks and slats in the wooden walls, coming from three directions at once to render the interior in a dim, unsettling light.

Whatever this place had once been, it had been abandoned for years. Rubble, broken planks and unidentifiable debris littered the squalid, narrow rooms. Insects droned about in the hot night, exploring the carcass of a dog that had recently expired here.

'Where is he?' Cailin asked sharply, seeming to direct the question at nobody in particular.

'Down,' Yugi said. 'Come on.'

He led them through a series of similarly deserted rooms until he came to a hatch, which he pulled up to reveal a set of wobbly wooden steps. A light burned somewhere below.

'It's us,' he hissed down, before descending. The others followed carefully.

It was a cellar. The warm, damp air tasted of mould, and the stone of its walls looked aged and crumbling in the lantern's glow. The man holding the lantern was murmuring with Yugi as Kaiku came down into the room. He was thin and slightly gaunt, with a worried expression on his brow. His short hair was greying towards his fortieth harvest.

The last man down closed the hatch behind them, shutting them in.

'We're all here? Good,' said Yugi. 'May I introduce the man who will be guiding us the rest of the way. There have been doubts voiced from the start as to whether a group of men – and ladies – such as us could even get *into* the Imperial Keep, let alone to the Heir-Empress herself. But *this* man did it alone, and unaided; and he got close enough to the little Heir-Empress to cut a lock of her hair. This is Purloch tu Irisi.'

The five men of the Libera Dramach burst into amazed exclamations. Kaiku and Tane, who had never heard of him, kept silent and glanced at each other. Tane gave Kaiku a reassuring squeeze on the shoulder. He was just as nervous as she was, yet his presence made her feel a little safer, and she was glad of it.

'Through there,' Purloch said, motioning to a shadowy

alcove in the wall. He raised his lantern obligingly, and they saw that a narrow hole had been knocked through it. 'The city's sewer pipes run against this cellar. They also run up the hill, and beneath the Imperial Keep. I used them before to get in, though there's no telling whether they found out and shut off the way. I don't think so. Nobody goes down there unless they have to.'

One of the men went to the hole and peered through, into the dark. 'What's down there?'

'I don't know, and I don't want to find out,' Purloch said. 'But I heard them last time, on my way out.'

'Heard *what*?' the man demanded.

'It doesn't matter what,' Yugi answered sternly. 'Light your lanterns. We're going down there. Ladies, I must apologise in advance for the stench, but—'

'Don't be an idiot,' Cailin said, crippling his gallantry. 'Do not think us frail. Either of us could collapse your heart with a thought.'

Yugi grinned, but there was uneasiness at the edge of it, and he was lost for something to say for the briefest of moments. His eyes flickered to Kaiku, appraising her anew. What Cailin had said was not strictly the truth, at least where it concerned Kaiku; but it gave Yugi pause.

'With such pleasant company, then, this journey will simply fly by!' he declared, recovering admirably.

The dank underworld of the city sewers was not a place Kaiku had ever imagined finding herself. Their world was circumscribed by a wet arc of light that curved over the tunnel walls ahead of them, and beyond it was only a black abyss which threw back a starfield of tiny glimmers as lapping water or moist bricks caught their lanterns' glow. The stench was indescribable. Tane had vomited almost immediately upon entering the sewers, and retched frequently even after his stomach was more than emptied. Several of the other men were similarly afflicted. Kaiku felt permanently on the verge of bringing up her last meal, but somehow the cloying reek never quite made her stomach rebel. Cailin appeared unaffected. Nobody was surprised.

The sewers of Axekami were a network of channels, dams and sluice-gates, flanked by wide stone paths for the sewer workers to use. With the unrest above, they were confident that nobody would be working tonight; but the thought of what they might find instead preyed on their minds.

Kaiku kept her eyes on Purloch as they walked the wet paths with the murky effluent of the city flowing past them. He was plainly terrified, his eyes skittering to every shadow, jumping when a rat scrabbled or a piece of junk in the water bumped against the lip of the path. What had he encountered down here that had scared him so? Had this man really penetrated the Imperial Keep? And if so, then why was he ready to do it again? What had turned him to the cause of the Libera Dramach? It was while musing on this question that she remembered the words of Mishani, on an occasion when Kaiku had asked her the same thing during their time in the Fold.

You only have to see her to know, Kaiku. She will win you with a glance.

Was that it? Had Purloch been so touched by the Heir-Empress? Was she truly such a transcendental creature?

None of them spoke as they walked through the endless dark of the sewers. Existence dwindled to the circumference of their lantern light, and the irregular ticks, patters and splashes of the diseased things that lived here. Purloch was leading them from memory, taking them up slanted inclines, through bottlenecks, over thin metal bridges. The omnipresent nausea that their surroundings induced compounded their misery, but there was nothing to do but plod on. They would be walking till dawn warmed the earth above, so Purloch had told them; but it was necessary to be in place under the Keep by the morning, for that was when the plan would be carried out.

Kaiku was crowded with doubts. Tane walked before her, and her eyes ran over his shaven skull and lean back. The sight of him brought a faint tinge of guilt. She had thrown herself recklessly into this affair, without knowing what she was getting herself into; but that was all right, that was her way. She had ever been headstrong and stubborn. Stubborn enough to walk alone into storm-lashed mountains, anyway. She had never really considered the chances of success then, nor did she now; they were not factored into her way of thinking. Yet her decision to come meant Tane had come too, and that was another matter.

She was not oblivious to what he clearly felt for her. He had followed her since the Forest of Yuna, stood by her side even after he discovered she was the thing he most abhorred. He loved her, she saw that. And she could not deny the desire he provoked in her. It was a heady thing to know that she could have him with a word, that he would come to her bed at her command. And yet it was a dangerous game, to play with men's hearts, and she was not so cruel. It would not be right, not now, not when she was still coming to terms with herself, with her power and her new life as an Aberrant, with Asara . . .

The memories of that night in Chaim caused her to flush. The heat of the moment had been overwhelming, but it had been too brief to make sense of it. Giddy with Asara's assertion that she should unshackle herself from the restrictions men had made for her, she had acted on a foreign impulse and subsumed herself in it. But all too soon the moment had been interrupted by Mamak . . . no . . . by the terrible feeling she had experienced when Asara had kissed her that final time, the awful *hungriness* of her, and how it had seemed her very insides were being wrenched free.

She was too confused to think on it now. Just as she dared not truly consider the implications of what she had learned in the Weavers' monastery. There was too much, too much, and she knew that if she looked at it all at once it would crush her.

She would think only of what was in front of her, going one step at a time. It was the only thing she could do.

Her thoughts scattered and her blood froze as an ungodly noise sawed through the silence. For a moment, nobody moved. Everyone was listening. It came again, echoing from a different tunnel this time. A creaking screech like the turning of a vast and long-rusted wheel.

'It's them,' Purloch whispered.

'It's what?' demanded one of the other men. 'It could be anything. A sewer pipe . . . a gate opening . . .'

'No,' Cailin said quietly. 'I sense them. They are coming.' She looked up, her eyes passing down the line to rest on Kaiku. 'We cannot face them here. Run.'

A third screech was her reply, louder than the last and closer. Purloch took flight, his boots skidding on the slippery floor in his haste to get away. The others followed closely, running as fast as they dared. The paths that ran alongside the flow of sludgy water seemed suddenly narrow now. The lantern light swung wildly around them, glinting off the bright, black eyes of rodents and other, less identifiable things that scattered at their approach. The screeches began to come more frequently; inhuman, malevolent sounds that could not have been made by any natural thing. They reverberated through the darkness, seeming to come from all directions at once. Kaiku felt them, a creeping sensation at the base of her neck. Demons.

Shin-shin? she thought, and a sudden wild panic gripped her.

They raced up a set of steps that ascended alongside a series of foul waterfalls. Tane stumbled and retched on his way up, falling to his knees. Kaiku crashed into him from behind, and immediately began pulling him to his feet, fear making her rough. He scrambled up, tangling himself in the rifle slung across his back. The others were already racing ahead, leaving Kaiku and Tane behind, taking the light with them. Neither Kaiku nor Tane carried lanterns.

'Wait!' she cried, as she wrenched Tane's arm out of his rifle strap and righted him. An explosive cacophony of howls sounded from the darkness behind her, terrifyingly close now.

'Come on! Up here!' Yugi cried down the stairway to them, and Tane finally got his feet under him and ran. Kaiku was close on his heels. She heard a scraping sound from behind, as if something were crawling on to the stairs, but she dared not look back. Her breath came in frantic gasps, and Tane could not move fast enough for her.

They burst out into a large, star-shaped chamber into which five tunnels opened. The water here was shallow, and a great circular drain lay in the centre of the floor, its rusty slats open to drink the putrescent water. Between the efforts of the drain and the way the hard stone floor rose up here, the water was only thigh-high. A narrow path ran around the edge of the chamber, but the intruders had already forsaken it and gathered in the water, around the drain, back to back. The creaking wails echoed around them, coming from the dark maws of the tunnels. Kaiku and Tane splashed into the water and joined the others, Tane retching anew at the cold touch of the effluent and the seeping of human waste that soaked his legs.

And then, as one, the wailing stopped. Silence fell, but for the stirring of the water around their feet. Purloch began to mutter a prayer to himself. Swords and rifles were held ready, all eyes on the five passageways. The light of their lanterns seemed to gutter, reminding them of how frail the margin was by which they were allowed their vision. If the lanterns were dropped or extinguished, they would be left in the endless dark, and nothing could save them then.

Kaiku became aware that she was shivering. Not with cold, but with tension. Her *kana* lay quiescent inside her, suppressed by whatever method Cailin had used to stop her being a danger to others; but she wished now that she had at least that to fall back on. Anything, anything to avail her against the things she felt creeping on the edge of the light.

It rose slowly from the water before her, just inside the mouth of the tunnel they had come from. A black, bedraggled shape, hunched over with its filthy hair hanging across its face, dripping putrid water. From its mouldering robe, its hands were curled into claws, white and bloodless and scabbed. A single eye glittered behind the matted curtain of hair, fixing Kaiku with a paralysing gaze. It exhaled a long, rattling breath.

'Gods! There's one here too!' someone cried, and Kaiku tore her attention away for a moment to glance at the second creature that had limped into the light from another tunnel. This one was emaciated and skeletal, a half-rotted corpse with its lower jaw hinged only at one side, and hanging together by a few strips of decaying flesh. It jerked along upright, its head lolling, but the sharp light in its eyes never left the people gathered in the centre of the chamber.

'What are these damned things?' Yugi whispered.

'Maku-sheng,' Cailin replied. 'The spirits of unclean water. They have taken the dead they have found down here and made them their own.'

'Another!' someone cried. It was grotesquely fat and naked, one side of its belly a gaping green wound through which the rotting slither of its intestines was wetly visible.

'And here!'

'Here, too.'

They were surrounded. The demons made no move to approach, only glared at them balefully. A whisper seemed to run around the chamber, a susurrus of hissing. The creatures were conversing at a pitch just outside human hearing. Kaiku was trembling uncontrollably now.

Suddenly, the long-haired demon raised one grimy hand and pointed, an ear-splitting howl coming from her. Her hair fell back from her face, and Kaiku glimpsed a horrifying visage of wrinkled, sagging flesh and long, decaying teeth; then the demons attacked.

All around them, the creatures came through the tunnels,

bursting from the darkness and lunging into the chamber, loping and jerking as their atrophied muscles carried them inward. Yugi's rifle roared first, the report of his weapon echoing away in all directions through the sewers. The fat maku-sheng's head exploded in a wet shatter of bone fragments and clotted fluids, and it fell backwards into the water. Those who held lanterns brought their swords to bear, swinging them into the oncoming tide of dead flesh, slicing effortlessly through marrow and sinew. The long-rotted creatures came apart beneath the edges of the blades, toppling into the water; but a moment later the same creatures they had cut in half were coming back at them again, flailing through the murky water while their severed legs twitched uselessly behind them.

'They will not stay down!' someone cried, and a moment later he screamed as one of the things fell on him, its teeth biting into his throat. His scream became a gurgle and his lantern fell into the water with a hiss. The light dropped a notch in the chamber, further cloaking the broken shapes that surrounded them.

Kaiku hastily fumbled her rifle up to fire at the long-haired demon advancing on her, but the shot clicked dead. Her ignition powder had got too damp to light. Baring its foul teeth, the demon lunged at her, and then Tane was there with a cry, his sword stabbing deep into the creature's breast. Kaiku scrambled back, dropping her rifle in the water and wrenching free her own sword; but the demon had already pulled away with a shriek, snapping Tane's blade with the twisting of its body. It retreated a few steps, its eyes glimmering with malice, and a moment later another of them burst out of the water, right in front of Tane. Cold hands clawed at him, and crooked teeth sunk into the meat of his leg.

He cried out in agony, staggering back and swiping downward with the remaining length of his blade; but though he hewed through most of the dead thing's throat, still it held on to him, pawing at his thigh and worrying the chunk of flesh it had in its mouth. Kaiku's sword seemed to elude her panicked grasp, but she somehow swung it down across the thing's shoulder blades, hacking it hard enough for it to make an involuntary shriek and release Tane. As it splashed beneath the water, Tane raised his injured leg and stamped on its head, crushing its skull against the floor in a vile bloom of dark fluid.

Kaiku felt the stir of the Weave around her, and realised suddenly that Cailin had entered the fray. Her eyes were the deep, sulphurous red that heralded the use of her Aberrant power. Three of the maku-sheng went flying to smash bone-lessly into the chamber wall, thrown away by her *kana*. The surrounding creatures recoiled, screeching, then attacked with redoubled fury a moment later. The knot of defenders around the centre of the room broke under the assault, splitting apart. The lantern light swung away from Kaiku, plunging her into darkness. Something lunged at her; she parried it, and felt a spray of something cold and foul-smelling across her cheek as her sword bit into dead flesh. Retreating in horror, she tripped against the covering of the drain in the centre of the room. There was a moment of sickening inevitability, and then she felt her balance desert her and she fell. The chill, polluted water closed around her head with a splash.

She flailed, gagging, and broke the surface for the merest of seconds; but then the long-haired demon was on her, its scabrous hands at her throat, forcing her back under into the lightless murk. There was no breath in her to scream. She kicked and thrashed, but the force pressing her down was too strong, relentless. Animal panic seized her. Her lungs burned, reaching for air that was not there. Unconsciousness swarmed at the edges of her vision, a sparkling blanket that encroached further and further towards the centre. She was dimly aware of underwater sounds, the splash and babble of her own weakening resistance, the noise of a rifle shot, the sound of howling as Cailin annihilated another swathe of demons. But it was all fading, receding, and behind her eyes she could see the Weave again, the glittering path that had led her once to the Fields of Omecha and the gatekeeper, Yoru, took her to the Gate but no further. Perhaps this time, she thought, as her struggles ceased . . . perhaps this time . . . she might join her brother on the other side . . .

But in the Weave of her body, something was stirring, thrashing. A knot was fraying. Consciousness fled her, but there was still something awake inside, fighting and twisting, picking at the fibres of Cailin's artistry. Her *kana* had been bounded and suppressed, but not beaten. Even as Kaiku's brain accepted her death, the creature within her fought against it, unravelling its bonds frantically, until with a snap they slipped free—

'Kaiku!' Tane cried. He had been casting about frantically for signs of her, having lost her in the chaos of the battle; but only a single lantern remained, held like a treasure by one of the Libera Dramach men, and it was barely light enough to see on the periphery of the luminescence. Now his eyes settled on the demon, hunched over in the water, pressing down on something; and he caught sight of the limp hand floating on the surface next to it. With a howl of anguish, he leaped at the thing. It raised its head in alarm, but at that moment Kaiku's *kana* finally loosed itself. Tane fell backward, shielding his face, as the demon shrieked and exploded. A blaze of fire threw yellow light across the murky water. The creature's burning, broken husk staggered away a few steps, animated by some shreds of remnant life; then it teetered, and plunged into the water with a hiss.

The other maku-sheng were squealing anew, having felt the force of the blast. Tane paid them no mind, picking himself up and forging over to Kaiku. He dragged her out of the stench and foulness, and her face came up pale, open eyes gazing crimson and sightless, hair plastered to her cheeks.

'Not her! No!' he shouted, though to what god or aspect of

fate he addressed his denial he could not say. He sheathed his broken sword, heedless of the demons swarming about in the darkness, and hooked his arms under Kaiku's armpits, towing her through the water to the path at the edge of the chamber.

Cailin was a fearsome sight in the shifting light of the single lantern, her black hair straggled and her eyes burning red. She looked like a demon herself. She flung her hands out again and again, sending her *kana* racing along the threads of the Weave to tear and knot and twist, rending apart the bodies of the maku-sheng. With each one she destroyed, she sensed the demon spirit fleeing invisibly from the now-useless corpse, rippling away through the foul water in search of a new host. Yugi fought stolidly alongside her, guarding her back, his rifle firing again and again, repriming between each shot with remarkable speed.

And then a single, keening howl rose from the demon pack. They halted in their attack, drawing to safe distance from the huddled defenders, glaring at them with their shining eyes from the shadows. The whispers began again, though no mouths moved. Yugi kept his finger tensed on the trigger, Purloch standing close to him. Four of the five men of the Libera Dramach floated amid the putrid mass of re-killed corpses. The last, a man just out of his youth called Espyn, held his lantern high and his gore-streaked sword ready, but the tip trembled perceptibly.

There was a stirring, and the demons retreated, backing out of the light into the shadow as smoothly as they had arrived, being swallowed by the tunnels around the chamber. In moments, they had disappeared.

Yugi breathed out a shaky sigh. 'Gone?' he asked Cailin.

'They will come back. We should not be here when they do.' She looked up suddenly at a movement, and saw Tane heaving Kaiku on to the path at the chamber's edge. 'Gods,' she breathed, and waded through the thigh-high water as fast as she could go. 'Espyn! Bring the lantern!' she commanded, and he scuttled to obey.

Kaiku's lips were blue, her red eyes glazed, her hair lank and sodden. Tane was reaching into her open mouth and pulling out some unidentifiable detritus from her throat as they arrived, haste and fear making him panicky.

'Is she breathing?' Purloch asked, casting quick glances at the tunnels behind them in case any of the maku-sheng should return.

Tane ignored him. 'Can *you* do anything?' he demanded of Cailin.

'She slipped my conditioning, got through my barriers,' Cailin said, with something like wonder in her voice. 'Heart's blood, she has a greater talent than I thought.' She looked at Tane. 'Without her conscious control, her *kana* would rebel if I tried. It would kill her.' She missed the irony of her statement, but nobody felt like making a joke of it.

'Then I will do it,' Tane replied. He crossed his hands and pumped her chest with the heel of his palm, then put his lips to hers and blew breath into her lungs. How cruel that it should be like this, he thought; their first kiss, so cold and foul-tasting and passionless. But then he was at her chest again, pumping, breathing, pumping, breathing, while the others looked at him as if he was mad. None of them knew the technique for reviving drowning victims, but Tane had learned it from Enyu's priests long ago.

'Wake up, for the gods' sake!' he shouted at her, pumping again. 'This is not the end of your path! You have an oath. *An oath.*' Another breath, blowing hot life into her waterlogged lungs. Then pumping. 'You're too damned stubborn to die like this!' he cried.

And as if Omecha himself had reached down and touched the dead woman beneath his hands, she jerked and spasmed into life, rolling on to her side and vomiting bilious sewer water across the path. She retched and retched, cleansing herself agonisingly, as Tane laughed with joy and tears ran down his face and he gave praise to the gods. Yugi clapped him on the back in congratulation, calling him a miracle-worker. Kaiku's retching gradually subsided, and she lay gasping like a landed fish, weak but unhurt.

Cailin shook her head in amazement, a smile on her lips, and wondered how many lives her potential apprentice had left.

THIRTY

Dawn came, and the battle raged on.

The forces of Blood Kerestyn had made little headway in breaching the city walls. The mighty western gates were closed against them, and their ladders were thrown back time and again. Had it been only the Imperial Guards they were facing, they might have overwhelmed the defenders by sheer strength of numbers; but they had been counting on the Guards to have their hands full keeping the riots in the city to a minimum. Instead a large portion of the cityfolk had united in defence of their home, little caring for politics in this matter. Whatever their feelings about the Heir-Empress, it was a point of pride that no one would be allowed to invade Axekami, and so the defenders' numbers had been swollen manyfold. Grigi tu Kerestyn spat his frustration throughout the night, and redoubled his efforts at assault when Nuki's eye peeped over the horizon, but the forces of Blood Batik were marching rapidly from the east, and they would be in the city before nightfall. Once there, they would be immovable, and Blood Erinima's safety would be assured.

Anais sat on her throne next to her husband, icily calm. The sun beamed through the high, unshuttered windows of the room, an unbearable swelter even though the morning had barely begun. Servants fanned air with great ornamental sails, but it did little good; Imperial Guards sweated and itched abominably inside their ceremonial metal armour. The purple and white pennants of Blood Erinima hung slackly against the walls. Braziers leaked perfumed smoke.

Durun was in a foul mood. He had been carousing last night. The Empress had been fighting for the very survival of her family, organising tactics, dealing with reports, and he had stolen away to drink. He had come to her bed and she had spurned him. The memory of their fiery argument combined with the morning's heat, his hangover and the fact that he was wakened so early and dragged to the throne room had all combined to make his temper far shorter than usual.

The doors were opened, and a Speaker announced:

'Mistress Mishani tu Koli of Blood Koli.'

She entered wearing a robe of midnight blue, her immense length of hair tamed with strips of leather in a matching colour. Her pale, thin features were composed in their courtly mask, serene and revealing nothing. Walking behind her and at one side was Asara, dressed in simple white, her hands folded before her in the manner of a handmaiden. The streaks of red that had run though her black hair had disappeared, for they were too ostentatious for a position so humble; and she had artfully shifted the pallor of her skin to take the edge off the remarkable perfection of her features. They walked along the patterned *lach* path that led to the thrones of coiled wood and precious metal, where the slender, fair Anais sat next to her tall, stern and dark-haired husband, who was dressed all in black.

'You have some nerve, Mishani tu Koli,' Durun said, before any formal greetings could be made.

Mishani's eyes flickered to him. None of the frank amazement at his rudeness touched her face.

'Blood Empress Anais tu Erinima,' she said, bowing. Then, to Durun, with a lesser bow, 'Emperor Durun tu Batik. May I know why my presence has caused such offence to you?' She was using the Saramyrrhic mode reserved only for the Emperor and Empress, but Durun's mode was far less polite.

Anais regarded her coldly from her throne on the dais. 'Do not play games, Mishani. It is only because of the special circumstances attending this day that I have agreed to see you. Speak your piece.'

This was wrong, Mishani thought to herself. Terribly wrong.

There was something happening here that she did not know about. Her visit to the Empress was ostensibly a friendly one, though its true purpose was more elaborate. She had asked to see Anais immediately upon her arrival, forsaking the usual politenesses, because it was essential to the Libera Dramach's plan that she was not with Lucia this morning. Everything could be ruined if the Empress – and her attendant retinue – were present when they tried to kidnap the child; for secrecy was the most important aspect of this operation, and no one must know who was responsible. Everyone else could be accounted for, but not the Empress; if she chose to visit Lucia today, kidnap would be impossible. There would be too many Guards. Mishani's function, using her noble birth as a lever, was essentially as a decoy.

But what had she done to warrant this hostility? This did not bode well.

'I come to offer you my allegiance,' she said. Durun barked a laugh, but she ignored him. 'When last I visited yourself and Lucia, my intentions were unclear. And though I know my father has opposed you and allied himself with Sonmaga tu Amacha, I would have you know that you may rely on what support I can offer you. Please forgive the urgency of this meeting, but I demanded to see you so that I might tell you this before the scales of this conflict have tipped. Whichever way they go, you and your daughter have my loyalty.'

'Your *loyalty*?' Durun cried incredulously, getting to his feet. 'Gods, I must still be drunk! Here stands the Koli child offering us her strong right arm, when her father not a day past has betrayed Sonmaga and even now assaults the walls of our city! What do you know of loyalty? You yourself are betraying your father by going against his will! His same traitorous blood flows in your veins. What will you offer us, Mishani? Will you call your father away from the attack on Axekami? Answer me! What will you offer us?'

Mishani was shaken. She understood it now, grasping the situation immediately. While her father had been on Son-

368

maga's side, he had been essentially defending the city by keeping Kerestyn out. If things had been as they were when she set off from the Fold, Anais would have accepted her friendship in good grace. That was all that was necessary. Even now, the Libera Dramach would be inside the Keep and hunting down the Heir-Empress. If all had gone to plan.

But all was not going to plan. Mishani had not known of the secret alliance between her family and Blood Kerestyn; her father had kept that from her. He was one of the invaders, and she was still his daughter in the eyes of the world. She had just stepped into a den of enemies. She glanced about nervously, and saw the Barak Mos by the side of the dais, his arms folded across his broad chest, watching her.

'Speak, Mishani tu Koli,' said Anais, her voice angry and hard. 'Why have you come to us this way?'

Mishani said the only thing she could. 'My father's actions shame me,' she said. She knelt and bowed low, her hair falling over her face, in abject supplication. Asara automatically followed suit, as a good handmaiden should do. 'And they shame Blood Koli. On the one hand, I have my loyalty to my family; on the other, to my Empress. When I learned of his intentions, I turned my back on him. Though he is my father, he is a man without honour. I throw myself on your mercy. I would stand with your daughter against whatever may come, for though I am Blood Koli by name, I am forever apart from them now.'

Anais stood, a frown of disbelief creasing her brow. 'You know better than this, Mishani. The fate of a noble family is bound together. The crimes of the father are your crimes also until retribution is exacted.' She opened her hands. 'You know better,' she said again, almost apologetically.

Mishani did know better. Such an unjust trick of the gods, to put her in this situation. It should have been so easy, civilised, a simple distraction tactic; she would have been gone before the Empress ever realised her child was missing. And now . . . now . . .

Anais shook her head sorrowfully. 'I will never understand what possessed you to come here, Mishani. You were always a shrewd and ruthless player at court.' She sat back down, and waved a hand at her guards.

'Kill them.'

Kaiku's eyes opened to the sound of a metallic creak. She started, scrambling awake from a nightmare of the maku-sheng, dreaming their terrible cries like the squeal of rusty gates echoing through the sewers. Tane caught her, his arms around her shoulders.

'Calm yourself,' he whispered. 'Calm yourself. It was only a dream.'

She relaxed in his grip, listening to her pulse slow. Gradually her surroundings made sense to her again. They were in a small, dank antechamber, lit by the single lantern that lay in the corner. The room stank of their sewage-soaked clothes, and Kaiku had a vile taste in her throat that would not go away. Sodden and dejected, the others were getting to their feet as Kaiku awoke, gathering themselves to go. She did not remember falling asleep. But she remembered the cold tongue of the sewer water forcing itself down her, and the glittering eyes of the thing that held her under . . .

The creak came again, and she realised it was the sound of a key. The door that had blocked their path was being opened. It was time to move.

She recalled an argument, somewhere in the black depths behind them. A conversation about what to do with their dead. Yugi would not leave them for the maku-sheng to have; but they could not bring them either. She thought they compromised by severing their heads from their bodies so the demon spirits could not inhabit them, though that might have been a nightmare too. Tane had argued for taking her back, but something had made her protest that she could go on, and it was a moot point anyway. There was one lantern, and that was going to the Keep.

The maku-sheng had not troubled them again. They had had enough of Cailin's power, and dispersed to seek less taxing prey. Kaiku had staggered on, borne up by Tane's taut shoulders, following the light like a moth. He limped slightly himself, suffering from the pain of being bitten in the leg by one of the foul things; but the bite was not serious, and he had bound it well. She remembered little of the rest of the journey, only an all-enshrouding weariness and misery interspersed with occasional moments of regret. When they had come to the antechamber that she now awoke in, Cailin had declared they were still early.

'I suggest you sleep,' she had murmured. 'In the morning, if all is well, we will be met by the leader of the Libera Dramach. He will take us onward.'

Tane professed his curiosity, for Cailin had mentioned him several times before, and always refused to reveal him for fear of endangering him.

'It does not matter any more,' she said. 'For after today, all deceptions will be over.' And yet, for all that, she had still not told them his name.

Kaiku had slept, but the few hours in the grip of oblivion had seemed only moments. And now Tane was pulling her up and asking meaningless questions about how she felt. But it was Tane who appeared to be suffering more than she was; he looked pallid and shaky, his skin waxy and his eyes bright with fever. He was ill, having picked up some infection from the foul sewer water or the bite of the maku-sheng. Kaiku considered it faintly miraculous that she had not succumbed herself – having swallowed a good deal of the effluent when she was drowning in it – but she doubted that any disease could survive the scouring of her *kana* through her body, and she put it down to that. Besides, she felt so bone-weary and burned-out that she would have been hard pressed to notice even if she *was* sick; she could scarcely feel worse than she already did.

The lock of the iron door disengaged with a clunk, and it

swung open, spilling the light from a new lantern in to mingle with their own. Holding it was a middle-aged man, tall and broad-shouldered, with a close-cropped white beard and swept-back hair.

'Cailin. Yugi,' he said by way of greeting. 'What happened to the others?'

'We ran into trouble,' Yugi replied. 'Good to see you.'

'Come through,' the stranger urged, and they did. He shut the iron door behind them. They were in a dank cellar that reeked of disuse, cobwebs and mould. He surveyed the ragtag mob assembled before him. Six were left of the original ten that had entered the sewers.

'We go ahead as planned,' he said. 'Your noble friend entered the Keep safely this morning. Even now the Empress and her idiot husband should be meeting with her in the throne room. The Heir-Empress is wandering the roof gardens, as usual. I have servant clothes ready, and there is a place where you may wash. Your condition would bring the guards down on us in a moment.' He looked Kaiku over. 'I expected only one woman. My apologies. You will have to make do.'

Kaiku was too relieved at the mention of Mishani to respond with more than a nod. Her friend had slipped her mind in the horrors of the sewer, and though she had the safest task of all of them, Kaiku could not help but worry.

'I do not recognise some of you,' the man said. 'Let me introduce myself, then. I am Zaelis tu Unterlyn, tutor to the Heir-Empress Lucia tu Erinima. I am also the founder of the Libera Dramach, and as much a leader as it can be said to have.' He seemed about to say more, to explain himself for the benefit of those who did not know him, but he thought better of it.

'Time is short. Come with me,' he said, and they went.

They were in an old, disused section of the prison dungeons, as it emerged; a long-forgotten place, by the looks of things. Tane wondered how many hundred years it had been since it was sealed off, how many Emperors and Empresses had not known of the small, innocuous iron door that led into the sewers. Time was the greatest concealer of all. He glanced at Purloch, and marvelled at how this man had found it out, had made his way through those sewers alone, with no guide, and had not only broken into the Keep but found his way to its most closely guarded prize. Purloch clearly felt he was pushing his luck too far by bringing them here; but he had brought them anyway, for Lucia. He felt he owed her that. Though Tane did not know it, he blamed himself as the author of the calamity that had seized Saramyr. He had taken Sonmaga's money and exposed Lucia for what she was; but now the weight of his guilt tore at him nightly. He would not be able to live with himself if that serene and unearthly child died because of his greed.

Zaelis led them to a small, dark room that had once been a washroom for guards and prisoners alike. A pair of rudimentary showers belched and splattered water on to the black, slick stone tiles. Clothes were heaped on a low stand in one corner.

'The water still runs, as you see. I managed to make it work; unfortunately I cannot turn it off again. Be quick,' Zaelis instructed.

They showered in pairs, the women first. The water was lukewarm and clean, heated by the sun through pipes high above. Once she had sluiced off as much of the foulness as she could, Kaiku dressed in the clothes of a male servant while Cailin attired herself more appropriately. Kaiku cared little. She fit men's clothes as well as women's, and she doubted it would raise a comment. Attired in simple grey trousers and loose shirt – folded right over left in the female fashion – she emerged from the washroom looking reasonably clean.

The others showered and dressed, and Zaelis instructed them to leave those weapons that could not be concealed behind. There was consternation at this, but Zaelis silenced them with a glare.

'Servants do not carry swords and rifles!' he snapped. 'Our objective is stealth. If it came to a fight in the heart of the Empress's Keep, I very much doubt any of us would survive it, weapons or not. Purloch will look after them.'

Kaiku glanced at the cat-burglar, who seemed almost shamefaced about staying. But he had done his part; he had got them into the Keep, and he would not risk himself further. Zaelis could get into the roof gardens far more easily than he could. Besides, he was their guide out of the Keep, and too valuable to lose. He would wait here, and lead them when the time came, back through the sewers to freedom.

The six who were left made their way out of the disused prison section, finally clambering through a large grille that led into a stockroom full of jars of dried food. The grille was set at ground level, hidden behind a pile of sacks in a corner. Kaiku suspected the entrance to the old prison had been built over long ago, but this sly back way had survived.

'Beyond this point, you are servants,' Zaelis instructed. 'Behave as such. My presence will be enough to deter questions.'

With that, he took them out of the stockroom and into the Keep.

Behind his bronze Mask, the Weave-lord Vyrrch's myopic eyes flickered open.

He was in his chambers. A scrawny jackal roamed about nearby, chewing on what morsels it could find. Vyrrch had demanded he be brought a jackal two days ago now; for what reason he could not remember. The canny creature had managed to stay alive while trapped in here, evading his clutches. He suspected he had brought it in to track down that girl who was still hiding somewhere hereabouts, but it had evidently not been one of his more sensible ploys.

He had not seen the girl for weeks now, and he was reasonably sure he hadn't killed her. He still came across signs of her from time to time, objects moved from their rightful place, food gone missing. She was somewhere in the many rooms of Vyrrch's domain, seeking a way out, finding none. Yet how crafty she was, to have stayed out of sight for this long. He almost respected her.

Another strange shiver in the Weave, and Vyrrch was reminded what had jarred him. Concern flickered across his malformed face, though the expression was unrecognisable on features warped by long exposure to the witchstone dust in his Mask. Since dawn, he had been preoccupied, spreading his consciousness thinly over the Keep. There were many elements to bring into play here, and he was the overseer of all of them. It was vital that he be ready to correct the slightest slip in this day's events, for the future of the Weavers rested upon them. By nightfall, the Weavers' position would be secured.

And yet there had been stirrings. Last night he had sensed a tugging in the Weave, a foreign thing, like the footstep of another spider on the edge of his web. It was slight, this disturbance; too faint to be a fellow Weaver. He had been asleep at the time, and slow to wake, for he was heavy with the amaxa root he had smoked the night before in a post-Weave craving. By the time he was ready to seek it, it had diminished and disappeared.

He could not imagine what it could be, but it had been close. It gave him cause to worry.

Now he felt something again. Much fainter this time, but because he was actively looking out for it, there was a thrill of recognition; and with it, sudden dread.

Whatever had disturbed the Weave last night was inside the Keep. And it was not the Heir-Empress.

He closed his eyes again, sinking back into the Weave. He searched down the tendrils of the threads, sending his consciousness out, searching, probing; then, like an anemone at the touch of a hand, the presence closed up and was gone.

It had *sensed* him, and concealed itself.

Vyrrch felt his skin grow clammy. Something that was not a Weaver, manipulating the Weave? Impossible! Not even Lucia could manipulate the Weave like a Weaver could; her powers were more subtle, less direct.

But he had felt it. And it knew he was looking for it.

Sudden alarm seized him. There could be only one explanation. Whatever it was, it was sent to thwart him, to meddle with his plans! If it was no artifice of the Weavers, then it must be an enemy. He searched for it frantically, but it had disappeared like a ghost.

His decision was immediate. All around the Keep the last of his bombers waited by the bombs they had constructed. Servants and handymen, their minds skewed gradually in the manner of the army Unger tu Torrhyc had supposedly led, their bombs concealed in baskets, in cupboards, in vents or strapped to their bodies.

He could wait no longer, not with that *thing* inside the Keep. It must be now.

Down the Weave, he sent the command to begin.

Zaelis led the intruders through the corridors of the servants' quarters, in the lowest levels of the Keep. In contrast to the elegance above, the servants' quarters were of bare stone and devoid of ostentation. It was unbearably hot and stuffy down here, for there were no arched windows or screens to catch the day's breeze, no bright, open state rooms or *lach* floors. The muggy air from outside found its way in to mingle with the steam from clothes presses and kitchens and the exhalation of a thousand people working. The light came from lanterns that sat in alcoves in the walls, and while they provided enough illumination, they reinforced the closeness of the cramped rooms. This was a part of the Keep that was still underground, buried inside the foundations of the hill; and here was where all the unpleasant and unseemly tasks of running such a vast building were carried out.

They walked with purpose but without hurry, following

Zaelis's lead. The servants who squeezed by on errands of their own paid them no mind, beyond a swift bow at Zaelis. The heat and sweat had dishevelled them all enough to make them look like servants – and conveniently disguised Tane's illness – but Zaelis's finery marked him out as a man of importance. Kaiku began to relax a little, content that they would not be instantly decried as intruders. She kept her eyes low as a servant should, and walked on.

She felt the twitching of the Weave at the same time Cailin did, but her perception of it was far more vague. It could only be the Weave-lord Vyrrch. She saw Cailin stiffen slightly, and then felt the slip and sew of her response, hiding herself away within the Weave. Cailin glanced back at Kaiku automatically. The muzzling of her *kana* would have rendered her invisible to the one who was probing them; but it was loose again, and wild, and so Cailin extended her protection to include Kaiku. Kaiku met her gaze, and a flicker of surprise crossed her face. Cailin's eyes had darkened from green to red-brown. If she used any more of her power, they would become the freakish Aberrant red, and the game would be up.

'Zaelis,' she hissed, in a rare moment when no servant was nearby. 'Vyrrch is searching for us. Get me to a safe place. I cannot deal with him here.'

Zaelis's reply was the barest nod. He steered them off the main corridor, into a narrower thoroughfare along a row of rooms where tubs of clothes soaked in hot water, and women stirred them with great pestles. Kaiku felt the creeping sensation of being watched. Did the Weavers somehow know of her? Could they sense the oath she had given to Ocha to avenge herself against them? The very air seemed pregnant with movement now, scurrilous fingers running just beneath the surface of sight, invisible manipulations that registered only to her Aberrant instincts. She could feel herself trying to slip into the Weave, her *kana* stirring in response, and she gritted her teeth and fought to hold it back.

And then time seemed to slow suddenly, a premonition of

disaster settling on her shoulders like a leaden shroud. She stumbled, not sure where it was coming from, only that something was about to happen, something inevitable. Her senses had warned her too late, and all she could do was wait with sickening dread for that something to arrive. She saw Cailin turn towards her, moving as if through treacle, and as their eyes met she knew the Sister had felt the same thing.

A moment later, the bombs exploded.

THIRTY-ONE

For one dreadful second, Mishani thought that the Empress's Imperial Guards were going to behead her where she knelt like some common servant, without any of the rituals of execution used to honour a noble adversary. Then she felt rough hands on her, pulling her upright. Asara was being treated similarly. Anais and Durun were sitting on their thrones, looking down. Anais's face was dispassionate, Durun's a smirk. She would be led to the proper place, and there her head separated from her shoulders. She was noble, even if an enemy. She would be allowed to die in a dignified fashion with her handmaiden alongside, and not on the floor of the Empress's throne room.

The Barak Mos stood to one side of the dias, watching her blandly. She met his eyes, and saw nothing there. There would be no help for her, or Asara. Her time had truly come.

Then, chaos.

The sound was a deafening roar that shook the Keep from its foundations up. The Guards who held Mishani and Asara stumbled backward to regain their balance. A moment later, a second bomb exploded, nearer to hand. This one made the room buck, and a scatter of loose stones showered down from a ceiling that had suddenly become spidercracked. The Guard by Mishani went down, and pulled her over with him. Shouts of alarm cluttered the air, suddenly multiplying as a third, more distant explosion rumbled through the room. Durun tried to get to his feet and had to grab on to the arms of his throne for support. The Barak Mos was casting around wildly in confusion, with an expression of what looked like anger on his bearded face.

'What is this?' Anais cried, mingled fear and outrage in her voice. '*What is this?*'

'The Keep is attacked!' someone cried.

The main door to the throne room burst open, and in ran several dozen Imperial Guards, their swords drawn. Mishani, who had squirmed out of the grip of the man who held her, thought for a moment they had come to join the Guards already inside; but it took only that moment to see she was wrong. They were not here to guard anything. They were here to kill.

Swords swung high through the morning sun and smashed through armour, muscle and bone. Those Imperial Guards who had been unbalanced by the blasts did not react quickly enough; they were hacked down before they had even got to their weapons. The throne room erupted into turmoil, Guards running this way and that to take position in defence of the Blood Empress. The man who had held Mishani grabbed her ankle as she crawled away, unwilling to let her go; but in the scramble Mishani kicked him viciously in the face, feeling gristle crunch as his nose broke, and he slumped and went limp. Suddenly Asara was there, pulling her to her feet; her own Guard lay supine, having suffered a similar fate to Mishani's.

Blades were crashing together all around them and men were shouting. They were in the midst of a surging tide of white and blue armour, with no way to tell who were the Empress's and who were the imposters who had stormed the throne room. Mishani shied in fright as someone backed into her and turned automatically, his sword raised to strike. Whether the Guard would have struck or not when he had recognised the noble lady cringing before him was a question never answered; Asara rammed her hand into his throat, fingers rigid, and crushed his oesophagus with a single blow. He collapsed trying to clutch at air that would not come.

'Get out of here!' Barak Mos cried to his son, standing on the steps of the dais with his great, curved sword held before him. His choice of weapon reflected his style of politics: force over finesse. Behind him Anais was calling useless orders, her voice unheard over the tumult. She seemed robbed of her imperial strength now, and all the uncertainty, fear and worry she had suffered since this ordeal began showed on her face. She was betrayed somehow. Someone had got into the Keep. And if they were in the Keep, they might get to—

'*Lucia!*' she cried, as her husband grabbed her arm.

'Come on!' he snapped, pulling her away from the throne. The imposters had broken through the main door, but there was another door at the back for the Emperor and Empress, beyond which were stately rooms where they could arrange themselves in their finery before emerging to give audience. The Imperial Guards who were loyal had formed a defensive barrier, clearing a way to that door for Durun and Anais to escape.

They were hurrying down from the dais when a Guard suddenly broke through the struggling mass, an imposter masquerading as one of the loyal defenders, and ran for the Empress. He met the sword of Barak Mos instead, who leaped to interpose. The man hesitated, taken off-guard by this unexpected opponent, and Mos hewed him down. He fell with an expression of comical surprise on his face.

'Rudrec!' Durun shouted as he led his wife to safety. One of the Guards, wearing the colours of a commander, broke away from the defensive line and ran to him. 'Go!' he hissed, so that nobody but they three would overhear. 'Find Lucia and bring her to the Sun Chamber.'

Rudrec grunted and left without bothering to salute in his haste. He was a hoary old campaigner with little time for niceties, but he was also one of their most trusted men. Anais took some small comfort in that. She clung to her husband, suddenly glad of his strength. She had ever been a formidable woman, despite her pale, elfin looks and slight stature, but she had never been threatened with physical violence in her life beyond the bedroom games she played with Durun. Now he was the one with the power, brandishing his sword in one hand as he led her with the other.

Six men joined them as they hustled out of the door and away, a retinue of bodyguards. Alarm bells were being rung in the high places of the Keep as they fled, and Anais felt a terrible sinking in her heart, a void of uncertainty that whispered her folly to her, ever to think that she could dare to put her daughter on the throne and live through it . . .

Kaiku coughed and choked as she stumbled through the smoke, her boots sliding on loose rubble. Nearby she could hear the rumble and growl of fire, the heat scorching her through the dark pall that filled the corridor. Someone was wailing somewhere; other people shouted orders and instructions, rendered incoherent by the ringing in her ears. She shielded her face with her arm and narrowed her streaming eyes, clambering forward through the hot murk, seeking.

She had lost sight of the others within seconds of the explosion. The bomb had been terrifyingly close, destroying a large portion of the nearby scullery and devastating the surrounding corridors. Kaiku had been knocked flat by the concussion and bruised by rubble that fell from above, and she had been rendered temporarily deaf by the noise. When she had regained her wits, she had found the already unfamiliar corridors in ruin, and disorientation had been immediate. Desperate servants hunted through the burning rooms for survivors; smoke made it impossible to see. Kaiku was picked up and then bustled out of the way when it was clear she was unhurt, pushed into a side corridor and told to make her way upstairs. By the time she knew where she was, she was lost.

The most frightening thing about the explosion was the abject panic it had provoked in the servants. Those running past her were scared out of their minds, unable to understand why their previously stable world had suddenly turned to smoke and fire in an eyeblink. Several were blank-faced and staring, zombie-like with shock, as if the explosion had wiped their brains from their heads. She had never seen people look so utterly *void*.

The fires were becoming too much now; the flames had spread and become fiercer and she could barely approach them without her skin burning. She was beginning to doubt whether she would find any of the others in this madness, much less find her way out; but she kept looking. It seemed the only thing she could do.

Over the squeal in her ears there came the sound of a man screaming. She considered for the briefest second that there was nothing she could do for him, that there was nothing she could do for *anyone* here and she should save her own skin, for her mission was more important than all of them. It did not matter. She could not ignore him.

Doggedly, she forged on into a room with walls ablaze. She kicked away a smouldering chair and ducked low to snatch a breath of lung-scorching air, then headed through the small doorway at the other end.

It had once been a kind of laundry room, she supposed; but the water in the washing troughs was boiling now, and the clothes and sheets heaped here had turned to ash. The far wall was almost totally demolished, and she could see through the smoke to what was left of the rooms beyond: a great disorder of rubble, for the roof had fallen in and the room above had tumbled down on top. She glanced up nervously at the ceiling beams, and saw they were bowing and splitting in the heat.

The scream again, and her tearing eyes picked out a man laid in one of the washing troughs, his skin blackened and one leg a bloody stump. The burns on his body were horrible. He had been caught by the blast, and somehow crawled into the trough, seeking the protection of the water; but the water was boiling, cooking him like a lobster. He went under and surfaced again, shrieking. Kaiku could not help him, but she could not turn her back either. Her eyes welled with fresh tears of sympathy and sorrow.

And then she saw a new movement, at the other end of the room.

She caught her breath at the sight. It was a little girl, dressed in a simple robe. Long, light hair fell in curling tumbles down her back. She had a round face with a curiously lost expression on it. But this was no thing of flesh and blood; she was a spectre, a spirit, that blurred and rippled as she moved as if she were a reflection in disturbed water. She walked across to the man in the trough, heedless of the flames. Kaiku watched, transfixed, as the spectre put her hand in the water, and it stopped boiling instantly like a pan removed from the heat. The man in the trough turned to look at her and on his ravaged face there came an expression of joyous gratitude. Then the spectre laid her small hand on his head, and his eyes closed. With a sigh, he sank beneath the water.

The spectre turned to Kaiku then, her features settling into those of a wide-eyed and dreamy-looking girl.

((. . . help me . . .))

The words seemed to come from far away and were very faint, arriving seconds after the spectre had mouthed them. The roof creaked above her, and Kaiku looked up in alarm. She darted back through the doorway just before the ceiling beams gave up with a tortured bellow, and a rage of stone and flame thundered down into the room, belching hot smoke through the doorway.

Kaiku shielded her face, squinting at the room where the spectre had been buried. There was only rock there now; and the weight was making the walls of this room bulge as well.

'Get out of there!' someone cried, and she turned to see a red-faced man at the other doorway, beckoning her through. He disappeared from sight, leaving a vacant arch; and across that arch, a moment later, walked the spectre.

Kaiku clambered back through the blazing room and out into the corridor beyond. The spectre was a glimpse through the smoke. Coughing, she followed, running close to the floor to avoid the black river of murk overhead. Other people were shouting now, the general theme being that they should get out before the place collapsed. Kaiku ignored them, intent on following where the spectre led. She had a sense that it was very important she should do that, and she was learning to trust her instincts more and more of late.

'Kaiku!' came a voice, and Tane grabbed her shoulder. She clasped his wrist to acknowledge he was there, but she did not take her eyes from the girl, nor slow her pace.

'What is it?' Tane asked, bewildered, hurrying alongside her.

'Can you not see it?' she asked.

'See what?'

Kaiku shook her head, impatient. 'Just come with me.'

'What about the others?'

'They can take care of themselves,' she replied.

The spectre was mercifully leading Kaiku away from the worst of the destruction, and after a few corners the air had become clearer and she could breathe again without pain. Tane walked with her, not asking for an explanation, convinced by the determination on her face. Always the translucent figure was ahead of them, just entering a passageway or flitting across the end of a corridor. They never seemed to catch up. Soon the fire was behind them, and the ways they hurried down were more and more trafficked by running Guards and administrative scholars. None of them saw the phantom girl as she passed among them. By their manner, Kaiku guessed there were other commotions in the castle besides the explosions she had felt, but she had no time to care what. Where the spectre went, she followed.

Cailin, Zaelis and Yugi pushed through the confines of the smoky corridors, away from the fire to where the walls still stood and the fug was thin enough to breathe easily. Most of the servants had fled to whatever imagined shelter they could when the explosions began, so the intruders could travel more quickly here. Cailin found that agreeable enough. Solitude was what she needed.

'In here,' she said, and they followed her into a cramped, windowless kitchen, where a cauldron of stew simmered over a fire and the stone walls seemed to sweat. Iron pots and pans hung untidily from pegs, some of them having fallen to the floor when the blast dislodged them. Cailin looked about. 'This will do,' she said.

'Do for what?' Zaelis asked. 'We should get further away from the fire.'

'I need to be undisturbed. Nobody will come here. We are far enough away from the blaze for the moment.'

'Gods, did you see Espyn?' Yugi coughed, running a hand through his soot-blackened hair. 'What about the other two?'

Cailin had indeed seen Espyn, lying twisted in the rubble, his face bloodied and his body broken. He had caught the fringe of the blast by sheer bad luck, and had not survived it.

'Tane and Kaiku must fend for themselves,' she said coldly. She did not abandon Kaiku lightly, with all the hope she had invested there; but there were more important things to do now.

Zaelis was frantic with worry. 'Bombs? Bombs in the Keep? Heart's blood, what is going on here? This is a disaster.'

'This is Vyrrch's doing,' Cailin said.

She pulled aside some chairs to clear herself a space, and then stood facing the cauldron. They watched silently as she took a breath, relaxing her shoulders. The smell of stew filled the air, and Yugi's skin prickled from the heat, but neither appeared to bother the Sister. She closed her eyes and splayed her fingers out where her hands hung by her sides. Her head bowed, and she let out a sigh; and when she raised her head again and opened her eyes, her irises were the colour of blood, and they knew she was seeing things beyond the reach of their vision.

'I will deal with the Weave-lord. You two go to the roof

gardens. Find the Heir-Empress. We are not defeated yet. This confusion may yet serve to aid us.'

Zaelis nodded once, and then he and Yugi were gone, the door slamming shut behind them.

Cailin drifted in an ocean of light, millions upon millions of tiny golden threads shifting in minuscule waves. As always, the euphoria struck her upon entering the Weave, gathering under her heart and lifting it, stealing her breath with the beauty and wonder of this unseen world that surrounded them. She allowed herself a moment to enjoy it, and then her long-practised discipline channelled the feeling away, dispersing it so it could not hook her with its false promises of eternal bliss.

Clear-headed again, she sent her consciousness out among the fibres, picking between them with infinite care, dancing from strand to strand like the fingers of a harpist. She was seeking those fibres which were being twisted out of true, those lines of light that had become marionette strings to the unwitting puppets in the Imperial Keep. Someone was manipulating events here; someone was coordinating from afar. She could sense the corruption of the Weave that surrounded several people in the Keep, and knew they were under the influence of another. They thought they were the instigators of the confusion they sowed, but the *true* instigator was out of their sight. And would remain so until Cailin hunted him down.

And so she darted between the threads, finding this one and that, gathering them up, each string giving her a stronger link to the fingers of the puppeteer. And finally, when she was ready, she began to follow them to their source.

Vyrrch had not moved since dawn from his customary spot, cross-legged on the floor in the centre of his bedchamber. The old lady whom he had chopped into meat had been heaved to the side of the room, from where the enterprising jackal had sneaked a few mouthfuls when it thought it was out of Vyrrch's reach. Of course, it was never really out of his reach; nor was the girl who ran loose somewhere nearby. He could have used the Weave to search for them, to simply stop their hearts or shatter their joints. But that was childishly easy, and Vyrrch was not so unsporting. He was impressed that the girl had been wise enough not to try and attack him when he was Weaving or sleeping, for no matter how comatose he looked, she would have been dead before she got within a yard of him. If she was not cheating, then neither would he. Let her go on with her hide and seek. The only key to the door was around his neck; she could not get out. It would be amusing to see how long she lasted.

Women. They were a crafty breed. Altogether too crafty, if the evidence of the past was to be believed. The Weavers' membership had been exclusively grown men for a reason: children were too undisciplined, and women too *good*. It had become very obvious during the earliest days of the witchstones' discovery that the female talents far outstripped those of men in the manipulation of the Weave. The Weave was the essence of nature, and men could only force nature to their will, clumsily and callously; women were part of it, and it came to them like the cycles of the moons. In those first years of madness, hidden at the settlement in the mountains where the great monastery Adderach now stood, the women had almost surmounted the men in power; but it was a mining village, and women were few in number there. The slaughter was quick. Once the men had felt the witchstones' touch, what lingering consciences they had were swiftly cast aside. From that day forth, only adult males had been accepted into the brotherhood, men who came seeking knowledge or power or sublimity.

It had been the same thinking that prompted the practice of killing Aberrant infants these last centuries, when it was suddenly noticed that girl children were being born with a rudimentary ability to control the Weave. Somehow, through the witchstones' influence on their parents and their parents' diet through the corrupted soil, the foetuses were gaining an instinct that the Weavers had had to learn. And it was as natural to them as breathing. But the Weavers were already well established by then, and the common folk were afraid of the freakish powers the infants displayed: so the practice of murdering Aberrants began. Not just the ones who could Weave, for that would make the Weavers' intentions too plain. All of them had to die, to keep the Weavers' secret.

But he had no time for such musings now. He scoured the Keep with one portion of his consciousness, searching for the anomaly in the Weave that had so alarmed him before. The bombers were out of the picture, annihilated by their own creations. Vyrrch had been forced to take direct control in those final moments, for there remained the possibility that the cat's-paws might balk at suicide. Vyrrch saw that their will remained strong until the fiery end.

The intruder had briefly dropped its guard after the bombs had exploded, but Vyrrch had been busy dealing with other things and, frustratingly, he could not pounce on it. Now he bent all his attention to the task of locating it again. With the Keep in chaos, the rest of the plan would run its course. His most pressing concern was this unknown enemy in their midst.

But Vyrrch had been a Weave-lord too long; he was too used to moving unchallenged, unaccustomed to opposition. He spun and threaded the loom of the Weave, but he did not notice the black widow creeping up the strands of his web until she was almost upon him.

Too late, he realised his mistake. This was no clumsy blundering like that of a lesser Weaver; this was an altogether different class. Even the most powerful of Weavers left tears where they went, snapped threads and tangled skeins; but she was like satin, gliding through the Weave and leaving no trace of her passing. This was a woman's way through that bright world, and Vyrrch saw they had been right to fear it.

He drew himself back suddenly, in terror, knowing that she

was inside his defences. Desperately, he struck at her, but she moved like a breath of wind. She feinted and dodged, plucking threads as decoys and then sliding nearer when his attention was elsewhere. The Weave-lord began to panic, trying to recall the old disciplines he had known so well before he became complacent, the arts that would drive her out of him; but madness had robbed them from his memory, and he could not piece his thoughts together again.

'Get away from me!' he shrieked aloud into the silence. The jackal started and fled in a scrabble of claws.

He turned his thoughts inward, feeling her gossamer progress along the threads that linked him with the outside world, the suck and flow of his breath, the touch of his skin against his clothes. Frantic, he began to knot, setting up traps, corrals of fibres that led into labyrinths that would lose her for an eternity. But he could barely feel her, let alone stop her, and all he was doing was delaying the inevitable anyway. He could not afford even the slightest portion of his mind to trace her threads back to their source. He did not know who or where she was; he had nowhere to strike.

And she seemed to come from all directions at once, darting here and there to nip and tug, sending false vibrations thrumming down the glittering fibres of their battleground. He flitted to and fro in the grip of increasing panic, laying tricks and feits for her; but nothing was effective, and he realised in despair that he had no other methods to use. He saw then how one-dimensional his command of his powers were; he, the greatest among the Weavers. For so long had he enjoyed supremacy that his ability to adapt had rotted and fallen away. He could not beat her.

With that realisation, he dropped his defences. This, more than anything he had done so far, caused the intruder to hesitate in uncertainty, and it gave him the time he needed. He drew in the Weave as if he was gathering a vast ball of yarn, sucking it into his breast. Too late, his attacker saw what he meant to do, but by then she could do nothing to prevent it. He threw out the spool, putting every ounce of his strength into it, and it unravelled and spawned a million threads that flew away across the landscape of the Weave, curling and spinning randomly and everywhere. A great clarion call, a deafening broadcast to every Weaver and sensitive in Saramyr and beyond. The intruder reeled with the potency of his cry, a wordless shriek of warning to all his brothers. *Beware! Beware! For women play the Weave!*

But Vyrrch was clever, and amid the uncountable threads was one that was different, one that was tautly focused and directed. And in the depthless dark where they hid from the daylight, four demons of shadow raised their heads as one, eyes blazing like lamps.

The message was simple. An image of Lucia tu Erinima, Heir-Empress of Saramyr, layered with impressions of scent, location, the near-imperceptible vibration that was her presence: all the things the shin-shin needed to track her. And with it was a simple command, phrased not in language but in an empathic blaze of intent.

Kill.

Then Cailin struck, the bite of the black widow coming from nowhere, and he realised she had slipped past his every wall and reached his core. His senses were paralysed, his control of the Weave gone. He was helpless. There was a moment of utter and abject horror as he felt her coiling in his brain, taking the thread of his life in her fingers, toying with it. Then, with a twist, she snapped it.

In his chambers, the Weave-lord screamed, spasmed, and slumped forward on to the floor.

There was silence again. It lasted perhaps an hour before the jackal plucked up the courage to emerge once more from where it had fled. It was another hour or more before the girl appeared, her clothing tattered and torn, her face covered in grime. She peered around the doorway, trembling in fear and hunger. There had been no noise but a soft lapping sound for what seemed an eternity.

The Weave-lord was face down, naked beneath his rags. Thick blood from his nose, eyes and mouth had pooled inside his Mask and run out on to the filthy tiles. The jackal was licking at it still.

She stood there watching, hardly daring to hope. She feared a trick. Only when the jackal began to eat Vyrrch's fingers did she believe it was not. He was dead.

With a sob, she approached him. The jackal retreated with a growl. Around Vyrrch's throat, hidden under the rags, was a brass key. She slipped it off him, ready to run at any moment if he should move. He did not. She stared at him for a while, and finally spat upon him. Then, fearing she had gone too far, she ran away, heading for the locked outer door and freedom, while the jackal returned to resume its meal.

THIRTY-TWO

'Who could do this?' the Empress demanded of her husband, who strode along the high corridors of the Imperial Keep, his long black hair stirring with the movement of his shoulders. 'Who could attack us in our own throne room?'

'Whoever it is, they will suffer,' he said. 'Now hurry.'

Anais had a crawling feeling in her belly. They were in the less-travelled areas of the Keep now, the domain of the scholars and the guest rooms and aged, empty chambers once used for social functions. Six men walked with them, swords drawn, as bodyguards. One, Hutten, she had known for many years, and he was as loyal a retainer as she could imagine. Another, whose name was Yttrys, she did not know so well; but she remembered his face, and she was convinced he was not one of those false guards who had attacked them in the reception room. The rest were familiar also, but she could not remember their names.

Yet despite the Guards, she was afraid. The riots, the explosions, the sudden assault; it was an orchestrated plan, but a plan to what end? Did they seek her life or Durun's? Or was it her precious child they were after? Here, with only six Guards, she felt terribly vulnerable. Whoever had started the trouble down in the city had known exactly what they were doing; the Keep had been drained of most of its soldiers, sent to deal with the mobs or to defend the walls against Blood Kerestyn. Blood Batik's troops would be inside Axekami by nightfall, but it was not yet midday and help seemed a terrifyingly long way off.

'Lucia,' she moaned, unable to contain her concern. 'Where is Lucia?'

'I sent Rudrec to get her; didn't you hear?' he snapped. 'She'll meet us.'

He was right. It wasn't safe where Lucia was. She had been hidden, and hidden well; but too many people knew where. If there was an enemy within, as she suspected, then it was best to have her with her parents, hiding somewhere that *nobody* knew.

She glanced at her husband. Durun was a boor and a layabout, but in his towering anger he was quite impressive. He had repeatedly sworn elaborate revenge on those who had attacked him – though not *her*, she noted – as they had been whisked away from the violence. She believed he would do it, as well, if they crossed his path. She felt an inappropriate stir of ardour. Sometimes, in his passions, she almost saw a man she could love; but those passions were rare and burned out fast, and then he was the sluggard she had been wedded to for many long years.

Durun drew them to a halt in the Sun Chamber. Anais had almost forgotten this place existed; but even amidst all that was going on, she found herself regretting that she had not come here more often. It was a place of true beauty, a great dome of faded green and tarnished gold, with enormous petal-shaped windows that curved symmetrically down from the ornate boss at the apex. The light of the morning splintered into layers of colour as it spread across the webbed glass, bathing the chamber beneath in a multitude of hues. The floor was a vast circular mosaic, and the walls were lined with three galleries of wood and gold. These had once been where councils had stood while a speaker held court in the centre, or where an audience would look down on performers below. Now, like so many of the Keep's upper levels, the chamber was empty and musty, a ghost of its former glory.

'Where's Lucia?' she fretted. She could hear how she sounded, no longer the Blood Empress but the weak woman they all wanted her to be. She hated herself for it, but she was powerless to stop. The attack on the throne room had shaken her to her core; for the first time she had looked in the eyes of men who intended to kill her. It made her authority seem a joke, a game she had been playing, issuing orders that governed the life or death of her subjects while safely shielded from it all inside her impregnable Keep. Now someone had struck at her, close to her heart, and the mortal terror she had felt was not easily washed away.

Who was it? Vyrrch? Most likely, but then she had a thousand enemies now. The bombs suggested Unger tu Torrhyc's vengeful army. She thought she had wiped them out, but maybe there were more, ready to deal retribution for the death of their brothers . . .

One of the six doors to the room was opened, and in came Rudrec with Lucia. She drifted after him, her eyes far away, bearing that look she always wore, the combination of bewilderment and deep curiosity mixed with a hint that she knew far more about the object of her attention than she should.

Anais gave a cry of joy and ran over to her daughter, kneeling and hugging her in relief. She dared not think what might have happened if the attackers had taken the life of her beautiful child. Trembling, she held Lucia tight, and Lucia stroked her hair absently. The Heir-Empress seemed pre-occupied, looking wide-eyed up at the windows above, but Anais was too overcome to notice that her mind was else-where.

'Give me news of the battle downstairs,' Durun demanded. They had come up several levels from the throne room. 'What about my father?'

Rudrec frowned, momentarily puzzled. 'I left when you did, my Emperor, and I went directly to the roof gardens to collect Lucia, then to here. I have spoken to no one. I have no news.'

Durun appeared satisfied. 'Good. Then nobody but us knows we are here? Matters should stay that way until we find out who is responsible for today's outrage.'

'No one knows we are here,' Rudrec affirmed. 'Shall I return to the throne room and search for the Barak?'

'No, stay,' Anais said quickly, getting up. 'We need another guard.'

Durun nodded his assent. Lucia hung on to her mother's dress.

'We should go,' Durun snapped suddenly. 'We can't be sure who to trust until the enemy is found.'

'I suggest we go to the Tower of the North Wind,' said Yttrys. 'There is only one door there, thick and easily barricaded. My Empress and Emperor will be safe until we can gather the Guards and root out the assassins.'

'Agreed,' said Rudrec. 'My Imperial Mistress?' he queried, looking for confirmation.

Anais made a neutral noise that they took as an affirmative.

The Tower of the North Wind could be reached from the Sun Chamber by a long, straight bridge spanning a dizzying drop. The bridge was plated on its side and underneath in a latticework of gold which caught the sun in blinding lines of fire. Its interior surfaces were no less fine, the parapets scattered with murals and the floor veined in dark lacquers. Beneath them was the sloping edge of the Keep, for it stood at the corner where two of the Keep's many-arched sides met; level upon level jumbled up towards them from the ground far below, sculptures lunging out to gaze off over the vast panorama of Axekami's streets. Ahead was the thin finger of the tower, a smooth golden needle rising before them, its tip raking the sky as a monument to the spirit that made the north winds blow. Its sister towers rose behind them, at the west, east and south corners of the Imperial Keep.

They stepped out into the open air, feeling the hot wind rustle their clothes, and there they halted.

The roof of the tower was black with ravens. They perched on the tapering apex, or waited on the sills of the arched windows that pocked its length. Closer to hand, they lined the ornamental parapets on either side of the bridge, and carpeted the floor near the far end, shifting restlessly. Every one of them had its black, bright eyes on the newcomers, watching them with an uncanny avian intelligence.

Anais felt a chill run to her core. She heard Rudrec breathe an oath. Durun cast an accusing glance at Lucia, but Lucia was not looking at him; she was gazing at the birds.

'What should we do?' Yttrys said, addressing Durun.

'Heart's blood!' Durun cried. 'They're just *birds*.' But he sounded less confident than he would have liked, and it came out as bluster.

He took Anais's arm and pulled her ahead with him, leading the group out towards the centre of the bridge. The hot breeze plucked at their clothes as if searching for a grip to throw them off and pitch them to their deaths. To their right, Nuki's eye was a bright, glowering ball, peering malevolently through wispy, slatted clouds.

Durun had evidently been hoping the ravens would scatter at their approach. They did not. They bobbed and shuffled, preened themselves or flexed their black wings, but always they watched.

'This is *your* doing, isn't it?' Durun growled, throwing Anais roughly aside and grabbing Lucia's tiny wrist. 'These are your accursed birds!'

Suddenly he snorted, released Lucia and drew his sword, plunging it into Rudrec's breast before the Guard Commander had time to react. Hutten and Yttrys drew their blades at the same time, but while the former was readying himself to strike at the Emperor, the latter drove his sword under Hutten's ribs. He cried out in surprise and pain, but his voice turned to a gargle as blood welled in his throat, and he slid to the ground with sightless eyes.

The birds began to caw, setting up an almighty and terrifying racket; but Durun had swept Lucia into the crook of his arm, with the point of his sword at her throat.

'You call them off!' he shouted. 'The first bird to take wing will cost your life, you Aberrant monstrosity.'

The ravens' cawing died, and they did not move, but it seemed that the searing summer day suddenly became chill under their baleful regard. Yttrys stepped over to Anais, guarding her with his blade. The other four Guards watched dispassionately. It was evident they were on Durun's side also. Only Rudrec and Hutten had not been in on it, and they had died for their ignorance.

Anais's eyes were fixed on her husband, hate shining through a salt-water sheen. It had happened in only a moment, but now the evidence of her senses had overcome her shock and was pummelling her with the truth. The raw betrayal, the disbelief . . .

Durun. All this time, it had been him. Her own husband.

And she had invited his troops into her city.

Her legs went suddenly weak, and she staggered back a step, her gaze never leaving that of her husband. She saw the whole picture then, and the extent of her ruin crushed her. Barak Mos and his son, working in unison with . . .

'Vyrrch,' she whispered. 'You were working with Vyrrch.'

Durun allowed himself a slow smile. 'Of course I was,' he said. 'The Weavers were most unhappy when you insisted on keeping Lucia in the line of succession. He was only too willing to help. But don't think it started there, wife. How long do you expect it took to find so many men loyal to Blood Batik, to integrate them into your Imperial Guards without anyone finding out? Eight years I've been planning this, Anais. Eight years, since this *thing* was born.' He squeezed Lucia tighter in his grip.

Eight years? Anais felt dizzy, as if the bridge were yawing wildly beneath her, threatening to tip her off. The immediacy of the situation clutched at her, pressing the breath from her lungs. The sheer scale of his bitterness, nursed for eight long years, bled through every word.

'I knew how you felt, Durun,' she said, bewilderment in her voice. 'I knew how you felt. An Emperor in name only, wedded to me for your family's advantage, part of a deal. I knew how frustrated you were, but *this* . . .'

'This isn't about me, Anais,' he replied, glancing at the ravens and then back to her. 'This is about our empire. You'd let us tear ourselves apart for the sake of your little girl.'

'*Our* little girl!' she cried.

'No,' he said. '*Your* little girl. Don't you think I have wenched my way around enough? Strange, then, that there have never been any bastard offspring to bother us, to make their claims to the throne. Strange how we tried so long for an heir, yet you became pregnant only once.'

'What are you accusing me of?' she cried, shamed that this should be aired in front of their subjects, terrified at what would happen to her and Lucia now.

'I have no seed, wife, nor ever had!' he spat. 'This monster in my arms is someone else's spawn, and every sight of her reminds me how I have been cuckolded.'

There it was, then; and suddenly it made sense. Anais felt her eyes welling, angry at herself that she should be weak enough to weep. Nuki's eye glared accusingly at her from behind the thin scratches of cloud in the east: *he* knew what she had done, and here was the long-feared retribution. So long ago, and she thought it had passed into the shadows of history and been forgotten. But Durun had known. And it would cost her and her family dear.

She wiped away the tears, defiant. She had suspected, always suspected . . . but never been sure until now. Well, she would not lie or beg forgiveness; not from him. 'Yes, I slept with another!' she shouted. 'Did you think it easy for me, that the whole castle knew my husband consorted with whores and maids? How was it that I was expected to tolerate your scabid antics, while I was to remain pure and for you only on the occasions when you decided to notice me? I am Blood Empress, curse you! Not some half-educated, placid little fishwife!'

'So who was it?' Durun snapped, silencing her. 'A salesman? A travelling musician?' He looked down at Lucia's face. She was calm, like a doll. 'No, she has noble features. A Barak, perhaps? Someone of high birth, surely.'

'You'll never know,' she sneered. But she did, and Lucia did too. By some instinct she had recognised her father the instant she saw him in the roof garden. And he had recognised her, she believed. The Barak Zahn tu Ikati. A brief affair, a tempest of lovemaking, ended all too quickly. It was as if her womb craved a child, desperate with malnourishment from Durun's empty issue; despite the herbs she had taken to prevent it, she had become pregnant almost immediately. She broke it off as soon as she knew, terrified by the implications. Was it really Zahn's? Or could it be Durun's, for she had made bedplay with him intermittently during the early stages of the affair, driven by a misplaced sense of guilt at deceiving him. What if it *was* Zahn's, and grew to resemble him? What if he tried to lay claim to what was his?

And yet, for all the magnitude of her mistake, she would not end the pregnancy. After trying for so long, a child – *any* child – was too precious to give up, whatever the circumstances. How could she dare to think it was not her husband's? Easier to believe it was his, and say nothing to Zahn. Against the subsequent discovery that the child was Aberrant, her lineage paled into insignificance; and it was surprisingly easy to convince herself that Durun was the father, even to the point where she had forgotten about the other possibility. She resembled her mother, and not Zahn or Durun.

'It does not matter who you prostituted yourself to,' Durun said, and she heard again in his voice the depth of his spite. 'Your polluted bloodline ends here, Anais. A treacherous attack by Unger tu Torrhyc's men, and the Empress and heir lie dead. As the only survivor, I will reluctantly become the *Blood* Emperor, true ruler of Saramyr.' He was beginning to enjoy himself now. The ravens were checkmated; Anais was at last his. So many years as the puppet on the throne, so many years in the shadow of a woman, a cuckolded husband without power. He would not let her die before she knew how totally he had outmanoeuvred her. 'By nightfall, the Imperial Guards will owe their allegiance to me as the only surviving member of the Imperial family, and my family's troops will have the city. Grigi tu Kerestyn can batter himself senseless against our walls, but he'll see it's a hopeless task. The council will accept me as Blood Emperor because they will have no choice. Truth be told, I think they'll be relieved that this whole debacle with you and Lucia is over.'

'And Vyrrch? What did you promise *him*?' Anais cried.

'Vyrrch is dead,' Lucia said quietly.

'Silence,' Durun snapped.

'The dream lady beat him,' she said.

'I told you *silence*!'

The ravens stirred, a black ripple through the blanket of beaks and feathers.

'My Emperor,' said Yttrys nervously. 'Let us be about our business and gone from here.'

Durun was about to reply when his hand exploded.

Anais screamed as hot blood splattered her, but her scream was nothing to the roar of agony that came from her husband as he drew back the blazing stump of his sword arm. Lucia darted out of his grip, her long blonde hair afire, screaming also. At the same moment the ravens took flight as one in a vast black cloud, and the air was filled with the beating and thumping of their wings.

Yttrys was too paralysed by fright at the sight of the birds to pay attention to Anais as she ducked away, grabbing Lucia and slapping at her head to put out the flames. Durun's own hair was alight now, the silken black gloss rilled with licking waves of fire. He beat at himself helplessly. Yttrys, suddenly realising what had become of his prisoner, ran to where Anais was crouched over Lucia. He hesitated for the briefest of moments, constrained by the last vestiges of her authority; then he plunged his sword into the Empress's back with a cry.

Anais screamed, a shriek of pain that overwhelmed the cawing of the approaching ravens. The agony was indescribable, but worse was the sudden, swamping cold that settled on her body like a shroud, numbing her. She barely felt the jerk as the blade was pulled from her, tearing through organs and muscle and skin to come free in a spray of dark arterial blood. She was already sinking into the grey folds of unconsciousness. Desperately she clutched Lucia to her, looking at the pallid face of her child, and tears fell from her eyes as the wet stain on the back of her dress swelled in ugly osmosis.

Yttrys turned to run, but in turning he saw Tane and Kaiku at the other end of the bridge; the shaven-headed man and the young woman with her eyes the colour of blood. The sight caused him to halt, to re-evaluate for a moment. Were they friend or enemy? Could he kill them both? Had they been responsible for what had happened to Durun? It was an automatic soldier's instinct, a second's pause; and that was all it took for the ravens to reach the Imperial Guards.

Yttrys shrieked as they enshrouded him, clawing at his nape and scalp and face, a thousand tiny knives raking and pecking at his flesh. He opened his mouth to shriek again, but they slashed and plucked at his tongue. They tore through his eyelids and gorged on the soft jelly of his eyes. He fell and thrashed and wailed, but they were relentless, attacking every inch of his body until there was no part of him that was not bloodied. The other Guards suffered similar torment before they died.

At the same time the ravens bombarded the Emperor, wings beating at his face, pummelling him, battering his body. Still flailing at his hair to put out the searing torch that was crisping the skin of his back and neck, he stumbled backward, and with a wail of fear he toppled over the parapet and plunged off the bridge. His final scream faded until they could hear it no more.

By the time Kaiku and Tane had run over to the fallen Empress, the quiet had returned. All about was the shifting of wings from the ravens, the soft wet smacking as they devoured the corpses of the Guards. Anais sobbed and gasped, lying across her daughter. Her back was soaked in a great dark patch, and blood had run down her arms and dripped from her sleeves, spattering sinister blooms of red on to the bridge. Kaiku crouched next to her, touched her shoulder with a gentle hand.

'Is she alive?' Kaiku asked.

Anais drew back, her moist eyes never leaving her child. Her face was grey, and seemed to have aged terribly. Lucia lay still, her eyes closed. Her back had been terribly burned through the green dress she wore, the fibres of the clothing having blackened and snapped and curled away from each other. Her breathing was shallow, and a pulse fluttered at her throat, but she would not wake when Anais rocked her.

The spectre that had led them through the Keep, that had brought them here; it was this girl. She had drawn them to her intentionally. She must have known she was in danger.

But it seemed they had come too late.

'Help her. She's . . . my daughter,' Anais gasped. She seemed oblivious to her own mortal wound.

Kaiku nodded, and for the first time Anais saw her, saw the crimson irises of her eyes. She coughed, and blood ran from her mouth. Kaiku felt tears coming. This, the Empress of all Saramyr. For so long she had been an almost mythical creature, holding the power of a vast empire in her hands. Millions would fight and die at her command, armadas would sail the oceans for her; she was as close to godhead as humanity would allow. But in the end, only human after all. She seemed so small now, just a frail dying woman. Kaiku listened to Tane murmuring rites to Noctu and Omecha, final benedictions for the soul of their ruler, and she felt a sense of tragedy overwhelm her.

Suddenly Anais clasped Kaiku's hand in her own, a grip so strong that Kaiku might have been an anchor to keep her from floating away. Her eyes were unfocused, and she was not seeing.

'I am frightened . . .' she sobbed. 'Gods, I am frighten-ed . . .'

Kaiku stroked her hair, smearing a trail of blood into it. 'Shh,' she said. 'Dying is not so bad.'

But whether the Empress heard her or not, she never knew, for the light in her eyes had gone out, and with a final sigh she sagged.

'Good journey,' Kaiku whispered, and tears fell from her lashes. It was only when she looked up again that she saw the ravens, surrounding them in a black tide, a blanket of feathers and beaks and eyes, all turned to the Heir-Empress.

'We must go,' Tane said suddenly. He rolled the Empress ungraciously aside and picked up the child, hefting her easily despite the illness that had weakened him. The ravens fluttered in consternation, but he ignored them. 'I can't help her here. She needs a physician.'

Kaiku did not reply, but she rose to her feet, her gaze still on the dead woman that lay before her. She was beginning to feel the incipient burn of using her *kana*, coming on savagely in response to the effort it had taken to focus her energy on such a small target – the Emperor's hand. What thoughts passed through her then, even she could not say; but then she turned and followed Tane as he ran back into the Keep, the fallen heir to Saramyr couched in his arms.

THIRTY-THREE

The Imperial Keep was in turmoil.

The bombs that had been set to sow chaos and confusion had been more effective than any of the usurpers could have imagined. Scholars raced to save precious manuscripts or works of art from rooms threatened by flame; servants rushed to and fro with water from the pipes to quench the hungry fires; children ran bawling in search of their mothers. The Imperial Guards were in disarray. Since they were unable to trust even their own ranks, they could not mount any kind of coherent operation. The Imperial Family had been taken away into hiding, and none knew where they were. A body had been discovered at the base of the Tower of the North Wind, but it was so flayed by ravens that there was little more than a bloodied skeleton remaining. It would not be for many hours that the rings on the corpse's fingers would be recognised as those of Durun tu Batik, former Emperor of Saramyr. The Empress's body was discovered shortly after; but by then it was far, far too late.

It had all got out of control. The bombs and the madness were necessary to provide a cover so the Empress and her Aberrant spawn could be killed in secret, and their murder credibly blamed on somebody else. Now it worked against its instigators, for amid the confusion nobody stopped for two servants carrying an injured girl. Not many in the Keep had ever seen the Heir-Empress, and few would recognise her in this state if they did, with her clothes burned and her face covered by her hair. Slightly more remarkable was the fact that one of the servants was a woman dressed in man's clothes, and that she stumbled along with her eyes bound by a torn rag of cloth and her hand on her sickly-looking companion's shoulder, evidently blinded by some shard of stone thrown by an explosion. But better the people of the Keep should see that than an Aberrant; for Kaiku's eyes were blood-red in the aftermath of using her *kana*, and would not fade for hours yet. The concentration involved in focusing her power to destroy only Durun's hand had drained her to exhaustion; and even then, she had failed. The Heir-empress lay unconscious and burned because she could not control the force within her well enough, and if she died it would be on Kaiku's head. She did not think she could bear the weight of that guilt.

So they hurried along as best they could, following Tane's memory back to the servants' quarters where Purloch waited for them. They had no time to think what might have become of the others. There was only flight.

((*Asara!*))

Asara pulled Mishani to a halt, dragging her to the side of the corridor behind a statue of Yoru, guardian of the Gates of Omecha, with his wine jug raised high. The cool, austere thoroughfares of the Imperial Keep had become manic now, and servants and soldiers rushed and clattered by, to and fro, boots clicking on *lach*, shouting commands and questions. They were in one of the interior corridors, where there were no outside windows, and even high-ceilinged and wide as it was, it felt terribly claustrophobic.

Both of them were sweaty and dishevelled. Their escape from the throne room had been a narrow thing, but the Imperial Guards had no interest in a noble lady and her handmaiden while they were locked in combat with each other. The loyal and the traitorous had become mixed and mingled hopelessly, and after Barak Mos had fled the battle-ground degenerated into a free-for-all. The robed advisors and scribes trapped in the room were ignored, and Mishani and Asara slipped away with them once their route was clear. One Guard had raised his sword to stop them, but Asara had killed him bare-handed in an eyeblink. Mishani still could not credit what she had seen, but astonishment was something that would have to wait. For now, she wanted only to escape this place. The pronouncement of her execution had shaken her enough so that she cared little about the Heir-Empress or the plans of the Libera Dramach at this moment; she needed only safety and sanctuary.

'What is it?' she asked, a little shocked at being roughly taken aside by Asara. She was not accustomed to being manhandled like that by anyone. The Aberrant lady hushed her.

((Asara.))

It was Cailin. This was not the first time the Sister had spoken to Asara from afar, and it did not perturb her now as it had in the beginning.

She concentrated a stream of images, recalling in a jumbled order what had happened to them, making it as clear as she could. There was no way for her to speak directly to Cailin – she did not have the mechanisms in her to send words – but impressions would be enough.

Cailin understood. She replied with another set of images, these ones embedded with instructions and information.

'What *is* it?' Mishani persisted.

Asara blinked, and the contact was gone. 'Cailin,' she said. 'She has done away with Vyrrch, and she has a free hand across the Keep. She is our eyes now.' She turned back the other way. 'We have something we must do.'

'What *must* we do?' Mishani's tone made it clear that she was not moving, and certainly not back towards the heart of the Keep.

'Kaiku and Tane have the Heir-Empress,' Asara said. 'We have to find them. Cailin will lead us there.'

'Kaiku?' Mishani said, and they were on their way.

*

Another explosion rumbled through the Keep, making the walls shake. This one was no bomb, but the stores of ignition powder down in the cellars. Kaiku stumbled and fell as they were crossing an intersection between two corridors, into the path of a frightened group of servant women who almost trampled her. The sound of running feet and the clank of armour came after, and Tane saw with a thrill of horror that a group of Imperial Guards was racing towards them. He shifted Lucia's weight to one arm and used the other to grab Kaiku and haul her to one side, then huddled down with her, shielding the Heir-Empress with his body as the Guards rushed by. They paid him no attention.

Kaiku's eyelids were drooping behind the cloth rag that concealed her eyes, her head lolling forward on to her breast. 'I cannot go on,' she said. 'I am so tired.'

Tane would not listen. The fever that had settled in his bones only seemed to make him more determined not to tire, more unforgiving of weakness; his or hers. Though he sweated and his skin seemed taut and yellowish, he would not allow himself to succumb, and was driving himself ever harder. Relinquishing Lucia for a moment, he dragged Kaiku to her feet. She moaned in protest. 'Be quiet,' he hissed, at the sound of new footsteps. He lifted Lucia up, put Kaiku's hand back on his shoulder, and they went on.

For Kaiku it was a descent into nightmare that was becoming all too familiar. The awful burning, the empty void left inside her after her *kana* had broken free stole her will to do anything but lie where she was and sleep. One day, unless she learned to tame it, it would be the death of her. It might already have been the death of the Heir-Empress, and the hopes of the Libera Dramach. She staggered in Tane's wake, hating him for forcing her to run when she could be asleep, hating herself for being so selfish when there was a child in his arms who could be dying even now.

Tane moved with certainty; after many years of finding his way through forests, the ordered corridors of the Keep presented no problem to him. Under his guidance, they made their way rapidly down into the lower levels, heading for the servants' quarters. Every new person that passed them by brought a fresh dread; every pair of eyes looking them over might recognise the child he carried, and that would be the end for them. But time and again their luck held, and they passed through the confusion unchallenged.

'Tane! Kaiku!'

They jumped at the sound of their names, but trepidation turned to relief as they recognised the voice. They paused on the narrow stairs they were descending, and from behind them came Asara and Mishani. The reek of hot smoke rose from below, but that was to be expected; they were almost into the corridors where Cailin waited.

'Kaiku, are you hurt?' Mishani cried, seeing the binding around Kaiku's eyes. Kaiku slumped, but Asara caught her and bore her up.

'She has used her *kana*,' Asara said. 'It drains her. She just needs sleep.'

Mishani's eyes flickered from her friend to the child in Tane's arms, then to Tane himself. He looked sick; his gaze was grey and bleak. He feared for the Heir-Empress.

'There is no time to waste,' Mishani said, deciding all questions could wait. 'We must go.'

And with that, they plunged down into the depths of the servants' quarters. Poisonous fumes undulated in thin veils along the ceiling. Distant wails and calls for help reached them faintly, even over the dull whine that had muted Kaiku's ears after she had been near-deafened by an earlier bomb. The walls had reverted to rough brick rather than varnished wood or *lach*; bits of rubble were scattered around their feet. People they passed were grimed with smoke and sweat, and the heat was almost intolerable. It was not so cramped here as the first time Kaiku and Tane had passed through it, for those who could escape had already done so, leaving behind only the wounded and those who were willing to try and help them.

They were beginning to hope they might make it back to the old donjon where Purloch waited when they ran into three Imperial Guards.

It was pure bad luck that placed them in the path of the four companions and their supine burden. The Guards had escaped the fighting in the throne room, their courage failing them in the confusion of not knowing who was an ally and who was the enemy, and they had fled down into the servants' chambers to avoid the bloodshed going on above. Their intention – if they were faced with a superior officer – was to offer the explanation of digging out those trapped by the blazing rubble; but ill fortune had brought the kidnappers right to them, and whether they were loyal or traitors, they would not allow the Heir-Empress to leave the Keep if they recognised her.

Tane, in the lead, almost bowled into the Guards as the companions rushed into a plain, square stone room that formed a junction between three corridors. Wooden drying racks hung from the ceiling, and clothes hung from them in turn, now bone-dry and crinkling in the heat. The coarse brown bricks of the walls had cracked in places from nearby bomb-blasts, and the floor was dusted with powder and chips of rock.

They were too surprised by the presence of soldiers down here to keep the guilt off their faces. Mishani was the honourable exception, but her efforts did no good.

'What's that?' one of them said, his rifle already aimed at Tane. The other two raised their own rifles, more in alarm at the violent arrival of the newcomers than in any expectation of a threat. They were jumpy, for it would mean their necks if their cowardice were discovered. The three of them were sweating heavily, baking inside their metal armour, the white and blue lacquer streaked with dirt.

'She is hurt!' Tane cried. 'Let us by!'

'I saw you in the throne room,' said one of the other Guards, his eyes ranging over Asara. They flicked to Mishani. 'You too. The Empress sentenced you to death.'

Neither Tane nor Kaiku reacted to the news. Tane's mind was racing through options of escape, but it was sluggish with fever and would not deliver; Kaiku was almost comatose on her feet.

'And you should be with her, not down here with the servants,' Mishani replied smoothly. 'Unless, that is, you are false Guards, like the other traitors who tried to take our Empress's life.'

Tane quailed inwardly at her boldness, but it made the Guards pause for a moment. They were evidently weighing their loyalties, deciding on the best response to the accusation.

'That girl,' said the Guard who had spoken to Tane. 'Look at her clothes. She's no servant.'

'It's the Heir-Empress,' the second one said, his voice dull with menace.

'It can't be!' said the third.

The second narrowed his eyes. 'I've done duty in the Heir-Empress's chambers before,' he said. 'It's her.'

Tane felt a nausea creep into his gut as the first Guard turned a sickly smile upon Mishani.

'Indeed,' he said. 'Then Shintu smiles on us, for that child is a monster, and she must die.' He put the rifle to his shoulder, pointed it squarely at Tane and pulled the trigger.

Nothing happened. The powder did not ignite. It was a misfire.

The expectation of the shot caused everyone to hesitate; except for Asara. She had covered the distance between her and the nearest Guard in a moment, her elbow smashing into his jaw as she grabbed the barrel of his rifle with her other hand, twisting it out of his grip. It fired with a percussive crack, blasting a spume of grey dust from the stone wall next to his companion's head, causing him to shy back with an oath of alarm. Tane shoved the child into Kaiku's arms, who was too weak to hold her, and the pair of them tumbled to the ground. By then the Guard who had misfired had his sword drawn, his rifle cast aside; but Tane was ready for him. He darted inside the Guard's thrust, grabbing him by the arm and swinging him heavily into the wall. There was not enough force behind it, his fever-burned muscles failing him. The Guard grunted and lashed out with an armoured knee, catching Tane in the gut; it hurt, but it did not knock the breath out of him. Mishani pulled Kaiku out of the way, dragging her into the corner of the smoky room, leaving the unconscious Heir-Empress lying where she had fallen.

Asara's enemy was putting up more of a fight than she had anticipated, and whereas her first blow would have finished most men, this one was particularly resilient. He threw her back, trying to get his rifle in between them, but she knocked it away again. Quicker and stronger than she seemed, she grabbed his forearm and levered it up his back, then tripped him so he fell with his full weight on it. The bone snapped loudly, and his scream of pain was silenced as Asara drove her sandalled foot into his face, smashing the gristle of his nose into his brain.

At the same time, Tane shoved his own opponent away from him, pushing him off-balance towards Asara. He was about to make a follow-up strike while the advantage was his when out of the periphery of his eye he saw the third Guard raise his rifle, and looked to see what he was aiming at.

His first thought was that it might be Kaiku, but she was too weak to be a threat, and her eyes were still bound. Mishani had her in the corner, out of harm's way. It was not them that the Guard was aiming at. It was the Heir-Empress, lying unprotected in the middle of the floor.

Tane howled an oath, sprinting at the Guard; but he was too far away, too late to prevent the trigger from being pulled, the hammer to fall, the powder to ignite. But he was not too late to fling himself in front of it.

The force was like a giant's hand slapping him in the chest, blasting him back to tumble over the small body of Lucia, knocking his breath from him in a white blaze of agony. He was aware of falling, but the air had turned to a cloud of feathers and he seemed to float slowly down; and while the impact of the floor hurt more than he could have imagined it would at that speed, it was overwhelmed by the soft cushion of shock that had settled into him.

He heard someone scream his name, but all he saw was the incomprehensible, idiot shapes of the washing above him, hanging from the drying racks and swaying in the smoky haze.

A gun fired, primed, fired again; two bodies fell. Mishani and Asara jerked about as one to find the source of the sound, and there was Yugi, a rifle in his hand, and Zaelis next to him in the doorway. The last two Guards lay inert on the stone floor. Kaiku had scrambled across the room, tearing off her blindfold, desperation lending her strength from some untapped reserve, and she was screaming Tane's name. Tane could barely hear her. All sounds had become dull, muffled. His body felt numb.

Mishani pulled the child out from under him and handed her to Zaelis. His expression was grim as he looked her over; he exchanged a glance with Yugi. They had feared for the Heir-Empress when they had reached the roof gardens and found that Lucia had been taken away by Rudrec at Durun's command; but hope had returned when Cailin had contacted them and directed them to where the others were. Now he saw how badly hurt Lucia was, and that hope faded again. Things looked graver still.

'Bring him back! Asara, bring him back!' Kaiku was crying.

Asara came to stand over her. She looked down at Tane. His eyes were on something above them, focusing and unfocusing wildly. His tanned skin had gone ghastly and pallid. A bright bloom of black and red soaked his chest, and she could see from the way it ran out from beneath him that the rifle ball had gone right through.

'I cannot,' she said.

'Bring him *back*!' she screamed, picking him up and holding him. If she had possessed an ounce of *kana* she would have used it, no matter what the consequences. To try and stitch his wound, sew up his insides, make him whole again. She had taken him so much for granted, this man; he had been her companion since he had found her in the forest, and she had given him nothing back, closing herself off from him. In that moment when she held him, she knew it was too late to make amends. Though her tears and her voice denied it, she knew his time was come, and no artifice of hers or anyone else's could undo it.

Tane had no breath to speak, even if he had the words. His thoughts were turned inward, spiralling into a void like water down a drain; but those he could snatch and piece together were enough to provide him with the answers he needed. All this time, all this questioning and wondering and uncertainty, and all he needed was to have faith. He had not failed. He had trusted his goddess, against all his doubts and fears.

Why was he here? Why had she spared him from the shin-shin, set him on his path to walk with the Aberrants? He knew now, and the answer was so clear that he marvelled at his ignorance in not seeing it before.

She had sent him here to die, in the place of the Heir-Empress.

I owe the gods a life, he thought, *and at last my debt is paid*.

His eyes focused on Kaiku then, her irises red like a demon's. Aberrant eyes, yet he found them no less beautiful for it. After all, he had sacrificed himself for an Aberrant, to safeguard their futures. And as the clutter of his mind swirled away, what was left was only truth. This was bigger than his beliefs; the Heir-Empress was precious to the world, even to the gods. She was important to them all. If by his life he had saved her, then it was worth giving up.

He drank in the features of Kaiku as she held him, and even contorted in grief as they were he could not look away, not even when they seemed to fade, and beneath them there was a stitchwork of golden fibres, a brightness and an ecstasy such as he had never imagined. He had done his work, and done it well, and the Fields of Omecha waited to receive him in splendour.

And if he might have felt a little resentful at being a pawn in the game of the gods, a sacrifice to be made for another's sake, then at least they let him die in the arms of the woman he loved.

THIRTY-FOUR

They escaped Axekami at nightfall, passing out through the south gate under cover of darkness. It was simple enough. All eyes were on the Keep and the east gate, where the armies of Blood Batik were flooding into the city. Fires still raged unchecked in the great truncated pyramid that brooded on Axekami's highest hill. The rioting had redoubled at the sight of the city's figurehead edifice belching smoke and glowing with flame against the gathering dusk, and Blood Batik's forces had responded savagely. In amid all of this, nobody noticed a covered cart drawing up to the quiet south gate. The sentries had their orders, of course; but oddly, after exchanging a few words with the hooded woman who sat next to the driver, they ignored them. The gates were opened, the cart drove through, and the kidnappers left Axekami behind them to boil and churn in its own anger.

Two miles south of the city, they turned off the road to a disused quarry. There they left the cart and took seven of the twelve fast horses that were being held for them there. The man who had guarded them looked worriedly at the child as she was passed into Zaelis's arms.

'Is it she?' he asked reverently, his eyes glittering in the green-edged moonlight. The air felt charged tonight, and the fine hairs on their skin were standing up. Tomorrow, or the next day . . . it could not be long till the moonstorm struck. They would have to ride hard to outpace it.

'It is,' said Zaelis. 'We must go. Every moment we waste brings her closer to death.'

The man swallowed and nodded, and watched as they rode off through the quarry, heading overland. He returned

416

to the ramshackle hut he had been sheltering in these last few days, previously owned by the foreman of this cheerless place. It was one of several stops along the route the kidnappers would take, to switch horses. Speed was of the essence, for all plans had relied on one factor – that the kidnappers would vanish with the Heir-Empress and leave no clue behind them. Even the tired mounts they left behind would be carefully hidden away until they regained their strength. If their escape was marked and they were followed, the Fold would be placed in great danger, and there were too many innocent lives at risk for that. Most of the populace did not even know of the mission, and were ignorant of the schemes being played out beyond the broken lands of the Fault; the Fold was unprepared and unable to defend itself against the might of the Imperial forces. He was left wondering if they had managed to steal the child without anybody knowing, or if even now there were armies sallying forth from the capital in pursuit.

He tried to sleep, but for most of the night he had no luck. Only towards dawn he began drifting in and out of a drowse, and his dreams were vivid and confusing. When he awoke the next morning, he could not be sure what he had imagined and what had been real; but one image stuck with him, and refused to fade in the manner of nightmares.

He could have sworn to the gods that he saw things moving on the lip of the quarry, just before the dawn. Stilt-legged things with eyes like burning lanterns.

They rode hard, long into the morning. When finally Zaelis called a halt, their horses were lathered, flanks steaming and lips flecked with spittle. They had left the road entirely, racing overland, and were deep in the gently rolling plains and hills of the trackless Saramyr countryside. They took shelter under the vast, ancient boughs of a jukaki tree, which stood alone on a slope, and there they rested. The air hummed with insects and the sun beat down on the grass, brightening the colours of the world. It was an incongruously beautiful day, and it did not match their mood.

Kaiku was asleep the moment she dismounted. She had been driven past endurance, almost falling out of her saddle several times, and she had held back the wave of unconsciousness far too long. Yugi began a fire for cooking. Zaelis laid Lucia on the grass, and he and Cailin crouched by her. Mishani, Asara and Purloch sat in the shade, sore and tired.

They had done it. They had snatched the Heir-Empress out from under the noses of the Imperial family, and nobody had seen them; at least nobody who had lived. Luck had made their timing perfect. The explosions in the Keep and the coup pulled off by Blood Batik, the fact that Durun had intentionally taken Lucia and Anais away in secret so nobody knew where they were when he killed them; it was entirely possible that the Imperial Guards had not even discovered the Heir-Empress was missing yet, and that they still thought she was hidden somewhere in the Keep. In the midst of the shambles, the kidnappers had plucked the child away and left no trail to trace.

And yet it did not feel like a victory, for the child lay there on the grass, hovering between life and death. If it fell to the latter, it would all have been for nothing.

Lucia lay raggedly before them, her breathing shallow. A large portion of her thick blonde hair had gone, and the edges of the surviving fibres were singed black and broke off at a touch. When Zaelis carefully brushed it aside, they saw the terrible burns on her upper back and the nape of her neck, the flesh cracked and oozing.

'Why is she like this?' he asked softly. 'Why won't she wake?'

'The burns go deep,' said Cailin. 'Near the spine.'

'You cannot heal her?'

Cailin shook her head. Even without her sinister makeup, she possessed poise and gravitas. 'I dare not. She is an unprecedented creature. We must hope her strength holds until we get back to the Fold.' She glanced at Kaiku, curled up and asleep. Without her the child would be dead. Yet because of her, the child might still die. Cailin refused to consider the responsibility she would share for allowing Kaiku to come, when she knew how dangerous her powers were.

Mishani was exhausted and miserable, for reasons beyond even her concern for Kaiku and the state of Lucia. She had almost been executed not one day past. Her father's change of heart had caught her in the backwash. Wasn't that what she had once loved about the court, that if you took your eyes away for a moment everything might change? Well, it had, and it had nearly cost her life. It had certainly cost her family. There was no going back, not ever. Not to court, not to Mataxa Bay. She was an outcast.

She looked at Kaiku, her face tranquil in sleep. *But at least I am not alone*, she thought, and found a small measure of comfort in that.

They cooked and ate while they rested, using the supplies provided in the horses' saddlebags. Zaelis drizzled warm honey mixed with milk into Lucia's mouth and was gratified that she reflexively swallowed. He gently prised open her eyes and they reacted to the light. But she saw nothing; she seemed to have gone dead inside, cut herself off in reaction to the pain of the burning. Such a sensitive thing, so fragile . . .

'I have to go,' said a voice at his shoulder. He looked up to see Purloch.

'I understand,' he replied. 'You have my thanks, and hers. You did a brave thing, to lead us back into the Keep and out again.'

Purloch nodded, unconvinced. The journey through the sewers had been harrowing, but mercifully there were no maku-sheng on the return journey. His nerves were frayed and tattered, and he felt strangely empty. If not for him, maybe Lucia would have grown up well, would have learned to disguise her powers and taken the throne. If not for him.

'My debt is paid,' he said. The words seemed hollow, but he said them anyway. There was a limit to his courage, and he had reached it. 'I will retire, I think, and go east. You won't see me again.'

'I wish you luck,' Zaelis replied.

'And I you,' Purloch said, and meant it. He glanced once at the stricken child, and then left to take a horse and ride away across the hills.

Then, too soon, it was time to leave again. They put out the fire and wakened Kaiku, who ate a few morsels of food before mounting up. She was still bone-weary, but the few hours of rest had done her much good. They put heels to their horses and galloped south, towards the Xarana Fault and safety.

They changed horses in the evening, and rode late into the night. Kaiku remembered little, for she drowsed in and out of semi-consciousness while her body kept itself barely righted in the saddle. Mishani rode alongside her, constantly concerned that she might fall. It was a dangerous way to go, but they could not afford to have someone lead her horse as Asara had once in Fo, or to have someone ride with her. They could not slacken the pace for anyone.

They camped again in the lee of a low and sheltered rocky outcropping, and there made a small fire, confident it would be invisible from afar. They had no need of the heat against the warm night, but they had to cook and boil water. Yugi had herbs that would either help them sleep deeply or keep them alert and awake, depending on whether they were on watch or not. He drank a large quantity of the latter, knowing he would not sleep until they were back in the Fold. Asara joined him on his vigil, for she needed little rest and could get by perfectly well without it. The others lay out under the triangle of moons that loomed in the northern sky and sank into oblivion.

The journey from the north edge of the Fault to Axekami

took several days at normal travelling speed. Zaelis estimated they could make it in two, which put their time of arrival at the broken lands around nightfall the next day. The Heir-Empress was worsening visibly now, becoming feverish and pale, shivering and muttering. If Tane had been here, he might have used his knowledge of herblore to ease the burn, to clean the wound and keep it from becoming infected; but they had no such knowledge, and even Yugi's expertise only extended to a few simple infusions. All they could do was mop the child's brow and tear strips of rags to use as dressings over the burnt flesh at her nape. Cailin sent a message ahead to her Sisters in the Fold, ordering them to have a physician and men to meet them at the northern edge of the Xarana Fault; but looking at the Heir-Empress, she had her doubts if the child could even make it that far.

The next day was plagued with troubles. Mishani's horse broke its leg in a rabbit hole, throwing her off. She was unhurt, but the horse had to be slain. She rode with Kaiku after that, who had become much more her normal self after a night's rest, though she spoke little and sometimes wept in memory of Tane. They were forced to slacken pace a little, but Mishani was very light and the horse was still strong and rested; the difference did not amount to much.

Nuki's eye was abominably intense towards midday, and Mishani became woozy with sunstroke. Zaelis did not stop, even to eat. He himself was beginning to suffer from sunburn across his nose and cheeks, but he drove them on, counting their discomfort a minor thing against the Heir-Empress's life.

As dusk fell, they were hungry and exhausted, and Lucia's breath had become a shallow wheeze. They watched with mounting dread as the dull white disc of Aurus loomed behind them, and small, bright Iridima arced up from the west, chased at a faster pace by Neryn. The air began to tauten and took on a metallic tang. Clouds raced in, drawn seemingly from nowhere, heading north in contradiction to the breeze.

They had reached the periphery of the Xarana Fault when the moonstorm struck at last.

It announced itself with a scream that made the horses whinny and shy, the sound of the air being torn under conflicting gravities. Purple lightning flickered between the clouds as they were shredded in the maelstrom of invisible forces, high up in the atmosphere. The land rose around them suddenly, great shoulders of rock dislodged by the ancient cataclysm that had swallowed the city of Gobinda and the Cho bloodline. Time had smoothed the edges with grass and soil and erosion, but it was still possible to trace the borders with the eye, the point where the unbroken earth suddenly descended into turmoil. They rode into its shelter with the screeching of the moon-sisters in their ears, just as the first spatters of warm rain began to dot the earth. In moments, it thickened to a deluge, and the sky opened to deliver a ferocious payload upon them. Zaelis hastily wrapped a blanket around the child he held in his lap, but he would not let them slow. They darted between enormous rocks, slithering down shallow slopes that were already turning to mud, and disappeared into the maze of the Fault.

Full dark had fallen by the time they pulled to a halt in a clearing surrounded by enormous boulders that hunkered around them like mythical stone ogres. Eerie purple light flickered across the scene, followed by an angry shriek from the sky. Mishani, who was riding with Yugi to give Kaiku's horse a rest, flinched at the sound.

'Why are we stopping?' Kaiku called over the noise of the storm, water dripping from her cheeks and chin.

Zaelis whirled his mount, looking first one way and then the other, his eyes scanning the boulders. 'Cailin?' he queried.

'They are meeting us here,' she confirmed. 'The physician, and stretcher bearers. They know better than to be late.'

'But they *are* late,' he said.

'I know,' she replied neutrally.

The sound of Asara priming the bolt on her rifle framed their concerns neatly enough, without the need for words. Yugi glanced about nervously.

Kaiku's eyes fell to a rivulet of water, gently trickling and dripping into a tiny pool formed by the cup of the rock below. She could not have said what instinct made her narrow her eyes and look closer, but at that moment a flash of eerie lightning flickered across the night, and she saw that the clear rainwater was mingled with something darker, flowing from somewhere behind the rock. In the poor light, it was impossible to tell what it was by sight, but she recognised it by its slow, lazy swirl in the pool. Blood.

'Your men are dead, Zaelis!' she called, as every sense she had clamoured at her to get away from there. 'It is a trap! Ride!'

Perhaps it was the conviction in her voice, or the fact that they were all on edge, but they reacted instantly and without thought to question. It was what saved their lives.

They raced out of the clearing at the same moment as two of the shin-shin leaped from hiding, springing down upon where they had been waiting brief moments ago. The remaining pair of demons were already racing along the rim of the boulders, their blazing eyes fixed on their prey as their spindly stilt-limbs propelled them rapidly over the uneven terrain. Lightning stuttered purple light across them, silhouetting them against the clustered moons, and then darkness fell again, and there were only the twin lamps of their eyes as they came after the Heir-Empress.

'Scatter!' Cailin cried, the reins of her mount gathered in one fist, wrenching it around to avoid sliding on the wet mud and crashing into a looming hunk of rock. The broken stones here provided a thousand routes to follow, and a person might lose themselves forever in this maze; but Cailin was not concerned about that now. Escape was the only option for them. She could not protect them against four shin-shin without her Sisters to help her.

Zaelis wheeled his horse, spraying rainwater from its flanks, and hunching over Lucia he spurred it through a narrow passage between two enormous slabs of granite. Kaiku went that way too. Asara was too late to check her momentum and squeeze through; instead she aimed for a short, muddy slope downward. Yugi followed with Mishani. Cailin went another way.

The sky screamed as if in thwarted fury, and Kaiku hunched her shoulders against its rage as she fought to control her mount. Zaelis was riding at a reckless pace, dodging through the rocks and trees with inches to spare while the rain conspired to blind them with wet gusts. Twice he almost dashed Lucia's brains out against an unforgiving bulge of stone, for she lay clutched to his chest with her head lolling to the side. Kaiku focused only on Zaelis's back, taking her cues from his movements. She scarcely dared to breathe as she whipped through gaps that threatened to smash her kneecaps, and she could not afford a second to look back and see where the shin-shin were.

You'll not get me now, she thought to herself with surprising venom. *I beat you once, and I will do it again.*

They broke out into a short, flat stretch, a strip of sodden grass mottled with patches of stone. Thundering towards a line of trees ahead, Kaiku found a few moment's grace to glance over her shoulder.

There were three of them that she could see; one racing along the ground after them and two darting between the boulders and outcrops that formed the walls of the maze their prey rode through. They were like living shadows, skinny patches of darkness that the eye refused to focus on, lunging through the rain with insectile speed.

She heard Zaelis cry out ahead of her. The fourth shin-shin had appeared from the trees, blocking their path, rearing up on its stilt-legs with a screech. Zaelis's horse brayed and swerved aside to avoid the demon in its path. Its hooves found a patch of slick stone and skidded, and Kaiku watched in horror as it twisted and went down. Zaelis took the brunt of the fall, cushioning Lucia with his body; Kaiku heard the snap as Zaelis's leg went, crushed under the flank of the horse. He bellowed in pain, but Kaiku was already bearing down on him, leaning from her saddle.

'Give her to me!' she called desperately, slowing as much as she dared.

Zaelis, understanding dimly through the fog of agony, lifted the child up as far as he could; and Kaiku snatched her, the weight of the dying girl smacking into her arms and almost pulling her from her saddle. She reined around, righting herself, and came face to face with the shin-shin that had emerged from the trees. She took a single gasp—

– and then Asara's rifle cracked out across the night sky, and the shin-shin was blown aside by the force of the shot. It flailed on the ground, its black stilt-legs pawing spastically. Its three companions looked up at where the shot had come from, and one of them erupted into flame with a howl. Cailin was there, emerging from another gap in the rocks, her eyes blazing red.

'Go!' Zaelis roared, his molten voice breaking under the pain as his horse thrashed itself upright and left him lying there.

Kaiku needed no second prompting. She spurred her mount savagely, and it leaped away towards the trees, chased by the sawing shriek of the storm as the moon-sisters watched her go.

She plunged into the dark, wet world of the undergrowth, where every shadow was a hard face of wood and every wrong move promised a sudden end. Her ears filled with the sinister hiss of branches as they waved under the onslaught from the sky, slapping her shoulders as she passed. She was riding one-handed, the other arm crooked around Lucia, the Heir-Empress's head jogging against her chest.

The ground suddenly dropped before her and her horse reacted before she did, turning to take the slope at the best angle it could. Kaiku held on for her life as her mount slid and slipped through the trees and rocks, and it seemed their luck could not hold, that every near-miss and narrow dodge brought them closer to the moment when they would collide with a tree and she would be broken like a twig doll.

And yet somehow the slope gave up before her horse did, and they bolted out into a narrow gully, with a stream running along its bottom. They pounded through the shallow water, throwing splash and spray up behind them. Kaiku knew they were beyond help now. There was no way the others could have followed her down here, much less find her again. She could only hope that the other shin-shin had suffered the same fate as the one Cailin had burned; but she dared not wait around to see. Whether it was her or her burden the shin-shin sought, she fled.

The walls of the gully seemed to narrow, and when the storm shrieked again she shrieked with it, for the sound was amplified and deafening along this corridor of rock. Her eyes were narrowed against the pounding rain, yet she seemed to be able to see almost nothing, and had no idea whether she was heading toward level ground or a cliff that would send her to her death.

It was the latter. Some instinct warned her, some part of her subconscious that recognised the change in turbulence of the stream ahead, and she reined her mount in hard enough to bruise its mouth. The stallion whinnied in pain, scrabbling to a halt. Kaiku leaned back in her saddle and held Lucia tight to avoid being tipped over the horse's neck, down the fatal plunge to moon-washed treetops below. Hooves skidded on wet stones, and Kaiku felt a sickening lurch as she realised that they might not stop in time; but then her mount found its purchase, and they came to rest inches from the precipice. Kaiku gazed out over the dark landscape, so far down, and her stomach churned at the thought of toppling through that endless space, the jagged rocks of the cliff wall rushing by, rains dashing against her face, hurtling towards the ground below . . .

With a rough tug, she pulled the stallion away, looking over her shoulder as she did so. Two of the shadow demons dropped from the treetops into the gully behind, their lantern-eyes trained unwaveringly upon the child in her arms.

'You will not have her!' Kaiku spat into the howling wind. Then her horse tugged left, against the reins, and she saw that the gully had crumbled enough at the cliff edge to form a ragged, unstable slope that they could use to clamber out. The horse wanted to try it, motivated by the terror of the things behind; but Kaiku knew better. Its hooves were not equipped for such uneven terrain. But her feet were.

She swung down off the horse and slung Lucia over her shoulder like a sack. Her arms and legs were aching, and the child needed better care than this, but she had no time to be gentle.

'You will not have her!' she screamed again, and the moonstorm keened in response. With that, she scrambled up the broken slope, inches from the precipice to her right. A thin film of water slipped and hurried past her feet, and twice she stumbled and had to put a hand down to keep her balance, but she gained the lip of the gully, and saw there were trees again, crowding up to the edge of the drop. Her lungs burning, she threw herself into the dark shelter of the branches; though she knew that from the shin-shin they provided no shelter at all.

Her breath came out in pants, her heart thudding in her ears, as she pushed though the dark, dripping netherworld of the trees. She could not outpace them like this; she could only hope to hide until daybreak or until help could arrive. A wild thought came to her. If she could find an ipi, like Asara had that first time she had met the shin-shin . . . but ipi dwelt only in the deep forests, and this was little more than a dense fringe of woodland.

You cannot hide. You cannot outrun them. Think!

Her mind flitted traitorously to her *kana*, the sleeping thing lurking within her that had caused her so much pain.

Though she might have used it as a last resort, even knowing it had nearly killed Asara and may yet account for the death of the little girl that jounced and jerked against her shoulder, she knew she did not even have that option now. She had not rested enough since the last time it had burst free; there was nothing inside her to draw on. She had drained herself.

There would be no reprieve this time.

The trees gave up suddenly, discharging her on to a flat table of rain-battered rock that jutted out into the night sky. The three moons glared at her, arrayed directly ahead, their edges overlapping amidst a nest of churning cloud and jagged tines of purple lightning. Their luminescence reflected wetly on the cold stone at her feet. She staggered to a halt.

'No . . .' she whispered, but even from this distance it was possible to see that she had cornered herself. The table of rock ended in another precipice; she could see by the curve of its edge that it ran all the way round to either side of her. She had been fleeing along a steadily narrowing promontory, from which there was only one way out: back the way she had come.

She heard the shin-shin wail from the trees behind, and whirled in terror. That was no option.

Frantically, she fled across the bare rock to its edge. Perhaps there was a way down, perhaps it was not as bad as it seemed, if there was even a lake or a river there then she might dare to jump . . .

But the precipice fell on to a jumble of rocks below, a maw of wet and broken teeth that waited hungrily.

She spun round, the limp form of Lucia still in her arms and wrapped in the sodden blanket, but she knew what she would see before she looked. The shin-shin were there, creeping out of the trees, three of them. The creature Asara shot had not stayed down, and they had escaped Cailin before she could inflict any further damage on them. They came prowling into the moonlight, their bodies slung low between their stilt-legs, yellow eyes glittering like burning jewels.

Kaiku clutched the child tight, feeling Lucia's small heart beat against her breast. The creatures had slowed, knowing their prey was helpless and at their mercy. Kaiku took a shuddering breath and looked over her shoulder at the fall behind her, the rain plunging past to plash on the stone far below.

Dying is not so bad, she thought, remembering her words to the Empress. But she had so much still to do. An oath unfulfilled, a new life to begin. She did not want to die here.

Lucia stirred against her, whimpering.

'Shh,' she murmured, her eyes never leaving the steadily approaching demons. She found the lip of the precipice with her heel. 'I will not let them take you, Lucia.' The wind whipped and teased around her, pulling her, and she thought what it would be like never to feel such a wind again on her face, and wanted to cry.

The shin-shin stiffened suddenly, frozen. They turned their heads to the sky, raising themselves up on their tapering limbs as if sniffing at the air. Kaiku watched them in mingled puzzlement and terror. What was this?

A gust of wind blew a sheet of rain across the rock table, and as it passed something seemed to glimmer within it. It was gone so fast that Kaiku doubted it had been there at all; but the shin-shin reacted, the focus of their gaze shifting to where the glimmer had been. One of them took a hesitant step back, uncertain.

Kaiku looked behind her for the briefest of instants, suddenly convinced there was something over her shoulder that she could not see. But all there was was the massive, blotched face of Aurus, seeming big enough to swallow the sky, and beside her was the white disc of Iridima with the blue cracks and lines that gullied her skin, and hiding behind and between them both, peeping out, was the clear green ball of Neryn.

She turned back, and gasped. For now she *could* see something, a faint iridescence that seemed to hang in the air.

Before her eyes, the shimmering coalesced and separated into three. The moonstorm screamed in fury behind her, and the shin-shin's pointed limbs tapped on the stone as they skittered back a few steps, heads bobbing in confusion.

The disturbances were taking on form now, towering to twice Kaiku's height. Slowly the sparkling rain began to gain coherence, knitting shape from the falling droplets of water and merging into a spectral mass.

The very air seemed to go still as the spirits took shape, and Kaiku's breath died in her throat.

They were slender, but great cascades of hair like feathers fell down their backs, and their radiance was a cool, cold light. Long robes, at once magnificent and ragged, tangled around their ankles and wrists, shreds of swirling fabric and strange ornaments swaying as they moved. Their skin was too taut, stretched across them in mockery of human form. They were women in shape, but terrifying of aspect, their features shifting and melting like the moons' reflection in a disturbed pond. They seemed emaciated yet somehow *smoothed*, joints and angles too curved, not prominent enough, like waxworks softened by the sun's heat. Long, hooked fingernails sprouted from thin, cruel hands. They looked down on Kaiku and the child, and in their eyes was a malice, an incomprehensibility of purpose that made Kaiku's body weak and her soul shrivel. It was like looking into eternity, and seeing only the void.

Yet in her terror she knew them for what they were, for there had been legends told of them since long before she was born. They came only on nights like this, sometimes to wreak vengeance, sometimes to bring spite; other times to heal, and protect and save. Their motivations were beyond human ken; they were mad, as the wolves who howled at their mistresses in the darkest nights. The spirits of the moonstorm. The Children of the Moons.

They turned to the shin-shin, and the shadow demons retreated warily, flattening themselves in submission. But the

Children of the Moons were not so easily placated. The shin-shin mewled and writhed, and Kaiku was appalled to see the creatures she had so feared abase themselves before these monstrous spirit-women, how much greater the magnitude of the Children's power must be. The shin-shin seemed robbed of their demonic arrogance, cringing helplessly as the spirits approached them. Bright swords slid from beneath shredded, incandescent robes. The shin-shin responded in a frenzy, but like pinned butterflies they could only thrash. They could not escape. The swords glittered, rising in an arc.

The massacre was short, and ugly. The shin-shin jerked and spasmed as they were cut and torn, their bodies rent and dismembered, their blood steaming and turning to vapour as it spewed from them. The Children of the Moons hacked the demons apart, taking them to pieces with their shining, rain-wet blades. Kaiku's view of the killing was obscured by the dreadful sight of the spirit-women, but she could hear the repulsive – and surprisingly human – impact of blade against flesh, the breaking of bone, the crunch of gristle. The joyous, grating shrieks of the Children mingled with the shin-shin's wails and drifted into the storm-torn sky.

In moments it was over, and the demons had faded into nothingness like a dream.

Kaiku shivered in the rain and the wind, the girl still clutched to her, her terror not lessened in the least by the departure of the shin-shin. For the great spirits now turned their ghastly eyes back upon her, and they came close until they loomed over her again. She had nowhere to go, not even an inch she could back away to without plummeting to her death.

She squeezed her eyes shut. Gods, would it have been better to have jumped than to face this? Were these creatures any better than the shin-shin? She felt as if her soul could take no more, racked as it was with fear and pain and weariness. Get it over with, then. Have it done.

She opened her eyes again, and found herself face to face with one of the Children of the Moons.

The spirit was down on one knee, bringing herself to Kaiku's level. Her vast and fearful face was only a foot from Kaiku's own, her nose and cheeks seeming to dissolve and reform with the slight inclinations of her head, her eyes like pits into the aether. Kaiku felt her blood cool and slow as she looked into them.

Then the spirit brought her hand up, and with the long, curved nail of her index finger she touched the bundle in Kaiku's arms, the lightest pressure on the blanket that enwrapped the Heir-Empress. Kaiku felt a shudder run through her, a soft charge of something so sublime that she had no name for it. She felt herself lifted from within, as if her body had become suddenly buoyant, a rush of ecstasy such as she had only felt before when she had touched the hem of death and looked into the Weave. A joyous awe threatened to swallow her whole, and she saw suddenly the nature of these awful beings that stood before her, saw them for the unfathomable, magisterial *vastness* they embodied, so far beyond humankind's understanding that she felt like a mote in the ocean in comparison. She saw into the world of the spirits for an instant, and it humbled her.

And then a gust of wind blew a stinging wave of rain across her face, and she shut her eyes against it. When she opened them again, the Children of the Moons were gone.

She stood on the edge of the precipice, the rain swirling around her and the moonstorm slashing the clouds with lightning in the sky behind. Shakily, she stepped away from the drop, staggering to the safety of solid ground. The trees rustled emptily, a hollow audience to the wonder and terror of the last few moments. She raised her face to the sky and felt the rain lick it with warm spittle, and she could not think of a single thought or word that would sum up the experience of gazing into the face of one of the great spirits, of being touched by it. Stunned with awe, she barely noticed the child in her arms stir, nor did she see when the Heir-Empress opened her eyes. She only noticed Lucia was awake when the child put her arms about Kaiku's neck and hugged her.

'Did you meet my friends?' Lucia asked, and Kaiku nodded and laughed and cried at the same time.

THIRTY-FIVE

Weeks glided into months, and the summer grew old.

The Libera Dramach maintained a perpetual readiness in anticipation of any retaliation from Axekami, their spies ever alert in the streets of the capital and all over the Xarana Fault; but as time drew out they began to believe they had no need of such rigid vigilance, and they relaxed somewhat. The Heir-Empress really had been stolen away unobserved. Saramyr was a vast place, and a thousand men might search for a thousand years and never find her. She had vanished without trace, and out of the sight of the world.

Most of the Fold had no idea who the new girl was. A large proportion of them had taken to this life amid the pleats and valleys of the Fault simply to escape their fetters outside, or to avoid the Weavers. Their interest in the politics of the Libera Dramach was non-existent; they simply had lives to live, and they had found a place to live them. And so it was only the core of the Libera Dramach who knew the secret of the girl in their midst, knew of the power she wielded and who she truly was. For the common folk of the Fold, Lucia was just another new girl, another refugee from one conflict or another, and that was not unusual.

Lucia herself recovered from the burns she had suffered, but she never lost the scars. Her upper back and the nape of her neck were wrinkled and puckered, and though the redness faded over time, they were still an abomination against the clear, unspoilt skin that surrounded them. Lucia, converse to expectations, chose not to grow her hair back to its previous length, but instead had it cut boyishly short. When Zaelis gently pointed out that long hair might hide her

434

scarring, she simply gave him one of her unfathomable looks and ignored his advice.

At first, Zaelis was protective of Lucia and acted as a father to her. His broken leg had healed badly and left him with a pronounced limp, but it did not stop him keeping her apart from the other children and away from harm. Of all people, it was Mishani who finally talked him into letting her run free. Lucia had never tasted freedom, never lived a life outside a gilded cage, always too important to be risked. But on the day of the new Emperor's accession to the throne, Mishani went to Zaelis and spoke with him. She was ever the persuasive one.

'She is not the Heir-Empress now,' Mishani pointed out. 'And she should not be treated like one. You'll make people suspicious.'

Zaelis finally demurred, and allowed Lucia to enrol in the school rather than be taught by him. Kaiku and Mishani took it upon themselves to act as elder sisters to her. She was a strange and distant girl, but there was something about her that drew people in, and within days she had been integrated into the close community of the Fold children, scars or no scars. Zaelis fretted and worried until Cailin pointed out the ravens that had taken to gathering on the rooftops of the buildings lately, and which roosted in the trees in the next valley.

'They will look after her much better than you can,' she said.

For herself, Kaiku found an odd sort of happiness after the kidnapping of the last of the Erinima line. Here she no longer thought of herself as Aberrant. It was a meaningless term now, and one that had lost all the connotations of shame and degradation it had carried for the greater part of her life. For the first time since the Weavers had murdered her family, she could simply be herself, to drift for a while without a pressing purpose to spur her on. Her oath to Ocha was there, of course, always present in the back of her mind; but she had her whole life in which to fulfil it. And besides, she had already struck her enemies a crucial blow. Her discovery that the witchstones were responsible for the blight on the land, for the Aberrants themselves, had caused a furore among the Libera Dramach, and plans were already afoot to deal with the problem. Let them plan, she thought. She found she could hold her cares away for a while in the lazy days of late summer. The Weavers could wait. Their time would come.

But first she had to learn. She applied herself to Cailin's lessons, and those of the other Sisters, who periodically returned from their secretive errands in other parts of Saramyr. Gradually her *kana* became less of an enemy and more of a friend, and she learned not to fear it but to treasure it. Though mastery of her abilities would be a long and arduous journey, she had taken the first steps, and they brought her greater joy than she might have imagined.

She and Mishani shared a house, in one of the middle tiers of the cascade of rocky plateaux that formed the backbone of the Fold. It had stood empty for a long while, so Zaelis gave it to them in recognition of their actions, and they took it and made it their own. The friendship between them was better and stronger now than it had been for years, since Mishani went to the city to learn the ways of court. They supported each other through the days when they felt bleak, when they grieved for the loss of their families or friends. Kaiku remembered Tane often, more often than she would have liked. For someone who had been such a brief episode in her life, he had made more of an impact on her than she would have believed at the time. Only when he was gone did she realise it, and by then it was too late.

Her father's Mask lay in a chest in her house. She took it out once in a while to look at it, and sometimes she felt a tugging, a strange urge to put it on, to have the scent and memories of her father back again. At times it seemed to whisper to her in the darkness of the house at night, calling her to it. Those nights she lay awake, but she never went to the chest. There was something in the call she disliked, something like a craving that she did not want to succumb to. Occasionally she thought of throwing it away, but somehow she always forgot about it soon after.

For Asara's part, she left soon after it became clear nobody was going to follow Lucia to the Fold. The easy days of peace Kaiku and Mishani enjoyed were anathema to her, so one warm evening as they sat on the slopes of the valley she announced to them that she was going. Where she went or when she would return, only she knew. But Kaiku remembered the look that had passed between them as they hugged their goodbyes and kissed each other on the cheek, the moment of uncertainty when it seemed their lips might brush, the awkward swell of repulsion and desire intermingled. Then Asara dropped her eyes, smiled a strange sort of smile and left. That smile haunted Kaiku sometimes. She found she wanted to see it again.

And so it went for them, safe in their sanctuary. The days passed, the summer wore on, and they built themselves new lives and lived them, like the other folk of the Fold. But all were conscious at every moment that there among them was a small bloom of hope, a child upon whom their futures rested. A child who still might take the throne, and change their world for the better.

She was growing. All they had to do was wait.

The new Blood Emperor of Saramyr strode out of the council chamber of the Imperial Keep, the roars of disapproval ringing throughout the corridors. His face was dark as thunder, but he had expected nothing less in reaction to his announcement. The very nobles who had cheered his accession with joyous voices, who had been there as he was proclaimed and all Axekami hailed him, had turned against him today. Yet more potent than the outrage against the laws he had declared was the knowledge that they could do nothing about it. The council was weakened. The nobles teetered, gathering themselves in, fresh from the memory of the recent conflict and keen not to be involved in another one. There was nobody to unite behind against him. Blood Amacha had been all but been annihilated with their defeat outside Axekami. Kerestyn and Koli had expended most of their forces in the attempt on the city, and been forced to retreat empty-handed. They knew better than to show their faces at court now. They hid and licked their wounds.

The Blood Emperor Mos tu Batik swept through a pair of double doors into his private stateroom, and knew there were none left to stand against him.

It was the same room in which he had once met the former Blood Empress, when he had warned her that Vyrrch and Sonmaga were plotting against her. She had little suspected that it was not Sonmaga but he and his son who were conspiring with the Weave-lord. Deception and deceit did not sit easily with a man of Mos's bluntness, but he could rise to the challenge when the occasion demanded.

The room was much as it had been then. It had escaped the fires that burned a portion of the Keep and ruined many precious artefacts. Another consequence of the shambolic execution of their plan. Vyrrch was supposed to have been there to coordinate the dampening of the fires after the coup, using his ungodly powers to help extinguish them. Instead he had been killed, somehow. The door to his chambers had been opened from the inside. And if the Weavers knew anything about it, they weren't saying a cursed thing.

He hadn't wanted this. He had wanted his son to be in his place, the Blood Emperor for the glory of Blood Batik and his family. It wasn't right that it should have gone this way, that the father should take the role of the son, while Durun lay in the catacombs, an unrecognisable corpse. But he would not let Durun's death be for nothing. Blood Batik were the ruling family now, and there would be changes.

He looked about, clearing his head of the bitter thoughts that swirled around it. The enormous ivory bas-relief of two rinji birds crossing in flight dominated one wall; a partition let out on to an open balcony, beyond which the hot breezes rose from the city below. Two couches sat by a low table of black wood. His visitor, as he had expected, had declined to sit on them.

'Emperor Mos,' he said, his voice a slow creak behind the cured-skin Mask.

'Weave-lord Kakre,' Mos replied.

Mos went to the table and poured out a glass of wine for himself, not thinking to offer his guest one. He drank it in one swallow. The new Weave-lord maintained an expectant silence, his face like a corpse amid the ragged bundle of furs and hide that was his robe.

'It's done,' Mos said at last.

The Weave-lord watched him disconcertingly for a time. 'You are a man of your word,' he said. 'Then our pact is complete.'

Mos poured, drained, nodded. 'The nobles can't oppose me. The Weavers will be given all the concessions and honours of a noble family, as if you were all one Blood. You will be allowed to be present at court, and at council. Your vote will carry the same weight as any other noble. You will be allowed to own land on the plains of Saramyr, instead of living up in the mountains where no land laws apply. You are no longer merely advisors and tools for communication, you are a political force in your own right.'

'And, of course, you will not forget the aid the Weavers have given you,' Kakre said. 'You, the Blood Emperor of Saramyr, will not forget who put you on your throne.'

'Heart's blood!' Mos swore. 'We made a deal, and I have my honour! I'll not forget. We have a partnership. See that you do your part, and keep me here.'

Kakre nodded slowly. 'I foresee a long and mutually beneficial relationship between Blood Batik and the Weavers,' he said.

'Indeed,' Mos said, but he was unable to hide the curl of

disgust in his voice. Kakre gave no indication that he had detected it. He bade farewell and left Mos to his thoughts.

Mos filled his glass for a third time. He was a big and broad man, and alcohol took a long time to affect him. He took the glass out to the balcony and felt the heat of Nuki's eye on his skin, bathing the streets of Axekami in a balmy evening light. *His* city. He had put it to rights, brought order to the people, and given them a leader they could believe in again. Blood Erinima was ousted, and peace had returned.

He let his eyes range down the hill that the Imperial Keep stood on, over the Imperial Quarter, past the bustling Market District to the docks and the sparkling sweep of the River Kerryn, then beyond, to the plains and the distant horizon.

The body of the Heir-Empress had never been found. She had gone, without a trace, without a trail or a clue. His best men had turned up nothing, and though they searched even now, he doubted they ever would. Like a phantom, a vapour, she had disappeared. There were a thousand ways she might have died in the chaos that had seized the Keep that day. He did not believe any of them.

If only Vyrrch had waited until his troops were in the city, as they had planned. Mos might never know what had caused the Weave-lord to set the bombs off early. He might never know what had happened on that bridge between the Keep and the Tower of the North Wind, from which his son had fallen. They had found the Empress there, stabbed through the back, and while every soldier who lay with her had been picked almost clean of flesh, she lay untouched. Whether some devilry or some grotesque trick, it mattered little. What mattered was who had done it. And what they had done with Lucia.

He looked out as far as he could. Somewhere out there, the disenfranchised heir was hiding, growing, gathering support. He could sense it. She would not be found until she revealed herself.

One day she would return, and that day would shake the foundations of the empire.